MORNING
SKY

To my husband,
Jim—God's amazing gift to me

A MESSAGE TO MY READERS

I hope you will join me on my continuing journey to explore the struggles and growth of Nicodemus and Hill City, Kansas, through the lives of the Harban and Boyle families. As the towns experience expansion and development, the character and fortitude of the inhabitants are stretched and tested in their fight to survive the harsh Kansas prairie.

Both of these towns were formed in the late nineteenth century by a group of African-American and Caucasian men with a vision to settle western Kansas. Their plan called for one city, Nicodemus, to be predominately settled by African-Americans and the other community, Hill City, to be predominately settled by Caucasians.

While grounded in fact, *Morning Sky* is a work of fiction and not a historical documentary. However, I have made every attempt to honestly portray the harsh circumstances these early settlers faced and the intense courage they displayed as they struggled to settle on the western plains.

Both of these towns continue their crusades to survive. Nicodemus is the only African-American frontier town in existence today.

For additional information about these communities, you may visit the Kansas Historical Society Web site at *www.kshs.org* or the National Park Service Web site at *www.nps.gov/nico/*.

The path of the righteous is like the first gleam of dawn,
shining ever brighter till the full light of day.

—PROVERBS 4:18 NIV

CHAPTER

Nicodemus, Kansas • June 1880

Nicodemus? Surely not!

Lilly Verdue traced one finger along the deep V-shaped neckline of her bright red dress. The crimson shade of her gown highlighted the mind-numbing drabness of this town as much as it accentuated her soft toffee-brown skin. What a wretched place.

Dust billowed from beneath the wheels of the freight wagon as it slowed to a stop. This couldn't be the town where Ezekiel had chosen to settle with his family, could it? Stunned into an uncharacteristic silence, Lilly stared down the street. A livery stable, a sod church, and a pitiable general store that appeared to double as the local post office lined one side of the street. On the northeast corner of Washington Avenue and Third Street, she saw a frame drugstore flanked by a small sod building advertising hotel rooms for rent. Lilly nearly laughed aloud as she read the signage. The building more closely resembled a ramshackle privy than a hotel or boardinghouse. Who would even consider paying to room in such a place?

Farther down the street, she spied another sod church, a lumber merchant offering limited supplies of wood, and a real estate office. A torn broadside nailed to the door of the real estate office boasted fair prices for farmland in Nicodemus Township.

"Little wonder!" Lilly muttered. "They'd have to pay *me* to own land in this forsaken place." No millinery shop, no dress shop, and no saloon or dance hall—yet a church on each corner.

Yes. This *would* be a town Ezekiel would choose for his family.

Lilly pulled a lace handkerchief from her beaded reticule and waved at two men standing outside the blacksmith's shop. As the wagon passed by, she straightened to full advantage, enjoying the stares of unrestrained interest. Perhaps she didn't need to worry about her age— it seemed she still had enough flair to garner attention from members of the opposite gender.

Dismissing the driver's condemning look, Lilly settled back against the hard wooden seat and sighed. "Any of these dwellings or businesses belong to Ezekiel Harban?"

The driver shook his head. "No, but you's lucky. Ezekiel's place is only a couple miles outside of town."

Lilly arched her perfectly shaped brows and curled her upper lip. She wouldn't argue with the driver, for if he thought there was good fortune connected with living anywhere near this place, he wasn't apt to understand a word she could say. Why waste her breath? Obviously this man was no different from her brother-in-law. He likely thought life must be filled with nothing more than hard work, austere surroundings, and religion. Oh yes, lots and lots of religion—the kind that was filled with a generous measure of fire and brimstone.

———

Mouth agape, Jarena Harban gawked at the flamboyantly attired woman. She could neither close her mouth nor turn her eyes from the mysterious sight. The strange visitor sat patiently, lips pursed and hands folded, while Jarena's father walked around the freight wagon and reached up a hand to assist her down from the conveyance.

Though her father's eyebrows were knit together in a fuzzy worry line—which was not a good sign—the woman appeared completely unruffled. In fact, she seemed the personification of tranquillity. With her tawny skin and perfectly coiffed sable hair, she was a vision to behold in a dress of red silk adorned with countless tiny beads. The stitched embellishments shimmered like diamonds as the woman slowly sashayed toward Jarena and her younger sister Grace. The woman came to a halt only inches in front of Jarena, who inhaled deeply and then lifted her nose into the air. Her nostrils filled with an unidentifiable scent—sweet, yet not too sweet—a most enjoyable experience.

A gleam of satisfaction shone in the woman's eyes as she appeared to notice Jarena's actions. "My own mixture," she announced proudly. When Jarena said nothing, the visitor pulled off one glove and extended her wrist until it hovered directly beneath Jarena's nose.

"The perfume—it's my own mixture," she explained. "I'm Lilly Verdue. *Aunt Lilly* to you and your sisters. And I suggest you close your mouth. Otherwise, you'll soon be catching flies."

Jarena immediately smacked her lips together. The woman nodded once, and Jarena let out a breath. For some inexplicable reason, the woman's sign of approval was important. Jarena wanted to impress this stranger, yet she wasn't certain why. Most of all, she didn't want to appear ill-mannered to such a stylish-appearing relative.

However, a quick glance at her father proved he didn't share her concerns. His eyes burned with anger, and his craggy features were twisted into a dark scowl. Jarena looked back and forth between her father and the outlandishly clad woman and waited for him to say something—anything. Instead, silence hung in the air like the stillness before a storm.

Unnerved, Jarena turned her attention to their guest. "So *you're* Aunt Lilly? Why didn't you tell us she planned to visit us, Pappy? We could have made arrangements before her arrival."

A throaty laugh escaped Lilly's lips, and Jarena noted it was one of those evocative sounds that caused men to take notice. Unfortunately for Aunt Lilly, Jarena's father didn't seem impressed in the least. Nor did he bother to answer Jarena's question. Without fanfare, he hauled Lilly's trunk from the back of the wagon.

As their father passed Jarena and Grace, he tilted his head toward the wagon. "Grab them other two satchels, gals."

Jarena stepped forward and grasped the worn straps of the larger bag while Grace picked up the smaller satchel. As she made the proper introductions, Jarena led her aunt toward the house and explained that their sister, Truth, had taken employment in Hill City. She glanced over her shoulder with an apologetic smile. "Had I known you were coming, we would have been better prepared."

Ezekiel frowned at his eldest daughter. "An' how wouldja prepare? We eat what we eat, and we sleep where we sleep. Ain't nothin' or nobody gonna change them things, so what's to prepare?"

Jarena could feel the heat rise beneath the frayed collar of her wrinkled calico dress. Her father's sullen behavior was uncalled for—so far as she was concerned, anyway. No matter how much her father disliked Aunt Lilly's past behavior, she was still their kin. Allowances were made for kinfolk. At least that's what her mama had always told her.

"Your father knew I was scheduled to arrive. Didn't you, Ezekiel?" Aunt Lilly's voice had the timbre of a cat's purr.

Jarena sunk her teeth into her lower lip. If Aunt Lilly thought batting her lashes and speaking in a sultry tone would endear her to the patriarch of their small family, she was sadly mistaken.

"I got yo' letters—*all* of 'em," her father replied curtly before striding off toward the door of their sod house.

With a determined step, Jarena hurried after her father. "*What?* But the only letter I ever knew of from her was the one that arrived shortly after we moved to Nicodemus—and I penned a reply. Who read the other letters to you, and why didn't you mention them?"

Before Ezekiel could reply, Lilly stepped forward. She wagged her index finger and frowned at him as though he were an errant schoolboy. "You didn't tell the girls I wanted to keep in touch with them? Ezekiel! Jennie's daughters are my only living relatives."

"There weren't no need to discuss you or dem letters with nobody. Anyway, I know what each of dem letters said—every last word. Iffen there was anything important, I woulda tol' the girls. They's *my* daughters, and I know what's best."

"But you can't read, Pappy," Jarena whispered.

"Didn't have to. Dr. Boyle and Moses read 'em. They even wrote answers to them letters for me. I tol' you the girls was doin' fine, Lilly. But it weren't jest the girls you was interested in, and we both knows that, don' we? Ain't heard you mention my last letter, Lilly. You gonna tell me you never did get the mail I sent you?"

Lilly traced one long painted fingernail along the folds of her silky skirt while peering at Ezekiel from beneath charcoaled eyelids. "Why, Ezekiel! Would I lie to you?"

Ezekiel came to an abrupt halt in front of the door. "Hmmph! Wouldn't be the first time, and I doubt it'd be the last."

Lilly shook her head as she gently patted Jarena's shoulder. "Don't you mind what your pappy says about me. He always did have a hard heart toward me."

Ezekiel grunted as he edged through the doorway and dropped the humpbacked trunk onto the dirt floor. "You ain' answered. Did you get my letter?"

Jarena followed Lilly into the house and watched as the older woman surveyed the dreary interior of the room. Jarena sighed. "As you can see, living out here in the middle of the prairie forces folks to live in strange habitats. But this soddy is much nicer than the dugout we called home until we moved from town. At least our sod house is completely above ground."

Scorn came into Lilly's eyes. "Those few stores and churches aren't a town! New Orleans—now there's a town."

Jarena frowned, considering her response carefully. "Folks around these parts have worked hard, and we're making great progress. The town may be small, but it's growing. Why, only three years ago there was nothing here but open prairie. With all the folks that moved here from Mississippi in the last couple of years, we'll likely expand to the size of Ellis in no time."

Obviously unimpressed, Lilly shrugged and continued to scrutinize the soddy before directing a pitying smirk at Jarena. "Your father never was one to care much about the home he provided for my dear sister or you children. I gave him plenty of opportunities to come down to New Orleans and make a decent living, but do you think he'd listen?"

"That's enough, Lilly! Don' need to be fillin' the girl's head with your half-truths and empty promises. You still ain' answered me. Did you get my letter?"

"Which one? I received several. Let's see . . ." She thoughtfully tapped her index finger on the tip of her chin. "There was a letter about three years ago. If memory serves me, Jarena penned that one. You'd only been in Kansas for a short time, and you said I shouldn't plan to visit. Then there was a brief missive about a year ago saying much the same thing—I believe someone named Moses wrote that one for you. I don't recall that I ever received a letter penned by any Dr. Boyle. In fact, when I didn't receive a response to my latest letter, I assumed you were prepared to welcome me with open arms."

"I sent my last letter a couple months ago. Ain' no reason why you shouldn'ta got it long ago."

Lilly pulled one of the rough-hewn chairs away from the wooden table and flicked the seat with her lace-edged handkerchief before sitting down. Jarena flinched at her aunt's conduct. Did the woman believe their furniture required dusting before it could be sat upon?

15

Their house might be primitive, but it wasn't dirty. She and Grace exchanged a look.

"I departed New Orleans shortly after posting my last letter to you," Lilly explained. "I suppose that could account for my not receiving your reply. Land alive, but it's hot inside this . . . this . . . ."

"Soddy," Jarena finished.

"Soddy." Lilly shuddered as she repeated the word.

"Don' know how you can complain 'bout the heat in Kansas," Ezekiel said. "Reckon it's sweltering down in New Orleans. How come you didn't mention you was gonna be movin' after postin' your last letter? How'd you expect me ta get word to you?"

"I made my decision rather . . . umm . . . hastily."

Ezekiel directed a harsh look at his sister-in-law. "What you's truly saying is that some folks caught on to your schemin' ways and run you out of town. Ain't that right?"

"Not exactly." Lilly looked at Jarena and Grace. "Come on over here, girls. Jarena, why is a beautiful girl like you still living at home and taking care of her pappy? You should be married and tending to babies of your own."

Jarena stopped in her tracks. Grace quickly dropped onto one of the empty chairs with a sturdy thud. "How come *you* don't have a husband, Aunt Lilly?"

"I did. He died a long time ago. I've never found another man who could measure up to my Henri."

"Ha!" Ezekiel slapped his beefy hand on the table. "Truth is, Henri Verdue died two weeks after you married him, and you ain' never found another man willing to marry you—an' we both know why."

The air crackled with tension. Jarena stared at her father in stunned disbelief. His eyes shone with disdain. She knew he didn't approve of Aunt Lilly—she'd known that fact for years. Yet she obviously hadn't realized the depth of his anger and contempt. She'd never known him to harbor such opinions against another person, especially a woman.

"What about children? You have any children?" Grace asked.

Before Aunt Lilly could reply, Ezekiel forged on with his barrage. "You ain't foolin' me, Lilly. You got yerself in some kind of trouble and come runnin' out here to hide among strangers. Thing is, with them fancy clothes and your eyes charcoaled an' cheeks rouged, you's gonna stick out like a sore thumb. We's hardworking, plain-livin' folks."

Lilly waved her handkerchief as if to shoo away the comments. "Not to worry, Ezekiel. I think I can adjust in due time. I'm certain to find some opportunities out here in the West. Now tell me, Jarena, do you have a beau?"

Jarena worried the edge of her threadbare apron. "I'm corresponding with a soldier—Thomas Grayson, but we're not yet betrothed."

"Then you need not waste your time on him. Surely there must be some other eligible young men in this . . . wilderness. Furthermore, I could tell you stories about soldiers that would make your—"

Jarena's father pointed a warning finger at Lilly. "That's enough! Thomas is a fine young man. Ain't no cause for you to be suggestin' otherwise. Jest 'cause you kept company with the wrong kinda folks all your life don't mean you gotta imply the worst 'bout others."

Aunt Lilly grinned slyly. "I do admit to leading a much more colorful life than you and Jennie."

At that, Ezekiel grabbed his worn wide-brimmed hat from a peg near the door. "We both know what you been doin' down in New Orleans—you was involved with them voodoo witches or whatever they's called." He turned to his eldest daughter. "There's chores that need tendin' to. I'll be back in time for supper, Jarena. You gals ain't got time to be sittin' around talkin' all afternoon."

Jarena and Grace agreed and stood in unison. The moment their father was out the door, Jarena waved toward the door and asked Grace to bring in the laundry. Jarena announced she needed to snap the beans for supper and then would begin cleaning off a few shelves for their aunt's belongings. Grace lingered, digging her toe into the hard dirt floor as she longingly glanced toward Lilly's trunk—likely believing the hefty container was filled with wondrous treasures.

"Tell you what," Lilly offered to Grace. "How about if Jarena clears off the shelves and then she and I will come outside to snap the beans and talk with you? It's too hot to remain indoors. I can unpack that trunk later."

Grace's eyes sparkled with excitement. "Then you're gonna stay on for a while?"

Lilly beamed an enchanting smile at the younger girl. "Of course! You didn't think a few cross words from your pappy would run me off, did you? Now hurry on outside, and we'll soon join you."

Grace flitted out the door as if her feet had sprouted wings. Jarena pondered how to use the next few minutes with her aunt. She didn't want to offend Lilly, yet if they were all going to live under the same roof and maintain some modicum of peace, she'd best speak up now. Jarena sucked in a deep breath. Carefully choosing her words, she asked that Lilly refrain from questioning her father's authority, live by their rules, and wear modest attire. She exhaled a sigh of relief after completing the requests.

Lilly's dark eyes glimmered with amusement. "Is that it? I thought you were going to give me chores. Do you suppose your pappy would prefer that I help with the womanly duties, or shall I plan to work in the fields? Which do *you* think more appropriate for a woman of my many talents and abilities?" The words slipped over her aunt's tongue like butter melting on a hot biscuit.

Jarena stared at the woman. Perhaps her father's assessment was correct—perhaps Aunt Lilly did enchant people and place them under her spell. Though she couldn't be absolutely certain, Jarena felt as though someone else had taken control of her being. She couldn't think of a single thing to say.

Lilly snapped her fingers in front of Jarena's face. "Cat got your tongue?"

Hoping to clear her mind, Jarena shook her head before finally looking up to meet her aunt's piercing gaze. "I think Pappy would rather you spent your time helping with the housework. Grace helps in the fields sometimes, but I don't think you'd easily adapt to such strenuous work."

Lilly chortled. "I won't easily adapt to housework, either. I'm accustomed to a more . . . umm . . . leisurely life."

Jarena shifted her focus to the dirt floor. "Then you've truly come to the wrong place, for Pappy will never allow you to sit idle. From what you've told me thus far, I can't imagine why you came here at all. I'm sure you realized you wouldn't find a life of luxury and ease out here on the prairie in a town that's only been in existence for three years."

Lilly brushed the folds of her dress. "I knew life would be less than comfortable—just as I knew your father would attempt to sweep me from his doorstep. I came to Kansas because I couldn't think of any-place else where I would be out of harm's way." She leaned closer and lowered her voice. "Aside from you and your sisters, your mother was my last living relative. And even though we were as different as night and day, I never felt so alone as the day I received the letter saying she had died. Your mother was never willing to compromise her beliefs in order to gain advantage." She grinned mischievously. "I, on the other hand, found the practice of give-and-take quite advantageous."

Jarena clasped her hands together; she didn't want Aunt Lilly to see them tremble. "What do you mean about being out of harm's way? Was Pappy right? Are you in some kind of trouble?"

"Let's just say there are people who *encouraged* me to leave New Orleans. You surely know there are those who take pleasure in blaming others for their difficulties. Throughout the years, I've become a favored target. That fact sometimes places me in a perilous position."

Jarena licked her dry lips. "What kind of difficulties?"

Lilly shrugged. "Anything from lost fortunes to the death of a loved one."

"But how could anyone truly believe that you have the power to influence such things?"

A combination of anger and triumph flashed across Lilly's face, and though the temperature in the soddy remained sweltering, a shiver coursed through Jarena's body. Her aunt squared her shoulders and peered across the table with an undeniable intensity. Jarena knew her question had been misguided.

"Don't underestimate my powers, Jarena. Many have suffered from such folly."

"No disrespect, Aunt Lilly, but if you hold such power, why did you leave New Orleans? Couldn't you have cast one of your *spells* on those people who threatened you? Not that I think such behavior is acceptable under any circumstances."

Lilly arched her brows. "So you don't believe in voodoo or any of the magical spells associated with witchcraft?"

Jarena shook her head. A tapping noise at the front door was soon followed by Miss Hattie's familiar voice. The old woman glanced about the room as she entered. "Who you talkin' to, Jarena?"

"Afternoon, Miss Hattie. This is my aunt Lilly. She's come from New Orleans for a visit."

Miss Hattie plopped her ample body onto one of the too-narrow chairs and cautiously eyed the newcomer. "A visit, huh? You brought a lot of baggage for a *visit*. Hope you brought along some decent clothes, 'cause what you got on ain't proper garb for these here parts." She added under her breath, "Ain't proper nowhere, for that matter."

"I believe my clothing is quite acceptable most anyplace, though after seeing the attire you ladies wear, I'll admit I am a bit overdressed."

"Um-hum," Miss Hattie confirmed.

Jarena watched the scene unfold with curiosity. Both Miss Hattie and Aunt Lilly were strong women, she knew that much, yet they were opposites—like spring rain and summer drought.

Jarena flashed a look of caution toward her aunt. "Before you arrived, Miss Hattie, Aunt Lilly mentioned she knew that she needed to change into more suitable attire. And she's already planning to help with the household chores."

"So you done seen the error of yer ways," she said, her features beginning to relax, "and you come out here to begin a new life—that the way of things?"

After a long moment of hesitation during which Jarena fidgeted nervously, Aunt Lilly said, "Something akin to that, yes. At least that's my plan for now."

Miss Hattie bobbed her head up and down. "Then there ain't no time like the present to begin learnin' 'bout your new life. Get outta them clothes and come on outside when you's changed. I's gonna make a special effort to teach you all we's learned about survivin' out here on the prairie. That way Jarena won't be slowed down teachin' you while she's tryin' to keep up with her chores. Come on, Jarena. Reckon we got us beans that need snappin' and clothes to be folded."

The older woman used the heavy wooden table for leverage as she lifted her body from the narrow chair. "I know your pappy made these chairs hisself, but they is the most uncomfortable thing I ever set on."

Lilly bent over her trunk and unlatched the metal hasp. "A woman should always take care with her appearance. After all, it's beauty that provides us our greatest advantage."

"Hmmph! Men is more interested in fine vittles than that fancy-smelling perfume you's wearing," Miss Hattie retorted.

"You can go on believing that nonsense about a man and his stomach, but I know better," Aunt Lilly replied.

Jarena looked back and forth between the two women as the sparring began again. Life was going to be interesting with Lilly Verdue around!

CHAPTER

2

New York City • June 1880

Macia Boyle carefully straightened her shoulders, arched her neck, and thrust her chin forward. Her hands were properly folded in her lap as she concentrated upon Mrs. Wendall Rutledge, matron of the Rutledge Academy of Arts and Languages—a school of distinction for young ladies. At least that's what the advertisement on page twenty-two of *The Ladies' Treasury* boasted. Macia now rued the day she had handed the magazine to her mother. She'd purchased the publication to help her mother while away a few hours. Instead, Macia's mother had planned for her daughter a summer filled with French lessons and social gatherings at Rutledge Academy. Macia had voiced her disagreement with the plan, but the entire matter had culminated in Macia's enrollment.

As a result, Macia now found herself sitting across a highly polished desk facing an austere Mrs. Rutledge. Wisely, the advertisement had depicted the academy rather than the beak-nosed woman with a tight knot of hair perched atop her head.

A sheaf of papers sat neatly stacked in the center of the broad desk. Mrs. Rutledge tapped the pages with her bony index finger. "I see you've been teaching school out on the prairie for the past couple of years, Miss Boyle." Her eyebrows crinkled into two question marks.

"That's correct."

Mrs. Rutledge pursed her thin lips into a pout. "I can only assume you've found your abilities lacking since you've come to us for further education."

The muscles tightened in Macia's shoulders. "Actually, I believe my teaching skills are exceptional. I am attending your academy at my mother's insistence."

"Yes. Her letter conveyed a hope that you will expand your horizons and perhaps find a young man who is your equal in society. She also mentioned that you'd been considering marriage to a blacksmith. Disheartening! And it is most distressing that your father forced his family to leave a lovely home and move to uncivilized country. It's difficult to imagine a man of education and wealth behaving in such a foolhardy fashion."

For the next fifteen minutes, Macia adamantly defended her father's decision to move west. And although Jeb Malone hadn't yet requested her hand in marriage, she also defended her right to marry him. Ironic, since she had so vigorously argued against the move to Kansas and had turned up her nose at the likes of Jeb Malone only a few years earlier.

Perhaps it was Mrs. Rutledge's condescending attitude that only the uneducated or poor would consider living west of the Mississippi that forced the angry rebuttal—or the judgmental woman's pitying look. But no matter the reason, Macia argued with a vengeance that surprised even her.

Mrs. Rutledge tilted her head to the side. "Based upon your spirited defense, I can only assume your father has converted you to his school of thought on this particular topic."

Macia pulled a handkerchief from her tapestry bag and twisted the lacy square between her sweating palms. "Then you will be surprised to learn that my parents concurred in their decision regarding my attendance at your school, Mrs. Rutledge."

The woman beckoned toward the two gentlemen who stood near the doorway. "Do come in and meet Miss Boyle."

The two men drew near and patiently waited while Mrs. Rutledge introduced them as her husband, Wendall, and a distant cousin, Marvin Laird. Mrs. Rutledge pointed at the paperwork on her desk. Rising from the chair, she requested her cousin complete the tedious duty.

Mr. and Mrs. Rutledge moved to the chairs on either side of Macia while Mr. Laird circled behind the desk. While he shuffled through the papers, the couple turned their full attention upon Macia. Their questions flowed like a swollen brook after a spring rain and Macia shifted back and forth as she attempted to keep pace. Their ongoing inquiry continued while Mr. Laird shoved several printed pages across the desk and held them in position with his open palm. He lifted the top page and tapped the nib of his pen along a blank line at the bottom, requesting Macia's signature.

Macia gingerly tugged on one corner of the page. When Mr. Laird didn't immediately release the documents, she curtly informed him she'd sign once she'd had opportunity to review the papers.

Mr. Laird sighed wearily as he slid his hand away from the sheaf of papers. "Merely a formality stating that you plan to remain with us throughout the summer months."

The cover page was emblazoned with the name and address of Rutledge Academy, and Macia's name had been inscribed in the middle of the sheet in a delicate script. Before commencing her review of the form, Macia informed Mr. Laird that she thought her father had completed the school's required paperwork long ago.

Mrs. Rutledge scooted to the edge of her chair. "In my haste to send the information to your father, I failed to enclose a few of the documents." The older woman's voice quivered as she spoke. "I fear I've become somewhat forgetful in my old age."

As Macia scanned the document, Mrs. Rutledge began to sniffle. Moments later, the woman's husband bent forward and peeked over the top of his wire-rimmed glasses with a look of concern in his eyes. "You're not old, my dear. I specifically recall you were in a hurry the day you posted the letter to Dr. Boyle. Purely an oversight. Happens to all of us from time to time."

Macia didn't miss the gentle plea in the older man's voice. Tears had begun to pool in his wife's eyes. Perhaps she suffered from bouts of dementia and her husband was attempting to protect her. If so, Macia understood. After all, hadn't her family spent the past several years attempting to protect her mother during recurring bouts of illness?

Mr. Rutledge handed his wife a handkerchief. The older woman began to dab her eyes while Macia attempted to console her. She'd given the paperwork a cursory review. No need to have Mrs. Rutledge reduced to tears over such an insignificant matter. If signing the documents without a fuss would allay the woman's concerns, so be it. Taking pen in hand, Macia hastily signed where Mr. Laird indicated and shoved the papers back across the desk.

Mr. Laird tapped the pages into a neat stack. "Do you anticipate your parents or other family members might visit while you're in New York, Miss Boyle?"

She shook her head. "No. My mother suffers from poor health. The journey would prove difficult for her—especially when I'll be here only twelve weeks."

"And your brothers? Your application indicates you have two older brothers."

"Yes. Carlisle and Harvey. However, Carlisle serves with the army and is now stationed in Virginia. Harvey is currently traveling abroad."

Mr. Laird removed his glasses and tucked them into his jacket pocket. "A shame. We encourage families to visit the school in order to observe the fine educational opportunities offered their children. Of course, few are able to do so—particularly those who send their daughters from great distances."

Seemingly recovered from her bout of tears, Mrs. Rutledge picked up a small brass bell perched on the corner of her desk. "We serve tea at three o'clock." She jingled the bell, and the young Negro servant who had met Macia at the train station hastened to the doorway. "Silas will assist you with your baggage and see you to your room."

Macia had obviously been dismissed, for when she inquired if any of the other students had arrived, Mrs. Rutledge ignored her question and once again declared that tea would be served in the drawing room at three o'clock. Macia shrugged. Clearly, Mrs. Rutledge was once again in control. The woman was a complete mystery, with her moods changing as rapidly as the prairie wind.

When they arrived in the upper foyer, Silas led her midway down a hall. He stopped outside one of the rooms and nodded. "This here's your room, ma'am."

Macia turned the knob and pushed open the door. The room was smaller than she had anticipated, though well appointed and nicely arranged. Without a word, Silas placed her bags inside and then hurried back down the stairs. A short time later, he returned with her remaining trunk. After thanking Silas, Macia inquired how long he'd been working for the Rutledges.

The young man inched toward the door as he muttered a response.

Macia could barely hear what he'd said. "Five years? Then you must enjoy working for the school. Have the other students arrived?"

"Ain't seen no one else, but that don't mean nothin'. Folks come and go 'round here all the time. Mr. Rutledge says I'm s'posed to go to the train station again this afternoon."

"Do you live here at the school?"

He took another step toward the door, his fear palpable. "I got a room in the carriage house at the back of the property. I gots to go, miss. I ain't supposed to visit with the students. Mrs. Rutledge don't allow that." Before Macia could question him further, he was out of the room and heading down the hallway.

Macia stared at the closed door and wondered why the employee of a girls' school would harbor such obvious fear. *Strange!*

She pushed thoughts of Silas and his fears aside. She eyed her trunks and fleetingly longed for Truth Harban's assistance with the daunting task of unpacking. Her journey had been tiresome, and the bed was inviting. Nonetheless, Mrs. Rutledge would likely consider her an uncivilized westerner if she didn't immediately unpack her baggage and prepare for tea. Though her mother and Truth would have taken more time with the process, Macia quickly yanked the dresses, shirt-waists, skirts, and nightgowns from her luggage and hung them in the wardrobe or shoved them into the wooden chest of drawers. She hoped Mrs. Rutledge wouldn't perform a neatness inspection, for she would surely fail. The bell rang for tea as she slipped the last of her sewing supplies and handkerchiefs into a drawer. Taking only a moment to peek into the mirror and pat her hair into place, Macia hurried out the door and down the stairs. She hoped she could elicit some information about the other students and the school's schedule during tea.

Though Macia was the only guest, Mrs. Rutledge presided over the afternoon tea as though overseeing an event of grand proportion. Her mood had greatly improved, and she insisted Macia drink several cups of the acidic brew. Macia had barely finished her final cup of tea when Silas entered with several young ladies in tow. Macia stared in astonish-ment when Mrs. Rutledge immediately rang for the young maid and ordered the tea cart removed.

Remembering her weary journey, Macia motioned for the servant to leave the cart. "I thought the arriving students might find a cup of tea refreshing after their travels."

Mrs. Rutledge frowned at Macia and the servant. "*I* said to remove the tea."

The maid scurried to collect the cart, and Mrs. Rutledge turned to greet the new arrivals. Her icy gaze instantaneously thawed and radiated warmth as she began introductions. The woman was completely unpredictable. If she truly suffered from a mental condition, should she be operating a school for young ladies? Yet she did have the assistance of her husband and cousin and the school's instructors. . . .

One by one, each girl was escorted into the office while Macia remained in the parlor and visited with those awaiting their turn. Amanda, Lucy, and Rennie were from Massachusetts, while Janet and Inez had traveled from Maryland. Not one of them was pleased to be spending the summer at boarding school.

Inez plopped down on the settee beside Macia. "When Mother inquired if I would like to spend the summer in New York, this is *not* what I thought she had in mind. I was planning a summer of unchaperoned pleasure. Instead, I have twelve weeks of French lessons and Mrs. Rutledge's prying questions."

Rennie giggled. "She *is* rather meddlesome, isn't she? All three of them, for that matter."

Amanda nodded. "They wanted to know if my parents would be visiting me this summer. I laughed. My parents use their precious time to travel here and visit me for a few hours? They would find the idea ludicrous. Besides, they've already sailed for Europe."

Rennie tucked a blond curl behind one ear. "I think my family may actually come for a visit, though I'm uncertain exactly when they'll arrive. Mrs. Rutledge said I should encourage them to set a date that won't interfere with my classes."

Moments later, Mr. Rutledge appeared at the parlor doorway to announce the baggage had been delivered to the girls' respective rooms. "You will have ample time to unpack before supper."

Rennie grasped Macia's hand. "Do come with me, Macia. I want to hear all about life out west. You're the first person I've met who has traveled beyond the borders of Ohio."

CHAPTER

— 3 —

Nicodemus, Kansas

Ezekiel swung his hoe into the ground with more force than necessary. Better to alleviate his anger out in the fields than in front of his daughters, he told himself as he continued to chop at the weeds. His attempts to remain civil toward Lilly had fallen short—way short. The woman had a way about her that brought out the very worst in him. Perhaps because she managed to outwit him or avoid his questions with the agility of a fox. She used all her energy seeking ways to make life easier on herself. Yes, Lilly was the epitome of selfishness. Hadn't he learned that lesson long ago when his Jennie had been dying?

What about forgiveness? The small inner voice nudged him away from his angry hoeing. Yanking the handkerchief that loosely hung around his neck, Ezekiel wiped the mounting sweat from his face. He leaned against the hoe's hard wood handle and looked heavenward. Billowing clouds floated overhead to form a tranquil blue and white canvas. The serene image pricked his conscience.

As the years had passed after Jennie's death, he'd attempted to forgive Lilly. In fact, until his sister-in-law arrived at his front door, he thought he'd been somewhat successful. However, all his old anger and fear had resurfaced the moment she'd arrived wearing that flaming red dress.

Once again Ezekiel began prodding weeds from the dirt, swinging the hoe a bit harder with each stroke. "Who's she think she is, coming out here 'specting me to provide a place fer her to live? That woman's gonna be nothing but trouble; I can feel it in my bones." A brown squirrel turned a quizzical look in his direction and then scampered away. The hoe clunked loudly against a sharp rock, and he ceased his chopping to examine the pockmarked metal. If he didn't quit thinking about Lilly, he'd soon need to replace the tool.

But try as he would, he couldn't dispel his remembrances of Lilly and her heartless disregard for Jennie during that last year of Jennie's life. Hadn't he and Jennie helped Lilly in her time of need? She could have done the same for them. Sending off that pleading letter to Lilly had been more difficult than most anything he'd done in his life. After all, he had never been one to beg—not even in his early slave years at the plantation when the lash of a bullwhip would slice into his back. As far as Ezekiel was concerned, begging was evidence of weakness—unless you were addressing the Almighty, of course. With the exception of his prayers, that letter to Lilly was the only begging he'd done in his lifetime.

Truth be told, had it not been for Jennie's tearful pleas, he never would have asked for Lilly's help. To his thinking, Lilly and the past were best left behind. But he couldn't refuse Jennie, so he'd pushed aside his fear and pride and slowly dictated the letter to Jarena. He watched his daughter carefully pen each word—and then he listened just as carefully when Lilly's letter of response finally arrived. He asked Jarena to read the letter several times, initially unwilling to believe the harsh refusal. Lilly didn't even care that her own sister was dying and needed her. She was involved with her own self-indulgent life in New Orleans. Surely Ezekiel didn't expect her to leave her home and affairs to come and help care for Jennie—moreover, being around illness depressed her. So instead of Lilly coming to their aid, Jarena was forced into the roles of mother, nurse, teacher, housekeeper, and cook for their beleaguered family.

Lilly's refusal wounded his dear Jennie—and whatever upset Jennie cut Ezekiel to the quick. Merely seeing the distress in Jennie's eyes caused an overwhelming anger to well up inside him. When Lilly didn't attend Jennie's funeral, he was relieved. Had she appeared, he might have done something rash. His devotion to Jennie was replaced by an incomprehensible sense of loss that even he could not have imagined. After her death, there were days when he thought he couldn't possibly go on. Yet he had three daughters depending on him, and as time passed, his pain began to lessen. Time, however, hadn't erased his feelings of bitterness toward Lilly.

Once more, Ezekiel leaned on the handle of his hoe and gazed at the sky. "D'you remember me askin' you to never send that woman my way?" he called out toward heaven. "You know that woman ain't nothin' but trouble. You knows that better'n anyone." Save the chirping of a meadowlark, silence surrounded him. Not that he'd expected a response. But maybe, just maybe, Lilly would be gone when he returned home for supper. That would be right nice.

He trudged back from the fields, murmuring his despair to God. As he neared the doorway, a tiny glimmer of hope banked his cold heart, a hope that Lilly was headed back to New Orleans. Instead, she was sitting in his house, still wearing that indecent dress and acting like she'd been invited to some highfalutin' afternoon tea.

An ache of hopelessness filled Ezekiel's heart before his anger slowly seeped back in. "You been here all afternoon and *still* ain't found no decent clothes to cover yerself with? Jarena, give her one of your dresses to put on."

Lilly stood up, completed a pirouette, and cast her brother-in-law a defiant look. "I *did* change, Ezekiel. That just shows how little you pay attention to details. I was wearing a red dress when I arrived. As you can see, this one is blue and white."

"Only thing different is the color. That garb ain't no more proper than the red dress you was wearing earlier today. You need to cover yerself. I have a mind to take you to the train depot down in Ellis come morning." A pang of guilt shot through him like a piercing arrow. He knew his words and deeds weren't a proper reflection of the faith he espoused, but he didn't apologize.

"Tomorrow's Sunday, Pappy," Grace reminded.

Lilly winked at the girl. "I'd wager your father would be willing even to miss church if I agreed to take the train tomorrow. In fact, you'd be willing to do anything to get me out of here, wouldn't you, Ezekiel?"

He dipped his hands into the tin washbowl and doused his face with tepid water. "No, Lilly, not *anything*. I gotta meet my Maker one of these days. You might give some thought to that fact, too. You's gonna be answerin' for your devilish ways in the hereafter," he warned while drying off his face and hands. Unfortunately, Ezekiel's sharp words only served to confirm that Satan had a tight hold on *his* actions right now.

Lilly tilted her head to one side and laughed—a low seductive ripple that softly ebbed and flowed like the call of a whippoorwill on a summer's eve. "You seem to forget that Jennie and I were taught those same lessons at our mother's knee—all that fear of hell and damnation. Somehow Jennie took it all to heart, but I never did. And look what it did for her! She lived a life of poverty and died young. I, on the other hand, remain in good health and have managed to enjoy many of life's pleasures."

Grace leaned on the table. "But you don't have anyone who loves or cares about you. I'd rather be poor and know that my family loves me."

"*Love?* Love doesn't buy pretty dresses or a fine house to live in. Once you've experienced the finer things in life, you'll see the error of your ways. Of course, I don't know how you'll ever have that opportunity unless you get out of this place." Lilly suddenly clapped her hands like a small child. "When I'm ready to leave Nicodemus, perhaps you can come with me."

Ezekiel crossed the room in three long strides and leaned down until he was nearly nose to nose with his sister-in-law. "You best stop right now with them ideas. You didn't want nothin' to do with these gals back when your sister was dyin', and I won't let you steal them away from me now that they's almost grown."

"You think Truth and Moses will stay for the noonday meal?" Grace asked as she struggled to fasten her dress.

"Of course. It's the first Sunday of the month," Jarena replied. "Come over here. I'll help you with your dress." Jarena fussed with the bow. "You know Truth wouldn't miss her visit—especially with you."

Jarena patted Grace's cheek and gave her a bright smile. Though Grace and Truth had been living twenty miles apart for more than two years now, Jarena knew the separation was still difficult for the twins. Truth had always been the more boisterous, outgoing twin while Grace tended to hide in her sister's shadow. Yet this long period of separation had forced Grace to develop on her own. Though her spirit remained gentle, she had surprised them with her desire to work in the fields and with her ability to cultivate her own vegetable and flower gardens. Her hands were callused, but her heart remained soft and pliable. And, like her flowers, Grace continued to blossom.

Lilly peered into a small looking glass and carefully adjusted her hat, which was festooned with a plethora of feathers and ribbons. "At the very least, I would think your father would have chosen to remain in town so you girls could be around someone other than him—and each other, of course. We've had little opportunity to discuss your sister Truth. Why is she permitted to live in Hill City while the two of you are forced to remain out here on this farm?"

"Living in Hill City's not so wonderful. I'm certain it isn't anything like living in New Orleans. Besides, I didn't want to go and live in Hill City, and neither did Jarena. We like it out here on the farm. And we get visitors. Why, if you remember, Miss Hattie was here only yesterday. She comes to visit us at least once or twice a week. And sometimes Nellie brings her children, too. I like it when Nellie brings little Nathan and the baby."

"Sounds enchanting," Lilly responded disdainfully. "But you still haven't told me why Truth is living in Hill City."

"She went over there to work for Dr. Boyle and his family not long after we moved to Nicodemus," Grace explained. "At first, she gave Pappy all the money she earned—to help us get by until our first crops came in. But once we were doing a little better, Pappy told her she should keep some of her wages for herself.

"As for living in Hill City, Pappy said it was up to us to decide. I was afraid to move away, but Truth's never been frightened of anything. She said she wanted to go. Later, when Moses arrived and set up his newspaper office in Hill City, she continued working for the Boyles. But now she works for the newspaper, too. She writes articles for both the Hill City and Nicodemus newspapers. Sometimes she even sets type," Grace proudly announced.

Lilly tucked her mirror back into her trunk and then looked at Grace in surprise. "There are *two* newspapers? Hill City can't be such a small town if it produces two newspapers."

"Moses prints a weekly newspaper for Nicodemus and one for Hill City, but both are printed in Hill City," Jarena clarified. "When he first moved west, he planned to set up his newspaper in Nicodemus, but the printing machinery and an office were for sale in Hill City, so he set up over there."

"And he hired your sister to work for him? I am pleased to find you girls well educated. At least my sister did something well."

"Your sister did everything well!" Ezekiel's voice boomed as he walked through the doorway. "You're not even fit to say her name. You girls get in the wagon. You, too, if you're plannin' on riding with me, Lilly."

She brushed past her brother-in-law. "I do hope today's sermon is based upon Christian love and forgiveness. Don't you, Ezekiel?" Each word dripped with sarcasm.

Jarena's fine features crumpled into a frown as she hoisted herself into the wagon. She sat down beside her aunt and leaned close. "Please don't keep aggravating Pappy, Aunt Lilly. Why do you say such things to him? He's a good man, and he deserves your respect."

A curt nod was the woman's sole acknowledgment.

Her aunt had either been offended by the request or struck by a fit of conscience. Given Aunt Lilly's silence, Jarena doubted it was the latter. Attempting to thaw the tension, Jarena carefully related the names of each settler's family members, the size of their farmstead, the length of time the family had been residing in Nicodemus Township, and the family's state of origin as they passed each farm. Although Jarena knew her aunt wasn't interested in where the Beyers, the Kembles, or any of the other families lived, she didn't want her father's mood to worsen before they arrived at church. After all, they would have precious little time to visit with Truth and Moses, and she didn't want it marred by incessant wrangling between her father and Aunt Lilly.

When the horses finally lumbered into the churchyard, Grace

pointed at a shiny black runabout with the top folded down. "There's Truth and Moses!"

While Ezekiel tied the team to a post, Jarena grasped Lilly by the elbow and propelled her toward Moses's buggy. "Come along. I'll introduce you to Truth. I'm certain she's already dying of curiosity."

"That's quite the young man she's snagged for herself. If I didn't know better, I'd think he was white. He could pass easily enough—at least with most folks."

Jarena gave her aunt a sidelong glance. "But not with you?"

"Not with me—I can always tell." There was a note of authority in her voice. "Was he trying to pass when he came out here?"

"No, though the folks in Hill City initially thought he was white. So did Truth. But he wasn't trying to deceive them."

Lilly chuckled in a smooth, velvety tone. "That's what they all say."

Truth hurried toward them, obviously entranced with Lilly's fashionable attire.

"This is Aunt Lilly. She's come for a visit," Jarena said as Moses came to a halt alongside Truth. "And this is Moses Wyman, Truth's intended."

Lilly fluttered her eyelashes at Moses as she wrapped Truth in a tight embrace. "I'm *very* pleased to meet both of you. Jarena tells me you'll be joining us after church. I trust we'll have time to become better acquainted." She grasped Moses by the arm and flashed him a beguiling smile.

"Truth mentioned that she had an aunt—living in New Orleans, if memory serves me correctly."

Lilly squeezed his arm. "Why, I'm flattered Truth would even think to mention me. After all, I haven't been an important part of the girls' lives."

"Now dat's a fact," Ezekiel said as he approached. "Let go of the boy's arm, Lilly."

Her eyes gleamed, and Jarena wondered what she was thinking.

4

Following Sunday meeting, Jarena watched in silence as Aunt Lilly used her feminine wiles to win Moses's attention. There had been little doubt of the older woman's anger when she had been intentionally shuffled to the end of the church pew—as far away from Moses as possible. Her father's purpose had been as obvious as Aunt Lilly's flirtatious behavior.

The moment the final amen was uttered, Aunt Lilly elbowed Jarena aside and positioned herself beside Moses, immediately clasping his arm and leading him to a quiet spot in the churchyard. Truth, who was completely uneducated in the art of seduction, had left Moses's side and was chattering gaily with her twin, far from the secluded location chosen by Aunt Lilly. Poor Moses looked like a cornered animal seeking a path of escape.

When her father didn't arrive to separate the twosome, Jarena decided she could watch no longer. With quick strides, she approached the pair. "Did you find this morning's message enlightening, Aunt Lilly?"

"What? Oh, the sermon? It was much the same as all the others I've been subjected to. If you've heard one, you've heard them all."

Moses attempted to use the opportunity to extract his arm, but Lilly quickly tightened her hold. "Now, don't you try to get away from me," she cooed. "I've only just begun our discussion."

Undeterred, Moses deftly loosened her hold. He waved to a gentleman across the churchyard and, without giving Lilly opportunity to object, strode off.

Lilly pursed her lips into a girlish pout. Had Jarena thought this was a game, she would have laughed aloud at such childish behavior from a grown woman. She hoped her suspicion was incorrect, but it truly appeared as if her aunt had some plan in mind, one that obviously included Moses, which Jarena found both frightening and appalling.

"Now there's a man worth his salt! He's educated, handsome, charming, ambitious—"

"And engaged to marry my sister."

Lilly chortled. "A fact I find totally amusing. What could a man such as Moses Wyman possibly see in your little sister? She has absolutely nothing to offer him. She's much too young for a man of his maturity and sophistication. Moses needs a woman who can stand by his side and help him get ahead in the world. A woman who knows how to entertain and who won't embarrass him in public—and a woman who knows how to lavish affection on him."

Jarena narrowed her eyes and leveled a warning glare at her aunt. "A woman like you?"

Lilly gathered her skirts into her hands and began walking. "No, of course not. But you must admit that Truth is an unlikely choice for a man such as Moses. In our brief conversation, it was immediately apparent that Moses needs a mature wife, someone who can help him develop to his fullest potential. Someone like you, Jarena."

"Me? Don't be foolish. I love Thomas Grayson. Once he completes his assignment with the army, he's going to return to Nicodemus and we're going to be married. His acreage adjoins ours. Did you know that?"

Lilly shot Jarena a look of disgust as she looped arms with her. "Farming! You're no more suited to be a farmer's wife than I am. You're bright and quite beautiful, I might add. You need to expand your horizons and look to the future. What kind of life will you have out here on the prairie? With a man such as Moses, there's no limit to your future. Think of it, Jarena—you could help shape him into a man of importance. With Moses, you could see the world, travel to Europe, and mingle with people of importance. You'd be able to go places and experience a life most colored folks can only dream about."

Jarena yanked her arm loose as she stopped in her tracks. "How can you even think such things? Truth is my sister. She loves Moses, and he loves her. He obviously thinks she'll make the perfect wife. All of that aside, I have no desire for any man other than Thomas Grayson."

"And what if Thomas never returns to Nicodemus? What if he dies out there in Indian Territory fighting for some white officer who's only too happy to send him off to battle? From what I observed in church this morning, there are very few suitable unmarried men in Nicodemus."

Her aunt's words struck like a blow to the stomach. Already, Jarena worried daily about Thomas, crying herself to sleep when an expected letter was late arriving—or didn't arrive at all. Didn't she already fear the worst for him? She didn't need her aunt's cruel reminder that he was constantly in harm's way.

Grace jogged up beside Jarena, obviously noticing her faraway look. "You thinking about Thomas? Come on, Jarena. Pappy says we need to get started home."

Jarena shook off the worrisome thoughts and forced herself to speak. "Yes, I was." She turned and watched Lilly approach Moses and Truth. She'd been so caught up in her own feelings she'd not even realized Lilly had left her side. "Run over and tell Aunt Lilly that Pappy wants her to ride with us," she ordered. "You can ride with Moses and Truth if you like."

"But Aunt Lilly said she was going to ride with them."

"I don't care what she said. You go on now, and do as I said."

Jarena watched as Grace sprinted off to deliver the message. When Lilly turned to glare in her direction, Jarena merely smiled and waved her aunt forward. For the time being, she decided she would do what she could to keep Aunt Lilly away from Truth and Moses.

After Jarena and Lilly had boarded the family wagon, Jarena's father tipped his hat and cautiously maneuvered his wagon around the Beyer family. "I invited Miss Hattie and Nellie and Calvin to come over this afternoon for a visit." His comment was spoken in a calm, even tone though his expression was hard as he studied Lilly.

"Oh, that was a wonderful idea, Pappy!" Jarena said. "I haven't had a chance for a visit with Nellie in a long while."

Ezekiel smiled and nodded. "Know'd you'd be happy to hear they was coming, Jarena. Tol' Miss Hattie they should plan to stay and take supper with us. She said to tell you she'd be bringin' some vittles along with 'em, so you shouldn't worry none 'bout having enough food for everyone. Hope she brings one of them red raspberry pies . . . or gooseberry. Um, um, that might be even better."

Jarena laughed along with him. "If Miss Hattie doesn't bring one, I'll go berry picking next week and bake you a pie."

Ezekiel flashed his sister-in-law a toothy grin. "You be sure and take your aunt Lilly along. That way she can learn where all the best berry patches is. Thataway, she can keep us supplied with berries the whole time she's visitin' with us."

"I'm simply not one for spending my time outdoors." Lilly's words were as smooth as the silk ribbons that decorated her lavish hat.

"You'll adjust. I'll see to that. You best enjoy yourself today, 'cause come mornin' you's gonna start earnin' your keep, jest like the rest of this here family." Ezekiel pulled back on the reins as they neared the house. "See to it that you act proper this afternoon, Lilly," he cautioned as he helped her down from the wagon.

"What are you afraid of, Ezekiel? You think I might be able to do something to break up your little kingdom out here in the middle of nowhere?"

When Truth and Moses approached in their wagon, Lilly rubbed her hands together with far too much glee—at least that's what Jarena thought. There was little doubt this day would be filled with worry.

As they walked into the house, Lilly slipped by Truth and positioned herself alongside Moses. "I'd be most interested in hearing about your life back in Boston, Moses. I realize everyone else knows all about your past, but I would like to learn about your early years. In fact, we could go and sit outdoors so we wouldn't disturb the others."

Ezekiel frowned and pointed to a chair. "Seems you was tellin' me only a few minutes ago that the outdoors don' agree with you. Best you stay put inside the house. Anyways, we don' mind listening to Moses tell 'bout his life afore he come to Kansas. Do we, girls?"

"No, not at all," Jarena hastily agreed.

Moses turned an apologetic look toward Truth. "And what about you, Truth? Are you weary of this story?"

She smiled in return and shook her head. "You go ahead and visit with Aunt Lilly."

Lilly clapped her hands with obvious delight. "Good! First of all, I want to know about your parents. I told Jarena you could easily pass for white—at least in the North, where folks aren't so familiar with mixed bloodlines. Down in Louisiana, you might have a lick of trouble if you tried to pass."

Moses shifted in his chair beside her. "I'm not ashamed of my ancestry, Miss Lilly. In fact, it seems to make whites more uncomfortable than anyone else. As you've so perceptively noted, I am of mixed bloodline—more white than colored, I'm told. Both my grandmother and mother were of mixed blood. My mother and I were sired by the same man—the vile owner of a Louisiana plantation. My mother had jumped the broom with another slave, but that meant nothing to the plantation owner. He continued to have his way with her."

Apparently unimpassioned by the sordid revelation, Lilly continued her inquiry. "So how did you end up in Boston and get educated?"

Leaning back in the chair, Moses told how his small family's freedom had been purchased by the Houstons, a wealthy family living in Lowell, Massachusetts. He explained that Mrs. Houston had grown up on a cotton plantation in Mississippi but had never believed in slavery—which led to her subsequent activity with the abolitionist movement. Consequently, on one of her journeys to the South, Mrs. Houston had managed to strike an agreement with the plantation owner and secure their freedom. Though Moses was quick to add that his story was much more involved, he didn't elaborate further except to mention his thanks that he'd been spared a life of slavery.

Lilly sat forward, hanging on each word of Moses's unusual tale. "What an exciting story—and so Mrs. Houston simply handed you your papers?"

"No. The Houstons offered work on their horse farm as well as a place for us to live. I was but a small child at the time, and the Houstons had a young son, Spencer, who was the same age. We became friends, and the Houstons extended me the same educational advantages as those given to their own son. I was privately tutored alongside Spencer; later we attended school together."

Lilly waved her hand eagerly. "Do go on. I want to hear everything."

Moses shrugged. "There's not much more to tell. After graduating from college, Spencer and I briefly went into business together, but soon our lives took us in differing directions. While Spencer wanted to continue the operation of his family's horse farm and involve himself in several production ventures, I wanted to try my hand in either the newspaper business or politics."

Lilly's eyes widened at the mention of politics. "Truly? You *are* a man of vision."

Though he quickly admitted political office wasn't widely accessible to coloreds just yet, Moses declared people must be prepared to step forward when the opportunity finally arose. With that thought in mind, he had taken a position with a Boston newspaper, but feeling as though he'd reached his goals, he found himself restless and ready to accept a new challenge.

"So you came to this vast wasteland?" Lilly's words were spiked with disdain and bewilderment.

"Indeed! I investigated stories that had been circulating about the development of several all-colored communities, and I determined it would be an excellent opportunity to begin a new chapter in my life," he enthusiastically replied.

Lilly looked at him as though he'd lost his senses. "And?"

"And it has! Though my original plan had been to set up a newspaper office in Nicodemus, I became acquainted with a young lieutenant on the train coming west. He introduced me to his father, Dr. Boyle, who in turn directed me to the widow of the previous newspaper owner in Hill City. I was able to purchase the building and equipment. Now I print papers for both Hill City and Nicodemus. And, quite possibly, there could be a political future for me here in Kansas. Of course, the best part was meeting Truth," he added, glancing at his bride-to-be.

"Truly?" Lilly asked.

Moses smiled broadly and gazed lovingly at Truth. "Absolutely. If ever I doubted God's hand in sending me to the prairie, when I met

Truth, I knew without doubt why He'd sent me."

Lilly's lips tightened into a disgusted sneer. "You are an educated man, Moses. Please don't tell me you came traipsing out here because God told you to. Such a statement would make you sound downright foolish."

He laughed. "I gave up caring whether I sounded foolish long ago, Miss Lilly. I care more about what is right and wrong, good and evil. However, if you're asking if God actually whispered in my ear, the answer would be no. But I knew I was supposed to leave Boston, and I knew He was directing my path. I try to keep my eyes and ears open to His leading. Simple as that. Now, then, I believe it should be your turn. Tell me about yourself and why *you've* come to this vast waste-land—that *is* what you called it, isn't it?"

Lilly pushed away from the table. "I should likely be helping the girls prepare the noonday meal."

Jarena immediately took advantage of the break in their conversation. Like Moses, she was anxious to hear Aunt Lilly recount her past. Jarena motioned for her aunt to remain seated and then added her own appeal that Lilly relate her story. Both Grace and Truth echoed the sentiment and drew near, asking for details about life in New Orleans.

Jarena noted her father's look of smug satisfaction as he turned his attention to Lilly. "Go on, Lilly. Tell 'em 'bout your life down there in New Orleans. 'Member you said they's all growed up now—they's able to hear the truth. If you's able to speak it, that is."

Aunt Lilly drew a deep breath and then slowly exhaled through pursed lips. "Well, all right then. I suppose I can rightly entertain you until our noonday meal is ready. My sister Jennie, that would be your mama—we were born to the same mother, but we had different fathers."

Jarena dropped the knife she'd been using to pare apples. "Mama never mentioned that." She glanced at her father.

Ezekiel nodded. "That's true."

As Moses had done earlier, Lilly settled back in her chair. All eyes were focused upon her as she stated that she, too, had been sired by a white man. She told how her early years were spent on a plantation in Virginia, living in the big house, where her mama was a house servant. She shot a look at Ezekiel as she added that life had been a little easier for them than it had been for the field slaves.

"A *whole* lot easier," Ezekiel said.

"A whole lot easier," she conceded. "Our mama, your grandmother, was a cook at the big house, and I spent my time playing with the master's young daughter. Course, at the time, I didn't realize I was his daughter, too; that's why I was chosen to be Sarah's playmate."

With her elbow resting on her knee, Grace cupped her chin in her hand. "But you were privileged to be at the big house."

Lilly sighed. "I suppose you could say that. Sarah and I were together all day long. Every day. So when the tutor came to teach Sarah her lessons, I sat over in the corner and listened and learned right along with her. Sarah even had me do her schoolwork for her each day after the tutor went home. At night, when I returned to our little room off the kitchen, I'd teach my sister, your mama, what I'd learned that day. She was a year younger than me, but she was a smart child—learned easily."

"You got that right," Ezekiel agreed. "And she know'd right from wrong, too."

Lilly kept her attention on Jarena and her sisters. "As I was saying, your mama learned quickly, and I'm pleased to see she made certain you girls received some education. Now, where your mama and I differed is that I used what I learned to get ahead in the world, while she chose to get married at a young age."

"And we're surely glad she made the choice to marry Pappy, or we wouldn't be here," Grace put in.

"And how did you end up in New Orleans?" Moses inquired.

"That happened after we were sold and living in Kentucky. There was a fine gentleman that came to the plantation one day—a white man. He was taken with my beauty and intelligence and offered to purchase me right there and then. The master refused at first, but eventually they struck a bargain and he took me to New Orleans."

"And is that the man you married?" Grace asked.

Lilly arched her brows and looked at Grace as though she were a bit slow. "No. He was already married—to a white woman. But he gave me my freedom and—"

"You weren't no more free in New Orleans than you was workin' in the big house back at the plantation," Ezekiel blurted. "That man still owned you. He put up the money for your keep, but you repaid him with your soul."

The rebuke brought Lilly to her feet. "I repaid him with my body, but not my soul! My soul still hangs in the balance, Ezekiel. I haven't yet decided if I'll give that to God or the devil."

Ezekiel stood, too. "That's what ya say now, but that's not what you was tellin' Jennie in them letters you used to write her—telling her ya could heal her if she'd come to New Orleans and let ya practice some of that voodoo magic on her. And don' ya try and deny that, neither. She read them letters to me, and Jennie weren't no liar."

Lilly slowly lowered herself onto the chair, clinging to her lace-edged handkerchief.

Jarena watched the older woman. There was little doubt Lilly was embarrassed. A haunting look of desperation filled her eyes as she attempted to retain a sense of decorum. And much as Jarena loathed Lilly's behavior, she could not in good conscience continue to watch the woman struggle any longer. "It won't be long until dinner's ready," Jarena said. "You men go on outside while we set the table and dish up the food. I'll call you when we're ready to sit down."

Lilly brushed past Jarena on her way to retrieve a serving bowl. "Thank you."

The words were no more than a whisper, but Jarena heard them clearly—and they sounded sincere. Perhaps her simple act of kindness would carve a chink in Aunt Lilly's hardened heart.

CHAPTER

— 5 —

Though the conversation throughout their meal had remained stilted, Jarena noted Aunt Lilly seemed to regain her composure as the afternoon wore on. Shortly after Miss Hattie and their other guests arrived, it appeared as if the earlier discussion had been completely forgotten.

Miss Hattie busied herself cutting a slice of raspberry pie while Ezekiel stood over her, holding a plate. She stopped short of dishing up the slice and turned her rheumy eyes on Moses. "So when you an' Truth gonna finally jump the broom? Seems like you been talkin' 'bout marryin' that gal forever, but you still ain' done nothin' 'bout it."

Moses grinned and extended his hand toward Truth. "It's not me that's holding up the plans, Miss Hattie. Truth says she wants to wait until September."

The old woman squinted and then frowned at Truth. "Why? You

two been courtin' for nigh onto two years now, Truth. Seems as though you'd know if he's the one by now."

Ezekiel pushed his plate forward. "Could ya dish up that piece of pie, Hattie, or do I gotta do it fer myself?"

Hattie gave him a look before heeding his wishes. "You got no patience, Ezekiel Harban. Moses, you and Calvin come get ya a piece of this here pie and go on outside with Ezekiel so us womenfolk can get us some serious talkin' done. Now where was I?"

Lilly leaned forward and patted Miss Hattie's hand. "Attempting to rush Truth into marriage."

"Rush? Either she loves him or she don't."

"Sometimes people need to find out if they're truly suited, Miss Hattie. There's a span of fourteen years between them—and a number of other differences, also," Lilly asserted. "Personally, I think Truth is exhibiting a great deal of intelligence and good sense by waiting. After all, there's nothing worse than finding out you've married the wrong person after you've already committed."

Truth appeared both pleased and confused by the comments. "I don't doubt my love for Moses, Aunt Lilly."

Lilly patted Truth's hand as she launched into a maternal speech. She warned about confusing genuine love for a man with mere infatuation, especially in circumstances where one has never before had a beau. After all, an inexperienced girl, especially one who's never even traveled, couldn't possibly expect to understand the deep emotions a man and woman should have before they wed.

Truth frowned and shook her head. "But I've traveled, Aunt Lilly. We saw lots of places when we moved out here from Georgetown."

Lilly sighed wearily. "But you never truly *experienced* them, did you? Never lived anywhere else or learned about other people or cultures. In addition to the age difference between you two, you're immature in the ways of the world—unlike Moses, who has traveled and is highly educated. Why, I would speculate you didn't even enjoy being schooled, did you?"

Truth agreed her aunt was correct on that account.

Finding she could take it no longer, Jarena stepped forward to come to her sister's defense. "Don't you let anyone put doubt in your mind, Truth. You love Moses, and he loves you. The two of you have much in common. You've succeeded in publishing newspapers to two communities, which is a feat not many couples could accomplish. I'd venture that there aren't many folks who could work so closely together in harmony."

Truth clasped her hands into a tight knot. "And we're both fond of Kansas."

"I don't expect that a man of Moses's stature will wish to remain in this dreary place for long," Aunt Lilly put in. "Once he's proven to himself that he's accomplished his purpose, he'll be ready to move on. He's already indicated an interest in politics. And you, Truth, will *you* be ready to leave here? Could you face leaving your sisters and father behind to follow your husband to some unknown place? Perhaps even another country?"

The joy in Truth's dark eyes clouded with fear as she declared her concerns over leaving friends and family. However, she soon recovered and avowed Moses wouldn't force her to leave her home, saying she was confident he would remain in Nicodemus if that was her desire.

Jarena glowered at Lilly as she concurred with her sister and then added, "I feel certain Moses would prefer to rear his children out here in the West."

Lilly crossed her arms and glanced back and forth between the two sisters. "Truly? Don't you think he would favor sending his children to a school where they could receive a quality education and would be afforded the same opportunities he received as a young man?"

"She's likely correct," Truth hesitantly agreed.

"Oh, pshaw!" Miss Hattie spoke up. "This here's jest a bunch of nonsense to my way of thinkin'. Only God knows what's gonna happen in the future, Truth. You gotta follow your heart. Moses is a good God-fearin' man who's bound to do right by you. Best you get yourself married to him afore some other gal sets her cap for him."

Truth massaged her forehead. "What do you think, Jarena?"

"I've already told you what I think. If you want to get married tomorrow, we'll see to it!"

Miss Hattie tapped the end of her parasol on the dirt floor. "Now that's the kinda talk I like to hear!"

Lilly walked to the door, pausing to lay a hand on Truth's shoulder. "So far as I'm concerned, Truth's inability to make her own decision speaks for itself." And with that declaration, she stepped outside into the warm June sunshine.

———

Lilly spied the three men gathered under a lonely cottonwood a short distance from the soddy. Ezekiel was sitting on a bench while Calvin and Moses sat on the ground, both leaning against the tree trunk. Ezekiel glanced up as Lilly drew near.

She sat on the bench beside him, lamenting the fact that the women were discussing topics of little interest to her. Consequently, she had decided a breath of fresh air would be more to her liking.

Calvin tucked a long piece of buffalo grass into the corner of his mouth. After declaring that Lilly didn't look like the kind of woman who would be happy living on a farm, he inquired what she planned to do with herself now that she'd arrived in Kansas.

Lilly batted her lashes and gave him an appreciative nod. "Why, you flatter me, Calvin. It's nice to see that such a young man can recognize a woman who's accustomed to the finer things in life. Unfortunately, unless I can locate some type of employment, I'm afraid I'm destined to accept Ezekiel's hospitality. You see, I fell on hard times prior to departing New Orleans, and I'm afraid that I now find myself financially embarrassed."

Calvin scratched his head.

"She ain't got no money," Ezekiel clarified.

Moses mentioned that a new banker had recently arrived in Hill City and was looking for live-in help. He offered to put in a word with Mr. Nelson if Lilly was interested in the position. Lilly was quite eager to say yes until Moses mentioned the couple had small children—possibly two or three. The mere thought!

Ezekiel slapped his knee and guffawed loudly. "Now that there would be a sight!"

Soon the other women joined them under the cottonwood. Jarena cradled little Annie Harris in her arms. With her bright eyes and dimpled chin, the baby girl was a picture of Nellie. On the other hand, young Nathan, with his sturdy build and quick smile, closely resembled his father. The boy trundled through the tall prairie grass and made a squealing headlong dive at his papa.

Miss Hattie motioned Ezekiel off the bench. "What you laughing 'bout?"

Ezekiel shoved his hat back on his head and chortled. "Lilly workin' as a housekeeper and mammy for some banker and their young'uns over in Hill City."

Well, that did it. Lilly jutted her chin forward and squared her shoulders. "I believe I'd be interested in the position, Moses. And I'd be most grateful if you would speak to Mr. Nelson when you return to Hill City. Tell him I could begin work immediately—so long as he can make arrangements for my travel to Hill City."

The entire group stared at her until Miss Hattie finally spoke. "'Scuse me? You's gonna go tend house for white folk? I don't believe it. You gonna wear them dance hall dresses to cook supper and chase after chil'ens? You ain't fit to be lookin' after no young'uns."

Lilly shifted on the bench. "Oh, but I *do* mean to seek the position. As for my clothing, I'm certain the banker's wife will find my apparel quite acceptable—and fashionable, I might add. As for the children, I believe Mr. and Mrs. Nelson will discover that I have much to offer their children, both educationally and socially. Don't you agree, Truth? Surely the Boyles have entertained these newcomers in their home— what did you think of them?"

Truth sat on the grass beside Moses. "Mrs. Nelson has come calling only once, and I've never met Mr. Nelson or the children. As for enter- taining, Mrs. Boyle has recurring bouts of illness and hasn't been well these past months. Dr. Boyle insists she refrain from the effort of entertaining guests during those times when she is ailing."

A warm breeze rustled through the lone cottonwood as Lilly considered this. "It would seem Mrs. Boyle depends upon you a great deal, Truth," she said. "I doubt whether a sweet girl like you would want to leave such a kind woman without assistance. How could she possibly get by if you were to marry and leave her employ?"

Moses lurched to attention. "Your concern is appreciated, Miss Lilly. However, the Boyles's daughter, Macia, will soon be returning to Hill City—in September—to take up her teaching duties. She's more than capable of caring for her mother."

"But if she's off teaching school all day . . ." Lilly permitted her words to trail off as she directed an accusatory look at Truth.

A frown creased Moses's forehead. "The Boyles know that we plan to wed in September. If Macia isn't able to successfully manage both tasks, Dr. and Mrs. Boyle will make proper arrangements. I truly don't think this is a problem that warrants your concern, Miss Lilly."

"Of course, you're correct, Moses. I was merely thinking aloud. I do hope you'll forgive me if I've caused you any discomfort by discussing Mrs. Boyle's welfare, Truth. After all, you're a sensitive young lady, and I should have realized that you would have already considered Mrs. Boyle and her physical afflictions. And, of course, I didn't realize there was an unmarried daughter in the Boyle household—a schoolteacher, you say. A plain girl, I take it?"

Miss Hattie pointed a finger at Lilly. "You sure is quick to pass judgment on folks. Miss Macia's a right pretty gal—smart, too."

Lilly swatted at a fly that circled nearby. "Yet not overly concerned with her mother's medical condition, I take it?"

"Macia cares deeply for her mother. It was her mother who insisted she attend some special school in New York," Truth explained.

Lilly sighed. "Seems marriage is a difficult matter in this part of the country. On the one hand, we have Macia Boyle, who can't seem to find anyone willing to marry her. On the other hand, we have Jarena, with a beau who's run off to Indian Territory; then, of course, there's Truth, who isn't certain she should marry at all. My, my, things are—"

"Hold on a minute!" Moses exclaimed, looking directly at Truth. "Did I hear her right? Did she say that you don't want to get married?"

"No . . . I mean yes—she did say that. But I said . . . well, I mentioned . . . oh, I don't know what I said, but I do know that I want to marry you, Moses," Truth sputtered.

"No need to be upset, Truth. You're an unworldly girl and unaccustomed to making important decisions. Surely Moses loves you enough to wait until you've made up your mind about your future." Lilly leaned forward and rested an arm around Truth. "Trust me, you're not ready for marriage—especially to Moses," she whispered in the girl's ear before releasing her.

Ezekiel jumped to his feet. "That there's a bunch of nonsense, and we done had enough of that kinda talk. Them two is jumpin' the broom come September, and you needs to keep your fingers outta the pot, Lilly. You hear me now?"

Lilly nodded demurely. "Of course, Ezekiel—whatever you believe is best."

CHAPTER

— 6 —

Once Ezekiel had started a fire under the wash water, he and Grace departed for the fields. Jarena returned indoors to retrieve a bucket. She'd have sufficient time to gather berries while the water heated. Lilly, who had remained abed while Grace and Jarena had hauled water for the laundry, was now up and dressed, enjoying a cup of coffee. After hearing Jarena's plan, Lilly declared she'd like to join her. When Jarena gave her what she was sure was an astonished look, Lilly declared that berry picking, after all, was not an overly strenuous activity.

They'd gone only a short distance when Lilly tugged on Jarena's arm and pointed at a growth of wild sunshine roses. Jarena followed after Lilly, surprised to discover her aunt's interest in the prairie's floral offerings.

Lilly stooped down and plucked a purple bloom. "Look! There are violets, too. With these flowers and some items I have in my trunk, we can mix up a batch of perfume. I have everything else we'll need, and I'll teach you my special recipe."

Jarena knelt beside Lilly, suddenly wanting to impress the woman—once again feeling mysteriously drawn to her. Lilly's willingness to instruct her was even more exhilarating than inhaling the signature fragrance the woman wore each day. As she continued to pick the flowers, Lilly explained the simple perfume-making process and suggested that if they truly liked the mixture, the two of them might consider joining forces in a small business venture.

Jarena hadn't had time to digest the idea, much less formulate a decision, when Lilly laid out the rest of her plan. They would secure the services of an itinerant peddler who could furnish them with bottles and oil once they'd depleted the small inventory from Lilly's trunk. In addition, the peddler could market their product for a small commission. Though Lilly avowed neither of them would get rich from such a venture, they could at least earn a little pin money. And, Lilly noted, most of the women she'd met could benefit from the use of perfume. In fact, the two of them would be conducting an act of charity by producing such a product!

Jarena didn't think perfume production qualified as a charitable act, though she did like the idea of earning her own money. The funds could be put to good use when Thomas finally returned. Yes, she decided, there was a definite appeal to the venture.

As Lilly continued to extol the entrepreneurial scheme, the sun grew warm on Jarena's neck. With a start, she remembered the dirty laundry and boiling wash pot and bounded to her feet. The flowers she'd gathered in her skirt spilled to the ground as she hastily explained they must hurry home. Undeterred, Lilly agreed to follow once she retrieved the flowers Jarena had carelessly dropped. Anxious to be on her way, Jarena had taken but a few steps out of the thicket when Lilly called her back with an instruction to remove two buckets of boiling water from the vat before adding the soap. They would need the untainted water for their perfume, she advised.

If nothing else, Aunt Lilly remained focused upon her objective. The woman seemed to care little if the household tasks were completed or if supper was prepared. However, once away from Lilly's charming talk, Jarena's thoughts returned to her chores. An explanation would be due if the clothes weren't clean and supper wasn't on the table—and she was the one who would be required to answer. She doubted Pappy would think flower picking and perfume making an adequate excuse.

The water was at a full boil by the time she arrived home—probably had been for at least half an hour, Jarena surmised. Still, the idea of making Lilly's signature fragrance enticed her enough that she removed two buckets of water before she began chipping soap into the vat.

Jarena was hanging the last of the laundry when Lilly finally ambled back to the house carrying a big bundle of flowers and softly singing a tune. There was little doubt in Jarena's mind that her aunt had intentionally stayed away from the house until the work was completed. Likely she had been relaxing while staying out of view until the last of the laundry had been scrubbed and hung to dry.

Lilly picked up the two buckets sitting nearby. "I'll go inside and reheat part of this water. We can begin as soon as you finish hanging the clothes."

Wiping her hands on her apron, Jarena walked indoors. Numerous empty bottles lined the table along with a small container of oil and a tall bottle of liquor. Jarena considered mentioning that alcohol wasn't permitted in Nicodemus. In fact, her father had signed a pledge when he purchased his land. *Best to stop now*, the tiny voice of her conscience urged. But her aunt was already pulling blooms apart.

"Sit down and help me with the flowers. Be careful with the roses. I've already pricked my finger twice."

Unheedingly, Jarena grabbed one of the stems but quickly dropped it from her hand. A tiny puddle of blood appeared where a small thorn had embedded in her finger. Once again the voice pricked her conscience—once again she hearkened to Lilly's voice instead.

Lilly was explaining the use of unscented oils to enhance the fragrance of flowers when Jarena perked to attention at a sound outside: a wagon—and the familiar sound of Miss Hattie's voice. Nearly knocking her chair to the floor, Jarena jumped up and rushed to the doorway. The old matriarch was lumbering toward her carrying a freshly baked pie while Calvin Harris moved to the rear of the wagon and hoisted her father's plow to the ground. He headed off to return the borrowed plow to the barn.

Jarena quickly stationed herself between Miss Hattie and the front door. With any luck, Calvin and his grandmother-in-law would quickly be on their way. Jarena held out her hands to receive the pastry, but the old woman ignored her and marched on toward the house, the whole time explaining that Calvin had promised to return the plow today. Jarena bounded ahead of the woman, but Miss Hattie was like a wagon on a roll. You either moved out of the way or she ran over you. Jumping aside, Jarena managed to enter the house and take up a position in front of the table. She spread the folds of her skirt across the table, thinking she must look like a bird prepared to take flight.

Miss Hattie greeted Lilly and then explained Calvin had hoped to come by the house earlier. However, she'd made him wait until her pies were baked. After all, the least they could do was bring Ezekiel a pie to thank him for the loan of his plow. There was no doubt the woman was scanning every item on the table as she set her gooseberry pie on the sideboard.

After a long look at the table, Miss Hattie turned to Jarena. "We's needin' to have us a talk—in private." Miss Hattie pulled her along until they cleared the door and moved away from the house. When she finally released Jarena's arm, Miss Hattie's breathing was labored and there was anger in her eyes. "What kind of craziness you and that woman got goin' on in there?"

Jarena struggled to find the proper words. "We're . . . we're making perfume . . . to sell. I'm going to save the money to help Thomas and me set up housekeeping when he returns."

Miss Hattie touched a finger to Jarena's head. "You doin' any thinkin' with that head of yours or you jest using it for a hat perch? There's alcohol in your pappy's house. You think he's gonna be happy 'bout that?"

"No, but . . ."

"Ain't no buts 'bout it. You's headed down a crooked road that's gonna lead you to trouble for sure. Now if you's smart, you's gonna march back in that house and tell Lilly you done made a mistake and she best clear up that mess she's makin'—and get rid of that liquor. You knows your pappy could get hisself in trouble if folks find out he's got liquor in his house."

Calvin waved from the wagon, obviously anxious to be on his way. Jarena sighed, relieved Miss Hattie would soon be gone. No telling what might happen next if the old woman remained. She'd likely go inside and destroy the supplies herself.

Miss Hattie waved back at Calvin. "I's comin', jest hold on a minute. You mind what I'm tellin' you, gal. I ain' gonna say nothin' 'bout none of this to no one, but I expect you to do the right thing."

"Yes, Miss Hattie." Though she truly didn't want to agree, Jarena mumbled the obligatory words. "You won't say anything to Pappy, will you?"

"I ain't gonna say a word. Now go on inside and get that mess cleared away."

Lilly didn't look up from her handiwork when Jarena stepped back into the house. Without giving Jarena opportunity to speak, her aunt launched into additional ideas regarding their new perfume business. She would order special oils to create a longer-lasting perfume—one for which they could charge more money. And, of course, they could change the scent depending upon the available flowers. Lilly explained they would purchase only a few of the costly oils she truly preferred. After all, they would want to make a profit.

When her aunt finally paused, Jarena relayed what Miss Hattie had plainly pointed out. "I'm concerned that Pappy won't agree to this venture. Perhaps we should wait until I can gain his approval."

As she had earlier, Lilly continued working, undeterred by the remark. "I don't know why he would object. Didn't God create these flowers with wonderful aromas? I'm certain He'd want His children smelling just as fine as the flowers. Besides, what's wrong with making perfume? We're performing a service for the womenfolk on the prairie."

She has a point, Jarena thought. She forced aside Miss Hattie's warning and continued to ignore the small voice urging her to stop. She focused her attention on Lilly and her exacting directions. And when her aunt finally declared the mixture ready to be bottled, Jarena carefully funneled the sweet-smelling liquid into the shiny containers. She didn't notice the sun had begun to cast longer shadows across the hardened dirt floor—nor did she hear her father approach the house.

"What's all this going on in here?" he boomed from the doorway, the sun forming a golden halo around his floppy felt hat. "Sure don' smell like my supper cookin' on that fire." The bottle in Jarena's hand dropped to the floor. Glass shards scattered around her feet and reflected tiny prisms of light.

Jarena waited, hoping Lilly would respond. Instead, Lilly folded her hands in a saintly fashion and remained uncharacteristically silent.

"I's waitin' for an answer, gal." Her father crossed the room in four long strides, stopping directly in front of Jarena.

She stepped in front of the shelf where she'd placed the oils and alcohol. Pointing a trembling finger at the small bottles that lined the kitchen table, she regaled her father with the many attributes of their proposed business venture—as many as she could recall, at least. Her thoughts had scattered like rose petals in a gust of wind the moment her father had entered the house. He didn't appear convinced as he stepped forward and gently moved her aside. His gaze settled on the oils and then he picked up the bottle of alcohol. Without a word, he removed the lid, walked out the door, and poured the contents on the ground. His dark eyes bore down on Jarena as he set the empty bottle on the shelf.

Ezekiel moved to the table, his jaw twitching as he dropped onto the chair opposite his sister-in-law. "Lilly, what you got to say 'bout all this?"

With a demure shrug, Lilly explained there was little she could add. Jarena glared at her aunt. Nothing to add? Why didn't her aunt come to her defense? Why didn't she explain what a wonderful idea this was? Lilly could at least admit making perfume had been her idea.

"This was all my idea, Ezekiel." Lilly's insipid confession did little to deflate the crackling tension that filled the room.

"I never doubted that for one minute. My girls ain' never disobeyed me 'til you walked into my house, Lilly. Jest about the time I's thinkin' I been too hard on you, you go and prove me wrong. Liquor ain' allowed in Nicodemus. Jarena knows that—everyone who lives here knows. And I'd wager you knew it afore you opened that bottle. Ain' that right?"

Lilly didn't flinch. "I don't understand why you're getting all riled up. You're acting as though I invited folks over to purchase a shot of whiskey when all I've done is teach Jarena how to make perfume so she can earn a little money."

Ezekiel struck the table with his fist. "Don' you go trying to mix right and wrong, Lilly! There ain' no excuse fer none of this. Jarena don' need no extra money. She's got everything she needs right here— and that don' include you or your perfume makin'."

Lilly folded her arms across her waist. "Men aren't always the finest judge of what's best—especially where their wives and daughters are concerned." She grudgingly added, "However, I'll do my best to keep the peace and abide by your rules until I can find a job."

Ezekiel gave a nod. "That would suit me jest fine. Now get this mess off the table and let's see to gettin' some supper."

Jarena hastened to begin supper while Lilly returned the bottles and supplies to her trunk. Ezekiel went outdoors to wait. Lilly nonchalantly drew closer to Jarena once Ezekiel had moved away from the house. "If you like, we can still make the perfume. We'll merely need to begin earlier in the day and keep our actions secret. The flowers will still be fine tomorrow morning."

Jarena shook her head and declined the offer. If her aunt intended to continue the perfume-making business, it would be without her assistance. Jarena wasn't willing to break the rules set up by the town of Nicodemus. Predictably, Lilly seemed unruffled by the refusal.

CHAPTER

— 7 —

New York City

M acia slumped forward, unable to control herself. She gasped for air as her upper body came to rest atop the polished oak desk. The familiar scent of lemon oil filled her nostrils while the cool wood soothed her fevered cheek. In the distance, she heard a faint tapping—perhaps a woodpecker drumming his beak on the ancient walnut tree outside the window. The tapping grew louder and more insistent. A slight breeze dusted her cheek as a loud thwack sounded directly beside her ear.

Her eyelids fluttered open and she settled her bleary gaze upon the wooden rod lying beside her face. She wanted to lift her head—she told herself to move, say something, sit up, do anything—but all to no avail. The stick moved from sight and was replaced by her French instructor's face. Mr. Gautier's head was tilted to the side, and he looked directly into her eyes.

"*Est-ce que je vous dérange, Mademoiselle Boyle?*"

The words jumbled in her mind as Macia attempted to translate the question into English. "*Oui*, I must take a nap."

"*Levez-vous, s'il vous plaît!*"

"I can't sit up—my head."

She listened to the sound of Mr. Gautier's departing footsteps, but she was still unable to move.

Rennie grasped Macia by the shoulders. "Macia! You must sit up." Macia's dead weight settled against the chair back. "Mr. Gautier has gone to report you to Mrs. Rutledge. This is the third day he's caught you sleeping during class. He's very angry, Macia."

"I'm ill, Rennie. I can't sit here. Please help me upstairs; I must lie down."

Inez's voice came from a couple of desks away. "You'd best not, Rennie. You'll get in trouble, too. Macia's likely pretending to be ill again because she hasn't completed her lessons."

If she'd had enough strength, Macia would have hurled her lesson book across the room at Inez. The girl was frightfully mean-spirited and certainly not someone Macia would ever count a friend. In fact, finding fault, either real or imagined, with others was the only thing that seemed to give Inez pleasure.

Macia handed Rennie her lesson book. "You can turn this in for me, Rennie, but I'm going upstairs, even if I must crawl on my hands and knees."

Amanda hurried to Macia's desk and encircled Macia's waist with her right arm. "I'll help you to your room, Macia. If Mr. Gautier wants to refund my parents' money, I'd like nothing more than to return home. I didn't want to come here in the first place."

"We'll both help you." Rennie gathered their lesson books and handed them to Lucy. "Here, Lucy, please turn in the lesson books for all three of us."

Lucy took the books, though she was obviously vacillating between fear and admiration as she danced from foot to foot. "What should I say to Mr. Gautier?"

"The truth. Tell him we've assisted Macia to bed, and when we feel it's appropriate to leave her alone, we'll return to class—which may not be today." Rennie grinned. "Though you need not add my final remark."

Macia groaned as the girls helped her to her feet. Her legs felt as though they'd been pumped full of jelly. Her knees buckled with each step. Amanda and Rennie tightened their hold as she began to sink toward the floor. She could feel perspiration on her forehead and upper lip as the girls hauled her to the stairs. By the time they had reached the upper hallway, she couldn't move her own body. The last thing she remembered was the heavy breathing of her friends as they attempted to pull her along toward the bedroom.

When Macia finally opened her eyes, she was greeted by the soft glow of her bedside lamp. She was lying in bed, still wearing the navy skirt and white shirtwaist required by the school, and Rennie was sitting in a chair across the room. "What time is it?"

"Nearly midnight. How do you feel?"

"Somewhat better, I think. Have you been with me all this time?"

Rennie smiled and drew her chair closer. "Amanda and I have been spelling each other. She's scheduled to return at three o'clock; then I'll sleep until breakfast."

"I'm so sorry. You must be exhausted." Macia licked her parched lips. "I do hope the two of you didn't get in trouble with Mr. Gautier or Mrs. Rutledge."

Rennie poured a cup of water and lifted it to Macia's lips. "Here, take a sip. You need not worry about us. Mrs. Rutledge doesn't want to refund money to our parents, so she's not going to say anything—at least for the time being." Rennie set the cup on the bedside table. "We must discover what is wrong with you. I think Inez may be taking ill, too. Janet told Mrs. Rutledge Inez had taken to her bed after classes today and wasn't well enough to come down for supper this evening."

"I do hope she managed to complete her lessons," Macia said with a feeble grin.

Rennie giggled. "She is a heartless one, isn't she?"

"I think she's anxious to impress Mr. Laird."

"You think she's enamored with him? Oh, how fun! Inez besotted by Mr. Laird. He's too old for her, don't you think?"

"Some girls like older men. Besides, he's not so much older—perhaps twelve years."

Rennie wrinkled her nose. "I want a man my own age, not some stick-in-the-mud who wants to sit home by the fire with a wool throw over his knees."

"Oh, Rennie, I always feel so much better when you're around to make me laugh."

The door swung open and Mrs. Rutledge entered the room. "She's dressed to receive visitors," she told Mr. Laird, beckoning him forward.

"You've come to call on me after midnight?"

"We were concerned about your health. And why aren't you in bed, Miss Kruger? You'll be falling asleep in class tomorrow. After missing your lessons today, you can ill afford such lackadaisical behavior. Your parents deserve better—and so does Rutledge Academy."

Rennie shrugged. "I'm more concerned about Macia's health than a few French lessons. Besides, my parents won't care a jot. They've grown quite accustomed to my failing marks in school."

Mr. Laird stepped closer. "Instead of intruding in Miss Boyle's health problems, why don't you surprise your parents and attend to your studies—just this once. *We* are the ones entrusted to look after Miss Boyle."

Rennie remained in her chair. "Well, *you're* not doing a very good job. Why don't you telegraph her father and ask his opinion? He's a doctor."

Macia sat up a bit straighter. "Perhaps I should contact my father and set forth my complaints. He will likely have some idea of what ails me."

"No need, my dear," Mrs. Rutledge said. "We've already written a lengthy letter to your father explaining your illness. We don't want to overly upset him—after all, you've already explained he can't leave your mother. And you do appear to be feeling much better tonight."

"Yes, that's true. I suppose you're right."

"Of course I am. Rennie, why don't you go along to your room? Macia's feeling better, and you both need to sleep."

Rennie leaned forward and grasped Macia's hand. "I'm happy to stay with you for the remainder of the night."

"No need. You go along. We can both sleep for a few hours before breakfast."

Mrs. Rutledge took Rennie's hand and walked her to the door. "Sleep well, my dear."

The moment the door closed behind Rennie, Mrs. Rutledge drew near and put her hand on Macia's forehead while Mr. Laird poured a small amount of water into a cup. He held out the cup, and Macia took a small sip. Pushing the cup forward, Mr. Laird insisted Macia empty the contents, for she remained somewhat feverish. In spite of the foul taste, Macia drank the liquid, though she did ask if Rennie could bring her fresh water the next morning.

"We have servants to see to such things. Daisy will bring you a pitcher first thing in the morning. You should change into your night-gown. We'll see you at breakfast in the morning."

Macia waited until they departed and then removed her navy blue serge uniform. Her skin didn't feel warm, and she wondered if she truly had a fever. She didn't like Mr. and Mrs. Rutledge—or Mr. Laird. There was something disturbing about the trio that ran this school. Though she doubted whether sleep would come after a full day in bed, Macia slipped between the sheets.

The sun was beaming in her window when she finally awakened the next day. Surely breakfast had been completed hours ago. She stood up, and her knees wobbled as she crossed the room. Leaning her head against the doorjamb, she turned the knob and peeked into the hall. Daisy sat on the floor outside her door. She appeared startled but quickly gained her wits and inquired if there was anything Macia needed.

Macia frowned. "Has breakfast been served?"

The colored girl stood up and smiled. "Breakfast and dinner. It's almost two o'clock, Miss Boyle. I brung a fresh pitcher of water this morning, but you was fast asleep."

Dizziness once again overcame Macia, and she grabbed the doorknob to steady herself before attempting to send Daisy on her way. After all, there was no need for Daisy to sit outside her door all day. Macia certainly didn't want someone guarding her door. She'd feel as though her bedroom had become a prison cell.

However, Daisy was adamant she must remain. She'd been instructed by Mr. Laird to wait outside the door and report everything Macia said or did. Stating she would return as soon as she reported Macia was awake, Daisy turned to leave.

Macia grasped the girl's arm and had soon convinced her there was no need to tell Mr. Laird, for she would be asleep again within minutes. Macia invited her to stand watch until she'd fallen asleep.

The girl shook her head and motioned for Macia to go on to bed as Daisy slid back into position alongside the door. Macia leaned against the cool wood and gathered her strength before wobbling across the floor and falling into bed. She shivered in the warm room. Why was Daisy guarding her door and reporting to Mr. Laird? What was going on in this place?

CHAPTER

— 8 —

Nicodemus, Kansas

t the sound of an approaching carriage, Jarena dried her
hands on a worn cloth and walked to the open door of the
soddy. "Wonder who that could be." She could sense Lilly
following close on her heels.

"Let's hope it's someone who can add a bit of amusement to our
dull lives," Lilly muttered. She drew nearer and peered around Jarena's
shoulder.

"Maybe a few Indians will come calling. That would likely provide
you with enough excitement for several days."

Lilly grasped Jarena by the arm. "Do Indians still live around here?"

The distress in her aunt's voice brought a smile to Jarena's lips. So
there was at least one thing that frightened the woman. "Some," she

calmly replied. "They're mostly friendly—especially the Osage. In fact, had it not been for their kindness during our first winter in Nicodemus, we might have perished. They were good-hearted enough to provide us with a portion of their kill when they passed through our settlement after one of their winter hunts."

Lilly shuddered. "I've heard tell of the horrid things they do—savages."

Jarena glanced over her shoulder, unexpectedly remembering a frightening dream she'd had the night before. "The Indians we've encountered are much less frightening than the possibility of someone conjuring up voodoo curses."

"You're worried I've placed a curse on someone, Jarena?"

Jarena nodded toward the black velvet cord that circled Lilly's throat. "I've seen you babble gibberish and rub on that talisman hanging around your neck. But I know God's power is greater than any of your conjuring, so I've been praying for His protection—and that you'll soon see the error of your ways."

Lilly fingered the amulet and emitted a throaty laugh. "I'm thinking that fine-looking gentleman walking toward us is none other than Mr. Nelson. I may be out from under your roof sooner than either of us thought possible."

The man removed his narrow-brimmed bowler as he approached the soddy. "Good morning, ladies. I do hope I've located the proper homestead. I'm looking for the Harban family and Lilly Verdue."

Lilly stepped forward and beamed at the man. "You must be Mr. Nelson. Let me commend you, as your excellent sense of direction has led you to the correct place." When he didn't immediately reply, Lilly tilted her head and smiled. "You are Mr. Nelson, aren't you?"

"Why, how did you know?"

Lilly carefully tucked a wisp of hair behind her ear. "Moses said to expect a handsome gentleman."

Jarena rolled her eyes.

"Why don't we sit outdoors and talk, Mr. Nelson?" Lilly said, indicating the cottonwood. "It's warm inside—and quite cramped. I'm certain you would be more comfortable under what little shade that tree can offer us."

Jarena trailed behind the twosome. She hadn't been invited to join them, yet her curiosity was sparked by the fancy gentleman's visit. Besides, she wanted to hear the conversation firsthand. There was no telling what version Aunt Lilly might relate once the man departed. The woman was proving to be an expert at twisting the truth.

Mr. Nelson sat down on the wooden bench under the tree and balanced his hat on one knee. "Moses tells me you're interested in working as a housekeeper." He took a moment to appraise Lilly's appearance before he continued. "However, you don't appear to be a woman who would be interested in a housekeeping position. And, truth be told, we need more than just a housekeeper. My wife and I definitely need someone who can help care for our children, assist with meals, and generally help maintain our household—someone willing to live in so that when both my wife and I must be away, the children receive proper attention and care. Do you enjoy children, Mrs. Verdue?"

"Do call me Lilly," she replied. "Though I've enjoyed periods of prosperity in my life, I've fallen upon hard times. Therefore, I am exceedingly interested in the position, Mr. Nelson. I'm certain that

Moses spoke highly of my abilities. As you likely know, Mr. Wyman is nearly a member of the family and is highly regarded by all who know him."

She was avoiding his question—and doing so with such skill that Jarena wondered if Mr. Nelson would notice.

"There's no doubt Mr. Wyman is a fine man—intelligent, well educated, and an excellent businessman. However, I'm interested in *your* qualifications, Mrs. Verdue—Lilly. When I spoke with Moses, he stated only that you are Truth's aunt and that you are seeking employment in this area. He added that neither he nor Truth could vouch for your suitability—due to the fact that they had only recently made your acquaintance."

With a look of warning, Lilly swiveled toward Jarena and requested the girl give Mr. Nelson a recommendation. Undeterred by her aunt's attempt to control the situation, Jarena declined the appeal and suggested Mr. Nelson speak to her father instead.

Lilly squinted at Jarena before turning her attention back to Mr. Nelson. "Ezekiel—Mr. Harban—was married to my half-sister, who died several years ago. However, he's currently out in the fields and won't return to the house until dusk. If you'd like to wait for him, we could find you a cool glass of water and perhaps something to eat—if your wife won't be overly concerned about your late arrival home."

Jarena bit her lower lip, quietly observing while Lilly manipulated Mr. Nelson into making a hasty decision. The woman was both intelligent and canny. But above all else, Aunt Lilly was an expert at influencing and controlling others!

Mr. Nelson pulled a gold watch from his pocket and checked the time, immediately stating his concern that his wife might believe his carriage had overturned or he'd met with some other unforeseen disaster. Slipping the watch back into his pocket, he hastily offered the position for the sum of ten dollars a month along with room and board.

Lilly gasped. "Ten dollars?" Her words sounded as if they'd been scraped over river rock.

Mr. Nelson patted her hand. "I know I'm making a generous proposal, but Moses did mention your tutoring abilities. Your qualifications surpass those of anyone we had expected to find."

Hoping she could stifle a giggle, Jarena bit her bottom lip. The thought of her aunt managing three children while preparing meals and doing cleaning for the Nelson family could prove most entertaining. She wondered if Aunt Lilly's wages would be decreased the first time she overslept or scorched the griddle cakes. Not likely, she lamented. Instead, Aunt Lilly would likely convince Mr. Nelson to *increase* her pay by using the same method she had just now used to wrangle him into hiring her without a proper reference.

"How soon would you be prepared to leave for Hill City, Mrs. Verdue—Lilly?"

Jarena followed close behind the twosome as they walked toward the house.

"If you could give me twenty minutes," her aunt replied, "I would be pleased to return with you today."

"Truly? Why, that would be wonderful. My wife will be delighted when she sees I've met with such great success."

Jarena wondered if Mrs. Nelson would be delighted once she discovered the fact that Aunt Lilly's penchant for housework and children didn't run nearly as deep as the banker surmised.

"If you'll excuse us for a short time . . . I've not even had time to completely unpack my trunk since arriving, so I won't be long. Jarena will be happy to assist me." Lilly took Jarena by the wrist and pulled her along.

"Don't you ladies attempt to lift that trunk. I'll come in and fetch it," Mr. Nelson called after them.

Lilly stopped in her tracks and flashed the banker a syrupy smile. "Why, you are such a gentleman, Mr. Nelson. If you're not careful, I'll be thinking that I'm once again down south, where men take pride in civility toward their womenfolk." The honey-dipped words had barely escaped Lilly's lips before she jerked Jarena through the doorway.

Jarena wrested her arm free from Lilly's tight hold. "Have you gone completely mad? You sounded ridiculous speaking to Mr. Nelson in such a manner—as though you think you're the mistress of some southern plantation instead of a colored woman down on her luck and looking for work."

Lilly wagged a finger in Jarena's face. "You receive the amount of respect you *demand* from others. I have lived a life of prosperity as a courtesan to white men much wealthier than Mr. Nelson."

Jarena shook her head. "Respect is earned, not demanded or coerced. No decent woman would boast of living as a courtesan."

With a derisive laugh, Lilly unlatched the hasp of her trunk and lifted the lid. "You don't understand the way of things, young lady. With a few flattering words, I made that man happy. And now he's going to please me by lifting this heavy baggage. We're both happy, and all it took was a few sweet words."

"Manipulation," Jarena muttered.

"Um-hum, that's what's been happening ever since the Garden of Eden. It's the way of things in this world. The sooner you learn, the easier your life is going to be, Jarena. Just try it." Lilly patted Jarena's cheek.

Jarena pulled away. "No—what you do is wrong. You should go out there and tell Mr. Nelson the truth. Tell him you worked as a house slave back in your youth but haven't performed such duties in years; tell him you don't know much about cooking or tending children but you're willing to learn; tell him you've never tutored, but your education surpasses that of most schoolteachers in the West. You may be surprised by his reaction. In spite of everything, he may still hire you."

Lilly piled the last of her belongings into the trunk. "He's already hired me. What are you afraid of, Jarena? That I'll go to Hill City and cause problems? Maybe force Moses to face the fact that he's made an error by choosing Truth? Or that I'll convince Truth she's not the right woman for Moses? Best you keep praying." A gleam of satisfaction shone in her eyes as she lifted the amulet between her fingers and slowly shifted it back and forth across the velvet cord. "Now grab that valise and follow me."

Dust rolled from beneath the carriage wheels as George Nelson slapped the reins and urged his team of horses onward. Lilly was settled beside him, excited to be looking forward to a comfortable bed and fine house. After fighting off the constant encroachment of fleas and lice in the soddy, she was thankful to be leaving before the arrival of the heavy rains. Grace's vivid stories of storms that could dump enough rain to turn the soddy floor into a mixture of mud and muck within only minutes were enough to convince Lilly she would not remain in one of the crude houses for long—at least not by choice.

"Now that we have nothing but time, perhaps you'd enjoy telling me about your life down south—I believe Moses mentioned Louisiana, is that correct?" Mr. Nelson flashed her an encouraging smile.

"Indeed—Louisiana. Though I lived in Virginia as a girl, until after the war."

"Terrible thing, slavery," he muttered.

"Even worse for those of us who suffered in bondage," she replied.

"I hope you didn't . . . ah . . . suffer too much."

"My life was not so harsh as some endured. However, I find conversation about the war and slavery most depressing and dreary. Do tell me about your children. What are their names and ages? Are they bright? Do they enjoy their lessons?"

Although Lilly found the topic of Mr. Nelson's family boring, she tried to listen carefully as he launched into a detailed discussion of his wife and children. The revelation that she would be caring for two boys, Georgie and Joey, ages eight and six, and their five-year-old sister, Alma, was startling. She'd been around enough young boys to know they could prove to be a constant vexation. But she had ways of dealing with troublesome people—the Nelson children would be no different. A bit of convincing might be necessary, but they would soon learn she had far more power than any of them.

"This is Hill City?" Lilly inquired as they neared the outskirts of town. Dusk had now given way to nightfall, and with any luck, the

Nelson offspring would be in bed. Lilly possessed neither the desire nor the energy to cope with children this night. Instead, a light supper and comfortable bed would suit her nicely—especially if Mrs. Nelson prepared the food and turned down her bed.

"Yes, and this is our house." His announcement was filled with pride, though the house was far less opulent than Lilly had hoped for. "I'm sorry it's so dark, but tomorrow you'll see that we have a large area for the children to play in just beyond my wife's flower garden. And there's a vegetable garden, also. She'll be glad for your help with both," he added.

She hoped he couldn't see the severe frown that crossed her face. "I'm not an avid gardener; I've grown only a few herbs."

"Kate—Mrs. Nelson—will teach you. She takes great pride in her flowers."

Lilly didn't comment on that. "Shall I see to my baggage?"

"No, of course not. If you can manage that smaller valise, I'll take the other bag and then return for your trunk after you've met my wife. Come along. She's going to be very pleased."

Katherine Nelson wasn't what Lilly had expected. Instead of an elegant, proper lady, she was greeted by a maladroit, unfashionable woman. Her dress bore more stains than did the garb of most toddlers at supper, and her hair hung loose and unkempt.

Mrs. Nelson's startled expression was soon replaced by a look of gratitude and relief. "I'm so pleased to have you." As if to emphasize her pleasure, she repeatedly bobbed her head.

"Where shall I put my baggage?" Lilly hoped the question would stop the woman's continued nodding, for she found the behavior quite off-putting.

"Just follow me upstairs—I'll show you to your room." She skittered toward the stairs like a chicken attempting to escape a farmer's hatchet. "In here," she said, leading the way into a small yet nicely appointed bedroom. "This room is closest to the children's bedrooms and the stairway that leads to the kitchen. I do wish the children were awake to meet you, but you may greet them first thing in the morning. I trust you'll find your accommodations adequate."

Lilly looked about. "Rather small . . . but I suppose it will do—for now."

Mrs. Nelson opened her mouth to reply, but Lilly turned and walked out the doorway. "Our journey was tiring, and I am truly famished. I'm certain your husband is also anxious for some of your delicious fare. He tells me you're an excellent cook."

A blush colored Mrs. Nelson's pale skin. "Truly? It's nice to know he pays me compliments outside of my hearing. Our life here in Kansas has been more difficult than I had anticipated. I find little time for myself. But now that you've arrived to help with the house and children, life is going to be much easier."

"Perhaps," Lilly replied. "Now then, why don't we go downstairs so I can taste some of that fine food your husband has been praising since we departed Nicodemus?"

"Indeed. And I can point out where things are kept in the kitchen so you'll have no difficulty preparing breakfast in the morning. The children are fond of eggs and griddle cakes with warm molasses."

"That's good to know. However, I didn't plan to begin my duties just yet. I believe I'll need at least a day or two to acclimate myself. I've discovered that children don't adjust well when someone new arrives and immediately steps in. It upsets both their appetites and their behavior. It will be best if I slowly enter into their routine. Don't you agree?"

"I don't know . . . I suppose . . . well, if you think . . ."

Lilly patted the woman's shoulder. "Absolutely! You know, I believe we're going to get on quite well, Mrs. Nelson. And if you'd ever like me to assist you with your wardrobe, I do consider myself an expert where fashion is concerned."

Embarrassment filled Katherine's eyes as she brushed her fingers across one of the many stains that soiled her dress. Lilly knew she'd struck a chord with the woman. This new position in the Nelson household might require a number of distasteful tasks, but Lilly now realized that Mrs. Nelson would be easily manipulated. And that fact pleased Lilly very much!

"Supper ready?" Ezekiel asked as he walked through the door of the soddy that evening, stopping only long enough to rinse his hands in the washbowl.

Grace bounded forward like a puppy ready to play. She bounced back and forth from foot to foot as she told her father that Lilly had gone off to Hill City to live with the banker and his family.

Ezekiel dropped his bulky body onto one of the wooden chairs. He'd longed for Lilly's departure. Hadn't he daily hoped to send her packing? But to Hill City? Off to spread her wily ways among good, honest folks not far from his home. That wasn't what he had prayed for, nor was it what he wanted. He wanted Lilly back in New Orleans, or at least some other faraway place. No telling what kind of trouble she'd be conjuring up over in Hill City. "That woman ain' never been nothin' but trouble!" The tin dinner plates danced across the tabletop as he slammed down his fist.

Startled, Grace stood before him, all evidence of her earlier excitement wiped away by his angry outburst. "I thought you'd be pleased. You said you wanted her to leave."

Ezekiel rubbed his beefy hand back and forth across his brow before lifting his head to meet Grace's doe-eyed gaze. "That I did. But Hill City weren't what I had in mind. I was hopin' she'd skedaddle a lot farther away than that."

CHAPTER

— 9 —

Hill City, Kansas

ager for the sensation of freshly laundered linens beneath her body and the shelter of a shingled roof over her head, Lilly undressed and donned an expensive silk nightgown—one of Bentley Cummings's many gifts. She'd slept little during her stay at Ezekiel's farm. The thought of snakes or other undesirable creatures descending through the roof or crawling between the sod bricks to take up residence in the uncomfortable bed had been enough to keep her wide-awake most nights. If luck was with her, the Nelson children would sleep late and she would be able to enjoy a hearty breakfast before making a swift escape. She could easily fill a portion of her day visiting with Truth and Moses. Then, too, a few introductions about town might prove interesting.

Though the crisp sheets beckoned, Lilly sat down at the narrow writing table. She must write a note to Claire before she slept this night. With single-minded determination, Lilly hastily scribbled a message advising her friend of her welfare and whereabouts. Tomorrow she would mail the missive to New Orleans. Pushing away from the table, Lilly extinguished the bedside lamp and slipped into bed.

The muffled sounds of the sleeping children seeped through the bedroom wall and served as an immediate reminder of the duties she must eventually fulfill. The notion was disconcerting. She wasn't good with children. No, that wasn't exactly correct, for she had no true way to gauge her abilities with youngsters. After all, her life had revolved solely around adults—mostly men. But surely if she could manipulate the influential men of New Orleans, she could handle three small children.

Nestling between the sweet-scented linens, Lilly wondered what Ezekiel had said when he returned home and discovered she had departed for Hill City. Likely he had danced for joy—or at the very least, burst into song. She had expected a cool reception from her brother-in-law. And though his accusations had stung, more often than not they'd been accurate. There was no denying she had refused his request years ago. He'd asked for her help caring for Jennie and the children, and she'd turned him down. Oh, she should have helped. No doubt about that. Unfortunately, Ezekiel had been right. By law, she was a free woman, but in truth, she had remained a slave to the wishes of Bentley Cummings, the man who provided her living quarters and attired her in the dresses and jewels that had persuaded her to remain his courtesan for years.

Bentley! If it hadn't been for his philandering ways, she'd still be living in New Orleans. She'd heard stories through the years that Bentley had other women, but she'd ignored the remarks, choosing to believe it was mere jealousy that had delivered the unwelcome news to her doorstep on numerous occasions. However, it had been impossible to retain her aloof countenance when Sephra had knocked on her door and announced she was Bentley's favored woman. A sudden fury had embraced Lilly as the young, beautiful woman stood before her, attired in the latest fashion and holding her young son by the hand—a tawny-skinned boy, though Lilly refused to admit any noticeable resemblance to Bentley Cummings.

When Bentley arrived the next day and exhibited no remorse, Lilly angrily informed him a curse had been placed upon the woman. Oh, how she wished she had never uttered those words! For when Sephra's body was discovered in a nearby swamp one week later, Bentley immediately placed all blame upon Lilly, threatening to have her thrown into an alligator-ridden bayou if she didn't tell him what had happened to his young son.

Though she had no idea where to locate the child, Lilly promised to produce him by first light. And although convincing Bentley required her to draw upon all of her womanly wiles, Lilly finally succeeded in her ruse. By the time he finally departed her bungalow, she was exhausted. However, there was no time for rest. If she was to survive the ordeal, a hasty exodus would be required. She bribed the coachman who delivered her to the train station, though she was afraid he would be most pleased to take a few extra coins and divulge any information if Bentley might inquire.

As she shifted her weight, seeking a more comfortable position in her new bed, Lilly continued to hope Bentley and the coachman would never cross paths.

The night was warm, and the smell of honeysuckle clung to the light breeze wafting through the small window near her bed, yet she pulled on the crisp white sheet until it completely covered her head. For the moment, Lilly felt invisible, even a bit safe. Wouldn't the folks back home be amused to find her hiding under the covers?

Down in New Orleans, people believed she possessed the special powers of a fearsome witch or voodoo queen, but Lilly knew the truth and she could admit it—at least to herself. Why, she was as frightened by life and its mysteries as anyone else. Yet it had been the fear of those special powers that had earned her a measure of control and respect among her peers. That, and the fact that she was Bentley Cummings's courtesan.

And now what was she? Even more, who was she? An aging woman with no true identity, self-exiled to this vast wasteland called Kansas—but for what? To be tracked down and returned to New Orleans? To be made the fool by Bentley Cummings? Or to be forced into servitude to reimburse him for the years of upkeep he'd so willingly paid throughout the years? He would enjoy such an ending. That prospect alone would undoubtedly fuel his resolve to leave no stone unturned in his quest to find her and make her pay.

"Who is she?" a teeny voice whispered.

"How do you expect me to know? Maybe she's here to help Mama clean the house and cook our food." The second voice was slightly deeper and more authoritative—likely the older brother, Lilly decided.

"That can't be right, 'cause she's still in bed and Mama's cooking breakfast," the hushed girlish voice argued.

Lilly remained perfectly still with her eyes pinched together while the children's whispers floated overhead. With a scrap of luck, the Nelson children would soon depart her room. Otherwise, she might be forced to frighten them away from her bedside. Several ideas immediately came to mind, but she forced the notions aside. She had better not test Mrs. Nelson's forbearance just yet. The lady of the house might not tolerate such behavior from a newly employed housekeeper. Lilly inwardly cringed at the title.

"Come on, before Mama finds out we're in here."

Lilly forced herself to remain motionless until she heard the sound of feet clattering down the back stairway. With a sigh of relief, she opened her eyes and shifted to the side of the bed. Her feet had barely touched the floor when Lilly spied a pair of cornflower-blue eyes peering from behind the door.

She leaned forward and pointed at the child. "What are you doing in my room?"

With a muffled squeal, the girl skittered sideways and moved toward the doorway. Lilly leapt forward and encircled the child's thin arm with one hand. "Why are you running off now? Why didn't you leave with your sibling?"

The child stared at Lilly's painted fingernails. "What's a sibling?"

Lilly's laughter filled the room. "Your brother. Why didn't you go downstairs with him?"

The girl's eyes were wide with wonder as she looked up and down, taking in the length of Lilly's form. "I wanted to see you."

"Well, now that you've seen me, I think you had best leave while I dress." The child moved toward the door. "What's your name, little girl?"

"Alma." The child raced out the door and down the back stairway.

Alma would be easily enough handled—that much was obvious. But the boys. If they were like most of the little boys she'd encountered in her day, they would need to be infused with a smidgen of fear before they'd behave in proper fashion. And Lilly possessed the necessary tactics to instill apprehension in most anyone. After all, she didn't intend to spend her days racing about after miscreant children. There would be better ways to fill her time, even in this remote setting. She would either teach them respect or scare them out of their wits. With her plan set, Lilly decided upon a pale yellow print dress and a hat with yellow ribbons for her stroll about town.

When she finally walked down the front stairway, she knew she'd made the proper choice. Her clothing would be a unique complement to the bright summer day. She stopped at the oak-framed mirror in the lower hallway, admiring herself for a moment.

"Is that you, Lilly?" Mrs. Nelson held a bowl in the crook of her arm and was stirring the contents as she walked down the hallway. At the sight of her new housekeeper, Mrs. Nelson stopped and pointed her wooden spoon at Lilly. "You aren't planning on wearing *that* to do chores and care for the children, are you?" A dollop of batter dripped from the spoon as Mrs. Nelson awaited Lilly's answer.

"You don't like this dress?" Lilly turned her attention back to the mirror and smoothed the lace-filled square neckline.

"Of course, it's lovely. However, it's not what I'd expect anyone to wear while performing chores."

Lilly's gown rustled softly as she approached Mrs. Nelson and placed a light pat on the woman's shoulder. "You've forgotten that I don't plan to begin my position just yet. I intend to spend the day visiting my niece and becoming acquainted with the town. In truth, I was thinking it might be best if I waited until the first of the week to actually commence working. Breakfast would be most welcome, though, before I depart."

Mrs. Nelson handed the mixing bowl to Lilly before stooping down to clean the batter from the wood floor. "I find your plan unsatisfactory. You'll begin work tomorrow. And if you want breakfast, I suggest you come into the kitchen and fix it yourself."

Lilly silently chastised herself. She had misread Mrs. Nelson and pushed her too far. "You misconstrued my comment regarding breakfast. Why, I would never expect you to fix my meal. I merely thought that if there was a cup of coffee and a cold biscuit, I'd help myself. I don't know if Mr. Nelson told you, but this is the first time I've met my nieces, and I'm anxious to spend time with them. I wouldn't have accepted this position but for the fact that Truth lives in Hill City. You see, they're my only family."

Mrs. Nelson's features softened. "I didn't realize. No, of course I understand."

Lilly followed Mrs. Nelson into the kitchen. "From the moment I met you, I knew you'd understand. A woman who has children of her own values the importance of family."

"Let me introduce you to the children. Alma, Georgie, and this is

Joey." Mrs. Nelson placed a hand atop each child's head as she introduced them.

None of them mentioned having been in Lilly's bedroom earlier, though Lilly guessed it was Georgie, the older boy, who had accompanied little Alma into her room. He had a devilish gleam in his eyes. He would likely cause the most trouble. Lilly offered a brief greeting and then renewed her discussion with Mrs. Nelson.

After listening to Lilly's tale of woe, Mrs. Nelson scurried about the kitchen, now seemingly anxious to prepare the new housekeeper a hot breakfast. The food was edible, though not the fine fare Lilly had enjoyed in New Orleans. And Lilly was somewhat surprised at how easily she'd been able to bring Mrs. Nelson around simply by sprinkling in a few words about familial ties and misfortune. A short time later, Lilly departed, leaving a frazzled Mrs. Nelson and her children to fend for themselves.

With her parasol raised, Lilly examined the Hill City dwellings as she made her way toward town. The frame houses were outnumbered by limestone and sod, though most were larger than the ones she'd observed in Nicodemus. Of course, the residents of Hill City had likely come prepared for life on the prairie. From the stories she'd heard from Jarena and Grace, tools and supplies had been in short supply when the Nicodemus settlers had first arrived. Therefore, the disparity wasn't surprising. She continued onward, careful to maintain a lookout for either Moses or the newspaper office.

At the sound of her name, Lilly turned to see Truth waving and running toward her at full tilt. Lilly waved in return and waited for her niece. Both Truth and Grace were vivacious and pretty enough, but

Jarena was the real jewel of the family. Jarena had maturity on her side, but it was much more than that. Hidden beneath frayed collars and worn shoes, Jarena's sense of style and class shone through—just like her own, Lilly decided.

Truth's gaze flitted back and forth between Lilly's parasol and her hat. "When did you get to Hill City? Moses told me Mr. Nelson was going to go to Nicodemus to talk to you."

"I just arrived last night. I plan to spend the day acquainting myself with you and Moses, as well as this town."

"I thought you'd be hard at work caring for the Nelson children."

"I was coming to the newspaper office to visit with you and Moses. I thought you'd be pleased to see me. Instead, you're staring at me as though you've seen a ghost. Mrs. Nelson and I have agreed I'll begin my housekeeping duties tomorrow." Lilly took Truth by the hand. "Why don't you show me where the newspaper office is located?"

Truth was only too happy to comply, eagerly leading her aunt down the street and proudly gesturing when they neared the building. They hadn't been inside the office long when Lilly decided she would gain little attention from Moses. After a brief welcome, he had become completely absorbed in composing an article for the newspaper and totally ignored her presence. On the other hand, Truth had insisted upon explaining all of the intricacies of printing a newspaper—from setting the type to inking the handheld brayer and feeding the paper. It was when Truth suggested her aunt take up the composing stick and try her hand at setting type that Lilly made her escape. Though Lilly admired Moses's dedication to his work, it was obvious she'd not gain his attention while he was in his office. Furthermore, with Truth's youth and innocence, she would be more easily swayed than Moses. Lilly raised her parasol and walked off toward the general store. Where there's a will, there's a way: that was her motto.

————————

After making her way in and out of the various businesses in Hill City to explain her affiliation with Moses and Truth as well as her position with the Nelson family, Lilly strolled toward home. She had hoped to meet Dr. Boyle and elicit some information about his wife and family, but a note on his office door indicated the doctor wouldn't return until later in the day. The message stated he'd been summoned to lend aid to the victim of a farm accident. Though she didn't relish a return to the Nelson household so early in the afternoon, there was little else to occupy her time. At least that was true until she caught sight of a woman sitting on the porch of the Boyle residence.

Lilly tipped her parasol to the side and stepped closer. "Mrs. Boyle?"

The woman peered over the top of the book she was reading. She squinted her eyes and peered more closely. "Yes? Do I know you?"

"No, we've never met," Lilly replied as she stepped closer. "However, I was hoping to make your acquaintance. I'm Truth Harban's aunt—Lilly Verdue."

Mrs. Boyle tucked a crocheted bookmark between the pages of her book and snapped the volume closed. "Ah, yes. Truth mentioned her aunt had come for a visit. She's quite excited to have you here." She waved Lilly forward. "Please sit down. I understand you've come from New Orleans. Do tell me more about yourself."

Lilly didn't need any further invitation. She collapsed her parasol and perched herself on the wicker chair facing Mrs. Boyle. "I'm afraid you would be quickly bored by anything I have to say. Why don't you tell me about yourself, Mrs. Boyle? No doubt your life has been filled with much more excitement than my own."

Margaret studied Lilly's dress. "I'm not so certain. At the very least, it appears you're more in style with the latest fashion than I."

Lilly touched a finger to the neckline of her dress, pleased Mrs. Boyle had noticed her refined attire. "Merely the kindness of a friend before my departure from New Orleans. Truth tells me you have a daughter who teaches school."

Mrs. Boyle nodded. "Yes—Macia. She'll be returning at summer's end, unless good fortune should smile upon her."

"You don't want her to return home?"

"Don't misunderstand. I love Macia and truly don't look forward to separation from her. However, I'd like to see her meet a suitable man who could provide her with a life of ease and comfort. The thought of Macia living the remainder of her life here in Kansas is not what I would wish for her."

Lilly listened attentively as Mrs. Boyle discussed Macia's plan to return and possibly marry Jeb Malone. Although the older woman had convinced Macia to journey east and attend a summer session of classes in New York before making a final decision regarding marriage and her future, she held out little hope her daughter would ultimately be deterred from her plans.

Mrs. Boyle took a sip of her lemonade. "Unfortunately, from the letters I've received, Macia has been suffering from ongoing bouts of illness since she arrived in New York. Distressing news, since she's always enjoyed excellent health."

"She's likely suffering from a touch of homesickness coupled with a change in diet and daily routine. Likely nothing to worry over."

Mrs. Boyle picked up her fan and snapped it open. "I truly hold out little hope Macia will be deterred from her plans. Jeb's a fine young man, but Macia deserves a better life than he can provide."

Lilly nodded sympathetically. "I do understand. I hope the worry over your daughter hasn't caused you undue anxiety. Truth tells me you suffer from occasional ill health. I trust having her help has proved beneficial to you and your family."

"Oh, indeed," Mrs. Boyle said, fanning herself with enthusiasm. "I don't know how I would have gotten by without Truth's help. Once she marries Moses, we'll have to find someone else, for I can't seem to manage on my own. Perhaps Grace might be interested—I must remind Samuel to speak with Mr. Harban."

"I wouldn't hurry to do that. After all, Truth's wedding is months off, and who knows what might happen between now and then."

Mrs. Boyle's eyes widened. "Are they having difficulties? Truth hasn't uttered a word."

Lilly leaned close. "Trust me, Truth wouldn't easily confide such a thing. But if she realized how much you need her, it might aid her in making a final decision about her future. Please don't mention I've said anything. She would feel I've placed you in a compromising position."

"Oh, of course not. Poor girl. And to think I've been trying to reassure her I can get along without her these past months. I do feel terrible—my comments have likely been weighing heavily upon her. I'll begin hinting about the problems I'm going to face once she marries Moses."

"The minute I laid eyes upon you, I knew you were a woman I could count upon."

Mrs. Boyle leaned back in her chair and feverishly fanned herself. "How can I ever thank you for taking me into your confidence? I am truly grateful you've arrived in Hill City. Surely between the two of us, we can steer Truth toward the proper decision for her future."

"Indeed we will, Mrs. Boyle. Indeed we will."

The Nelson house was quiet when Lilly walked into the foyer. Perhaps Mrs. Nelson and the children had departed for an outing. She smiled at the prospect. Having time alone to reflect upon her thoughts and plans was one thing Lilly relished. And finding time alone would likely prove difficult in the future. She walked up the front stairs and down the hallway toward her room, the sound of her footsteps muffled by the wool carpet. As she neared her bedroom, Lilly traced the tip of her parasol along the spindled railing that ran the length of the upper hall.

Mrs. Nelson peered around the bedroom doorway, her unkempt hair sticking out in all directions. "Lilly! I wasn't expecting you. I was bringing . . . checking . . . to see that you had enough linens in your dresser." Plunging her fingers into her disheveled hair, Mrs. Nelson sent a hair comb flying down the hallway.

"You brought me fresh linens when I arrived last night. Why would you think I'd need more so soon?" Lilly brushed past Mrs. Nelson and into the bedroom. "I don't see any fresh linens, Mrs. Nelson."

Her face flushed the shade of strawberries. "Once I entered your bedroom, I realized I'd forgotten them."

Lilly pursed her lips as she surveyed the room. One of her dresser drawers was ajar and the hasp on her trunk had been opened. There was little doubt Mrs. Nelson had been snooping in her things. Lilly attempted to remain nonchalant as she stepped toward her trunk and then glanced over her shoulder at Mrs. Nelson. The woman looked like a child awaiting a reprimand. Though Lilly longed to voice an objection to Mrs. Nelson's behavior, she surmised her status in the household prohibited such conduct.

At present, all Lilly wanted was a few moments alone to examine the contents of her trunk to see if Mrs. Nelson had discovered the packet of personal papers and letters hidden in one of the small interior drawers. "If you would excuse me, Mrs. Nelson, I'd like to change my dress."

Mrs. Nelson turned away from Lilly and hastened toward the door. "Yes, of course. I'll fetch the linens." She reached to pull the door closed behind her.

"No need. I have plenty to last me the week, Mrs. Nelson."

The woman's feet clattered down the back stairway as Lilly lifted the trunk lid. She reached into the small drawer and wrapped her fingers around the bundle there. A sigh escaped Lilly's lips as she lifted and inspected the packet of envelopes and leather folder. The bundle was intact, but there was little doubt she must now find a safer place for her personal papers. Lilly paced the room like a caged animal. She must find the perfect hiding space. As she neared the center of the room, her toe caught on a loose floorboard. Her arms flailed like windmill blades as she attempted to remain upright. She sputtered an invective when she finally regained her balance. However, her anger was immediately mollified when she bent down to locate the spot. With a tug, she lifted the board. She pushed the leather folder into the space beneath the floorboard and placed the packet of letters on top. With a stomp of her heel, she forced the board back into place. The documents should now be safe from prying eyes.

Lilly considered herself an excellent judge of character, but this time her instincts had failed her. She had underestimated Mrs. Nelson. In the future, she would be more careful.

CHAPTER

— 10 —

Truth folded her hands in her lap and waited for Moses to say something—anything. She'd arrived at the newspaper office to advise him of her decision. His anger was obvious. Likely because she hadn't consulted him prior to making her choice. Truth stared out the window while Moses busied himself locking type into the chase. When he finally completed the task, he wiped his hands and sat down opposite her.

He rested his arms on his desk and leaned forward. "Did you even consider speaking with me before you entered into this arrangement?"

There it was! He thought she should ask for his permission. "We're not married yet, Moses. The Boyles have been good to me. It's the least I can do. I don't understand why you're upset in the least. The journey won't take long."

Moses leaned back and folded his arms across his chest. "Seems you were telling me only the other day you couldn't complete your news article because Mrs. Boyle was ailing and you were needed at the house. Tell me, Truth, who's going to take care of Mrs. Boyle if you make this journey?"

Truth hesitated. She hadn't thought about that. "Perhaps Jarena or Grace could come and stay while I'm gone."

"Perhaps Grace or Jarena could go and fetch Macia home—or Dr. Boyle could?"

"I don't think either of my sisters would agree to go. Besides, they don't know Macia as well as I do. And Dr. Boyle won't leave town when his wife is ailing. I couldn't ask him to leave Mrs. Boyle."

"Why doesn't Dr. Boyle just pay a nurse to accompany his daughter home? That makes more sense to me."

"It has been impossible to find a person of good reputation to make the journey. If there were some other way, I wouldn't go, Moses. I'm sure you can understand that they need my assistance."

Moses stood up and walked around the desk. "Your loyalty is one of the things I most admire, Truth. I think they are asking too much from you, but if you truly believe you must go, then I won't object."

He took her hand and they walked to the office door. "When will you depart?"

"I'm not certain, but once the plans are complete, I'll talk with you."

He nodded. "I'm going to Nicodemus tomorrow. Do you want me to speak with Jarena and Grace?"

"First let me ask Dr. Boyle. Could you come by the house later this evening?"

"Of course. Now, you'd best be on your way. You have Mrs. Boyle to care for, and I have a newspaper to print."

Truth gave a final wave as she hurried back toward the Boyles' house. She hadn't told Moses of her fears. Had she explained she didn't actually want to make the journey to New York, he would have insisted she stay home. She wanted to help Macia, but the thought of traveling alone by train worried her. However, Macia had successfully made the journey to New York City. Surely Truth could do the same. On the other hand, Macia was more accustomed to the details of traveling. But when Truth had expressed her fears and reservations, Dr. Boyle quickly reassured her she'd meet with no difficulty. Though the doctor's words were somewhat comforting, Truth longed to talk with someone— another woman—about her concerns.

She stopped midstep. *Aunt Lilly!* Her heart quickened at the thought. Aunt Lilly was a woman of the world. If Truth didn't tarry too long, there would be sufficient time to stop by the Nelson house for a chat. Her aunt would have a plethora of knowledge regarding travel by rail and coach. Truth hastened her step as she neared the Nelson home. If good fortune was with her, Mrs. Boyle would still be napping when she arrived home.

Truth lifted her skirts with one hand as she hurried up the Nelsons' front steps and knocked on the door. Moments later, her aunt yanked open the door. Little Alma clutched at Lilly's dress, and the sound of yelping boys echoed inside the house. Truth watched as her aunt attempted to disentangle Alma's grasp. In spite of Lilly's efforts, the child managed to maintain her hold.

Truth smiled at the twosome. "Good afternoon, Aunt Lilly."

Lilly sighed as she finally extricated Alma's chubby fingers from her skirt and grasped the child's hand. "It's good to see you, Truth. Do come in. What brings you visiting?"

"There's a matter I'd like to discuss with you. Do you have time for a brief chat?"

With a derisive laugh, Lilly said she did. The hollering boys kicked up the rug as they ran through the sitting room chasing one another. "Their mother has gone off for a meeting of her church ladies."

Truth was surprised her aunt would permit such unrestrained behavior from the boys. "Your first time alone with them?"

"Unfortunately not. I'm afraid they become exceptionally unruly when there's a distraction. I'll have them under control by the time their mother returns."

The words bore an ominous ring. Truth didn't question how her aunt would accomplish such a feat, for she didn't want to know. Instead, she told Aunt Lilly her news. "I'm going to be traveling to New York to bring Macia Boyle home. She's taken ill while attending school there, and her physician believes she needs someone to accompany her on the journey."

Lilly's eyes widened. "Mrs. Boyle mentioned her daughter had been ill. But why are they sending you? Don't they have a family member who can help?"

"They couldn't think of another plan." Truth glanced at the mantel clock. "I stopped to ask if you thought I'd have difficulty making the necessary transfers at the railroad stations. I'm frightened I might miss one of my connections."

Lilly winked at her. "You'll do fine. Just remember to ask someone which car you're supposed to be in. Some states don't let us sit with the white folks. You don't want to be sashaying onto one of those cars, because those white folks will be mighty quick to send you packing. Just open your mouth and ask what you need to know. Hold your head up and walk proud—folks respect that."

Truth fidgeted. "So you think I can do it?"

"Of course you can. What does Moses think about this?"

"He's unhappy."

Lilly hollered at the boys to settle themselves. "Can't say as I blame him. Who's going to be taking care of Mrs. Boyle?"

"I'm going to see if Dr. Boyle wants either Jarena or Grace to come over. I don't think Pappy will mind since I won't be gone too long."

Touching a finger to her lips, Lilly appeared to be deep in thought. "I believe Jarena would be the better choice. Grace will be busy working in the fields, don't you think?"

Truth shrugged. "I'm not sure. Moses is going to inquire when he goes to Nicodemus tomorrow."

"Nicodemus? Tomorrow? I do wish I could go with him. I haven't yet had an opportunity to make amends with your father."

"If Mrs. Nelson is willing to let you go, I'm sure Moses would enjoy your company."

Early the next morning, Mrs. Nelson and her three children stood side-by-side on the front porch as Lilly departed with Moses. They rode in silence for several miles before Lilly decided to speak. Long ago, she had learned there was great value in proper timing. She also realized that her presence alongside Moses served as an immediate reminder that Truth would be traveling to New York against his wishes.

Lilly adjusted her hat. "I must say I was surprised when Truth told me she would even consider the Boyles' request. And I was even more surprised that you had no objection."

Moses grunted. "Is that what she told you? That I had no objection?"

Lilly furrowed her brows as though deep in thought. "I believe she said that you had been quite understanding of her position. You're an indulgent man, Moses."

He laughed. "Perhaps indulgent, but not happy. I don't believe she should go. In fact, I don't want her traveling across the country by herself. I'm not certain Ezekiel can dissuade her."

She lurched to attention. "I didn't know you were planning to gain his support."

Moses shrugged and flicked the reins. "Worth a try. If he has no objection to her going, then I'll mention the possibility of Jarena or Grace returning to stay with Mrs. Boyle. To be honest, I doubt I'll gain Ezekiel's allegiance. He feels a debt of gratitude to Dr. Boyle."

Lilly frowned and shook her head. "On those rare occasions when white folks finally do help us, seems like they want to hold it over our heads for the rest of our lives."

"That's true of lots of folks, Lilly. I find that particular fault doesn't know any color boundary. People are either genuine in their desire to help or they're not. It's a personal characteristic, not a matter of color. And I don't think Dr. Boyle expects repayment for any good he's done for folks in Nicodemus. I think he's just a man who needs help."

"So you do agree with Truth's decision."

"No. But I won't stop her, either." They rode in silence for a moment. "How are you faring with the Nelson family?" Moses asked.

This was a man who wouldn't be easily controlled. He was turning the conversation away from himself with a practiced ease and agility. If she were going to satisfactorily manage this situation, she would need to play her cards very carefully. She had best not appear overly interested in his situation with Truth. For the remainder of the journey, she regaled Moses with stories of the Nelson family. Though Mrs. Nelson would likely give a completely different evaluation, Lilly spoke of her capable assistance to the entire household. Of course, she failed to tell Moses of the burned food, the scorched clothing, and the numerous chores she'd willingly left half done.

"Looks like there's some sort of celebration going on," Moses commented as they came into Nicodemus and passed a group of settlers gathered on Washington Avenue. "I'm guessing they must have completed sinking the well."

Lilly clapped her hands. "Oh, I didn't know. Now *that's* certainly something to celebrate." Her words hung in the air, dripping with unbridled sarcasm.

Moses hunched forward. "Water *is* something to celebrate. Folks in these parts work hard, Miss Lilly. They're interested in nothing but owning a piece of land, raising their crops, and rearing their families—water's an important part of that equation. It makes good sense that they'd celebrate. I know you've likely been in bigger cities than most of these folks have. Probably done and seen more, too—so have I. But that doesn't give anyone free rein to scorn them."

Lilly swallowed hard. If she didn't watch her mouth, she'd ruin this opportunity to win his confidence. Using her finest conciliatory tone, she hastened to mention it had been far too long since she'd given thanks for the simple things in life.

Moses drove the buggy to the nearby field where Ezekiel was hoeing. The older man began to wave and then stopped. He lifted one hand to shade his eyes as he focused on the buggy.

Lilly leaned close to Moses. "Ezekiel's seen me and he's not happy."

"I do believe you're right on that account, Miss Lilly. Let me help you down; then you can walk on out there and talk with your brother-in-law."

The only thing that was worse than visiting with Ezekiel was begging his forgiveness. But Lilly knew she must. If she was going to maintain any leverage in the family, she would need his blessing.

She stepped between the rows, her feet sinking deep into the soft dirt. Memories of her mama's vegetable garden returned as Lilly inhaled the freshly tilled soil. Before Ezekiel had time to speak, Lilly offered an apology and asked his forgiveness for running off to Hill City without so much as thanking him for his hospitality.

Ezekiel leaned on his hoe, his chin resting on his large hands. "Ain' never knowed of you to ask for no one's forgiveness, Lilly. What you got up your sleeve?"

Lilly bit her lip, annoyed that Ezekiel had questioned her motives. He might not be educated, but the man could read people better than most. He questioned that she would make a special journey merely to ask his forgiveness.

Tilting her head, she gave him a winsome smile and explained she'd taken advantage of the fact that Moses was coming to Nicodemus. While he pondered her response, Lilly declared a genuine desire to smooth the waters between them. When Ezekiel's features softened, she hastened to add that she'd been working hard at the Nelsons'.

"You planning on keeping the promise you made to me and Jennie years ago?" His voice carried a hint of suspicion.

"You mean . . ."

He nodded. "You know zackly what I mean."

"Yes, of course."

"Then I don't s'pose there's any good to come from holdin' a grudge. Better ta live in harmony than anger. You's forgiven—for that much at least."

Lilly wouldn't push for more. She knew there were some things he'd never forgive, but at least they had returned to speaking terms. "Thank you, Ezekiel."

"How you doin' with them young'uns of the Nelsons?" His voice was laced with amusement.

"Fine. The little girl's easy enough. But I told the boys if they didn't behave, I'd think about placing a spell on the both of them. Scared the daylights out of them."

A frown fell over Ezekiel's features. "I heard tell them's some ornery boys. Jest be sure you don' go no farther with that kind of talk."

She nodded. "Moses needs to have a word with you. You want him to walk out here, or are you ready for a few minutes of rest?"

"I'll come over to the wagon. Won't hurt me to set for a spell. Ain't nothing wrong, is there?"

Lilly walked toward the buggy, pretending she hadn't heard Ezekiel's question. Better that Moses explain. In fact, she proceeded to the back of the wagon and distanced herself from the men. Close enough to hear, yet far enough away to appear uninterested. Moses's assessment had been correct: Ezekiel wanted to help Dr. Boyle—even if it meant sending Truth halfway across the country by herself. Lilly rubbed her hands together. Hopefully, he would agree to send Jarena to Hill City.

Ezekiel wiped his face with an oversized kerchief and then tucked it into his back pocket. "I don' know 'bout sending Jarena. Grace ain' never been much of a cook. A man could plumb starve to death eating what that chil' prepares." He smiled.

Moses laughed and slapped Ezekiel on the shoulder. "I don't think it matters who returns with me. If you want Jarena to stay here and cook your meals, then send Grace instead."

Lilly took a step toward the men but stopped as Ezekiel slapped his hat back atop his head. "Naw. I needs Grace helping out in the fields. We'll make do 'til Jarena gets back home. Iffen you got time, I'd like to talk with you 'bout the problems with the cattle herders. Some of us was thinkin' maybe you could write another piece in the paper and even send it off to them politicians in Topeka. They been sayin' they's gonna get that herd law passed, but ain' nothing happened yet—least we ain' been told 'bout no changes."

"And from the looks of some of the fields I saw on the way over here, the cattlemen aren't going to voluntarily change their ways."

"Now that's a fact. You see Herman Kemble's crops when you come past his place? His winter wheat's ruined, and his corn, too. What them cattle didn't eat, they tromped over and destroyed. Like the rest of us, he was countin' on the money from that wheat. I'm tellin' ya, Moses, them cowboys ain' got no respect for nobody. I done tried my hand at talkin' to some of 'em, but they won't listen to reason. There's gonna be somebody killed afore long if this keeps up. We's worked hard to get these crops growed."

The hot Kansas sun had turned the green sprouts of early spring into an ocean of pale golden shafts that billowed and rolled in the soft summer breeze. Lilly had heard this was the most promising crop of wheat Ezekiel and the other settlers had planted since arriving in Kansas. And now they prayed the sea of grain would stand long enough to harvest. With each of their previous plantings, portions of the corn and wheat had been destroyed by cattlemen running herds through their fields. Each time the farmers planted seed, they vowed the destruction wouldn't happen again. Yet aside from their prayers, they remained helpless—unless they took matters into their own hands or the legislature passed the promised herd law.

"I don' want to see another incident like the one last summer when Herman Kemble an' John Beyer kidnapped a few of them cowboys."

Lilly drew close, amazed that this band of farmers would actually take the law into their own hands. "Do tell. I can't imagine any of those mild-mannered church-attending farmers actually defending a kidnapping. Why, that's a crime. Sounds like I'm not the only one in these parts who's immoral, right Ezekiel?"

He grunted. "'Cept for getting their cows back, didn't do the farmers no good. Gotta have fences if we's gonna keep them cows out. Breaking the law ain't the answer."

Lilly's brow furrowed. "I don't understand. Were they arguing over cattle or crops?"

Ezekiel shook his head in disgust. "Both. The crops was being trampled, and there was an argument over water rights down at the river. When some of John Beyer's cows was down there, the herders took 'em. John retaliated by gettin' Herman and a few other men to help him kidnap a few of the cattlemen. They held the fellas hostage until John's cows was returned."

"Then it *did* work," Lilly said with satisfaction.

"The crops is still being trampled, ain't they? You call that a victory?" Ezekiel didn't give her time to answer. Instead he turned back to his discussion with Moses.

Lilly was quick to note Ezekiel kept his back to her and his voice low while he continued. Some things never changed. Ezekiel still didn't believe women were bright enough to discuss anything more profound than cooking or cleaning. So be it. She stepped to the side of the buggy and patiently waited. Moses could answer her questions later. What she needed to focus on now was how to make Moses see that Jarena was the best choice of wife for him.

— 11 —

Jarena prepared Mrs. Boyle's tea tray and tucked the mail beneath her cloth napkin. For the life of her, Jarena couldn't decide exactly what ailed Mrs. Boyle. One minute the woman appeared to be fine, but the next, she'd take to her bed. The day after her arrival, Jarena had questioned Dr. Boyle about his wife's condition, but the conversation proved futile. Either Dr. Boyle didn't know the cause of his wife's affliction or he didn't care to disclose the information. Whatever the reason, it was difficult to anticipate exactly what would be expected from day to day. Jarena wondered how Truth had managed to help at the newspaper office with any regularity.

Balancing an ornate silver tray in one hand, Jarena knocked lightly before entering the bedroom, where Mrs. Boyle sat at a small circular table in front of the window. Without looking up, the older woman tapped on the table.

"You have a letter. Dr. Boyle asked that I bring it to you." After placing the tray in front of Mrs. Boyle, Jarena backed away.

"Sit down and read it to me."

Jarena sighed and dropped her hand from the doorknob. She sat down opposite Mrs. Boyle and examined the masculine script. "The letter appears to be from your son, Captain Boyle." Jarena hesitated. Surely the woman wouldn't want Jarena to hear the personal news her son had written.

Mrs. Boyle turned her gaze to Jarena. "Well, open the letter." The woman was obviously impatient to hear the latest news from her son. And, truth be told, so was Jarena. It had been some time since she had received a letter from Thomas, and she hoped Captain Boyle's letter would provide some insight.

Jarena stared at the address on the letter. "I didn't realize your son had been promoted and . . . reassigned. He's no longer at Fort Concho?"

"No. When he received his promotion, they sent him to Virginia—Fort Myer. I tend to think the promotion and reassignment were due in part to the letter I wrote Vice-President Wheeler." Mrs. Boyle's face suddenly sparked with life.

Jarena's eyes widened and her jaw went slack. "You wrote a letter to the vice-president of the United States?"

Mrs. Boyle straightened in her chair and squared her shoulders. "Indeed. I told him in no uncertain terms that I wanted my Carlisle sent back to the safety of civilization or he need not consider me among his friends. Of course, I didn't tell my husband I'd written the letter until after it was posted."

"Was Dr. Boyle cross with you when he found out?"

"Oh, he pretended to be upset for a short time, but deep down he was relieved. Samuel doesn't want Carlisle out there fighting those Indians any more than I do."

Jarena sobered at the older woman's reply. Of course the Boyles didn't want their son in some forsaken part of the country fighting Indians. She didn't want Thomas there, either. But she wasn't a friend of Vice-President Wheeler. Fact is, she didn't know anyone important enough to bring Thomas home. Unless . . . She hesitated, but she knew if she waited any longer she would lose her confidence.

"Mrs. Boyle, do you think you could . . . I mean, would you consider . . . that is, I'd surely appreciate it if you'd consider writing your friend the vice-president about Thomas. Thomas Grayson. He's the man I'm going to marry. When he comes home, that is."

"Oh yes, Thomas. I remember him. He went to Fort Sill with Carlisle, didn't he? Was Thomas later assigned to Fort Concho, also?"

Jarena bobbed her head up and down. "Yes. And I'm worried, Mrs. Boyle. I haven't had a letter from him in a long time."

Mrs. Boyle patted Jarena's hand. "That doesn't mean anything bad has happened, my dear. For the most part, I find that men don't enjoy letter writing."

"But he'd been faithful to write at least once a month before. If you'd consider writing Vice-President Wheeler, I'd be willing to forego my wages while I'm here. I don't expect him to reassign Thomas, but if he could find out if all is well, I'd be so grateful."

Jarena couldn't bring herself to say what she needed to know. Somehow she feared that speaking the words might make it so. A silly thought, but still she couldn't help herself—she wouldn't give voice to the thought that Thomas might be dead.

Mrs. Boyle studied her for a moment. "I'll see what I can do. Now, why don't you read me Carlisle's letter."

The letter was filled with tidbits regarding his new military assignment—the food was excellent, he regularly preached at a small chapel on the post, and there had already been two military balls since his reassignment. Mrs. Boyle beamed with satisfaction. Jarena hesitated as she began to read the final page. Carlisle's letter told of his former company—Thomas's company—heading off to take a stand against Indian renegades who had begun departing the reservation. He said casualties would likely be great.

Jarena tucked the letter back into the envelope. Tears rimmed her eyes as she handed the missive to Mrs. Boyle. "Thomas wrote that his company was going into New Mexico Territory. He said there were problems keeping Indians on the reservations. I haven't heard from him since."

"Don't you worry yourself. I'll write a letter this evening to both the vice-president and Carlisle asking for information."

"Thank you, Mrs. Boyle. If you'll excuse me, I haven't finished polishing the silver. I'll return for your tray later this morning." She wiped tears off of her cheeks as she scurried down the hallway.

———

A knock sounded at the front door as Jarena placed the final piece of silverware in the wooden case and closed the lid. Mrs. Boyle wasn't expecting company. In fact, no one had come visiting since Jarena had arrived. Likely because folks never knew when the lady of the house would be suffering from one of her mysterious maladies.

Before she could make her way to the door, the knocking resumed in earnest. Jarena trudged forward, her steps weighed down by fearsome thoughts of Thomas off fighting in Indian Territory. The dull thud in her head kept time with the incessant banging. She wished the caller would depart; right now she wanted to be alone with her thoughts. Neither a visitor nor a salesman was welcome.

"You look sour enough to eat lemons." Aunt Lilly stood before her in a red and gray print dress, holding Alma by the hand. "What took you so long to answer the door?"

"I was polishing the silver out in the kitchen." Jarena glanced over her shoulder. "I don't have time to visit, Aunt Lilly. I need to fetch Mrs. Boyle's tray from her room and begin preparations for supper. Shouldn't you be doing the same? And where are the two boys?"

Lilly smiled broadly. "Mrs. Nelson prepares supper three nights a week. I don't think Mr. Nelson is fond of my cooking." Her eyelashes fluttered in an exaggerated wink. "The boys were naughty and they've been confined to their room, so Alma and I thought we'd pay you a visit. I told Alma you might offer us some lemonade and cookies."

Jarena couldn't refuse Alma's pleading blue eyes. "Once I pick up Mrs. Boyle's tray, I'll return and set out some cookies."

"And lemonade," Lilly added as Jarena departed the room.

After retrieving the tea tray, Jarena shepherded her guests into the kitchen. Perhaps if she served them the obligatory cookies and lemonade they would be on their way.

Lilly directed Alma to a chair and then stepped to Jarena's side. "What's wrong with you, Jarena? If you're concerned the Boyles won't want you entertaining visitors, you just forget that notion. After all, you're doing them a favor by filling in for Truth. They have no reason to complain."

Jarena halved one of the lemons and squeezed a stream of juice into the glass pitcher before looking at her aunt. "They are paying me to perform household duties and care for Mrs. Boyle. Whether I am here for a day or a month is of no consequence. I was taught always to give my best, Aunt Lilly."

"When you get out in the world, you're going to find it's best to save yourself for those times when the reward is greatest." Lilly lifted her hand and turned an open palm toward Jarena. "No need to start quoting the Bible. I heard all those verses years ago. Life has taught me I'm the one who's correct on this topic—and many others, also."

After arranging a small plate of cookies, Jarena poured lemonade into three glasses. She handed Alma a napkin and offered the child a cookie before sitting down. "Are the Nelsons pleased with you—despite your inability to cook?"

"Obviously you weren't listening to what I said. I can *cook*, Jarena. But unlike you, I'm saving my talents for the proper time. Now, tell me what has disturbed you. I can see there's something beyond my unexpected visit that's troubling you."

Though Aunt Lilly wouldn't have been her first choice of confidantes, Jarena's thoughts had been running rampant since reading Carlisle's letter to Mrs. Boyle. She needed reassurance—a few words that would settle the unrelenting sick feeling in the pit of her stomach. Besides, who else would listen to her tale of woe? Carefully choosing her words, Jarena explained the contents of Carlisle's letter. Her aunt listened attentively until Jarena finished her story.

Lilly covered Alma's small ears. "I tried to tell you about men serving in the army. If Thomas is still alive, he's likely taken up with one of the female camp followers. Those trollops will even go into Indian Territory to service the soldiers. Most of them are hoping to find a husband, but they'll settle for less."

Jarena gasped. Fearing she might faint, she folded her arms around her waist and leaned down to rest her forehead upon her knees.

Lilly moved closer and rubbed Jarena's shoulder. "I'm sorry. That was thoughtless of me. No doubt, Thomas is fine." She flapped her fan in front of Jarena for several minutes before bringing the feathered accessory to an abrupt halt. "I know! You must go and visit with Moses. The newspapers always receive information before the rest of us. He may have some news; if not, he may know someone who can gain access to such reports."

Revived by the suggestion, Jarena sat up straight. "That's a wonderful idea, Aunt Lilly. I'll go and visit with him on my way to the general store tomorrow. Thank you."

Lilly smiled and nodded as she grasped Alma by the hand and led the young girl toward the front of the house.

Jarena stood in the doorway until her aunt and little Alma were out of sight. Perhaps she had misjudged Aunt Lilly.

CHAPTER

— 12 —

Early the next morning, Jarena hurried off to the newspaper office. Her palms were sweaty and her heart beat wildly beneath her cotton shirtwaist. Moses was operating the printing press, and though a small bell rang when she opened the door, he didn't look up. She waited a moment and then waved her handkerchief in the air. He smiled and pointed at a chair beside his desk.

She wanted to place her hands over her ears to muffle the noise but decided such behavior would appear unseemly. Instead she folded her hands in her lap and occasionally leaned forward to peek at the clock. Perhaps she should have gone to the general store before coming to the newspaper office. After all, Dr. Boyle was awaiting her return before departing for his office.

Five more minutes and then I'll leave. She stared at the clock, watching the small pendulum swing back and forth. As the final minute ticked off, the clamor of the printing press quieted.

"I won't keep you long," Jarena explained. "I can see you're very busy."

"Never too busy to visit with family. Well, almost family." He grinned as he dropped into the chair behind his desk. "How are things going with the Boyles? I've been meaning to stop by and check on you, but without Truth to help here at the newspaper office . . ."

"No need to apologize. I understand. Working for the Boyles has been satisfactory, though I wouldn't want to remain indefinitely. However, I'll be fine until Truth returns. If you have a moment, there's a matter I wish to discuss with you."

He nodded and listened intently as Jarena told him about the contents of Carlisle's letter. When she had completed her account, she leaned forward and rested her hands on the desk. "Do you think you could secure any information?"

Moses took her hands in his own and held them lightly. "I know there have been a number of skirmishes with a band of Indians led by Victorio, an Apache chief. As I recall, companies from both the Ninth and Tenth have been involved, but I've not heard many of the details. And you must remember that the efforts to contain the Indians on reservations have resulted in ongoing difficulty in those territories."

Jarena stiffened. "Would this Victorio be in New Mexico Territory?"

"Yes. However, I believe from the paper I read, he's attempting to lead his warriors back into Mexico to avoid being returned to the reservation. But that was a number of weeks ago and there's no telling where he might be now. Furthermore, Jarena, there are many soldiers who will never be involved in a skirmish."

She slipped her hands from his and leaned back in her chair. "You know that's not true for the buffalo soldiers, Moses. The army's keeping them stationed in the territories where most all of the fighting is taking place."

"Thomas is likely eating a warm meal while you're fretting."

Touching her hand to her heart, Jarena gazed into Moses's eyes. "I have a feeling inside that something terrible has happened, and I need to know."

He stood and stepped around the desk. "I can go to Ellis later in the week and telegraph Fort Concho. I'll inquire if they know of Thomas's whereabouts, if that would help."

"Oh, thank you, Moses." She once again checked the clock. "I had best be on my way. I must stop at the general store before returning to the Boyles'."

"I'll walk along with you. I need to mail this," he said, lifting an envelope from atop his desk. "If my friend Spencer doesn't hear from me soon, he's going to think I've forgotten him."

Moses took her arm as they walked down the street while excitedly discussing the possible date of Truth's return. There was little doubt Moses missed the joy and companionship Truth added to his life.

"I know how much you miss Truth, and if there's anything I can do to assist you while she's gone—writing an article for the newspaper or helping in any other way—you need only ask."

"I may take you up on your offer. Seems there's little time to accomplish everything, and having someone to write a piece or two would help tremendously. Are you certain you wouldn't find it an inconvenience?"

"Of course not. I'd be delighted to have something more challenging to occupy my mind than washing clothes and tending the flower garden."

Moses beamed as they stopped outside Walt and Ada Johnson's mercantile. "Good. In fact, I may bring over an assignment before I depart for Ellis."

Jarena nodded and moved forward to enter the store. Miscalculating the step, she tripped on her skirt and tumbled forward. Instinctively, she stretched her arms out, hoping to break the fall. Instead, she found herself locked in Moses's embrace as he jumped forward and caught her. Stunned, Jarena grasped the lapels of his waistcoat, holding tight until she could gain her balance.

"Now isn't this a lovely picture?"

Jarena whirled about at the sound of Aunt Lilly's voice. The woman had appeared just inside the open doorway from nowhere. She gave one of her exaggerated winks and stood beaming at them as though she were a proud parent. "Though I do believe the general store is a rather public forum for a display of affection."

Jarena gasped. "Whatever are you talking about? I tripped on—"

"No need to explain to me. I perfectly understand matters of the heart."

Her aunt was speaking louder than necessary and gaining the attention of several ladies. Jarena grimaced. Aunt Lilly knew that her outlandish comments would draw the interest of Mrs. Johnson's customers. Two or three ladies edged closer to the doorway and pretended to busy themselves reading the labels on bottles of paregoric and tincture of arnica. Jarena clutched her aunt's arm and endeavored to move her out the door.

With a firm yank, Lilly adroitly extracted her arm. "I'm not ready to leave just yet, Jarena. I haven't completed my order. And you and Moses haven't even begun your shopping, have you?"

Moses withdrew the letter from his pocket. "I'm going to post my letter and be on my way, Jarena. I hope to talk with you before I depart for Ellis. If not, I'll send word when I return."

Lilly moved to his side. "I'm sure Jarena would prefer to have you deliver your message personally—especially if the news is unwelcome."

Jarena offered Moses her thanks, glared at her aunt, and began to gather items from the store shelves with Lilly close on her heels. The woman was an absolute enigma—one minute acting kind and compassionate, the next creating chaos in others' lives.

Lilly gathered up the basket of purchases and slowly sauntered toward home. She didn't want to return to the house, where she would be greeted by noisy children and tedious housework. Even going to the general store was preferable to keeping the Nelson children in tow. But there was little choice this day. Mrs. Nelson planned to attend her temperance meeting at the church, a gathering Lilly figured was no more than a gossip session with a respectable title.

The street churned with dust as a colorfully decorated drummer's wagon drawn by a sleek dappled mare raced into town. The driver yanked back on the reins and brought the conveyance to a rocking halt in front of the general store. Lilly shaded her eyes to watch a well-dressed man step out of the buggy and sprint up the two steps and into the mercantile. She longed to know who the man might be—obviously a salesman passing through, but nonetheless, he might prove to be a diversion. If only she had time. She weighed the consequences but grudgingly turned and walked toward the Nelson home. For the time being, she needed her job.

Mrs. Nelson was pacing on the front porch when Lilly returned. "I was beginning to think something had happened to you. If you hadn't returned within another five minutes, I was planning to send Georgie to check on your whereabouts."

Lilly breezed past her employer, down the hallway, and into the kitchen. Mrs. Nelson was close on her heels as she placed the basket of groceries on the sturdy wood table.

"As your employer, I'd like to know the reason you were detained, Mrs. Verdue."

Surprised by Mrs. Nelson's brusque behavior, Lilly lifted her gaze from the basket. Every so often, the woman mustered a courage that caught Lilly off guard. And every time, Lilly was required to quickly regroup and change tactics. Assessing the situation, she played on Mrs. Nelson's sympathies by explaining she'd taken time to console poor Jarena, whose intended had likely been killed in an Indian skirmish in the southwest territories. It was obvious her tale had the desired impact.

Mrs. Nelson's eyes grew wide, and she clasped a hand to her bodice as she offered several apologies, each more humble than the last. And then, joy of all joys, the woman asked if there wasn't something she could do to help. Lilly nearly danced with delight. She'd gained an advantage with barely any effort or planning. Though Lilly declined the woman's assistance, she did mention it would bolster Jarena's spirits if she could visit the girl more frequently.

"Yes, of course. And I'll ask the ladies of the church to pray for the young man. What is his name?"

"Thomas. Thomas Grayson. He's serving with the Tenth Cavalry."

Mrs. Nelson rubbed her forehead. "Dear me! Isn't that Captain Boyle's group of men?"

Lilly quickly explained about Captain Boyle's reassignment as she continued to unpack the basket. "I don't think Captain Boyle should find himself in too much danger at his new military post."

"We'll pray for him anyway. He's hard at work trying to save the souls of those soldiers. He's got his work cut out for him. From what I hear, those men are more interested in alcohol and immoral women than the Word of God."

"Hard to imagine, isn't it?" Lilly asked with a wry grin.

Mrs. Nelson picked up her reticule. "Indeed. You would think that when a man is in the midst of flying bullets and arrows, he'd be anxious to hear about the afterlife. You know, seeking God and eternal salvation rather than a bottle of whiskey and . . . and . . ."

"A woman's embrace?"

Mrs. Nelson's cheeks flushed. "Yes. Now, I had best be on my way or I'm going to be late. Do make sure Georgie doesn't escape out the upstairs window again."

Lilly nodded and finished her kitchen chores before going upstairs. It had been quiet far too long, and though Alma would still be napping, the boys were likely engaged in their usual mischief. If only Joey didn't have his older brother to lead him astray, he'd be easily managed. However, Georgie was a problem that needed solving.

The carpeted hallway muffled her footsteps as she peeked inside the boys' bedroom. They were nowhere to been seen, and the window was closed tight. Yet she could hear their hushed voices, and it sounded as though they were coming from *her* bedroom. Lilly marched down the hallway, her anger mounting with each footstep. She pushed open her bedroom door, and the boys jumped up from their crouched position and watched her with wide-eyed attention.

Moving across the floor with the speed of a warrior after his prey, Lilly grasped Georgie by one ear. "What are you doing going through my belongings?"

The boy turned pale and attempted to wrest his ear from her pinching fingers. "We were going to clean your room for you."

"And you need to get inside my closet and go through my drawers to clean? Is that right?"

"N-n-no, but—"

"Quit your fibbing, Georgie. What is it you thought you'd find in here?"

The boy shrugged and then flinched when the movement caused Lilly's hold to tighten on his ear. Joey rushed forward and tugged on Lilly's skirt, obviously hoping to come to his brother's aid.

"We was stealing this." The child dug into his pants pocket and pulled out one of Lilly's handkerchiefs. He turned back the lace edging that surrounded the linen cloth and revealed a rabbit's foot and a glass ball.

"Is that an eye in there?" Joey asked. "Georgie said it was."

Lilly took the handkerchief and its contents from the younger boy. She released Georgie from her grasp. "Sit down. Both of you."

They both dropped obediently to the floor. One end of the rabbit's foot was crusted with dried blood, and Lilly held it in front of the boys. "Some folks think a rabbit's foot brings them luck, but it doesn't."

Joey tilted his head to the side, and his eyes widened with surprise. "It doesn't?"

"Wasn't lucky for the rabbit, was it?"

The boys shook their heads. "No. But folks say having one is good luck for *people*," Georgie pointed out.

"If it wasn't good luck for the rabbit, it won't be good luck for you, either. Besides, I found you in my room. Did the rabbit's foot bring you good luck?"

Georgie shook his head. "No, but how come you got it?"

"Someone gave it to me as a gift, believing that it brought good luck."

"What's that?" Joey placed a plump finger on the glass ball.

"An evil eye." Lilly made her voice low and ominous. "I had hoped I wouldn't be forced to use it when I came here to live. I thought I would be living in a house with well-behaved children."

Joey inched away from her. "You are."

"Oh, I don't think that's true, Joey. I believe you *could* be a good little boy. Instead, you allow Georgie to lead you into trouble, don't you?"

Georgie elbowed his brother, but Joey ignored the jab. "Uh-huh. But I won't do it no more. I promise."

"Good. Then you go to your room and stay there until I come and fetch you."

Joey ran from the room as though his knee pants were on fire, and

Lilly turned her attention back to his brother. "You remember when I told you to behave or I'd place a hex on you?"

Georgie slumped and stared at the floor. "Yes, ma'am."

"Then why do you keep on with your mischievous ways?"

The boy peeked up at her. "I wanted to see if Mama was right about you."

Lilly's mind reeled. "Right about what?"

"I heard her tell Papa she thought you were hiding something. I was trying to find it."

Lilly gave a nod, remembering the day she'd found Mrs. Nelson snooping through her belongings. Though Mrs. Nelson had pretended to be delivering linens, Lilly suspected the woman had been spying.

She squatted down and took hold of Georgie's trembling hands. "If you tell me the truth, you don't need to fear me, Georgie. What else did you hear?"

"Papa asked her why she didn't trust you."

"And?" Lilly urged, dropping the boy's hands.

"She said she saw things in your room she didn't like, but when Mama saw me listening, she stopped talking." He touched the rabbit's foot. "I figure she saw these things."

"Did you ever hear them discuss anything else about me?"

He wagged his head from side to side. "Can I go now?"

"No. We must reach an agreement, Georgie." Lilly removed the glass ball from the handkerchief and held it between her fingers with the eye pointed directly at him. "Do you see the evil eye staring at you?"

Fear shone in the boy's deep blue eyes. "Evil eye?"

"Yes. I use it to put a curse on those who don't do what they promise. Shall I say the words that will place you under the spell of the evil eye, Georgie?"

"No*ooo*! I'll be good. I promise."

"But that's not all. You must promise to tell me anything your mama or papa says about me. *Anything*. Do you promise?" Lilly slowly twisted her fingers as she moved the stone closer to the boy. The eye appeared to come to life, following Georgie's darting glance.

"I promise, I promise. I'll tell you everything I hear. Can I go now?"

She nodded. "Now go to your room. When Alma awakens, we'll go outdoors and you and Joey can play." The boy jumped to his feet. But before he could bolt out of reach, Lilly stood and took hold of his arm, shoving the glass ball at him one final time. "Don't forget, Georgie."

As the boys' bedroom door slammed shut, Lilly dropped to her bed with a laugh. She hoped her performance had been successful. Throughout the years, she had effectively persuaded countless individuals she could conjure spells. Lilly knew her true skill was not voodoo or witchcraft, however, but the power of persuasion.

Only the future would reveal if she had succeeded, but there was precious little time to dwell on the matter since Alma was now up from her nap and peeking out from her bedroom doorway. After safely tucking away the handkerchief and its contents, Lilly gave the room a fleeting glance. She truly needed a lock for her door.

She motioned to Alma and tapped on the boys' bedroom door as she walked by. "Come along, Georgie and Joey. Alma's awake. Let's go outdoors—and no trouble."

The boys needed no further encouragement. They bounded down

the stairs and out the front door before Lilly and Alma had cleared the upper hallway.

While Lilly prepared a plate of cookies and a pitcher of lemonade, Alma returned upstairs to pick out a favorite book. She held up a book of Grimms' fairy tales for Lilly's approval as the two of them walked to the porch.

"Excellent choice."

Alma beamed at the praise and snuggled close, carefully pointing at the pictures and turning the pages on cue. Lilly had nearly completed the first story when the sound of an approaching wagon captured her attention. She hastily read the final lines and then snapped the volume together, certain the horse and wagon belonged to the man she'd seen entering the Johnsons' general store earlier in the day. Lilly stepped off the porch and sauntered down the sidewalk as the buggy slowed.

The man tipped his hat and pulled back on the reins. "Lovely day."

She appraised the man for a brief moment. "New in town, aren't you?"

"Making my way to some of the smaller towns with my sample books. I'm hoping to discover whether I can turn a profit passing through once or twice a month."

Lilly wiped the beads of sweat from her lemonade glass as she further evaluated the man's appearance. His clothing spoke of money, but Lilly knew any salesman worth his salt dressed to exude prosperity. "And are you meeting with success?"

The man removed his hat and pulled a handkerchief from his breast pocket. "Not much." He swiped his forehead and nodded toward Lilly's glass. "I don't want to appear bold, but I could sure use a cool drink.

That lemonade looks mighty inviting."

"Then you had best come and have a glass. You can tie your horse to that post. Mr. Nelson won't be home anytime soon."

"Charlie Holmes," the man said as he approached. "Nice to see a smiling face. Can't say as folks around these parts have been too welcoming. Seems as though they'd rather wait till the train is due to arrive in Ellis and then take their wagons down there and collect their goods."

Lilly introduced herself and took the man's linen fedora. The inner band was greasy and discolored. Mr. Holmes clearly used an abundance of macassar oil to slick his wavy hair into place. But she wouldn't fault him. At least he cared about his appearance—unlike most of the men in these parts.

Mr. Holmes leaned against one of the ornate wooden columns flanking the porch stairs while Lilly went into the house to get a glass and then poured some lemonade for her new acquaintance. "Do sit down, Mr. Holmes."

Alma scooted off one of the cushioned wicker chairs and tugged at Lilly's sleeve. "May I go out back and play with my brothers, Miss Lilly?"

"Of course, Alma. But remember, you know right from wrong. If your brothers are doing something improper, you must come tell me."

The child's curls bobbed up and down, circling her head like a bouncing blond halo. "I will, Miss Lilly." Alma waved a chubby hand as she descended the porch steps and skipped off.

Lilly handed her guest the lemonade and permitted her fingers to rest on his a moment longer than necessary. "If only her brothers were so easily managed."

Mr. Holmes nodded before taking a deep swallow of his beverage. "Boys can be more difficult—more energy."

Choosing a nearby chair, Lilly sat down and carefully arranged the folds of her skirt. "You have youngsters of your own, Mr. Holmes?"

"Goodness, no. I've never married—too much traveling. I've been around my sister's boys, though—and of course I remember my younger years." His eyes glimmered with amusement.

"I'm sorry you haven't met with greater success during your recent travels. I suppose the life of a salesman can be most trying."

He blotted his upper lip with his kerchief. "No more vexing than that of a housekeeper and nursemaid. While I can take a brief respite from the drudgery of my daily travels, there is no escape for you." His look conveyed genuine sympathy.

Lilly fluttered her lashes and refilled his glass. "Thank you, Mr. Holmes."

He lightly touched her hand. "Please. Call me Charlie. I feel as though we've already begun to develop a kinship. I only wish there were some reason for me to return this way more often. Unfortunately, Mr. Johnson placed only a small order with me, though he suggested I stop in Nicodemus."

"Did he?"

The children's laughter floated from the backyard as Mr. Holmes scooted forward on his seat. "Perhaps you know some of the folks over there? I could explain that we're acquainted and it might help my sales."

Lilly stifled a laugh. "I'm afraid not, Charlie. Though my brother-in-law farms outside of Nicodemus, I came to Hill City shortly after my arrival in Kansas."

After draining the contents, Charlie handed her the empty glass. "I thank you for your hospitality, but daylight's wasting and I need to be on my way. With your kind permission, I would like to stop next time I pass through town."

Mrs. Nelson would frown upon such visits, but Lilly enjoyed the man's company. "Mrs. Nelson is away from home on Tuesdays. Otherwise . . ."

"I'll be certain I'm in Hill City every other Tuesday." He picked up his hat and offered Lilly his arm as she walked him to the front gate.

She patted his arm. "And in the meantime, I'll be thinking of some way to help you become more prosperous, Charlie."

— 13 —

New York City • July 1880

Truth followed the servant girl into the mahogany-paneled office and emulated a faint bow as the owners of the Rutledge Academy introduced themselves. They were a formidable group, and Truth once again wondered why she had agreed to make this journey.

Mrs. Rutledge twisted her lips into a knot as she examined the letter of introduction Truth had handed over upon being presented to the woman. "This says you've come to fetch Miss Boyle home."

"Yes, ma'am."

The younger of the two gentlemen stepped to the side of the desk and picked up the letter. "How are we to know this isn't a forgery or that you didn't take this letter from someone else?"

Truth cocked her head to one side. Were these people jesting with her? Why would anyone else want to come and take Macia home? "Macia can identify me, and if you fear the letter is a forgery, I believe you have other papers with Dr. Boyle's signature. I suggest you compare them."

Mr. Rutledge glanced at Marvin Laird. "She's a smart one, isn't she?"

Mr. Laird ignored the question. "How is it that Dr. Boyle happened to send you, Miss Harban? We wrote and told him that Macia was ill and that he need only send money for her treatment. Didn't he receive my missive?"

"Yes, he did. However, as he states in his letter, he will be more at ease caring for Macia himself. Had it not been for Mrs. Boyle's ill health, he would have come himself. I was hoping to begin our return journey tomorrow or by week's end, at the latest."

Mr. Laird laughed. "*You* may leave whenever you desire, Miss Harban, but Miss Boyle is in no condition to travel. I explained that in my detailed letter to Dr. Boyle. I trust he sent sufficient funds to cover her medical expenses?"

Truth fingered the clasp on her reticule and shook her head. "No. He said he would send you payment for the additional expenses once Macia arrived home."

The man's back straightened. "I don't believe you."

Truth pointed at the ivory stationery. "It's right there in the second page of his letter."

Mr. Laird snatched the paper from Mrs. Rutledge and ran his finger along the page. He looked up and glared at Truth before whispering something to Mr. Rutledge. The older man bowed his head in agreement, and both of them stormed from the room.

Truth fidgeted for a moment while hoping to gain her courage. "May I see Macia?"

Mrs. Rutledge didn't reply. Instead, she stared into the distance acting as though she'd not heard a word. Truth loudly cleared her throat, and Mrs. Rutledge startled to attention. "Well, I suppose Daisy can take you upstairs, though Miss Boyle is likely asleep. You shouldn't disturb her."

"Yes, ma'am. I'll be quiet as a church mouse."

Truth followed Daisy up the staircase and down the hallway. When Daisy reached to turn the doorknob, Truth touched her arm. "What's going on in this place? Why do those people act so odd?"

Daisy shrugged and pulled away. "I jest do my job and keep my mouth shut. I don't know nothing about nothing. Your mistress is in there." That said, Daisy shoved open the door and retreated at a lope.

The sight of Macia's sallow complexion and sunken cheeks sent fear coursing through Truth's body. She barely looked like the vibrant young woman who had departed Hill City just over a month ago. Truth paced back and forth with an occasional glance toward the canopied bed. She didn't know how to proceed. She'd come to New York fully expecting to begin her return journey within a day or two. Instead, her plans had begun to go awry from the moment she'd set foot in the city. Aunt Lilly's assurances that she would have little difficulty navigating in the city had proved untrue. Outside the railway station, the street had been jammed with carriages, wagons, carts, omnibuses, and trucks, all packed together in helpless confusion. People scurried about in ill-fated chaos while policemen waved and shouted at the passing parade of humanity. Hailing a cabriolet had been a daunting task, but dodging a racing omnibus had placed Truth's very life in peril. And as if to add insult to injury, the omnibus driver seemed quite jubilant when she'd dropped her valise while jumping into the cab.

Having survived the harrowing incident with the omnibus, she'd been treated as an interloper when she had finally arrived at Macia's school. How Truth longed for the assistance of some kindly soul who would direct her along the proper path. If only Macia would awaken, perhaps she could help. However, Macia wasn't stirring in the least. Truth plopped down in the oversized chair near Macia's bed and drifted in and out of a restless sleep until a knock on the bedroom door awakened her. Before she could answer, Mr. Laird and Mrs. Rutledge entered the room.

Mrs. Rutledge drew near and touched Macia's cheek. "Has she awakened at all?"

Truth shook her head. "No, ma'am, and she looks much too thin—and pale."

"Well, what did you expect?" Mr. Laird looked down his nose at Truth as he spat the words. "She's ill. We told you she's in no condition to travel."

"Maybe if another physician examined her, we could gain further information about her illness." Truth's suggestion was met with icy stares.

Mr. Laird brushed past Truth and neared Macia's bedside. "When I want your opinion, Miss Harban, I shall ask. In the meantime, I suggest you return to Kansas. There is nothing you can do here in New

York. Miss Boyle is well cared for, and you'll only be in the way. More-over, you can't remain in the room overnight—it's against the academy rules."

Truth's stomach lurched at the comment. "I-I don't have anywhere else to go. I'll sleep on the floor beside Macia's bed. There's nothing in the rules against someone remaining in the room to care for a sick student, is there?"

Mrs. Rutledge tapped her finger on her chin. "You are not a trained nurse. Our rules specifically state that only paying students may remain in the rooms."

"But I've traveled so far. Surely in this instance you could make an exception."

"I suppose you could stay in the servants' quarters with Daisy until you decide to return home," Mr. Laird allowed.

There was no sense arguing. She wouldn't win this battle. "So long as I can attend to Macia's needs during the day, I'll accept your kind offer to sleep in the servants' quarters. I do hope Daisy won't object."

"Daisy? She has no right to object to anything. She's a servant who knows her place, Miss Harban."

Mr. Laird's words stung like an angry slap. Obviously, he wanted Truth to argue. Instead, she decided to remain compliant and disap-point him. "Thank you, Mr. Laird. I accept your offer of accommoda-tions in the servants' quarters. Dr. Boyle will be pleased to hear how well I've been treated here at the Rutledge Academy. I'll simply plan to spend my days in this room with Macia. Does the doctor make daily visits?"

Mrs. Rutledge arched her eyebrows. "Doctor?"

"Yes. Dr. Anderson. Your letter to the Boyles said Dr. Anderson was caring for Macia. Dr. Boyle asked that I speak with the physician upon my arrival in New York."

"His schedule varies, though the two of you will eventually meet. Now go along and tell Daisy to show you to your quarters," Mr. Laird instructed. "She should be in the kitchen preparing supper."

Truth's stomach rumbled at the mention of food. She hadn't eaten anything since early morning. "What time is supper?"

Mr. Laird smirked. "I can't believe you were expecting to take your meals in the dining room with the students, Miss Harban. You may be able to find a few extra morsels in the kitchen."

Truth picked up her valise and opened the door. "I shall expect more than a morsel, Mr. Laird. Obviously, Macia isn't eating. I shall plan to eat her portion. After all, her family has already paid for her board at this *academy*."

Without another word, Truth strode off. She hurried down the steps, using the front stairway rather than the back stairs Mr. Laird had suggested. It was a childishly defiant measure, but one that pleased her nonetheless. After navigating the curved hall that meandered in several directions, Truth spied Daisy moving about in the kitchen. The girl looked up as Truth entered the room.

"Mr. Laird sent me. He said you would show me to the servants' quarters."

Daisy swiped her floured hands down her apron. "Do I look like I got time to take you out dere right now? I's busy fixing supper. It don't matter what Mr. Laird said I should do with you. There won't be no forgiving me if supper's late, and I ain't losing my position over some stranger."

Truth could wage an argument against Daisy's position—and perhaps even win. But what would be accomplished? She needed a friend, and maybe if she was kind, Daisy would be willing to help her. She set her valise in the corner and removed her cape. "Give me an apron and I'll help you, Daisy. I cook for the Boyle family, and I can follow your orders."

Daisy's eyes shone with suspicion, but she handed Truth an apron. "You can peel them potatoes."

Truth finished each of Daisy's assigned tasks without complaint. "You can help yourself to any of that food," Daisy said after they had completed the supper preparations, indicating the pots and bowls. "I always fix extra for me and Silas. Mr. Laird says we's only s'pose to eat the scraps. That man is crazy if he thinks I'm gonna gnaw on the bones while the rest of them eat the pork chops."

After helping with the supper dishes, Truth was exhausted but certain she'd made a friend. Daisy looped arms with her as they walked to the servants' quarters. "This here place ain't very nice—nothing like what you's been living in with that fancy doctor and his family."

"Once I've had some sleep, I'll tell you about some of the places I've lived, Daisy. I'm certain your room will do just fine."

As they neared the carriage house, Daisy called to Silas and asked him to bring a bed from the storage barn. "Miss Harban's gonna be staying in my room." Daisy led the way upstairs to the large rooms above the carriage house—much larger than what Truth had expected. "Me and Silas was sorry Miss Macia was one of the gals to get sick this school session. Miss Macia and Miss Rennie been right nice to both me and Silas. Not like some of them uppity girls. I was hoping it would be one of them snooty gals like Inez Barringer that got sick."

Daisy waved Silas into the room and helped him as he set up the bed. Silas pounded the wood frame together and topped it with a flimsy mattress. "Once in a while the snooty ones get sick."

Truth unfolded the sheet Daisy handed her. "You mean there are students sick during every school session?"

"Um-hmm. Mrs. Rutledge says it's the change in climate and water. Sure ain't my cooking, 'cause Silas ain't never got sick."

Silas laughed and rubbed his stomach. "Now that's a fact. And those pork chops tonight was really good."

Though Truth wanted to question the two of them further, Silas excused himself, and Daisy was soon asleep.

When Truth awakened the next morning, sunlight spilled through the two windows on the east wall, and there was no sign of Daisy. The girl had likely been in the kitchen working for several hours. Truth hurriedly dressed and then raced across the rear yard to the kitchen.

"Why didn't you wake me?"

Daisy gave her a lopsided grin. "I figured you was mighty tired what with your traveling and then helping me in the kitchen. Thought you could use the sleep. 'Sides, ain't nothing you can do for Miss Macia. Jest like all the other gals, she ain't gonna do nothing but sleep."

"Does Dr. Anderson come to check on her, Daisy?"

"He was here once. He don't never come too often."

"But he wrote that Macia's been having seizures. How does he know that unless he comes to see her?"

Daisy shrugged. "Don't know. I ain't never seen Miss Macia have no seizure. She jest sleeps all the time."

"Tell me about the other girls that have gotten ill," Truth urged.

Daisy glanced about. "We can talk tonight when we go back to my room. I don' like talking 'round here where people's always listening."

Truth wondered why anyone would be interested in listening to a servant's conversation, but she harkened to Daisy's admonition. She and Daisy would talk at length this evening.

Truth headed off toward the grand stairway but turned on her heel and walked to the back stairs. It was, after all, closer to Macia's bedroom. She was nearing the top of the steps when she saw Mr. Laird and another man exit Macia's room. She stood quietly, wanting to hear what they were saying. The stranger explained he would bring additional medicine. Was this Dr. Anderson? She absolutely must talk to him.

She stepped into the hallway. "Dr. Anderson?"

The stranger turned in her direction. "Yes? May I help you?"

Mr. Laird dipped his head toward Truth. "This is the woman I mentioned—Miss Boyle's servant."

Truth didn't correct the statement. She was, after all, the Boyles' maid and housekeeper, if only for a short time longer. "May I speak to you about Miss Boyle's condition?"

The doctor rubbed his index finger over his mustache. "Yes, of course."

"I'd like to accompany Miss Boyle home, where her father can attend to her medical treatment and restore her back to health."

The doctor shook his head. "She's unable to travel in her current condition. However, I'm sure your ministrations will be helpful. Perhaps in the next several weeks her strength will return."

The days marched on in blurry replication while Macia continued to fade in and out of a hazy stupor. Unfortunately, the meager amount of food Truth could force into her patient usually came back up, and her condition had changed little since Truth's arrival. Truth had been ever watchful, hoping there might be some way she could reverse the tide. None of her efforts had met with success, however, and Dr. Anderson soon proved to be as obstructive as Mr. Laird and the Rutledges. When her attempts with all of them had failed, Truth turned to Daisy and Silas.

After much prodding, they had agreed to reveal what little they knew about Macia's illness. Although Truth had hoped for more information, both of the servants were frightened to speak freely. And Truth understood their reticence—both of them stood to lose their employment with the school should they speak out of turn. But they had told her enough so that she'd begun watching Mr. Laird very carefully, and she'd now discovered a pattern in Macia's incessant sleeping. Shortly after Mr. Laird would arrive with fresh water and encourage Macia to drink, she would drop off into hours of sleep, followed by periods of lethargy. And just when she would become somewhat lucid, Mr. Laird would reappear with more water.

Truth now believed Mr. Laird was pouring medication into Macia's water to make her sleep. She didn't know, though, if the medication had been prescribed by the doctor or if the treatment was Mr. Laird's idea. Worse yet, she dared not ask Dr. Anderson, for he would likely tell Mr. Laird, who would surely send her packing.

After another day without any correspondence from home, Truth decided she must take matters into her own hands. The thought was frightening, yet she absolutely must do something to get Macia out of this place. As if being imprisoned in this dreadful school wasn't enough, she'd not received one letter from Moses or the Boyles. She'd been faithful to write Moses daily and Dr. Boyle several times. Mrs. Rutledge had at least been amenable to posting the letters—the woman's only act of kindness. Yet neither of them had bothered to respond. Pacing back and forth in front of the windows, she startled when Macia groaned and turned in the bed.

"What time is it?"

Truth hurried to Macia's bedside and grasped her hand. "It's nearly suppertime, and you've not yet eaten breakfast. Why don't I help you into the chair and I'll brush your hair."

Macia closed her eyes and turned away.

"Please, Macia. You absolutely must spend some time out of this bed. Let me help you."

Without waiting for Macia's approval, Truth leaned down and hoisted the girl's skeletal frame upward. Using her powers of persuasion, Truth dragged Macia to the nearby chair. Holding her shoulder with one hand, Truth retrieved a silver-handled brush from atop the dressing table. She began to brush Macia's hair in earnest, for she doubted her patient could tolerate sitting in the chair for long.

"I'm going to marry Marvin." Macia's words were garbled.

Truth looked into the mirror and met Macia's glassy-eyed stare. "Who is Marvin?"

"Mr. Laird."

"Mr. Laird? No, Macia. You're going to marry Jeb Malone when we return to Hill City. Remember?"

Although Truth knew Jeb hadn't yet proposed to Macia, everyone in Hill City expected a wedding would take place the moment Macia returned from New York—everyone with the possible exception of Mrs. Boyle, who still held out hope her daughter would marry a wealthy man with social standing.

Macia extended a wobbly finger toward the mirror. "Nooo. I'm going to marry Mr. Laird. He loves me, and he's going to marry me. He says I'm bea*uuu*tiful."

Truth patted Macia's arm and slowly repeated her earlier explanation as though speaking to a small child.

Macia slapped at the brush. "I know who I'm going to marry. Don't you tell me . . ." Before Macia could complete the sentence, she collapsed into uncontrollable sobs. "What has happened to me?"

Truth knelt down and cupped Macia's chin in her palm. She wiped away the tears that rolled down Macia's cheeks. "It's going to be all right. You're confused because you're ill, that's all. We're going to get you better and go home."

Macia's eyes reflected confusion, so Truth said nothing further about going home. Instead, she fashioned a dark blue ribbon into Macia's blond curls and spoke of the warm weather. When Mr. Laird arrived moments later, he appeared startled to see Macia sitting in the chair with her hair properly combed.

With his jaw tightly clenched, Mr. Laird approached Macia. "Look at you! It seems the two of you have accomplished more than usual today."

"Do you like my hair?"

"Indeed, it looks quite lovely, though I believe you've likely overexerted yourself. I'm going to have to give Truth a sound reprimand for having you out of bed much too long."

Truth knew his jovial tone was nothing more than a charade for Macia's benefit. The moment they were alone, Truth would be the recipient of his wrath. His jaw continued to twitch as he poured a cup of water. With his back turned, he pulled something from his pocket. Truth edged closer and saw him pour something into the glass.

"Here you are, Macia." Mr. Laird turned with the glass in his hand.

"I'll give it to her." Truth reached for the glass and knocked it to the floor, the contents spilling on the dressing table and wool rug.

"You idiot! Look what you've done!"

"Why are you so upset? It's merely water. I'll pour her another glass." Truth stooped down to wipe up the spilled liquid and winced as Mr. Laird's fingers dug into her arm. Her feet barely touched the floor as he yanked her toward the door.

Truth glanced over her shoulder. "I'll return in a moment, Macia."

"Don't count on it," Mr. Laird hissed as he closed the door. "What do you think you're doing interfering with Macia's medical care?"

"Medical care? A glass of water? It was an accident. I'm guessing you've had an accident from time to time, Mr. Laird."

"I want you to leave the academy, Miss Harban. Go back to Kansas—go anywhere—but I want you out of here. Do I make myself clear?"

"Very clear."

She hurried down the back stairway. She must think—she needed a plan.

CHAPTER

— 14 —

Nicodemus, Kansas

E zekiel arose before sunup. The night had been warm, and the wheat should be dry enough to cut by the time his neighbors arrived. He'd struck an agreement with several of the surrounding farmers, and they were joining together to harvest their fields. They'd finished John Beyer's crop yesterday. If all went well, Ezekiel should have half an acre cut and tied by noon. They could make better progress with more tools. However, the wheat was ripening throughout the township, and the farmers couldn't wait in hope of borrowing more implements. Ezekiel wasn't one to complain, though. Having help to rake and bind the sheaves made the work go faster, as did alternating their jobs. Swinging the cradle scythe was hard on the shoulders and arms, and he couldn't withstand it for too long. After thirty minutes he would switch out to rake or bind the bundles. Though some of the township residents had decided to hire a man to cut their grain by machine, Ezekiel and several others decided they'd work together and save the money charged by a cutter.

He'd planted five acres of wheat this year, the rest in corn. He hoped his crops would provide him with the necessary cash to purchase more livestock and a few more tools and perhaps a few items for the house. Last year he'd seeded only two acres with wheat and five with corn. But his yield had been good. From the money he'd made off his crops, he'd been able to purchase a cow and a few pigs. Though folks said a yield of fifty bushels was good, he'd been pleased to produce twenty-five bushels per acre last year. Again this year, the entire county had been short on rain. He'd be counting his blessings if his fields yielded thirty bushels per acre. Even if he set aside thirty bushels for the year's bread and seed, he should still make a tidy profit. But he'd not count on that until the greenbacks were in his pocket.

Before Grace set the coffee to boil, Ezekiel heard the sound of an approaching wagon. Tugging open the door, he was greeted by Miss Hattie.

"'Bout time you was crawling out of bed, Ezekiel. We's been up long 'nuff to eat our breakfast and drive all the way over here, but it looks like you's jest now wiping the sleep from your eyes. You got coffee to boiling, gal?"

Before Grace could answer, Miss Hattie was inside surveying the room. "Um, um. Don' look like you's been getting food prepared for these here men that's gonna be working for your pappy. I brung some chokecherry and sweet potato pies and a nice big ham, but you's gonna have to get busy, Grace."

The girl's shoulders slumped. "I was planning to help with the cutting."

"The cuttin'? What you thinkin', gal? You ain't got Jarena here to do the cookin'. Who you think is gonna feed the men?"

Grace shrugged. "I hadn't given it much thought." She glanced at her father. "And Pappy didn't say anything, either."

Miss Hattie narrowed her eyes and looked at Ezekiel. "Did Effie Beyer feed you when you was working with John?"

He nodded. "Course she did."

"Then how come you's not giving any thought to feedin' the men when they's here to work for you?"

"Plumb slipped my mind, Hattie. Jarena took care of such things last year, and I jest wasn't thinkin'. Me and Grace think about the crops, not the cookin'."

"Now that there's the first thing I heard that I can agree with. I tol' Calvin you wouldn't be ready. Course, he thought I didn't know what I was talkin' about. Grace, you git down to the root cellar and fetch some potatoes, maybe some yams, too." Hattie pulled an apron from a hook and tied it around her waist. "And you can ferget about goin' out in them fields. You's gonna be helping me and Nellie with the cookin' today. I figure the other women will be bringin' their share even though you didn't bring no food to Effie's."

Grace frowned. "But I worked in the fields as hard as any of the men."

"That's jest it, Grace—you ain't no man. You needs to be tendin' to womanly duties here in the house. 'Specially now that Jarena's gone over to Hill City. I sure do miss that chil'. What you hear from her anyway?"

"You want me to fetch the potatoes or tell you about Jarena?"

Ezekiel gave her a frown. "You's sounding right sassy, gal. You best watch how you talk to yo' elders. Go fetch the potatoes and *then* you can tell Miss Hattie 'bout your sister."

Miss Hattie nodded her approval and poured herself a cup of coffee. "How you an' Grace been farin' with Jarena gone?"

Ezekiel smiled. "We's getting along, but I ain't denying I miss her cookin'." He jumped to his feet at the sound of approaching wagons. "Sounds like the others is here."

While Grace and Effie Beyer peeled the huge mound of potatoes, Caroline Holt and Mildred Kemble snapped beans, occasionally sending their young daughters to fetch water and scrub the boards they'd set up for the noonday meal table.

Effie picked up another potato and began peeling. "You read that piece in the paper about all them Exodusters still pourin' into Topeka? Sounds like the only place for them to stay is penned up in some kind of barracks over to the fairgrounds. That story in the paper said the tools and lumber was stolen so's they can't build more housing for them."

Mildred nodded. "Them white folks don't want no more of them barracks built unless they's at least a mile out of town. Now ain't that jest something!"

Miss Hattie continued kneading a batch of dough. "Calvin says Topeka's full to overflowin' with all our folks migratin' from the South. He says the town cain't handle no more."

Effie frowned. "Cain't or don't wanna? They did all that advertisin' about comin' out here, and now they don' want us."

Grace leaned back and continued peeling as she listened to the women talk about the huge number of colored folks pouring into the state. She'd thought much like these women until Moses had explained that it wasn't the Kansas legislature that issued the call for folks to come—it had been men like Pap Singleton, who dreamed of a utopia where freed slaves could enjoy the same independence as white folks. He'd traveled extensively and expounded upon all the land and abundance Kansas had to offer. Of course, the land promoters had encouraged the migration, too. But now the capital city was faced with a daily influx of families migrating to what they hoped would be a better life, only to be greeted by worse conditions than they'd left behind.

Grace quartered the potato and dropped it into the kettle. "Maybe we should send a letter to the new governor telling him to send some of those Exodusters out here to Nicodemus."

All of the women looked at her as though she'd suggested an outrageous proposition. It was Miss Hattie who pointed her finger and said, "You gone daft in the head, gal? We can't be bringing folks out here if we ain't got nothin' to offer. We's jest now beginnin' to get settled ourselves."

"Tha's right," Mildred agreed. "Last thing we be needin' out here is a band of settlers who gots even less than we do. Why, we'd find ourselves back to askin' for handouts like we did that first year when we come out here."

Miss Hattie wagged her head. "Um, um, I don't never want to go back to dem days again. Nope, that ain't no kinda idea, gal."

Grace didn't reply. After all, Miss Hattie had spoken—even if Grace thought the older woman was wrong. Grace had lived through those tough days not so long ago. She'd struggled right along with the rest of them, going to bed hungry, nearly freezing through the winter, having to seek aid from others in order to survive. But they'd put all that behind them when they voted to end all appeals for help back in the spring of 1879. Surely they were now strong enough to lend other new settlers a hand up. After all, wasn't that what the Bible taught? She'd speak with her father instead of these women—she could trust his reasoning to be sound.

But when the men returned for their noonday meal, they were engrossed in their talk of crops and the weather—and Herman's reduced yield due to the drovers running cattle through his fields. Mr. Kemble infused his anger into their conversation at every opportunity. But who could blame him? With each field the men harvested, Herman was reminded he would have less yield than the others, especially wheat and corn. At least his sorghum remained in good condition, and perhaps he would be more pleasant during the fall, when the men harvested the cane. Then again, maybe not, since Grace didn't think he had planted more than one small field of sorghum. Each time Grace approached her father, he'd motion for her to remain silent or Miss Hattie would call out a command for her to fill the bowls or water glasses. Grace would be happy when the work crew moved on to the Holts' place, where she could go back to working out in the fields. She would talk to her father tonight.

By the time sundown came and the men finally stopped for the night, her father downed his supper and fell into bed. As she slipped between the sheets herself, she decided she'd speak to her father the next day. Rather than using her nightly prayer time to talk with the Lord about what to do about the Exodusters, or give thanks for daily blessings, Grace filled the time with pleas for help with Miss Hattie and her domineering attitude. As far as Grace was concerned, Miss Hattie needed her comeuppance. And God was about the only one big enough for that job.

Unfortunately, God didn't intervene the next day—and Miss Hattie didn't change her ways. When Grace mentioned the unfortunate Exodusters, Miss Hattie shushed her, and while they baked bread, peeled potatoes, and boiled ham hocks with beans, Miss Hattie steered the discussion toward the temperance movement, which was a topic near and dear to her heart.

Grace sighed. The women were always attending temperance meetings and rallying behind the cause as though liquor were available at every corner. "Why do you spend so much time talking about temperance, Miss Hattie? Liquor isn't a problem in Nicodemus. All the families have signed the prohibition petition."

Miss Hattie looked up from the kettle of beans she was stirring. "Don't mean whiskey ain't still a problem, 'specially in other towns where they ain't voted against liquor."

"With the legislature's amendment coming for a vote in November, all the taverns and dramshops will be closed. That's what Moses told Pappy. Moses said he's going to be doing some articles for the newspaper before election time comes around."

Miss Hattie swiped a shirtsleeve across her forehead. "I know you think that law's gonna take care of ever'thing, Grace. But I done lived a lot of years, and I can tell you it won't make no difference. Liquor gonna *always* be a problem. It's the devil's brew, that's a fact."

Grace widened her eyes. "If it's the devil's brew, how come doctors give it to sick folks?"

Miss Hattie pointed her dripping spoon in Grace's direction. "You's just beggin' for an argument, ain't ya? You's wantin' to show us how smart you is, but you best be rememberin' that pride's a sin—almost as bad as drinkin' that devil's brew."

Grace slumped in her chair. Her prayers had gone unheeded.

CHAPTER

— 15 —

J arena settled in the buggy beside Moses. She had hoped to move back home before the Fourth of July celebration, but it hadn't worked out that way. Perhaps she'd be home for good before the Emancipation Celebration the first of August. Well, at least she'd have a few hours to visit with Pappy and Grace today after church.

"I don't think Pappy's going to be happy about Truth's prolonged absence," she said as Moses pulled back on the reins and brought the buggy to a stop in the churchyard in Nicodemus.

"Nor do I, but let's wait until after church to tell him." Moses held out his hand to assist her from the buggy. Jarena waved as her sister raced to greet her.

Grace giggled as she pulled Jarena into a tight embrace. "I was hoping to see Truth in the buggy, too, but I suppose it's too soon for her return, isn't it?"

Jarena glanced at Moses. "Yes, I suppose so." She hugged her father and then took Grace by the hand. "Do sit beside me in church. I've missed you."

"You're coming back to the house for a visit afterward, aren't you?"

"Of course. I thought I'd have a chance to see how much your cooking has improved."

"You'll be disappointed. Miss Hattie doesn't think I'm much account in the kitchen. We didn't get on so well when the men were over to help Pappy with the wheat. I sure hope you're home before it's time to harvest the corn."

The two sisters walked into the church and scooted across a wooden pew. Jarena leaned close to Grace's ear. "I'm sure you did fine. Miss Hattie's more bark than bite. She likes to keep everyone on their toes."

"She's bossy and disagreeable. She argued with me about everything from the food to the Exodusters and the temperance movement. She doesn't agree with me about anything."

Jarena placed a finger to her lips. "We'll talk after church."

The limestone church that had been completed in early spring was soon filled with the sounds of a lively spiritual, and Jarena drew comfort from the familiar strains. It was good to be in her own church again. Though she attended Sunday services with the Boyle family in Hill City, she found the experience foreign. Much too stiff and formal. No one clapped their hands or shouted praises to the Lord—and the preacher delivered his message in a dreary monotone voice—nothing like Reverend Mason, who took pleasure in marching back and forth while waving his arms to make a point. She settled into the pew and wrapped herself in the warmth of her surroundings. She longed for the morning to last forever. But today it seemed as if the singing ended much too rapidly and the sermon was shorter than was the custom. Before she knew it, they were out of church and on their way to the farm.

Unwilling to be separated for the ride home, Grace squeezed into the buggy with Jarena and Moses. "I do hope you don't mind, but I wanted to talk to both of you about the Exodusters in Topeka. Pappy says you likely know more about them than most folks."

Moses flicked the reins and encouraged his horse into a trot. "What is it about the Exodusters that's captured your interest, Grace?"

She proceeded to explain her conversation with Miss Hattie and the others. When she had finished her lengthy summary of the heated conversation, she said, "So what do you think? Which is more important—temperance or the Exodusters?"

Moses pushed his hat back on his head. "They're both important issues, Grace. The others are likely more interested in the temperance issue because they've struggled with it in their own family and have suffered through the devastation caused by the abuse of liquor."

Grace nodded. "But they've suffered through the hardships of moving to a new state and nearly starving to death, too. I thought they'd feel compassion for the Exodusters. Instead, they're thinking only of themselves—not wanting folks coming out here unless they've already got the finances to establish themselves."

Moses stared into the distance as the horse trotted onward. "I think what you're hearing is fear."

"Fear? Fear of what? Having to share with folks who have less? Instead of being afraid, it seems folks would be anxious to help. Every one of us prayed for help when we were out here on the prairie with nothing. What if aid hadn't come from the East or if the Indians hadn't shared their food with us?"

"You make a valid argument. And you've given me an excellent idea for your sister's next writing assignment for the newspaper. I think a series of articles addressing this issue would be an excellent way to encourage folks to put their Christianity into practice. We can set forth the facts and hope folks will move to action."

Grace leaned forward on the buggy seat. "That's a wonderful idea. Truth can rally folks to action like nobody else I know."

"There's no doubt Truth could write some stirring accounts, but I was thinking I'd ask Jarena to write the articles. She's begun helping me at the newspaper, but I guess you didn't know that."

Grace gave her sister a sidelong glance. "Jarena would do a fine job, but Truth should be home soon. Maybe we should wait until she returns. I don't figure the Exoduster problem is going away anytime soon."

They pulled into the yard, and Moses helped the girls down from the buggy. "We don't need to decide right now."

Jarena followed her sister into the sod house while feeling as though she'd been away for an eternity. Granted, the Boyles' house was grand in comparison, but this was her home. And with the limestone extension her father planned to add after the fall harvest, this house would be better than any place they'd ever lived. Even Jarena was surprised by the affinity she now felt for the home she'd railed against only a few years ago. She ran her fingers across the rough-hewn table as though it were made of the finest mahogany and inhaled the scent of the sod bricks and dried sunflower stalks. Yes, this was home.

"Good to have you home, daughter."

"It's good to be home, Pappy. I only wish I could stay."

He patted her shoulder. "I's thinkin' Truth should be gettin' back any day now, don't you think? Any word from her?"

Moses drew closer. "Seems it's going to be a while longer before Truth returns. Dr. Boyle had a telegram from Miss Boyle's doctor. It seems Miss Boyle began to experience some type of seizures. The doctor thought it would be unsafe for her to travel just yet."

"Did he say how long afore she could come home? I ain't likin' the sounds of this." Ezekiel massaged his forehead. "Truth don' know nothing 'bout gettin' along in no big city."

Jarena patted her father's arm. "She's not alone, Pappy. Macia's there. And she's at the school, where there should be folks to help."

"If Dr. Boyle's gal is having some kinda fits, she ain't gonna be no help to Truth, and them other folks is strangers." Ezekiel shook his head. "Guess there ain't much we can do to change things, but I'm thinkin' I made a mistake lettin' her go."

Moses pulled a chair close and sat down opposite Ezekiel. "I have great confidence in Truth's ability, Ezekiel. She's intelligent and she's going to do fine. When she returns, she'll have stories to tell that will keep us entertained for weeks on end."

Ezekiel grinned, but it appeared forced. "I guess you's right. Don't s'pose fretting is gonna help. We all needs to be prayin' for her—and Macia, too."

As they prepared the noon meal, Jarena encouraged Grace to tell her more about what the ladies had discussed while at the Harban soddy while the men were harvesting the wheat.

"The ladies are talking about forming a temperance union," Grace related. "Miss Hattie's leading the charge and is already making plans to meet on the second Wednesday of each month. She got permission to meet at the church. But I see no reason to form a temperance union in Nicodemus."

"I guess I never gave it much thought."

"Exactly my point. Why do we need a temperance union when the town already prohibits liquor? Seems to me like a waste of time and energy. I think it would be more beneficial to work toward helping some of the Exodusters."

Jarena laughed as she heaped the steaming green beans into a large china bowl before placing it on the table. "And you appear to be as focused upon the Exodusters as the other women are upon the temperance union."

While the two of them continued to fill the plates and bowls with ham and potatoes, Jarena explained the finer points of the liquor legislation. Though Grace didn't appear overly concerned to hear that the prohibition bill had not yet been voted upon by the legislature, Jarena doggedly explained the risks that existed if the bill should fail. She wanted Grace to understand that many citizens were sorely concerned over such a possibility. If the bill didn't pass, those who had tirelessly worked toward its acceptance would be devastated.

"Both are worthwhile endeavors. Neither should be discounted as unimportant or undeserving of our best efforts. If you won Miss Hattie to your side, she could help, but you'd likely need to go to her with a compromise of some sort."

Grace pulled off her apron and hung it on a nearby hook. "What kind of compromise?"

Jarena scanned the table one final time, making certain all of the bowls and plates were in place. "Ask her if she'll attempt to influence some of the ladies to find a way to help one or two families move from Topeka. In return, you could offer to help influence the young women to become involved in the temperance movement. I think if all of you listened to each other with an open mind, it could work. Now go call Pappy and Moses before this food gets cold."

Grace giggled and glanced over her shoulder as she hurried to the door. "Not much chance of that happening in this heat."

The soft breeze fluttered the ties of Jarena's bonnet as she and Moses journeyed back to Hill City. "You miss Truth terribly, don't you?" she asked.

"No more than you miss Thomas. At least I know she isn't in danger of being ambushed by a renegade band of Indians."

Jarena shrank back at his words.

"I'm sorry, Jarena. That was unforgivably insensitive of me. I should think before speaking. Please accept my apologies."

He shifted on the buggy seat, and Jarena could see the embarrassment in his eyes.

"You know, I don't think I've told you what a pleasure it has been to have your company while Truth has been away. And I meant what I said to Grace. I want you to write a series of articles about the Exodusters. Perhaps it would be enlightening if I traveled to Topeka and observed the conditions for myself."

"I don't know when you'd find time to make the journey, but a first-hand account of what's going on in Topeka would be helpful. We would be confident the articles contained accurate information."

Moses flicked the reins. "I'll give it some thought. Incidentally, did you notice the two new limestone buildings going up in Nicodemus? We passed them on the way to the church earlier today."

Jarena thought for a moment and then nodded. "I was going to ask Grace who owned them, but it slipped my mind."

"Two new stores going in—almost directly across the street from one another. And both of them being opened by white owners. Nicodemus is no longer an all-colored community."

Jarena swiveled in the seat. "White men? And they want to open stores in Nicodemus? Who are they? More importantly, why do they want to open their businesses in Nicodemus? Why not Hill City or Stockton?"

Moses grinned. "You ask excellent questions, Miss Harban. You're a natural reporter. Now let me see if I can remember all your father told me."

While they continued their journey, Moses entertained her with information about the newly arrived entrepreneurs and their decision to settle in Nicodemus. He pointed out the obvious opportunity available to the new residents. With only one fledgling general store in Nicodemus, the newcomers would have plenty of customers vying for their wares.

"From what your father tells me, both men have purchased land and they're building houses. Seems they're settling their families in Nicodemus Township."

Though Jarena wasn't opposed to white folks settling in Nicodemus, and the town charter didn't prohibit members of any race living
in the town, it seemed odd that two white families that didn't even
know each other would both decide to build general stores in Nicodemus in the short time she'd been gone to Hill City. She wondered if it
was purely coincidental. Likely it was as Moses said: the men were
speculating upon growth in the area and hoping that the railroad would
eventually plan a route that passed through Nicodemus—a hope shared
by every resident of the township.

CHAPTER

— 16 —

Nicodemus, Kansas • August 1880

A s usual, the residents of Nicodemus had celebrated the Fourth of July with fervor, but it was the celebration of the liberation of the West Indian slaves by Britain that brought joy beyond compare. Better than the Fourth of July, better even than Christmas. Today they would celebrate Emancipation Day.

Moses, Jarena, and Lilly had arrived at the Harban farm two days earlier: Moses to witness and report the countless activities for the newspaper, Jarena to help prepare food, and Lilly to enjoy the luxury of a few days away from household chores and the Nelson children. My, how she needed the vacation!

The night before, the streets in Nicodemus had been watered to keep down the dust, and now excitement reached fever pitch as revelers lined the streets to await their first glimpse of the parade. Women and girls were dressed in lightweight muslin, while the men and boys sported their best bib and tucker. All of them cheered and applauded as the horse-drawn wagons decorated with brightly colored banners passed by. Children pranced with delight as a makeshift band marched down the street, the musicians having difficulty keeping step while playing their instruments. But no matter—the tunes were joyful, and the crowd responded with clapping and shouts of enthusiastic approval.

When the parade ended, the assembled crowd piled into their wagons and carriages and formed a lengthy caravan that snaked its way to Palmer's Grove, a cool coppice close to the Solomon River. A wood platform draped with colorful bunting stood sentry over the rows of tables that would soon be laden with food. An abundance of sweet potatoes, white potatoes, corn, onions, and wild herbs were added to the cooking pit where a hog donated by Herman Kemble had roasted throughout the night. Spirits were high, and children quickly organized to play games while the adults completed final preparations for the noonday meal.

Though Lilly had attempted to rearrange the seating at their table, Grace was the one who finally sat beside Moses throughout the meal. The two of them talked quietly together until the meal was nearly finished.

Lilly reached across the table and tapped her fork in front of Moses. "It would be nice if you two would include the rest of us in your conversation."

Moses served himself a generous wedge of Miss Hattie's gooseberry pie and waved at Miss Hattie. "Fine-looking pie, Miss Hattie."

Ezekiel nodded from his place at the head of the table. "Even better tastin'."

Lilly opened her fan and flapped it back and forth with vigor. "I do believe you're ignoring me, Moses."

"Not ignoring, Miss Lilly. However, my conversation with Grace was of a private nature, not something I wished to share with the entire group."

Lilly snapped the fan together and pointed it at Grace. "I wonder what Truth would think of your flirtatious behavior with her intended?"

Grace jumped up from the table. "*Flirtatious?* We were merely talking, that's all."

"Of course. I understand completely," Lilly said.

Without another word, Grace rushed off toward one of the other tables, obviously hoping to emphasize the honesty of her reply.

Moses folded his arms across his chest and shook his head. "You managed to run her off, didn't you?"

"I would say it's her own guilt and embarrassment that sent her scampering off like a frightened child." She stretched her neck to see what her other niece was doing. "It looks as if Jarena could use some help chopping ice for the lemonade."

"And I wish I had time to accommodate her. However, I've been asked to introduce today's speakers, and I believe it's time for the program to begin." That said, Moses strode off toward the platform, leaving Lilly to contemplate her next move.

For the most part, the speeches contained enough patriotic zeal to offset what they lacked in elegance, and those attending would agree they had all been reminded of the fact that they had much for which to be thankful. The orators' chairs emptied one by one as each speaker completed his speech and moved to sit among the crowd of onlookers. As the final speaker departed the platform, the crowd began to disperse.

Moses hurried to the center of the stage and waved his arms. "Hold up! We have one more speaker. One I believe you will be surprised and pleased to hear from. I'll wait until you're all seated and quiet before making the introduction."

Murmurs continued as folks looked about, eagerly attempting to see who among them had been enlisted to speak and had not yet taken the platform. Moses patiently waited until the only sounds were those made by the children playing in the distance and the meadowlarks perched in the branches overhead.

"I have a special surprise in store for you today, and I trust that you will be courteous and open-minded throughout this next presentation. Grace Harban is going to come to the stage and speak to you about the correlation between this Emancipation celebration and the Exodusters who have made their way to Kansas during the past year."

As Grace came to the stage, Moses clapped, and others followed suit. Although she didn't receive the same hearty ovation given the other speakers, there was a smattering of approval and an air of surprise when she began to speak. Though her voice momentarily quivered, she soon gave the impression she was quite comfortable in front of the audience.

With the crowd's attention focused upon her, Grace carefully outlined what she and Moses had learned regarding the plight of the Exo-dusters in Topeka. She asked that the residents of Nicodemus think back to their own early days on the plains of Kansas. "Remember our desperation and our prayers that others would reach out to help us. There are many living in pitiable conditions at the fairgrounds, packed into dismal quarters with little food or clothing, some suffering from dysentery and other ailments. They are without adequate funds to begin life anew and therefore must live in dismal conditions with little hope for the future."

With zeal and passion, she explained that the Topeka newspaper had begun to report a growing opposition to the Exodusters. "Materials and tools needed to build additional barracks and houses for the new arrivals have been stolen by whites who do not want the barracks built within a mile of the city. Many of the Kansas farmers are now unwill-ing to go into the fields alongside Negroes, and prejudice is beginning to rear its head."

For a full fifteen minutes, Grace held the attention of the crowd until one of the men shouted, "What you want *us* to do 'bout it?"

Grace didn't know who had asked the question, but the interrup-tion didn't deter her. "I'm glad you asked. I'd like to challenge all of the residents of Nicodemus to help the new arrivals to Kansas, and I've thought of several ways we can help. Certainly we should be praying for them. In addition, I believe we could take up a collection and send money, or we could send a portion of our crops—or both. We know what these folks need. After all, we needed the same things when we arrived in Nicodemus."

"Next thing we know, you'll be wantin' us to move 'em all out here!" one of the other men hollered.

Grace nodded. "I thought of that idea, also. We could sponsor several families and help them get started if they wanted to come on out to Nicodemus. Of course, we could celebrate Emancipation Day and just go back home and forget the fact that our brothers and sisters are suffering. I guess it's up to all of us what we'll do, but Moses has agreed to oversee any efforts that we decide upon."

As Grace stepped down from the platform, young Emily Kemble came running forward holding a few coins in her hand. "This here's my money from cleaning the chicken coop every day. You can have it to help them people."

Emily's spontaneous generosity was all that was needed. Soon others enthusiastically embraced Grace's idea and joined in with promises of assistance. When the crowd had finally scattered, Moses drew near and smiled. "What is it the Bible says? 'And a little child shall lead them'? I'm mighty thankful for Emily Kemble's generous heart."

"So am I. Before I stepped up there to speak, I asked God to open the people's hearts. I surely didn't expect Him to use one of the children in order to answer my prayer, but I'm glad that's how it happened." Grace glanced at Emily, who was now surrounded by a group of children. "And just look at Emily. She's pleased as can be that she was first to give her money."

"She should be proud of herself, and so should you, Grace. You gave an excellent speech. In fact, I think you even surprised yourself, didn't you?"

"I suppose you're correct. Now, let's hope folks don't soon forget that they've promised to help."

"No need to worry. I'll keep it at the forefront of their minds by including a story in the newspaper. I'll even put it on the front page, if you like."

Jarena drew near and clasped Grace's hand. "And your speech has prompted me to get busy writing those articles we discussed. I'm proud of you, Grace."

"Thank you."

Soon the band gathered on stage and began tuning their instruments as folks gathered around anticipating the entertainment. The air quickly filled with music, and each time the band stopped to rest, the crowd entertained themselves with singing and dancing. As daylight turned to dusk, a couple of men lit a huge bonfire and folks gradually grouped together, the young children drawing closer to their parents as darkness settled.

Jarena sat next to Moses and gathered courage in the nighttime shadows. "I wondered if you've received any additional reports regarding Victorio and his renegades."

Moses continued to stare at the blazing bonfire. "Only sketchy reports—nothing definite."

Lilly stepped toward them and sat down beside Jarena. "Let's don't forget that you haven't had a letter from Thomas in quite some time. It seems to me that you two have been cut loose and set adrift, what with Truth off enjoying herself in New York and Thomas hunting down Indians or perhaps . . ."

Jarena knotted her hands into tight fists. "Don't say it, Aunt Lilly. Thomas is *alive*. I know it! And certainly Truth didn't anticipate being gone more than two weeks. Seems as though you take delight in twisting the truth."

Lilly's laughter rippled in its usual manner. "Now, now, Jarena. I know the truth is difficult to accept, but there comes a time when one must face the facts of life. I'm merely pointing out that you and Moses have very likely been left without prospects for the future. Why not consider each other?"

"Aunt Lilly!"

Moses shook his head. "You'll get nowhere with your brazen matchmaking attempts, Miss Lilly. So unless you wish to alienate your niece, I suggest we sit back and enjoy the evening without any further discussion about Thomas or Truth."

Ezekiel strode toward them carrying a large piece of Miss Hattie's gooseberry pie. "Did I hear you mention Truth? You get a letter from her, Moses?"

"No, though Dr. Boyle has received several letters from the folks who operate the school, and they say Macia's still unable to travel. Dr. Boyle says they mentioned sending Truth back home without Macia. He didn't want that to occur, so I know he wrote a hasty response. I must admit that I don't understand why I haven't heard from Truth."

"She's likely thinking she'll soon be home and there's no need to write," Jarena said.

A light breeze carried a trail of smoke from the bonfire in their direction, and Lilly snapped open her fan. "Given any opportunity, I would think that a young woman planning to wed in September would return on the next train out of New York. Any girl who's anxious to marry, that is."

"Part of me tends to agree with Jarena, but I'm getting worried.

Perhaps I should have given her more detailed instructions about con-
tacting me while she was gone."

Ezekiel slapped Moses on the back. "No need to blame yerself.
Didn't none of us think she'd be in New York long enough to be writin'
letters."

CHAPTER

— 17 —

Hill City, Kansas

Enough! She'd had enough of this place and these people. Something had to change. Lilly stomped over to the chest of drawers to retrieve her nightgown. Today hadn't gone as she'd planned. Jarena and Moses simply would not listen to reason. They both continued to cling to the misguided notion that they were in love with some person who was off gallivanting around the country. Nonsense. Jarena and Moses belonged together.

As she removed her nightgown from the chest of drawers, Lilly noticed an envelope lying atop her dressing table. Her hand trembled as she examined the handwriting. She searched her memory, hoping to summon a remembrance of the unfamiliar script. Who could be writing to her? With the exception of Claire, her dear friend in New

Orleans, no one knew she was living in Kansas. Beads of perspiration formed along her upper lip as she sliced open the envelope with Bentley's silver letter opener, a beautifully engraved remembrance she'd removed from his valise on one of his many visits to her home. She pulled out the letter and immediately scanned the last page for a signature. Her tense body relaxed as she examined the name—Marian Bordelon—Claire's sister.

She moved the flickering lamp close to her bed and began to read. As she finished the second page, Lilly clasped a hand to her chest. Claire's lifeless body had been found near the bayou, and Bentley Cummings had left New Orleans. How could it be? Obviously, Bentley was determined to find Lilly—at all costs. Lilly had no doubt Bentley had either killed Claire or paid someone else to commit the murder. She also had no doubt he would kill Marian if he thought circumstances warranted such action. Lilly's hands had once again begun to tremble. She startled at the sound of Georgie thumping against the adjoining wall as the boy tossed about in restless sleep.

Surely Claire must have grown increasingly worried when Bentley had begun to follow her. Why hadn't she expressed those fears to Lilly or taken some measures to protect herself? Of course, what could she have done? Leave New Orleans? That had been Lilly's own decision, but it seemed unfair that Claire need even consider such an option. After all, Claire had done nothing to deserve Bentley's wrath. Nothing but remain Lilly's friend and confidante. Nothing but withhold information from him. And now Lilly was left to bear the guilt of Claire's death and accept the fact that Marian had also been placed in harm's way. She wondered if Marian had maintained her silence or if she had told Bentley what he wanted to know.

The room was stifling, and Lilly got up and crossed the floor. She raised the window and stared into the dark silence. "If I were Marian, I would have told him."

A coyote howled in the distance, and Lilly shivered. An omen? She hoped not. If she were a godly woman like her sister, Jennie, she'd now be on her knees in prayer. Of course, if she were like Jennie, she probably wouldn't be in this predicament and she wouldn't need to ask for such help.

Marian's letter didn't say when Bentley had left New Orleans—only that he had headed for Kentucky after remembering Lilly had told him of family living there. She wondered if the entire letter was a ploy. Had Bentley stood over Marian and dictated the words? A rush of fear exploded in her belly like water flooding a fractured dam. What if Marian had given Bentley her address? What if Bentley was on his way to Hill City instead of Georgetown? He could be arriving at any moment.

When sleep wouldn't come, she paced the length of her room and reread Marian's letter until the pages were dog-eared. What was it her mama used to say? Things always seem worse at night? Would it be better in the morning? Lilly didn't see how. If only her mind would settle long enough to develop some sort of strategy.

Dark circles underscored Lilly's eyes the next morning when she glanced in the mirror, and for the first time since she'd arrived in Hill City, she took little care with her appearance. She took the back stairway to the kitchen and prepared breakfast in a daze. The children arrived in the kitchen a short time later, and with the exception of

Alma's unkempt hair, they were presentable. Lilly noted Georgie's look of disapproval when she placed a bowl of oatmeal before him.

He glared at the congealed oats. "I want griddle cakes."

"The only way you're going to get griddle cakes this morning is if your mother prepares them. Now quit pouting and eat, Georgie. I've had little sleep, and I'm not going to argue with you today. That goes for all three of you."

Alma picked up her spoon. "I like maple syrup on my oatmeal, Miss Lilly."

Lilly retrieved the crock of syrup and placed a dollop in the center of all three bowls. "Now eat up, all of you."

Georgie scowled but did as he was told. When he'd finished eating, he pointed his spoon at Lilly. "How come you look like that today?"

"Like what?"

"Messy. That's how Mama looked before you came here. Now she comes to breakfast all neat and tidy, and you look like she used to."

Could this day get any worse? Lilly removed his empty bowl from the table. "Thank you, Georgie. On top of everything else, that's exactly what I wanted to hear this morning."

"What was it you wanted to hear, Lilly?" Mrs. Nelson walked into the kitchen and placed a kiss on Alma's plump cheek. "Oh my. With those dark circles around your eyes, you resemble one of those raccoons Georgie's been attempting to trap as a pet. From all appearances, I would guess that you must have gotten in quite late last night. Did you sleep at all?"

Wonderful! Now she had Mrs. Nelson, who had no sense of style or decorum, assessing her appearance. The nerve of the woman—saying *she* looked like a raccoon.

"Did you find the letter I placed on your dressing table?"

Lilly nodded.

"Not bad news, I hope. I didn't recognize the handwriting. Your other letters . . ."

Mrs. Nelson stopped midsentence. Apparently she'd been snooping again. Lilly wondered if Mrs. Nelson had steamed open and read Marian's letter before placing it on her dressing table. Lilly wouldn't put it past the woman. Oh, she looked harmless enough, but beneath Mrs. Nelson's broad pin-tucked bodice beat a meddlesome heart—of that Lilly was certain.

Once the children had scampered outdoors to play, Lilly poured a cup of coffee and joined Mrs. Nelson at the table. Though Lilly's behavior would have been considered unacceptable in most homes, Mrs. Nelson hadn't yet developed the art of setting boundaries for Lilly within the household.

After settling into her chair, Lilly took a sip of the hot brew. "I hope this will serve to keep me awake."

"I'm most anxious to hear about the celebration in Nicodemus. Do tell me about it."

The last thing on Lilly's mind was the Emancipation festivities, but if she hoped to elicit information from Mrs. Nelson, she'd need to spend a few minutes entertaining the woman first. Unfortunately, Mrs. Nelson had no meetings or appointments scheduled, and what Lilly had hoped would take only a few minutes to explain lasted much too long. The moment Lilly attempted to move the conversation in another direction, Mrs. Nelson quizzed her for more details.

Mrs. Nelson poured herself another cup of coffee. "And who pays for all of these festivities and the speakers to come to the celebration? I know Mr. Nelson was asked to donate funds to the Fourth of July celebration."

Finally a question Lilly could warm to. Money! "I believe most of the speakers volunteered their time, and the supplies were likely donated. I must say it was kind of your husband to contribute funds to help the community, although his generosity doesn't surprise me. From the first time I laid eyes on your husband, I knew he was a kind man who would help others. Of course, one must have the funds available in order to extend such kindness."

Mrs. Nelson stirred an additional spoonful of sugar into her cup. "'Tis true. George is one of the kindest men I've ever known. Sometimes he's much too kind and generous—always ready to give a handout to anyone who approaches him. I've told him over and over that one day he'll wish he had all the money he's given away."

"And I'm certain he disagrees."

"Of course. I told him if he keeps taking money out of that safe, one day there won't be enough to send the boys to college—that's my dream, you know. A good education at a fine eastern college for my boys."

"Your husband takes money from the bank? Isn't that considered stealing?"

"Whatever are you talking about? I said no such thing."

"You said he took money from the safe."

Mrs. Nelson gazed heavenward. "From *our* safe, not the bank safe."

Hairs on the back of Lilly's neck prickled. A safe! She hadn't seen a safe in the house. That piece of information was a very good reason to begin cleaning more thoroughly—and soon! With a little prodding, Mrs. Nelson might even reveal the general location of the safe.

"I apologize. I didn't realize you had a safe in the house. I improperly assumed . . . Of course, Mr. Nelson would never consider pilfering funds from the bank. . . . I do apologize for even mentioning . . ." Lilly hoped her stammering reply was convincing. She was weary, and it took every bit of effort she could muster to continue this charade.

"No apology needed. I truly wish George would place our personal funds in his bank. However, he insists upon keeping them separate. I believe it has something to do with a bank failure and depression years ago. His father lost everything, and he instilled this fear in George—at least that's what I believe."

"Very strange that a man who distrusts banks would enter the banking profession."

Mrs. Nelson nodded her agreement and then explained the plan she had devised years ago to help her husband overcome his doubts. When a position had become available at a local bank, she had insisted her husband apply for it. Soon thereafter, Mr. Nelson was offered the position, and though he had been loath to accept it, his wife had insisted. Mrs. Nelson had thought the new job would put an end to her husband's worries. Much to his wife's chagrin, Mr. Nelson's fears and mistrust remained intact, and through the years the banker continued to place a safe in each of their homes. Although delighted by the turn of events, Lilly offered the woeful responses Mrs. Nelson obviously expected.

When Mrs. Nelson offered nothing further regarding the location of the safe, Lilly forged onward. "One of the families I worked for in

New Orleans had a safe. They installed it directly into the wall of their mansion. I found the concept fascinating." She hoped the remark would spur a clue from Mrs. Nelson.

"At least George hasn't gone that far. I don't want holes carved into the walls. George purchased a steel safe shortly after we married, and when we moved to Hill City, he had it shipped by train—likely cost a fortune to have it delivered." Mrs. Nelson pulled the drapes back and peeked out the window. "I believe Alma is calling me, and you're probably eager to clear off and wash the breakfast dishes."

Breakfast dishes were far from Lilly's mind. Instead, she was concentrating on locating Mr. Nelson's safe. With a flitting wave of her hand, she encouraged Mrs. Nelson toward the door and her young daughter. She emitted a sigh of relief as the woman headed outside.

Intent upon surveying the room, Lilly startled when Mrs. Nelson returned and grasped her by the arm. "I was pleased to hear about the Emancipation celebration, Lilly. Mr. Nelson and I may attend next year and bring the children—unless we wouldn't be welcome."

"Everybody is welcome at Emancipation celebrations, Mrs. Nelson. And I know the committee would be pleased to receive a contribution from your husband."

Mrs. Nelson laughed as she returned to the hallway and headed toward the back door. "I'll be sure to tell him."

Once the door closed, Lilly hurried to Mr. Nelson's office. She'd spent little time in the room, giving it only a cursory dusting from time to time. Unlike his wife, Mr. Nelson didn't appear to notice whether Lilly dusted or swept the floors, and Mrs. Nelson seldom entered the room. Lilly entered the office and carefully pulled back the edge of the draperies. Good! Mrs. Nelson was busy in the flower garden with one of her frequent horticulture projects while Alma had busied herself picking blooms from several plants. No doubt Mrs. Nelson would be distressed once she discovered Alma's unceremonious ruination of her prized blooms.

Turning away, Lilly shook the draperies into place and began to search for anything that resembled a safe. She peeked into the large kneehole of Mr. Nelson's desk and then moved on. Dropping to her hands and knees, she flipped back the imported tapestry cloth that draped the library table. She crawled underneath, thinking the safe might be hidden in the dark recesses beneath the heavy table. Finding nothing, she stood and walked the circumference of the room, tilting several paintings that hung on the office walls as she circled the room. Perhaps Mr. Nelson *did* have a wall safe and Mrs. Nelson had been attempting to lead Lilly astray.

Once convinced there was no wall safe to be found in the room, Lilly dropped into one of the tapestry upholstered chairs and cupped her chin in one hand as she surveyed her surroundings. Her gaze settled upon the large oak cabinet she'd dusted on several occasions. The open upper shelves contained books and ledgers, but she had no idea what was behind the lower doors. Surely a safe would be too heavy to place inside such a cabinet. However, unable to find another place to investigate, she moved to the cabinet and knelt down. With a tug, she pulled on the knob, surprised when the door opened to reveal a black metal safe fronted by a large combination lock. There was little doubt the cabinet had been built to specification for the sole intent of hiding Mr. Nelson's safe. Lilly would give him credit—the cabinet was ingenious. And the safe was locked.

After another quick peek out the window, Lilly hastened from the room. If Mrs. Nelson returned inside and the breakfast dishes were still sitting on the table, she would expect a full explanation. Best to get the table cleared and then further assess the situation.

As she performed the mindless tasks, Lilly brooded over where the combination might be concealed. Mr. Nelson had gone to great lengths to hide his safe, and Lilly knew the combination would not be easily found. On the other hand, she couldn't imagine he would leave his wife without access to the steel monstrosity. What if something happened to him? Mrs. Nelson would need explosives to retrieve her inheritance! Lilly attempted to picture Kate Nelson setting fire to a stick of dynamite. The notion was more than even Lilly could imagine. The befuddled woman would blow up the entire household in the process.

Of course there was the remote possibility Mr. Nelson had documented the combination in his last will and testament. Lilly hoped he hadn't decided upon that alternative. Surely he wouldn't have given the combination to his lawyer. Or would he? The very thought that Mr. Nelson might have chosen such a plan was exasperating. No! She would not surrender to such a deflating thought until she'd conducted a thorough search. Besides, a positive attitude was always a stronger ally in the midst of difficult circumstances—and finding the combination was going to be tricky.

Lilly had nearly completed the dishes when Mrs. Nelson returned to the kitchen holding Alma's hand in a firm grasp. The woman's features tightened into a scowl as she announced Alma would be spending several hours in her room. As if to emphasize the child's misdeed, Mrs. Nelson declared both she and the boys would soon depart for an outing to the general store while Alma served her penance.

Though Lilly experienced a fleeting ache for Alma's misfortune, she was pleased to know she'd have the house to herself for at least an hour. The proposed outing would afford her time to scour Mr. Nelson's office. Once Mrs. Nelson was gone, she would mollify Alma with cookies and milk and then begin her search.

Lilly paced the length of the kitchen as she waited to hear the sound of footsteps on the stairs. A short time later, Georgie bounded into the kitchen with his hair wetted down and combed into place. He was immediately followed by Joseph, who was wearing a clean shirt and holding his mother's hand.

"We're off. Make certain Alma remains in her room. Do not take pity on her, Lilly. She must learn respect and proper behavior."

Wiping her hands on the worn apron, Lilly nodded her agreement and escorted the threesome to the front door. She waved until they were out of sight and then turned to find Alma sitting on the top step, her eyes swollen and red as she sniffed a remorseful apology for her misdeed.

"You don't owe me an apology, Alma. It's your mother who's unhappy with you. Now, I can't let you come downstairs, but I'll bring you a cup of milk and some gingersnap cookies if you promise to stay in your room until your mama comes home."

The child promised and then sniffled. Lilly handed Alma a handkerchief and then ordered her off to await the cookies and milk in her room. Alma obediently wiped her nose and trotted off down the hallway. Within a few minutes Lilly supplied the child with her promised treats. Appeased by the indulgence, Alma took a bite of her cookie and waved the damp handkerchief toward Lilly.

Retrieving the limp offering, Lilly tucked the hankie into her pocket, admonished Alma to remain in her room, and proceeded directly to Mr. Nelson's office. Leaving the door slightly ajar, she began her search in earnest, first going through the desk drawers and then pulling out each book and flipping through the pages. With each shake of a book or ledger, she hoped to see a scrap of paper descend like manna from heaven. But none was forthcoming.

Perhaps there was a secret compartment in the desk. She'd heard of such things though she'd never actually seen one. Returning to the desk, she pulled the center drawer out and up, hoping to remove the drawer. Unfortunately, it wedged and wouldn't budge further. Excitement pulsed through Lilly's veins in a heady rush. There must be something hidden behind or under the drawer. She tugged and shifted, but to no avail. Time was passing much too rapidly. She crawled under the desk and turned onto her back to see if she could push the drawer from underneath. Prodding with her fingertips, she stared at the bottom of the drawer. She couldn't believe her eyes—penciled onto the bottom of the drawer were the directions. *Spin lock three times, turn R to 35, turn L to 22* . . . Without taking time to read any further, Lilly scrambled to fetch a piece of paper. She banged her head twice in the process, stopping only long enough to rub the sore spot or utter a curse. When she'd copied the directions precisely, she edged from beneath the desk, tucked the paper into her pocket, satisfied herself the room was in proper order, and departed.

Pleased with her success, Lilly hurried upstairs, retrieved the plate and cup from Alma's room, and headed off toward the kitchen. The satisfying events of the past hour had wiped away her weariness. Now that she had located the necessary funds to leave town, she needed only the proper opportunity. She must get word to Charlie Holmes. He could provide her with transportation, and she could provide him with a substantial boost to his income. With any luck, she would be out of the state prior to Bentley's arrival and before Mr. Nelson discovered his loss.

— 18 —

New York City

Truth remained awake most of the night. With each new idea came an overwhelming obstacle. Sometime during the night she'd resorted to prayer and shortly thereafter had fallen into a fitful sleep.

"Best get up and get to Miss Macia's room afore Mr. Laird comes snoopin' around." Truth rolled to her side, and Daisy's voice faded. "Come on, Truth, you gotta get up. I's leaving to go over to the kitchen."

Truth forced herself to an upright position and waved Daisy on. "I promise I won't go back to sleep."

Daisy exited the room and then came back. "If you ain't over to the house in half an hour, I's gonna send Silas to come get you. You hear?"

"No need to send Silas. I'll be there in no time."

Forcing herself out of bed, Truth washed the sleep from her eyes and tucked her hair into place before donning a lightweight cotton dress. No telling how long she'd be permitted to remain at the school, but so far Mr. Laird had not forced her to leave.

Though she'd slept little for several nights, Truth had failed to develop a practical plan to get Macia away from Rutledge. Should Truth be required to immediately leave the academy, she had no strategy to save either Macia or herself.

After stopping in the kitchen long enough to prepare a tray of food, Truth hurried up the back stairs and into Macia's room. The drapes were closed, and as usual, Macia remained sound asleep. She placed the tray on a bedside table and gently attempted to rouse Macia.

When her gentle whispers were unsuccessful, Truth pulled back the covers, opened the heavy drapes, and began to vigorously rub the girl's arm. "Wake up, Macia!"

Macia's eyelids fluttered and then opened. "Truth?"

"Yes. Now let's get you up so we can have us a nice visit and eat some of this fine breakfast I brought for you. I know you're hungry."

Macia clutched the sheet and attempted to cover herself. "Why don't I just sleep a little longer?"

"I can't allow that. You need to eat and regain some strength. The only way you're going to do that is to get up and begin doing a little more each day. We've got to get back to Kansas, Macia. Your folks are plumb worried to death about you. They're not going to rest easy until I get you back home."

"Marvin will take me. We're getting married."

"You been talking 'bout marrying Mr. Laird off and on since I been here. You must be having some terrible hallucinations if you're thinking you want to marry that man."

Macia sunk back against her pillow and frowned. "Marvin's been learning all about me. He's been very nice to me."

"How do you know if he's nice to you? And how can he learn anything from you? All you do is sleep. We need to put an end to all this sleeping. Come on, I'm going to help you out of this bed."

Truth had managed to feed Macia only a small portion of her breakfast before she heard footsteps in the hallway. She held her breath, hoping one of the girls had returned from class to retrieve a book or pen. Instead, a light tap sounded at the door, and Mr. Laird entered. Truth waited for him to order her from the room. Instead, he warmly bid her good morning and encouraged Truth to continue aiding Macia with her meal. Mr. Laird sat down near the fireplace and watched until Macia had eaten her fill—which had not taken much time or food.

Macia placed her fork on the tray. "I must rest now. Help me back to my bed, please."

Had Mr. Laird not been present, Truth would have insisted Macia remain out of bed for at least a while longer. However, this wasn't the time to provoke an argument, so she did as Macia requested. Once settled, Macia immediately dropped off to sleep. The girl's drowsiness was puzzling, for Truth didn't think anyone had visited the room before she arrived this morning. Yet if Macia hadn't been given any additional medication, why was she so groggy now? Perhaps she truly had contracted some horrid illness. Truth didn't know what to believe. And now, instead of throwing her out on her ear, Mr. Laird was engaging her in conversation and insisting she join him downstairs for a cup of tea.

Truth followed hesitantly, all the while longing to run down the back stairway and visit Daisy in the kitchen. For the first time in her life, she much preferred the idea of peeling potatoes or scrubbing pots to visiting over a cup of tea. Jarena and Grace would certainly find that hard to believe.

Mr. Laird jerked three times on a cord in the parlor, and soon Daisy appeared. The servant's eyes were wide with surprise when she spied Truth sitting on the divan like any prim and proper guest who might come calling. Truth longed to speak, but she dared not say anything to Daisy.

"Bring us a pot of tea and perhaps some of those tarts that I like so well. Is it too early in the day for you to indulge in sweets, Miss Harban?"

Truth shook her head. "No, sir."

"Tea and tarts it is, Daisy. No rush. Miss Harban and I are going to visit."

"Yessuh." Daisy scurried from the room as though the carpet were on fire and the flames were licking at her heels.

Mr. Laird leaned back in his chair and tented his fingers. "I believe I would enjoy hearing a bit about your history, Miss Harban."

"My history?"

"Yes. You appear more educated than most of the coloreds I've known. And you're obviously trustworthy, since Dr. Boyle sent you to fetch his daughter. Not all coloreds can be trusted, you know."

Truth shifted and looked him directly in the eyes. "Not all whites can be trusted, either, Mr. Laird. People are people—some good, some bad."

"Yes, I suppose that's true. That fact aside, tell me about yourself. I find you somewhat of an enigma."

Truth wanted to tell him she found him to be a mystery, also. And she certainly found Macia's condition puzzling. However, she did as he requested, telling him of her roots in Kentucky and the family's subsequent move to Kansas. She shared only the barest of details, but he demonstrated a genuine interest in her background, asking questions and making courteous comments as she spoke.

While Truth continued to answer Mr. Laird's questions, Daisy set the tea tray on a nearby table and exited the room.

Mr. Laird stood and moved toward the rectangular cherry table. "So you're planning to marry Mr. Wyman in the near future?"

"Yes. In September."

"Excellent. He sounds like a fine man. And who's taking care of the wedding preparations in your absence?"

"I'll have to complete the arrangements when I return to Kansas."

He nodded as he lifted the teapot and began to pour. "Since it appears Miss Boyle is going to have a slow recovery, I do believe you're doing yourself a disservice by remaining in New York. If you haven't sufficient funds for your train ticket, I could advance the money and Mr. Boyle could reimburse me later."

"I have a return ticket. Mr. Boyle purchased it in advance—along with Macia's ticket."

"Then why not leave Miss Boyle's ticket with me, and you may plan to return in the morning? I'll be happy to escort you to the train depot.

You can report to Dr. Boyle that Macia is in excellent hands."

"No. I believe I'll wait until Macia is well enough to travel with me. I promised Dr. Boyle."

Mr. Laird didn't argue. He merely turned his back, poured another cup of tea, and handed it to Truth. "As you wish. Do have one of these tarts with your tea."

Truth ate the tart much too quickly and gulped down the cup of tea. She returned the cup and saucer to the table while firmly declining his offer for an additional cup of tea. Right now, all she wanted was to escape his presence.

That evening, Truth sat outside the carriage house with Daisy and Silas, both of them anxious to hear details of her conversation with Mr. Laird that morning.

"I ain't never knowed of Mr. Laird to allow no coloreds to take tea with him," Silas said. "And he's wantin' you to come to the parlor every day and drink tea? Whole thing sounds crazy."

"I think so, too, but I'm afraid if I don't agree, he'll say I can't stay here and care for Macia."

Daisy pulled at a loose thread in the hem of her apron. "I's glad it's you and not me. I sure wouldn't wanna sit and talk to that man. The Rutledges is all right, but Mr. Laird scares me."

Truth shrugged. "He acts as though he's interested in knowing about Macia's family, and he asked lots of questions, but if talking to him will let me stay, then I'm willing to spend time with him. I figure he'll soon tire of the idea."

Once the girls had gone up to their room and prepared for bed,

Daisy sat down on the edge of her cot. "I think Silas is taken a likin' to you. I see the way he looks at you when you's not watching."

Truth twisted around and faced Daisy. "No. He's merely being kind. Besides, he knows I'm planning to marry Moses when I return to Kansas."

"Don' mean he ain't hoping you'll forget 'bout Moses and start thinking 'bout him."

Truth reached down and pulled back the bedcovers, pretending she hadn't heard the reply. She truly hoped Daisy was mistaken. Not that Silas wasn't a kind young man—and handsome, too. However, she didn't need anything else to complicate her stay in New York.

Truth's expectation that Mr. Laird might forego their daily ritual of tea and conversation diminished. Each day he appeared and escorted her to the parlor, and each day he plied her with questions while he served her tea and tarts. To make matters worse, the Rutledges had come to expect her assistance with household chores and kitchen duties—to defray the cost of her room and board, they said. Though Truth was willing in spirit, she'd daily grown more fatigued and had taken to napping each afternoon. She prayed Mr. Laird might be out of the house on business this day, for she truly did not want to take tea with him.

Her hopes were dashed when Mr. Laird appeared in Macia's room at his regularly appointed time with his counterfeit smile and an affable greeting. "I'm not feeling well, Mr. Laird. My stomach is upset and I'm exhausted. I trust you'll understand if I don't join you for tea this afternoon."

"If your stomach is upset, I'll have Daisy brew a pot of peppermint tea."

No need to argue further. There was no denying the man, for he had an answer to every objection. Truth followed him into the parlor and quickly downed the tea, thankful he willingly excused her earlier than usual. After a brief stop in the kitchen to offer apologies to Daisy, Truth hurried across the grassy expanse to the carriage house. Suddenly overwhelmed by blinding dizziness, Truth pressed her fingers to her temples. Her knees buckled as she grasped the handrail.

A strong arm encircled her waist and lifted her upright. "You ain't gonna make it up them stairs without help."

"Silas." She breathed his name and clung tightly to his shirtsleeve.

Silas scooped her up in his arms and carried her up the steps and into her room. He gently placed her on the bed. "I'm thinking *you* got the sickness, Truth."

Fear overcame her as he spoke the words. "You've got to get help, Silas. Bring a doctor to see me. *Please*. Not Dr. Anderson—someone else."

Silas wrung his hands and nodded. "I will, but you sleep, Truth. We'll talk 'bout a doctor in the morning. I promise. You jest sleep."

Truth's eyes fluttered and then closed as she heard Silas's retreating footsteps. She willed her eyes to open and her lips to speak, but she could do neither. Pain seared through her belly like a fiery sword and destroyed all thought of sleep. How was she going to get Macia out of this place if she became sick herself? She pulled her knees to her chest and rolled to her side. When the pain increased, she rolled over onto her back. Tears trickled across her face and followed a downward path, plummeting into her ears like raindrops splashing into a well.

Truth abandoned herself to the surges of pain until, completely spent, she dropped into a fitful sleep. Darkness had fallen, and Silas and Daisy were sitting nearby talking when she finally awakened.

"She's awake," she heard Daisy tell Silas.

"How you feeling, Truth? Daisy brung you some supper. You think you's able to eat something?"

Truth attempted to sit up but immediately fell back against the pillow. "Just something to drink—water, not tea." While Daisy poured the water, Truth motioned Silas closer. "Did you go for a doctor?"

"We needs to speak 'bout that idea. Me and Daisy been talking. If Mr. Laird or the Rutledges find out I went for a doctor, I's sure to lose my job, and it ain't so easy findin' work in New York. Lots of immigrants coming in and taking all the jobs. This ain't nothing so fine, but I's got a place to sleep, food to eat, enough money for my needs—and I can even save me a little."

Truth grasped his hand. "They won't find out, Silas. The fact is, I think I'm going to die if I don't get help."

Daisy lifted the cup of water to Truth's lips. "You's asking an awful lot of Silas. When you's feeling good again, you can take yourself back home, but Silas will be left here wid nothing and nobody to hep him. Ain't fair to ask him to do something what could make him lose his livelihood."

Daisy was correct. Truth's request was selfish. Yet what else was she to do? If her health permitted, she would go herself. But such an idea was impossible now.

"If anything happens, you can come to Kansas with Macia and me. I give you my word."

Silas sat up straight and looked directly into her eyes. "You mean dat? For sho'?"

"Yes. I give you my word, Silas."

"What I gotta do?"

"Bring me a pen and paper. I'm going to write a letter for you to take to a doctor in town. Wait until the doctor reads the letter. I'm hopeful God will lead you to someone who will immediately return with you. If not, you must find out exactly when he'll come so we can be certain he won't be observed."

Silas retrieved Truth's writing supplies while Daisy enumerated the many reasons why Silas shouldn't be involved in a scheme that might jeopardize his position at the school. And although Truth understood Daisy's reasoning, she wished the girl would cease her talking. While Silas sat close by and Daisy paced the length of the room, Truth penned a letter setting forth the strange and difficult circumstances she'd experienced since arriving at the Rutledge Academy. She wondered if any sane man would believe the contents of her letter—she could only pray God would direct Silas to the right man.

When she had finally completed the letter, Truth handed it to Silas. "Before handing over this letter, you must explain that you work at the academy. Ask if the doctor knows Mr. Laird or the Rutledges. Do you understand?"

Silas ran a finger along the edge of the envelope. "What I gonna say if the doctor asks what difference it makes if he know 'em?"

"Just say you want to be sure you're at the correct office. If he says he knows any of them, you must walk out. If he says he doesn't know them, give him the letter."

Silas scratched his head. "I guess I can do that. I'll go tomorrow morning when I'm s'posed to be working over in the stables. Don't nobody check on me then. Still ain't fer sure how I'm gonna find a doctor's office."

Daisy folded her arms across her chest. "If you's set on doing this, I guess I don' want you wand'ring around all day lookin' for a doctor. There's a couple of doctor offices 'tween Seventh an' Eighth streets by the Bradbury Hotel."

Truth reached out and clasped Daisy's hand. "Thank you, Daisy."

She jerked away. "Don't be thanking me. I didn't do nothing. And if anyone asks either of you 'bout any of this, you best tell 'em I got nothing to do with any of it."

CHAPTER

— 19 —

Hill City, Kansas

Certain the Nelson children were napping, Lilly tiptoed into her bedroom and pulled a small carpetbag from the back of her wardrobe. After grabbing a letter opener from the top drawer of her chest, she knelt down and pried at the loose floorboard. The wood creaked as she finally raised the board. Shifting backward, Lilly rested on her haunches and listened for the children. When all remained silent throughout the house, she exhaled and lifted the packet of ribbon-tied letters from the narrow opening beneath the floor.

She caressed the tattered envelopes for a brief moment and then shoved them into her valise. Moving quickly, she replaced the floorboard and pressed it back into position with the heel of her shoe. With a perfunctory swipe of her handkerchief, she brushed away the loose splinters of wood. Although Lilly suspected Mrs. Nelson had already discovered the hiding place, she didn't want to draw attention to the spot.

Without a backward glance, Lilly rushed downstairs and into Mr. Nelson's office. Her heart thumped in a wild, erratic rhythm as she pulled open the doors of the large oak cabinet. The huge metal safe stood before her, a box of thick steel waiting to be conquered. She pulled from her pocket the scrap of paper bearing the combination.

Her hand trembled as she carefully followed the directions for spinning the dial and then moving it first in one direction and then the other, stopping at each designated number. She inhaled and pulled on the handle. It didn't budge. Beads of sweat formed across her forehead as she once again twirled the knob and followed the exacting directions. Again the handle remained fixed.

Lilly glared at the steel box and back at the combination. "Come on! I don't have all day." Determined, Lilly sucked in another deep breath, twisted the dial, and carefully moved from number to number as the directions stated. When the arrow pointed to the final digit, she heard a muted click. Her pulse quickened and her hands trembled as she reached for the handle. This time it moved. Bending forward, Lilly lifted the handle and pulled the heavy door outward.

She wanted to shout with joy but dared not make any noise. After all, she didn't want to waken the children or alert anyone to what she was doing.

After opening her carpetbag, Lilly turned her attention back to the safe. Amassed inside were neatly banded stacks of bills, a pouch filled with silver coins, and another pouch containing what she thought were gold nuggets. She opened a case that lay beneath the leather pouches and gasped aloud at the sight. Mrs. Nelson's jewels? How could that dowdy woman possibly have chosen the diamond-and-sapphire necklace and matching earbobs? They must have belonged to Mr. Nelson's mother, for Lilly couldn't imagine her employer ever having worn anything so strikingly beautiful.

Carefully lifting the necklace from the case, Lilly examined the piece. The twinkling gems beckoned to her like fireflies on a moonless night. All thought of leaving the jewelry behind immediately faded. The necklace would show to great advantage on her long, thin neck.

Moving quickly, she wrapped the necklace and earrings in her handkerchief and returned the velvet case to the safe. One by one, she situated the stacks of money along the bottom of her valise. As she dumped the contents of one pouch into her bag, footfalls sounded in the hallway. Lilly quickly tossed the leather pouches into the safe and jumped to her feet.

"Aunt Lilly! What are you doing?"

"Jarena!" Lilly attempted to gather her wits about her. She must remain calm. "You startled me. Do you make a habit of entering houses without knocking?"

"I did knock. The door was open, and I thought you were likely in the kitchen and didn't hear me. I knew Mrs. Nelson would be at the temperance meeting." Jarena glanced back and forth between the carpetbag and open safe. "What are you doing, Aunt Lilly?"

With an air of bravado, Lilly picked up the carpetbag. "I suppose you could say I was cleaning the safe."

Jarena remained in the doorway. "I think you are cleaning *out* the safe. Whatever are you thinking? You'll go to jail. Surely you realize the Nelsons will have you arrested."

"If you keep your mouth shut, it may be at least a week before Mr. Nelson realizes anything is missing from the safe. I can be far from Kansas by the time he discovers the loss."

Lilly reached for the bag, and Jarena promptly grasped her hand. "Don't do this! You'll regret it for the rest of your life."

"You listen to me, Jarena. I *must* leave town. Terrible things happened back in New Orleans before I departed—unspeakable things that now cause me to fear for my life."

"And you think *this* is the way to solve your problems?" She dropped her aunt's hand. "Stealing from the Nelsons? They've been good to you. Gave you a decent position so that you could earn a living and be a respectable member of the community. Is this how you plan to repay them? By stealing their savings and then running out?"

Lilly's harsh laugh echoed throughout the room. "You're young and naïve, Jarena. You have no idea about life outside the protection of your little world. There is no way I can make you understand the urgency of this matter. This money is necessary if I'm going to save my life. And if I remain in Hill City, the lives of others will be placed in jeopardy."

"And so you were going to empty the safe and leave the Nelson children unattended while you run off to some unknown destination to live on the Nelsons' money? And I'm supposed to believe this is all for the best? What can be so terrible that you would go to these lengths?"

The clock on the mantel chimed, and Lilly looked out the front window. No sense hoping to see Charlie pull up in his fancy wagon— a full hour remained until he was due to arrive. Lilly's plans with Charlie had been based upon her regular daily schedule. Most days the children would just now be falling asleep, but they had played hard all morning. If only they had maintained their normal routine, this confrontation with Jarena could have been avoided. But how could she have known that they would take an early nap today? Children were completely unreliable!

Jarena stepped into the room and drew near. "Won't you sit down and discuss this with me? Perhaps if we reason together, we'll be able to find a solution that won't cause harm to anyone."

Rejecting Jarena's suggestion could prove risky. If Lilly refused, Jarena would no doubt hurry off to seek assistance from Moses or, worse yet, the sheriff. With any luck, she could placate the girl by appearing repentant. Twisting the velvet cord that encircled her neck, Lilly motioned Jarena toward one of the leather-upholstered chairs in front of Mr. Nelson's desk.

"Why don't we sit down and discuss the matter. I don't think you fully understand the depth of my difficulties."

Jarena sighed. "Thank you. That's all I ask, for the moment—an explanation."

Keeping Jarena at bay for the next hour was going to take both creativity and a silver tongue. However, both were a part of the vast repertoire of skills and abilities Lilly had developed throughout the years.

She pulled a handkerchief from her skirt pocket and clutched the lace-edged square in one hand. "I truly do not know where to begin. Please give me a moment to gather my thoughts." She bowed her head and dabbed the cloth to the corner of one eye.

"Do take your time, Aunt Lilly."

Lilly spent several minutes sniffling and staring at the patterned wool carpet. When she realized Jarena would wait no longer, she wiped her eyes and looked up into the young woman's eyes. "You know, I've always wanted to do the proper thing, Jarena. And strange as it may seem, at those times when I've done what I thought was correct, I've later regretted my decision."

"Sometimes that happens to all of us, but you can't honestly tell me you believe it's the right thing to steal from the Nelsons, can you?"

"No, stealing isn't right. But I'm not taking their money because I covet their wealth. I need it to escape from Kansas."

Jarena pressed the folds of her skirt with one hand. "I don't know where you're planning to go, but it appears as if you've taken much more than enough to purchase a train ticket."

Lilly couldn't deny that Jarena had concluded the truth. Oh, she'd considered taking only enough for a train ticket and room rent until she could find work—far less than she'd finally stuffed into her case. But once the safe was open, the jewels had shimmered and winked in a seductive dance that caused her heart to race, and the crisp banded cash had tantalized her with thoughts of luxury and excess—with remembrances of her life with Bentley. How could she explain such thoughts to a girl who had lived a life of poverty and wanted nothing more?

"I hadn't planned to take so much. But I suppose if I'm going to be labeled a thief, I might as well be a prosperous one, don't you think?" Lilly's attempt at levity seemed to fall flat as Jarena solemnly shook her head.

"It's not too late, Aunt Lilly. If you'll just return the items to the safe, no one will know except you and me. I promise to never speak of this again, and I give you my word I won't tell a soul."

Lilly took Jarena by the shoulders and peered deep into her eyes. "Listen to me, girl. There's a woman dead and a child missing down in New Orleans. The man who's on his way here believes I killed that woman and had something to do with his son's disappearance."

Jarena pulled back, her eyes wide with fear. "And did you?"

"No need for you to know any details. Bentley believes I did, and that's all that matters. He won't hesitate to kill me. I've led a terrible life, Jarena—one you can't begin to imagine. And now my sins are catching up with me. I must leave Hill City, and this money is the only way out."

"You're only making matters worse. There's forgiveness for your sins, if you're willing. There are lots of verses in the Bible that I could show you. Maybe if you'd consider asking God to forgive you, things would turn around in your life." Jarena jumped up from her chair and grabbed the Bible lying on the far corner of Mr. Nelson's desk.

"Don't begin pointing out Scripture to me, girl. If you think everything is going to be fine because I throw myself on God's mercy and say I'm sorry, you've been wrapped in cotton wool way too long." Lilly held out her thumb and forefinger with just a small space between them. "You've got these little bitty wrongdoings that need to be forgiven, while me—well, I've got sins that are vile enough to make a grown man blush."

"Miss Hattie says sin is sin, and God will forgive it all, if we're truly sorry."

"And what do *you* say, Jarena? Do you think all sin should be forgiven?"

She nodded. "Of course I do. There's no sin too great for God's forgiveness."

"But what about *you*? I listened to all those verses when I was growing up. I know what the Bible says about God forgiving sin, but I don't see too many people willing to forgive each other for those sins."

"It's *God's* mercy and forgiveness we need, Aunt Lilly, not that of people."

"Sometimes we need both. For instance, let's say that a long time ago I asked God to forgive me for not coming to help out before your mama died. And let's say I believed God forgave me, but I knew your pappy was still holding a grudge. Isn't it hard to believe God's forgiven you when those you wronged are still angry—especially when they're the ones saying you need to get right with God?"

Jarena laid the Bible back on the desk. "When I was having trouble understanding forgiveness, I thought God should prove He had forgiven me by fixing everything. I wanted proof I was forgiven. I think it's the same with you. You think asking God's forgiveness will erase the past."

"How about you, Jarena? Do you always forgive those who wrong you?"

Jarena bobbed her head. "Maybe in the past I didn't do so well. However, God's taught me a lot about forgiveness since we moved to Kansas. If I expect Him to forgive me, then I've got to forgive others."

"Saying those words is easy, but acting on them is a whole other story, now, isn't it?"

"Yes, but that's what God calls us to do."

Lilly studied Jarena. Her eyes spoke volumes. She was a lovely young woman—so untarnished, so inexperienced. The girl truly believed she could forgive the transgressions of others with merely a word or a nod, a simple act of obedience to God. How little she knew.

Lilly heard the sound of a horse and wagon in the distance. She glanced at the clock and then bolted to her feet. It wasn't yet time, but Charlie was likely early—worried that all might not go according to plan or that she might need assistance. Lilly stooped down and grasped the handles of the valise.

"I'm sorry to disappoint you, Jarena. What you've asked me to do may be the right thing. However, I'm afraid it's impossible." Lilly flashed a smile as she looked over her shoulder. "Tell your pappy he was right about me all along—I'm no good."

Jarena lunged forward and grabbed hold of Lilly's arm. Her fingers clawed into the fabric of Lilly's shirtwaist. "Please don't leave like this!"

Lilly pulled loose and hurried down the hallway with Jarena close on her heels. Why wouldn't the girl accept the fact that she wasn't going to succeed? Lilly raced out to the porch and down the steps. It was indeed Charlie's buggy approaching from the right. She pushed open the front gate and ran forward. Her eyes widened and fear gripped her as she caught sight of an unrestrained horse and buggy careening toward her from the left.

Jarena screamed. A shrill, ear-shattering cry. The girl's piercing wail was the final sound Lilly heard as she crashed to the ground.

CHAPTER

— 20 —

Charlie Holmes had become a weekly regular at the general store in Hill City. Jarena had seen him plying his wares at the local mercantile or traveling house to house, stopping wherever he might make a sale. He had always been courteous, but they had exchanged no more than a few words during their brief encounters. However, when he jumped out of his buggy and raced down the street to lend aid, Jarena sighed with relief.

"Who does that runaway horse and buggy belong to?" Charlie came to a panting halt and dropped down on one knee beside Lilly. He stared at Lilly's lifeless form. "She needs medical attention."

"Dr. Boyle is in his office. Please go and fetch him—tell him to hurry!"

Jarena feared the horse had stepped on Aunt Lilly's midsection. In addition, her face was cut and swollen, and her clothing was ripped and covered in dust. Jarena cradled her aunt's lifeless form in the crook of her arm. She leaned over Lilly's face and listened. Her breathing was shallow and irregular. Jarena wanted to breathe for her, somehow make her more comfortable. After all, this was her fault. Had she done as Aunt Lilly bid and remained in the house, none of this would have happened.

"Dr. Boyle will be here soon, Aunt Lilly. You hold on." She doubted whether her aunt could hear what was being said. In fact, Jarena knew she couldn't. But speaking the words somehow soothed her and provided a sense of peace.

The sound of pounding feet coming toward her caused Jarena to look up. Dr. Boyle and Mr. Holmes were running down the street with Walt Johnson, Jeb Malone, and Virgil Kramer following close behind. Dr. Boyle dropped his black leather bag nearby and leaned down beside Lilly. He pushed back her eyelids and listened to her labored breathing.

Dr. Boyle signaled to the other men. "Let's take her to the office."

Jarena looked toward the house. "The Nelson children are alone inside. They're napping."

"You had best stay with them, Jarena. The men will help me get her down to my office, and there's nothing you can do for your aunt right now. I'll send word if there's any change. You can come to the office once Mrs. Nelson returns home."

Walt Johnson unfolded a long, narrow piece of canvas. They used the heavy cloth as a stretcher, with each of the men grasping a corner, while Charlie and Jarena stood in the middle of the dusty street and watched the bewildering sight.

Charlie leaned down and reached for Lilly's carpetbag. "I'll put this in my buggy and go down to Dr. Boyle's office to await word on Lilly's condition."

Before Charlie could gain a good hold on the bag, Jarena snatched it from him. "This doesn't belong to you, Mr. Holmes. I'll take care of my aunt's satchel."

His stare remained fixed on the bag for a moment. "I don't want any trouble, Miss Harban, but I do believe I'd like to take that with me."

Suddenly Jarena understood. Charlie Holmes knew what was in the bag. He was providing Aunt Lilly with a method of escape. Jarena narrowed her eyes and glared at him. "I don't think that would be wise. You see, I know what's in this bag, Mr. Holmes, and I wouldn't want to send the sheriff after you. You were planning to take Aunt Lilly out of town with you, weren't you? The two of you set up this entire thing, and that's the only reason you happen to be in Hill City today, isn't it?"

Charlie backed up a few steps and pointed his finger at Jarena. "You can't prove none of that. Now, I'm leaving town like you asked, but don't you start no trouble for me or I'll see to it that you pay—you understand?"

"I'll mention your abiding concern to Aunt Lilly once she's up and about."

The peddler tugged on the brim of his felt bowler and pulled it forward on his head. "You've got no reason to cast aspersions, Miss Harban. If you hadn't chased after her, your aunt would be fit as a fiddle. Besides, I doubt she's ever going to regain consciousness. Truth be told, I figure you'll be burying her in a day or two."

Jarena faded at the man's angry words. How could he utter such cruel remarks while her aunt lay unconscious on the way to Dr. Boyle's office? Obviously, he cared little for Aunt Lilly. Her aunt had partnered with a man willing to compromise honest behavior for his own gain— a man who would help her steal from the Nelsons—a man much like Lilly. What else could Jarena expect of such a person? Clasping the carpetbag in her hand, Jarena started back toward the Nelson home.

Mrs. Nelson should be back within the hour, and the children might awaken at any moment. Jarena hurried into Mr. Nelson's office. What if she couldn't open the safe? She stared at the black monstrosity and uttered a silent prayer before she pulled back on the handle. The heavy door swung open, and Jarena sighed with relief. Apparently Aunt Lilly had failed to secure the lock when she shut the door. Jarena opened the valise and then peered inside the safe. She had no idea how to arrange the items, but she would do her best.

After pouring the silver coins into one of the leather pouches, she placed the gold nuggets in the other pouch and returned the necklace and earrings to the velvet case. Only the cash and a packet of letters remained. She placed the stacks of money side by side and then balanced the jewelry case and pouches on top. The letters in the packet were addressed to her aunt, so she returned them to the valise.

Jarena dropped Aunt Lilly's bag behind the front door and stood nearby to greet Mrs. Nelson as she entered the house. "Good afternoon, Mrs. Nelson."

Jarena detected a hint of fear in Mrs. Nelson's eyes. "Jarena. Whatever are you doing here? Are the children all right?"

"Indeed. They're still napping. My only concern is that they've slept so long this afternoon, they won't sleep tonight. I had planned to awaken them within the half hour if you hadn't returned."

"Where's Lilly?"

"That's why I'm here, Mrs. Nelson. You see, Aunt Lilly met with an accident. She's being cared for by Dr. Boyle—at his office."

Mrs. Nelson removed her feather-bedecked hat and placed it on a table near the stairway. "What kind of accident? I didn't send her on any errands today."

"She noticed an acquaintance passing down the street. She had walked out front to speak to him when a runaway wagon coming from the opposite direction knocked her to the ground."

Mrs. Nelson clasped a hand to her bodice. "Dear me! I trust her injuries aren't serious?"

"I fear they are. She was unconscious when I last saw her. I'll go directly to the doctor's office when I leave your house."

Mrs. Nelson paled at the information. "If there's anything she needs or if I can do . . ."

Jarena patted Mrs. Nelson's arm. "No need to worry, Mrs. Nelson. I know Dr. Boyle is providing excellent medical treatment, and I can assist with her care. You have three children to look after."

"Please tell Lilly I'll be praying for her."

Jarena stepped back and picked up the carpetbag. "Yes, I'll be certain to tell her."

Once she was out the door and headed toward Dr. Boyle's office, Jarena exhaled a deep breath. Thankfully, Mrs. Nelson hadn't questioned her about the valise or its contents. Jarena had been prepared to say she had carried the carpetbag into the house—which was not exactly a lie since she'd carried it from the street into the Nelson residence. In addition, it contained Aunt Lilly's letters, and she didn't want to ask Mrs. Nelson to return the personal items upstairs to her aunt's room.

The waiting room of Dr. Boyle's office was empty when Jarena entered, though the doctor stepped into the room shortly after the bell jingled above the front door.

He smiled warmly and motioned for her to follow. "She's fading in and out of consciousness. I believe there's nothing more I can do—it's a matter of time."

"She won't . . . She isn't . . . I mean . . ."

Instinctively, Dr. Boyle patted Jarena's hand. "I don't know if she's going to live. Only time will tell. However, you're welcome to go and sit with her. I believe we'll move her over to my house this evening. That way you and I can both look after her. We'll put her in Macia's room."

"Thank you, Dr. Boyle."

After seeing her aunt's condition, Jarena realized sitting by the woman's bedside would accomplish little. Instead, she'd go by the Nelsons' to retrieve a few of Aunt Lilly's possessions and then return to the Boyle residence and prepare supper. Perhaps by the time the men carried Aunt Lilly to the Boyle home, she would be alert enough to eat some soup.

Though all had gone according to plan and her aunt was now safely ensconced in Macia's bedroom, Jarena felt helpless. Lilly's eyes occasionally fluttered open in a vacant stare, or she emitted an infrequent groan, but otherwise no signs of consciousness developed. Jarena wondered how long Lilly might remain in this lifeless state. Jarena sat in a nearby chair, mending a pair of cotton stockings while silently praying her aunt would at least have one final opportunity to accept Christ before she died.

"Jarena." The voice was but a faint whisper. Startled, Jarena dropped her sewing to the floor.

Hunching forward, she grasped Lilly's fingers. "Can you hear me, Aunt Lilly?"

"Yes."

The single word was barely audible, but Jarena heard it. She dampened a cloth and wet her aunt's dry lips. "If I lift you up, will you drink a sip of water?"

"Yes." The one word seemed all her aunt could manage, but at least it was something. Jarena slipped her arm beneath Lilly's shoulders and lifted the cup to her lips. Her aunt took only a small sip. Even so, the effort pleased Jarena.

"You're making great strides, Aunt Lilly. By tomorrow I'm certain you're going to want to eat some soup, and you'll be anxious to return to work." A feeble smile crossed the older woman's lips before she once again slipped into a state of semiconsciousness.

Later that evening, Dr. Boyle set up a narrow cot and situated it near Lilly's bedside. For the remainder of the night, Jarena lay near her aunt, listening to her muffled groans and uneven breathing. Although she was fatigued and her body ached from the uncomfortable bed, Jarena arose the next morning at daybreak. Weary or not, there were chores she must tend to.

After serving breakfast to the Boyles, Jarena prepared a tray for her aunt. Though she didn't think Aunt Lilly would partake of any nourishment, she hoped the smell of bacon and eggs would at least stir her into a brief period of wakefulness. She placed a small china teapot on the tray as a faint knock sounded at the front door.

Wiping her hands on her apron, Jarena walked toward the door. "Who could possibly be calling at this early hour?" She pulled open the door and looked down to see young Georgie Nelson looking up at her and holding a limp bouquet of pink and yellow roses. A smear of blood stained his right index finger.

The boy extended the bunch of roses. "I brought these for Miss Lilly. Can I see her?"

Jarena peeked around the doorframe, thinking surely Mrs. Nelson must be somewhere nearby, but no one else was in sight. "Does your mother know you're here, Georgie?"

"She said I could bring the flowers. I picked 'em last night, so they're kind of droopy, but I hope Miss Lilly thinks they smell good. She likes roses. She told me so."

Jarena stepped aside and ushered him into the foyer. "Why don't we put those in some water before we take them upstairs."

Georgie followed along and enthusiastically plunked the flowers into the cut-glass vase Jarena offered. "How soon will Miss Lilly be coming back to our house?"

"It's hard to say. It may take a while before she's strong enough to return. She's mostly been sleeping since the accident."

"Can we wake her up? I need to talk to her real bad." Georgie chewed on his bottom lip and picked a dry leaf from the bouquet.

"Is there something I can help you with, Georgie?"

"Nuh-uh. I just want to talk with Miss Lilly."

"Very well. Let's go upstairs and see if she's awake. I was going to take up her breakfast tray. You can carry the flowers."

They paraded up the stairs, down the hallway, and into the bedroom where Lilly lay just as Jarena had left her over an hour ago. Georgie walked to the side of the bed and placed the vase of roses on the bedside table with a loud thunk.

Lilly stirred and her eyelids fluttered. Georgie seized the opportunity. "I'm glad you're awake, Miss Lilly." He leaned down and whispered into her ear.

Aunt Lilly's eyes opened, shining with fear. She grasped Georgie's shirt and whispered a strained reply. The boy nodded and then pointed at the flowers. "I brought you some roses from Mama's garden. Pink and yellow—the colors you like. Can you smell 'em?"

Lilly's hands shook as she reached for Georgie's arm. "Yes. Thank you, Georgie. Now remember what I told you."

"Your hands are shaking, Aunt Lilly. Can I bring you a blanket?"

"No. I'm merely feeling weak."

Jarena stepped forward with a cup of tea. "Perhaps this tea will help to warm and strengthen you a bit. And I've brought you a breakfast tray with bacon and eggs. Do you think you could eat a few bites?"

Georgie stood near the doorway while Jarena assisted Lilly with her tea. "I'm going home now, Miss Lilly, but I'll be back to see you in a few days and bring some more flowers."

"Thank you, Georgie. You're a good boy."

Jarena furrowed her brows as the boy's footsteps clattered down the steps. "You truly must have injured your head if you're telling Georgie Nelson he's a good boy."

Lilly sighed. "I don't believe I'm . . . going to live, Jarena. I have a searing pain in my head . . . and I feel like a fire is burning in my belly. I'm so weak."

"You're better than yesterday, Aunt Lilly. And I want you to know that although I was required to wrestle your valise from Mr. Holmes, I was able to safely return all of the Nelsons' belongings to the safe before Mrs. Nelson returned home yesterday afternoon. I'm hopeful Mr. Nelson won't notice if the items are out of order. So there's nothing you need be concerned about except getting well."

Lilly turned her head and looked about the room. "My carpetbag? Where is it? There were letters . . ."

Jarena stroked her aunt's forehead. "After seeing the envelopes were addressed to you, I realized they hadn't come from Mr. Nelson's safe. The packet remains secure inside your valise—over on the floor by the chest."

"And Charlie? Did he take anything from my case?"

"No. I didn't give him an opportunity. I told him I'd send the sheriff after him if he didn't cooperate. He was unhappy, but he didn't argue any further. Now I want you to concentrate on getting well. Dr. Boyle will be up to check on you a little later, and I believe he's going to tell us you're on the mend."

"I don't think so, Jarena. I can feel my body weakening. I now know what folks mean . . . when they say you can tell when you're dying."

"I don't believe you're going to die, but I believe this may be a warning to you, Aunt Lilly. You need to make your peace with God."

"I don't think it's possible for me to make peace with God, Jarena." She closed her eyes and took a couple of shallow breaths. "I'm certain He doesn't like deathbed conversions. I doubt He even hears them. After all, it doesn't seem right that folks like your mother and father could live godly lives and then someone like me . . . who's been a disgrace all my life . . . could ask forgiveness at the moment of death and receive it all the same."

A sense of desperation filled Jarena as she clutched her aunt's hand. "This isn't the time for us to debate the ability or willingness of God to forgive your sins, Aunt Lilly. If you truly believe you don't have much time, you must ask Jesus to come into your heart—accept Him as your savior and repent of your sins. Surely you don't want to spend eternity in hell."

"Now you sound like one of those fire-and-brimstone preachers who came around sermonizing at revival time." A tear rolled down Jarena's cheek, and Lilly attempted to wipe it away with a shaking finger. "If it's that important to you, child, you tell me what to do and say, and I'll do it."

Jarena straightened her shoulders. Her heart swelled with joy: There was hope for her aunt. "Are you sure?"

"I said I'd do it, but I don't have the strength to keep talking. Just tell me what you want me to say and do."

— 21 —

New York City

Truth knew Silas wanted to help her. However, she had grown weary of his constant reminders that he must be careful. So far as she was concerned, his vigilance took up far too much time with his trying to plan everything down to the last detail. Even now, he was once again delaying the delivery of her letter.

Silas's exasperated sigh filled the room. "You gotta unnerstand that if I go to town 'ceptin' on the regular schedule, I's for sure gonna get in trouble. They's gonna know somethin's not right. If I's gonna help, you's got to be patient, Truth. I done tol' Mr. Laird you's still sick, and Daisy's gonna sneak upstairs and check on Miss Macia."

Truth paced the length of the carriage house with her arms tightly folded across her chest. She'd been able to spend several days feigning continued illness, but that meant leaving Macia alone. However, with Silas unwilling to go into town until his regularly scheduled trip next week, she must now return to look after Macia—which meant resuming the visits with Mr. Laird. She shuddered at the thought, yet she knew Silas was correct. They dared not draw unwanted attention.

"An' you cain't be spending time down here in da carriage house," Silas insisted. "What if Mr. Laird walks over here an' sees you?"

"Does he sometimes come here?"

"He been here once or twice, and with you sick, I figure he might be wantin' to check and see if I been lyin' to him. Ain't smart takin' chances."

"I'll go back upstairs in a minute. The days are long sitting up there with nothing to do. I told Daisy to bring me some mending from the house and I'd finish it for her." She looked directly at Silas. "Have you noticed that since I quit going to tea with Mr. Laird, I've been feeling much better?"

"Course. I'd be a fool not t' see that."

"Well, do you remember me telling you I thought I'd seen Mr. Laird putting something in Macia's water on several occasions?"

Silas picked up one of the harnesses, laid it flat on the wood table, and began spreading neat's-foot oil on the leather straps. "Um-hmm, I remember that."

"Well, I think that's what he was doing to me. Putting some kind of drug in my tea—or maybe in Daisy's tarts when she served them to us. I never actually saw him, but I think that surely must be what he did. Otherwise, why would I feel better since I've quit joining him for tea? What do you think?"

Silas continued applying the oil, carefully seeking out any spots he might have missed with the worn paintbrush. "So you ain' needin' me to go fetch the doctor after all? Is that what you's saying?"

"Even if I'm not so sick, we still need to have the doctor see to Macia. I can explain the ailments to him. I should go myself since I'm feeling somewhat better."

"That ain't smart thinkin'. What if Mr. Laird comes searchin' for you or you go lookin' for the doctor's office and get lost in da city. You ain't never found your way 'round no city big as New York, now has you?"

Truth recalled her arrival at the train station and the subsequent incident with the omnibus. Perhaps she couldn't navigate about the city on her own.

"You needs t' learn some patience. I's gonna fetch the doctor, but it ain't gonna be until next week. Promise me you ain't gonna do nothin' to get us in trouble."

His request wasn't unreasonable. Placing Daisy or Silas at risk was completely unfair, and Truth knew it. "All right. I'll wait, but that means I must return to see Macia tomorrow. If Mr. Laird insists I join him for tea, I'll watch him carefully."

Silas removed a bottle of castor oil from the shelf and poured a dollop into a separate container before adding a measure of the neat's-foot oil. Truth watched as he stirred the concoction and then thoroughly brushed the next harness. After replacing the bottles and cleaning his brush, Silas rubbed his stomach and nodded toward the stairs.

"You best go on. I's goin' over and see if Daisy saved me any victuals."

Truth stood at the small window in the bedroom over the carriage house and watched as Silas ambled across the grassy expanse toward the kitchen door. Taking up a pair of stockings from Daisy's mending basket, she threaded a needle and hoped Silas would soon return.

Truth completed the mending and, after a bit of searching, found a set of pillowcases in the bottom drawer of Daisy's chest. With nothing else to pass the time, she dug in the sewing basket, deciding to embroider a delicate border of pink and yellow flowers along the edge of the pillowcases. She hoped Daisy wouldn't think her actions too presumptuous. Though she longed for a book to read, Truth had been unable to convince either Silas or Daisy to remove a volume from the shelves that lined the Rutledge Academy classrooms.

When she finally heard the carriage house door open, Truth shoved the pillowcase into the sewing basket and waited, uncertain if it was Silas or Mr. Laird who had entered. Holding her breath, she tiptoed across the room, opened the door, and peeked downstairs. Silas was pulling a tin from the shelf, obviously preparing to continue his work on the harness straps. After she assured herself Mr. Laird hadn't accompanied Silas, Truth hurried below and greeted him while she made herself comfortable on one of the lower steps.

He returned her greeting and then dipped his brush into the neat's-foot mixture. As Silas brushed the leather, he told Truth he'd received his comeuppance from Daisy for eating the final remains of the noon-day meal without permission. With a mischievous grin, he spoke of the pork roast and large helping of fried potatoes he'd devoured.

However, the gleam faded from his eyes only moments later. "'Bout the time I finished eatin', I heard angry voices come into da kitchen. Then someone said your name."

"My name?" Truth startled to attention and prodded Silas on.

"He say you ain't nothing but trouble. Too smart for your own good—and that things need to be taken care of right away."

"What *things*?" Truth squeaked. She rocked back against the unyielding step. The hardness of the wood pressed through her thin dress. She wanted to lean forward but fear held her body tight against the splintered tread.

Silas stopped his paintbrush in midswipe. "You! You need to be taken care of right away is what they was saying. Mr. Laird said he been puttin' something in your tea but now that you's taken to your bed, he gonna have to start all over. Something 'bout the effects wearing off. Then Mrs. Rutledge got all upset and said she didn't wanna hear no talk 'bout what he been doing to none of the girls. Next thing I knows they's arguing 'bout getting money on account of papers the girls signed."

The information was far more than Truth had expected to hear. There was now little doubt that Mr. Laird and the Rutledges were up to no good. Guessing at reality was one thing, but knowing Mr. Laird had actually spoken of putting something into the tea caused Truth's pulse to quicken.

Truth mentally attempted to sift through the information, still uncertain what all of it might mean. Silas picked up a piece of the well-oiled leather and rubbed it with a soft cloth while he repeated additional snatches of conversation as they came to mind. "I think these papers they's havin' the girls sign has somethin' to do with all of this."

"What did they say specifically, Silas? You need to remember exactly what kind of papers they were. Macia didn't mention signing any papers."

He lifted the leather strap and examined his handiwork. "That gal ain't awake long enough to mention nothin' 'bout no papers."

"Think, Silas. What kind of papers did they talk about?"

He scratched his head and then leaned both hands on the worktable. "Somethin' to do with 'life.' I heard 'em say 'life papers.' I knows that for sure."

Truth stood. "When I go to see Macia tomorrow, I'll try and keep her awake long enough to ask her some questions. Maybe she remembers signing something."

"Jest be careful. Them folks is surely riled up, and if Mr. Laird hears you asking questions, no tellin' what might happen. Like I told you earlier, he's mighty angry wid you for causin' trouble. No tellin' what he might do."

The next morning, Truth slipped up the back stairs and into Macia's room. She hoped Mr. Laird had discontinued his habit of appearing in Macia's room each morning. She poured water into the washbowl and carried it to the bedside table. After dipping a cloth in the water, she wrung it out and wiped Macia's face. The girl stirred and attempted to push Truth away.

"Quit fighting me, Macia. You need to wake up."

"You're always bothering me, Truth. Go away."

Truth persisted. Though Macia fought her at every turn, Truth managed to eventually force the girl from her bed and into an overstuffed chair with the promise that she'd let her sleep in peace after they talked.

Pulling a chair opposite Macia, Truth plopped down and leaned forward, resting her arms across her thighs. "I want you to try and remember if you signed any papers when you first arrived at the school, Macia."

"Why?"

"It doesn't matter why, just tell me—do you recall signing papers?" Macia stared at the ceiling until Truth finally snapped her fingers. "Try to concentrate, Macia."

"They said Father hadn't completed all of the papers and I was required to sign something. That's all I remember. Now can I go back to bed?"

"Not yet. Did you read any of them?"

Macia shook her head. "No. Mrs. Rutledge was talking to me and Mr. Laird—Marvin—pointed to the place for me to sign."

"Did the papers say anything about your life?"

"My *life*? Why would they say anything about my life?"

Before Truth could respond, the door swung open. "Well, look who's here. I trust you're feeling much better, Truth?"

She dug her fingernails into the flesh of her palms as Mr. Laird crossed the room. "Yes, thank you. I was just going to help Macia get back into bed and then return to my room and get some rest myself."

He wagged his finger back and forth. "Not without some refreshments before you depart. I won't take no for an answer."

"Another time might be better. Today is my first day up and about and I'm a bit weary."

"I promise I won't keep you long. I've missed our little chats. Come along, now."

Truth reluctantly helped Macia get back into bed and then followed Mr. Laird downstairs. As had become the custom, they waited while Daisy brought the tray into the room. However, Truth would make certain he wouldn't fool her this time. She carefully watched as Mr. Laird prepared the tea, and although he dipped his hand into his pocket, she didn't see him withdraw anything. He carried the tray across the room and carefully situated it on the table.

"Do help yourself," he said, pointing at one of the teacups.

Without hesitation, Truth reached across the tray and picked up the cup and saucer on the opposite side of the tray. Mr. Laird appeared dumbfounded as she took a sip of the tea.

She picked up the other cup and offered it to Mr. Laird. He hesitated. "Please. I don't want to partake alone."

His jaw twitched as he took the cup and balanced it on his knee without taking a sip. When the brew had grown cold, he placed the cup back on the tray. "I have several appointments and must depart. We'll spend more time together tomorrow."

Truth forced herself to appear unruffled as she walked from the room. She maintained a steady, even gait until she walked out the kitchen door. But the moment her feet touched the grassy expanse, she raced pell-mell toward the carriage house and barreled through the doorway. "Silas! You were right! He's using something to make Macia sick—and me, too. Except this time I fooled him. We need to go to the police, Silas."

His eyes widened with fear. "Police?"

Truth dropped onto the bottom step. "Yes. Police, constable, sheriff, whatever name they go by here in New York—we must go and talk to them."

Silas squatted down in front of her. "And tell 'em what? That these fine white folks what run this expensive school for girls is bein' mean to us colored folks and may be killin' some of the white gals?"

She nodded. "Yes. That's exactly what we need to tell them."

"This may be the North, but if you think them constables is gonna listen to us, you better think again. They'd prob'ly say we was crazy and lock us up in that insane asylum on the other side of town. We can't be goin' to no police, Truth."

"You think they won't listen because the Rutledges are wealthy and own this school?"

"And 'cause rich folks send their daughters to this place, and 'cause lots of important folks know Mr. Laird an' Mr. Rutledge—and 'cause we's colored and they's white."

Truth rubbed her forehead. "Then what are we going to do?"

"If we's gonna get outta here, we gotta get us a good plan. I'm thinkin' we can't take no chance getting that doctor. So long as you can keep from drinking any more of that tea, you shouldn' be gettin' sick no more. And maybe it's better if Macia's sleepin' when we try and take her outta here—that way she won't wake nobody up with her yellin'."

"I'd rather go to the constable."

Silas grabbed both of her hands and held them tight. "You listen ter me, Truth. You got lots of book learnin'. Ain't no denyin' you's lots smarter than the likes of me. But if there's one thing I know, it's that we can't depend on no one but ourselves to get outta here. If you ain't willin' to keep the law outta this, then I ain't goin' with you. You gotta give me your word."

There was no choice to be made. She must have Silas's help or she'd never get Macia out of this school. She nodded. "You have my word."

"Good. Now let's make us a plan."

CHAPTER

— 22 —

Hill City, Kansas

Jarena opened the front door to young Georgie Nelson.

"Good morning, Miss Harban. May I see Miss Lilly?" He carried another bouquet of roses in one hand and clutched a small black folder in the other.

Jarena motioned him inside. "Does your mother know you're cutting her roses, Georgie?"

He shrugged. "I told her I was coming to see Miss Lilly, and she knows Miss Lilly likes roses."

"I see. Well, it might be wise to ask permission before you cut any more. I'm certain she works very hard to grow such lovely flowers. She may want to keep them to enjoy herself."

"She's the one who always says it's better to give than receive. Is

Miss Lilly awake? I need to talk to her."

Jarena knew she had best warn the boy that her aunt wasn't responding as well as Dr. Boyle had hoped, and her periods of consciousness grew farther and farther apart. "She's still not doing very well, Georgie, so even if she's awake, you mustn't expect her to talk too much." Jarena pointed to his hand. "What's that you're carrying with you?"

He gripped the folder more tightly, holding it against his chest. "Something I brought for Miss Lilly."

Obviously the boy didn't want to divulge what gift he'd brought, so Jarena didn't pry. It was likely a drawing or poem he'd written. Jarena thought young Georgie might find himself in a good deal of trouble if his parents discovered he had been cutting roses and borrowing his father's leather folder. However, she found his affection for her aunt both surprising and endearing. From all accounts, Georgie had been Aunt Lilly's nemesis, yet here he was coming to visit her sickbed and delivering gifts.

"Would you like me to put the flowers in water before we go upstairs?"

Georgie thrust the bouquet at Jarena and waited in the foyer until she returned with the flowers tucked into a water-filled vase. He followed her up the stairs. While Jarena placed the flowers atop the chest of drawers, Georgie tiptoed to Lilly's bedside. He dropped into the chair next to the bed and waited a moment. He hunched forward, leaned close to Lilly's ear, and spoke loudly. "You awake, Miss Lilly?"

If his boisterous voice didn't cause Aunt Lilly to stir, Jarena didn't know what would.

Georgie was peering down at Lilly when she opened her eyes. "Georgie! Move away from my face."

He jumped back as though he'd been hit with a round of buckshot. "I came to see you, Miss Lilly, and I brought you this, just like I said." He held the item in front of her face.

"Slip it under my pillow."

Georgie did as she bid.

"Thank you." She patted his hand. "Does your mother know you brought this?"

He shook his head. "I took it out of the hiding place when she was in the backyard with Alma."

"Excellent thinking on your part," Lilly wheezed as she panted to gain her breath.

"Am I safe now, Miss Lilly?"

Lilly gave him a weak nod. "Forever, Georgie."

"Thank you. Alma said to tell you hello and she hopes you come back to the house real soon. I brought you some more roses."

"Thank you, but you shouldn't pick any more of your mother's roses."

"That's what Miss Jarena said, too." Lilly's eyes closed as Georgie completed the remark. "Is she sleeping again?" he asked Jarena. She nodded, and the boy stood up. "Guess I'll go on back home, then."

Jarena accompanied him down the flight of stairs. "Thank you for coming, Georgie. It was very kind of you. I didn't realize you and Aunt Lilly had become such dear friends."

His mouth dropped open. "Friends? I came over here 'cause Miss Lilly used her evil eye on me. I had to keep my promise so she'd set me free from her curse before she died."

Jarena felt as though she'd taken a blow to the stomach. She grasped Georgie's shoulder. "You believe my aunt placed a curse on you?"

"You ever see that bloody rabbit's foot and her evil eye—and that thing she wears around her neck on the velvet ribbon? She's got special powers."

"No she doesn't. You were never under any spell or curse, Georgie. Do you believe me?"

The boy chewed on his bottom lip. "I feel a whole lot better now that she told me I'm safe." He ran down the steps and waved once he'd cleared the gate.

Jarena watched the boy race toward home and shook her head. So much for believing Aunt Lilly's tender care had endeared her to the Nelson children.

When she heard Jarena and Georgie going down the stairs, Lilly opened her eyes. She was glad to be alone—and awake. She reached under her pillow. Her fingers clawed at the pillowcase until she secured a firm grasp on the folder. She gasped for breath as she held the coveted possession to her breast. How could so little effort cause such exertion?

The thin leather cover had become brittle with age. But inside were Lilly's most valued possessions. First was the certificate of freedom she'd received after leaving Kentucky and moving to New Orleans. She had argued long and hard for the document, but that piece of paper had made her a free woman even before President Lincoln's Civil War.

And though being a courtesan had tied her life to white men, Lilly knew that, by law, she was free. She opened the folder and ran a shaky finger down the yellowed page. In her haste to rob the Nelsons' safe and leave town, Lilly had retrieved her letters from beneath the floorboards but had failed to reclaim her most important possession—the leather folder. How could she have been so reckless? Such foolhardy behavior!

Holding the papers to her chest, Lilly decided it was time to tell Jarena. Lilly would suffer Ezekiel's wrath for breaking her old promise, but Lilly had long ago grown accustomed to Ezekiel's anger. And there was likely no need to worry. The way she was feeling, she'd be dead by the time he found out, anyway. Her heart raced when she heard approaching footsteps.

"You're awake!" Jarena's voice was filled with happiness as she sat next to Lilly. "And you even gathered enough strength to look at the folder Georgie brought you."

Lilly took as deep a breath as she could manage. "Sit down, Jarena. I've got some things to tell you before I die."

"You're not going to—"

Lilly held up her hand to silence the girl. "I don't have the time or energy to argue. You need to listen real careful . . . because you're not going to like this—not one little bit."

Jarena moved her chair closer to the bed and nestled Lilly's hands in her own. "I think you must be exaggerating again, Aunt Lilly."

She ignored the remark. "You remember that talk we had back at the Nelsons'? The one about forgiveness?"

"Of course I do. How could I forget?"

"You still believe you can forgive anything that's ever happened to you?" The words were raspy and uneven as she struggled for breath.

Jarena lightly squeezed Lilly's fingers and nodded.

"Then this will be your test, Jarena." Lilly closed her eyes. Her strength was quickly waning. She forced her eyelids open and looked at Jarena—such a lovely young woman. "Jarena, I am your mother. Not Jennie—but me. You are *my* child."

Jarena snatched her hands away as though they'd been touched by a hot poker. "Aunt Lilly! That's not possible, and you shouldn't say such a thing!"

Pain settled in Lilly's heart as she opened the folder Georgie had delivered. She should have known that would be Jarena's reaction. She lifted out her certificate of freedom and then handed the folder to Jarena. She watched as Jarena stared at the birth document. "Georgie told me his mother saw these papers. I was afraid she'd tell everyone in town. I didn't want you to hear this from anyone else."

"This isn't possible. I was born in Kentucky, not New Orleans. This is something you made up and put on this paper."

Lilly heard the words but was without the strength to argue. She could no longer keep her eyes open. She slipped back into a state of unconsciousness.

———

Jarena held the paper between her fingers while Lilly's words repeated in her ears like a clanging bell. The unwelcome clamor refused to fade away. Jarena wanted to shake Lilly out of her unconscious stupor and force her to take back the claim. She tossed the piece of paper onto the bed and rushed downstairs.

She wanted to speak with her father, but that was impossible—at least until Sunday. There was no one else to talk to about this, and Jarena suddenly felt very alone. She dropped into an overstuffed chair in the parlor and folded her arms across her chest. She rocked back and forth while tears flowed freely down her cheeks. Through tear-blurred vision, she examined her arms. No one could deny her skin was several shades lighter than the twins', though she wasn't nearly as pale as Lilly. What about her father? Had he been white or colored? Her thoughts swirled as she dropped forward until her face rested in her lap. With her voice muted by the fabric of her skirt, Jarena sobbed—deep, heaving moans of agonizing pain.

A loud knock startled her, and Jarena sat up and wiped at her face with the corner of her apron. Had Georgie returned to bring even more proof of her heritage? She was sure her face was puffy and tear-stained, yet Mrs. Boyle would begin thumping on her bedroom floor if the knocking continued. Jarena kept her face turned downward as she opened the door.

"Jarena! I was beginning to wonder if anyone was going to answer."

She immediately recognized the voice and glanced up in spite of herself. "Moses." His look registered surprise, and she hastily turned away. "I must look a fright. Please forgive me."

"May I come in, Jarena?"

"Of course." She stepped aside to permit him entry. "Forgive me. I'm weary and am having a rather tearful day. I trust you won't tell Dr. Boyle. I wouldn't want him to think me incapable of caring for his wife and the house."

"And your aunt Lilly," Moses added.

"Yes—Aunt Lilly."

Jarena felt numb, as though she'd been sucked into a place where nothing could touch her, where nothing could make her feel better or worse. She wondered if this was how Aunt Lilly felt in her current state of unconsciousness—a part of the event and yet separate, somehow floating above and observing the entire scene.

Moses could not know. She must act as if nothing had happened. "Have you had any word from Truth?" Her question was silly. If Moses had received a letter, he would have been shouting with joy. Instead he appeared somber—almost sad.

"No, nothing. I don't suppose the Boyles have heard anything from Macia or the school?"

"Dr. Boyle hasn't mentioned a letter. I believe he would have come and talked to you." She felt ridiculous carrying on this inane conversation while her aunt lay upstairs professing to be her mother. The very thought made her want to scream. "Did you want to speak to Dr. Boyle? He hasn't returned home. I'm certain you'll find him at his office."

Moses pulled a handkerchief from his breast pocket and wiped his forehead. "Warm today, isn't it?" He folded the square and shoved it back into his pocket. "In reality, I came to speak to you, Jarena, but since you're not feeling well . . ."

"I'm feeling fine. Merely weary from tending to Mrs. Boyle and Aunt Lilly. Oh, you're wondering if I've completed my article for the newspaper. That's it, isn't it? I must apologize, for what with—"

"No, Jarena. I've . . . I've had word from Fort Concho."

She waited, not breathing, afraid that even one breath of air might make her shatter.

Moses reached for her hand and enveloped it in both of his own. "I'm afraid that the news isn't good. I've received word that Thomas's company engaged in a deadly skirmish while attempting to bring Victorio and his men back across the border from Mexico. Thomas and two other men didn't return from that battle."

Jarena stared at him, unable to make a sound.

"I'm so sorry to bring this news. I debated whether I should tell you. I pray I've done the right thing."

Moses's words were the last sound Jarena heard before she collapsed into his arms.

———————

Jarena roused to the acrid odor of spirits of ammonia. She lurched back and flailed her arms, hoping to escape the burning sensation invading her nostrils.

"Good! She's coming around. Can you hear me, Jarena?"

She sputtered and pushed at Dr. Boyle's hand. "*Please*. Take that away."

Dr. Boyle assured someone nearby that she would be fine. She forced her eyes open. Bright sunlight filtered through the sheer curtains and framed Moses's figure. He and Dr. Boyle had aligned themselves beside the divan, and they stood peering down at her.

"Why don't we see if you're able to sit up?" Dr. Boyle gently assisted Jarena into an upright position. "There! You're doing beautifully. Any dizziness? Do tell me if you feel as though you're going to faint again."

He adjusted a pillow behind her head and then leaned back to observe her. "Any previous history of fainting?"

Jarena returned his attentive look. "No. I've been quite weary of late."

"And little doubt, what with caring for my wife, your aunt, and this house. For a doctor, I haven't been very perceptive. I should have noticed the toll this was taking on you. And then, the news of Thomas. I am so very sorry, my dear." He gently patted her hand. "I believe you should go to your room and rest. I can look after Margaret and Lilly for a few hours."

"Thank you, Dr. Boyle. I appreciate your kindness. But I should be fine in an hour or so—a short nap should help." Jarena traced a finger across the tufted velvet of the divan. "Is there a possibility I might go to Nicodemus to see my father sometime soon?"

"Yes, of course. I can see to things here at the house, and I'm certain Betsy Turnbull would be willing to lend a hand."

Jarena pictured Betsy Turnbull serving her aunt and Mrs. Boyle their meals and nearly withdrew her request. Betsy cared little about personal cleanliness, and she consistently manifested that point of view. However, Jarena decided she truly did not care what Aunt Lilly thought, and Dr. Boyle should be able to placate his ailing wife for a day or two.

Moses leaned closer and offered an encouraging smile. "I'll plan to drive you over on Saturday, and we can attend church in Nicodemus the next day, if you like. I know your father and Grace will both be delighted to see you."

Brushing a stray hair from her forehead. Jarena accepted his offer.

"Now, if you'll excuse me, I believe I'll go upstairs and rest."

Both men jumped to their feet. She could feel their eyes on her as she walked out of the room. Obviously they believed a journey to Nicodemus would bolster her spirits. They had no idea why she truly wanted to go home.

She paused outside Lilly's door, surprised to see her aunt looking back from her bed. "Can we talk?" Lilly's voice was a hoarse whisper.

The faint scent of Lilly's perfume wafted through the doorway to remind Jarena of the woman's past. "You can say nothing I wish to hear, and there is nothing I wish to say to you." She turned on her heel and walked away.

Jarena fell onto her bed and covered her eyes. Her thoughts skittered back and forth erratically between Thomas and Lilly. A tight knot had taken up residence in her stomach and refused to dissipate. A tapping sounded on the wall that separated her room from Aunt Lilly's. Jarena rolled onto her side and covered her ears. Let her tap—she had a bell on her bedside table. Dr. Boyle would come and lend aid if she needed it.

When she could stand it no longer, Jarena jumped up from the bed and went to Lilly's door. Her jaw was clenched tight, and her fingers dug into the doorjamb. "What do *you* want?"

Jarena's venomous attack seemed to defeat Lilly with the accuracy of an asp striking its prey. Pain surfaced in Lilly's dark brown eyes.

"Only what you promised. Forgiveness."

Jarena swallowed a gasp as she hastened back to her room. Lilly's soft words hung in the air like a thundercloud waiting to burst.

Forgiveness.

~ 23 ~

Nicodemus, Kansas

Ezekiel paused for a moment and watched his neighboring farmers as they cut and topped the sorghum cane crop. He pulled his handkerchief from his pocket to wipe his forehead and neck. Once again they were sharing their tools and labor, just as they had during the wheat harvest. Harvesting the huge six- to twelve-foot stalks was difficult work, and early on, the men had learned that trading off jobs was essential in order to maintain their strength throughout the day.

Though Ezekiel preferred operating the thin-bladed stick that cut off the leaves, he also spent his share of time removing the head of seeds from each stalk or cutting off the bare stalks and loading them into the wagon. Except for John Lovell, most of the farmers planted only enough cane for their own use, so the harvesting didn't take too long at any one farm. John, who had brought his mill and evaporating pan from Kentucky, planted cane as his cash crop and traded the use of his mill in exchange for labor to harvest his large crop. Ezekiel secretly believed John got the best of their arrangement—he figured he was being paid less than nothing for the hours he worked in John's fields—but Ezekiel loved the taste of sweet sorghum over warm biscuits, so he didn't complain.

More than anything, it pleased him to see Grace enjoy her time with the womenfolk as they worked together feeding the cane into the mill, tending the fire, or skimming the boiling syrup. Grace missed the companionship of her sisters—of that there was little doubt.

Perhaps he should send word to Dr. Boyle that Jarena was needed at home. After all, he hadn't intended to have his eldest daughter remain in Hill City so long. If he insisted on Jarena's return, the doctor could likely find someone else to nurse his wife and help with the cooking. No one so skillful as Jarena, of course, but surely someone would step forward to assist. Ezekiel jumped down from the cane-laden wagon and began unloading the cumbersome stalks.

"What you thinking about, Pappy?"

Grace's question startled Ezekiel from his thoughts, and he dropped the heavy armful of stalks atop the waiting pile. "I's thinking 'bout the fact that Jarena's been gone from home way too long. Thinkin' maybe it's time I send word to Dr. Boyle that we's needin' her back home. I ain't wantin' to add to Dr. Boyle's problems, but I's ready for Jarena to come home. What you think 'bout me doing such a thing?"

Grace fed a few stalks into the horse-powered mill and then watched for a moment as the heavy rollers began to flatten and crush juice from the cane. "I miss Jarena—maybe even more than I missed Truth when she went over to Hill City. I reckon that's because now there's nobody left at home but the two of us."

He winked before grabbing another armful of cane. "And maybe 'cause you gots to do all the cookin'?" He continued with another armload. "Looks like John's gonna have a right nice yield on his cane dis year."

"Looks that way. I told Mrs. Lovell I wouldn't be helping tomorrow, and she's mighty unhappy. I figure since none of the men except you brought their womenfolk to help, I shouldn't have to be here every day."

Ezekiel noted that Grace was watching his reaction closely. "Ain't no denying we got work at home that needs to be done. Where is Mrs. Lovell?"

"Over by the fire skimming. She'll send me over there this afternoon when the sun's beating down the hottest. She got mad at me yesterday when I let the syrup in the evaporating pan get too thick."

Ezekiel unloaded the final shafts of cane. "Guess she can keep that batch fer her own use instead of selling it. I best get back out to the field afore they wonder what's happened to me. We'll talk more when we git home tonight."

However, further discussion was set aside. When they arrived home, Jarena and Moses were there waiting for them.

Jarena glanced over her shoulder as her father and Grace entered the house. She continued preparing supper as though her routine ministrations had never been interrupted by her temporary move to Hill City.

Grace rushed to Jarena and wrapped her sister in an embrace. "Pappy and I were just talking about you this afternoon, and now here you are."

"And what were you saying? That you miss having someone here to cook and clean for you?" The words were tinged with austerity.

Grace stepped back as though a hand had slapped her. "No! We miss talking and laughing with you. We miss your cheerful smile, and we dislike the emptiness in our family when you're not with us." She peered at Jarena suspiciously. "Is something wrong?"

Jarena ignored the question, overwhelmed by her own feelings of pain and rejection. She wanted to speak to her father first—alone. Tell him how she'd wrestled with her questions over the last several days. Tell him the innumerable feelings she'd experienced since discovering and accepting the fact that he wasn't truly her father. Tell him of her anger for the years of lies and deceit. And then force him to explain how he had so easily decided to cloud her life by a horrible lie.

So far as Jarena was concerned, her only family connection remained with Lilly—but Jarena didn't want Lilly! The very thought caused her spine to stiffen and tears to well in her eyes.

Her father placed his hat on a peg near the door and sat down beside Moses. "This here's a good surprise. Almost like you two knowed what I was thinkin' earlier today." Ezekiel proceeded to explain, and when he finished, he looked expectantly at Jarena. "What you think? You wanna plan on comin' back home, daughter?"

Jarena blended flour and melted butter into the chicken stew and then stirred as the mixture bubbled and began to thicken.

"You hear me, Jarena?"

"Oh, I thought you were speaking to Grace. Beyond praying the news regarding Thomas is incorrect, I have no plans. However, I don't think I'll be returning here anytime soon."

Ezekiel frowned and hunched forward to rest his long arms across his thighs. "What news? Ain't nobody told me 'bout no news from Thomas. What'd you hear from him?"

"Moses received word from the army that Thomas was involved in a skirmish with the Indians. He and a couple of other soldiers didn't return to the fort." Jarena recited the words in a dull, lifeless tone.

Her father looked shocked. "You's sayin' them words awful easy-like." He turned his attention to Moses. "You think maybe she's tryin' to hide her sorrow?"

"You don't need to talk as if I'm not in the room with you. I'm present and can hear what you're saying. Quite honestly, if I displayed all the pain I've been forced to bear over the past week, I'd flood this entire soddy with my tears. But my tears aren't going to change anything. Not about Thomas and not about *you*."

"*Me?* What you needin' to change 'bout me?"

"Lilly got herself run down by a carriage over in Hill City. She's wavering between life and death and had an enlightening piece of information for me. We'll talk after supper." Jarena watched her father closely and saw his jaw clench. He knew exactly what Lilly had disclosed.

Grace slumped in her chair. "Seems there's nothing but bad news coming our way."

"Now that's a fact," Jarena agreed.

Ezekiel patted Moses on the back. "Have you had any word from Truth? I'm getting a might worried 'bout that situation. Nearly time for the weddin', and that gal's still off in New York."

"I'm worried too, Ezekiel. Dr. Boyle had a letter from the school last week. They said Macia is still ailing and now Truth hasn't been doing well—they say that's why she hasn't written. The doctor was supposed to visit, and they said not to worry."

Ezekiel poured a basin of water and washed his hands. "How's a person s'posed to do that? Ain't been nothin' but worry since she got on that train."

After drying his hands, Ezekiel joined them at the table and prayed for the safety of Thomas, Truth, and Macia before helping himself to one of the flaky biscuits and a hefty serving of the chicken stew.

Although Grace attempted to keep the dinner conversation cheerful, the atmosphere during the meal was strained. Jarena blamed herself for the air of discomfort, but nonetheless she did nothing to lighten the oppressive mood. There were too many perplexing issues circling the table. Everything from Thomas and Jarena to Truth and Macia—each one of them dispiriting. Somehow, Grace's talk of Mr. Lovell's sorghum crop and the seven gallons of syrup harvested from their own small crop seemed unimportant and out of place tonight. So they poured the sorghum syrup on their hot biscuits and ate in silence.

When the meal had been completed, Grace got up to wash the dishes and Moses offered to keep her company, both obviously anxious to have Jarena and her father out of the room. When they were a short distance from the house, Ezekiel led her to his favorite resting place under the cottonwood tree.

"Why don' you tell me what I done that's troublin' you, Jarena?"

He'd barely completed the request when Jarena spun on her heel. "How *dare* you lie to me for all these years! Call me your daughter. Let me think of you and your wife as my mother and father. Let me believe that I had twin sisters. Push aside my questions about why I looked different from the twins!"

"Lilly done tol' you."

"Yes. Lilly done tol' me," she mimicked harshly. "How could you?"

He grasped her shoulders, but she yanked herself away. "What difference it make? You's the same to me as Grace and Truth."

"*What difference does it make?* I don't even know who I am! All these years I've been cooking and cleaning, caring for your daughters and your sick wife. During all that time, I believed they were my sisters and my mother. I believed you were my father. But that's all a lie. The only thing that's real is Lilly."

"That ain't true. Lilly's the biggest lie of all. She done broke her promise and tol' you what was never s'posed to be said. Now she's trying to turn you against me and yo' sisters. They's still blood—maybe not your blood *sisters*, but blood is blood, Jarena, and you's still one of this family."

Jarena tried to move away, but her father blocked her path. Each time she attempted to go around him, he moved in front of her. Her anger rising, she clenched her fists and stepped to the side. "Let me by! I have nothing more to say."

"You sit down, gal. I's gonna tell you the truth of what happened back when Lilly made her promise. What you's gonna hear from me is 'zactly what happened. After you listen, then you can decide 'bout who you is and iffen we's your family."

Jarena returned to the space under the cottonwood. Arms folded across her chest and her features taut with anger, she strengthened her resolve. Nothing he said would change her mind. Deceit and lies! She'd been taught to shun such sins all her life. Now he planned to convince her otherwise. Let him try.

He fidgeted and Jarena watched, enjoying his discomfort, wishing he could somehow feel the excruciating pain she'd lived with since Lilly's utterance—to know what it was like to have one's foundation stripped away.

"I ain't good with words like you, Jarena, so I's gonna speak from my heart and hope you's listenin' real good."

Settling his back against the cottonwood trunk, he rested his large hands atop bent knees and began his story. Speaking in a calm and even voice, he transported Jarena back to the early days of his life with Jennie, sharing their pain when she hadn't conceived a child early in their union and explaining how they had held to their faith, certain that God would bless them. And He did.

"It was close to Jennie's time to have the chil' when we had a letter from Lilly sayin' she was 'spectin' a chil'. Now I never did approve of Lilly, never liked her ways. She didn't have no husband, and she wanted us to take the baby and raise it like it was our own. We agreed after she promised never to lay claim on the chil'. She promised she'd never tell she was the one that birthed the baby. We figured God was givin' us a double blessing."

With a pained expression, he told how Jennie's and his child had been stillborn. Two days later, Jarena was brought to them by a man whom they'd never seen before nor since. Subsequently, everyone assumed Jarena was their child, and neither of them ever corrected that notion.

"I figure God was testin' me to find out if it was a chil' I wanted or jest proof of my manhood. When I accepted you and loved you like my own, I think God was pleased. Leastwise, that's what I decided when Jennie gave birth later to the twins."

Ezekiel wiped a tear from his cheek. He stared into the distance as he continued revealing what had happened so long ago—telling Jarena of the agreement with Lilly, the promises that had been repeated over and over to ensure that this day would never arrive.

"Jennie kept her word, and I woulda kept mine. Course, we always knowed there was a risk with Lilly, but we hoped jest once she'd do the right thing. And if she ever gets outta that sickbed, I'm gonna have me a word with her that she won't soon forget. I wanna know what possessed her to tell you. That woman ain't nothin' but selfish. She ain't never changed her ways." Ezekiel leaned forward and cradled his forehead in his palms.

"Maybe you should have told the truth from the start. Then all of this could have been avoided. Did anyone think about that?"

Ezekiel lifted his head and met her steady gaze. "Lilly was afeared your true father might hurt you. Don' know if that's a fact or iffen it's another one of Lilly's lies, but we believed her. We agreed it was best fer everyone. I still don' understand why she decided to tell you."

"Mrs. Nelson snooped in Aunt Lilly's papers."

"She never destroyed the birth paper, did she?" His eyes shone with sudden clarification. "She was afeared Mrs. Nelson would tell so she decided to do the tellin' herself."

Jarena pulled a long piece of grass and twisted it around her index finger. "She thought I'd forgive her."

"Did she say that?"

"Earlier I talked to her about God's forgiveness. Since I told her about God's forgiveness, I guess she figured I'd be willing to do the same."

"Not so easy, is it?"

She shook her head. "No. And the thing is, I don't even want to try and forgive her—or you. I'm not proud of how I feel, but at least I'm telling you the truth."

"And I's not proud of livin' a lie, Jarena. All I can say is we did the best we knowed how. Your mama and me loved you the best we could, and so far as we was concerned, you was and is our chil'. Ain't no piece of paper gonna ever change how I feel 'bout you." His eyes rounded as he looked off to the north. "Fire!"

As soon as he'd said the words, Jarena could smell smoke. Her father grabbed her hand and pulled her along toward the house. He hollered for Moses to begin wetting down burlap sacks as they neared the soddy. After ordering Grace and Jarena to fill the water barrels and protect the house as best they could, he and Moses hurried toward the fire, carrying a pitchfork and the wet sacks.

Jarena and Grace took all the buckets they could find and ran to the river. The men were still within sight when Grace began to anxiously question Jarena. Although Jarena was uncertain how much she should divulge, she tossed caution to the wind and truthfully answered all of Grace's difficult questions. When she had finished, Grace was teary-eyed, shaken by the startling disclosures.

Grace dipped her bucket into the river and watched as it filled with water. "But you'll always be my sister, won't you?"

A pain stabbed Jarena's heart. A part of her wanted to hurt this sweet doe-eyed girl she had nurtured throughout the years, for she wanted someone else to experience the keen ache, the anger and deceit, the deprivation of family that had transpired with only a few spoken words and a piece of paper. But she couldn't. "Yes, Grace. I love you, and you'll always be my little sister."

"If you want, I'll go back with Moses and take care of Mrs. Boyle and Aunt Lilly. That way, you wouldn't have to be around Aunt Lilly, and you and Pappy could mend your feelings."

"Thank you, but I don't think that's a good idea right now. I'd rather be in Hill City. Moses may receive further word from Fort Concho, and I want to be nearby."

Grace frowned as they hurried back to the house. "So you think there's still a chance Thomas is . . . ?"

"Yes, Thomas could still be alive. I'm not going to give up."

———

Ezekiel and Moses were nearly three miles from the house before they arrived at the blaze. At least ten sweating men were already fighting desperately with wet sacks, scoops, shovels, and anything else they could find, shouting orders and warnings, retreating when too hard-pressed by the flames, stopping occasionally to drink the water the women and children carried to them before beginning the battle anew.

An hour later, the men corralled the licking flames into the river's bend, where the fire eagerly leapt in a roaring blaze, threatening the dry grass that edged the far bank of the river. Before the blaze finally succumbed, a few unyielding sparks flew to the other side of the bank, but the burning embers were promptly smothered by several men waiting there with wet sacks.

Finally certain no danger remained, Ezekiel and Moses started back for home, with soot clogging their nostrils and smoke clinging to their clothes but thankful lives and crops had been spared this time.

The moon shone down as the two men silently trod back toward the soddy through the brown-black carpet of fire-scorched grass, each of them lost in his private thoughts. Ezekiel was sure Moses was thinking about Truth. Meanwhile, Ezekiel was thinking about his older daughter, worried that the anger burning in Jarena's heart would be far more difficult to extinguish than a blazing prairie fire.

— 24 —

New York City

Twisting her arm free from his wrenching grasp, Truth turned to see Marvin Laird's despicable sneer riveted upon her. He pinned her against the kitchen wall, his body quickly forming a prison from which she could not escape. Fear clawed at her throat and prevented even the slightest cry for help.

"You've been misbehaving, young lady."

She shook her head in wild abandon. "No." The single word was as much as she could force from her lips.

"You should remember that the bedroom occupied by Janet and Inez shares an adjoining wall with Macia's room. They tell me an entirely different story from yours. In fact, their tale is quite interesting. And though I didn't want to believe them, they have now convinced me that you are a devious young lady intent on leading others astray. You've broken my trust with your lack of character."

When Mr. Laird patted his chest as though heartbroken, Truth regained her pluck and dodged away from his hold. "*My* lack of character? I daresay you don't even know the meaning of character!"

"Be very careful, Truth. Remember that you are under my control, and I hold all of the advantages. Henceforth you will do exactly as you are told." His features suddenly relaxed, and he stepped back. "Those of us in charge of the school have decided you should sleep in Macia's room. In fact, you will be spending almost *all* of your time with Macia. I know this will please you immensely."

"Why are you doing this?"

He placed a finger to his lips and studied her. "I think you already know why. You've forced this upon yourself, my dear. When you begin plotting and attempting to undermine those in authority, you must surely realize your privileges will be withdrawn."

"Privileges? I'm not one of your students, Mr. Laird. I was sent here to accompany Macia Boyle back to Kansas, and that's what I still intend to do."

"You see? You're such a headstrong girl—downright defiant at times. In the future, you will lend minimal assistance to Daisy. You will not speak to Silas, nor will you go to the carriage house at any time. Have I made myself clear?"

Truth's palms turned clammy. Not talk to Silas? How would they ever finalize a workable plan of escape? They'd had little enough success even when they'd had their evenings together.

"I'll need to gather my belongings."

"Daisy has already seen to that. Your bags are upstairs in Macia's room, and I've had a cot placed near her bed." Mr. Laird pulled his pocket watch from his jacket and viewed the time. "In fact, you may go upstairs now. Do not leave the room unless you are summoned by Daisy or another member of the staff. And that does *not* include Silas. Have I made myself perfectly clear?"

Truth remained silent. If she spoke, she would likely say something she would regret.

Mr. Laird flicked his hand at her as though she were a pesky fly. "Go on now. I have other matters that require my attention, but remember what I've told you."

Hastening from the room, Truth could feel Mr. Laird watching her. She marched up the stairs, her anger mounting as she climbed each step. How dare Inez and Janet spy on her and then report their findings to Mr. Laird! They'd likely been holding a water glass to the wall and listening to every word uttered in Macia's room. She'd like to tell the two of them they were placing Macia's life in jeopardy, but that would do little good. They would report those words to Mr. Laird, too. Instead, she must be more vigilant—and quiet. However, the latter might prove difficult. As time passed, Macia had grown increasingly loud and belligerent during her waking hours—and much more difficult to calm. Somehow she must find a way—a way to keep Macia quiet and a way out of this house and back home.

Mr. Laird had been correct: Her baggage was in Macia's room, and a small cot had been set up alongside one wall. Of course, Macia was sleeping soundly. Truth opened her large satchel and lifted out a shirtwaist. Wait . . . perhaps she shouldn't unpack. If she and Silas were going to leave, she'd want to be prepared—and if anyone questioned her, she could merely claim an inadequate amount of storage space in the room.

Somehow this decision was a comfort, an affirmation that she would leave this place one day. As she refolded and tucked the shirt-waist back into her valise, Truth's finger scraped across a piece of card-board. She examined her finger and then dug into the valise for the cardboard sheet. A recent train schedule! Either Silas or Daisy must have placed it in her valise before delivering the baggage to Macia's room. Her excitement grew as she studied the list. Possibly Daisy would agree to carry messages back and forth to Silas, and they could continue to plan their escape.

As Macia began to stir, Truth quickly tucked the schedule back into her suitcase. She would locate a better hiding spot later. She stood beside the bed.

"Is there anything you need, Macia? A glass of water? Would you like to sit up for a while?"

"Yes, Truth. Please help me into the chair."

After she was situated, Macia grasped Truth's hand. "Earlier in the week, I was having nightmares. Terrible dreams. A man who looked like Mr. Laird was dressed in white and told me my parents had died. He handed me a paper to sign. I argued, saying I didn't understand, but he said he'd take care of everything if I signed the papers. It all seemed so real. My parents—are they dead?"

"They are very much alive. Would you like to go home and see them soon?"

Macia was more lucid than Truth had seen her in weeks. "Yes, I would. Why don't you make arrangements with the school for my departure? Do you think you could manage the task on my behalf?"

Truth stared at Macia, completely dumfounded by her change in disposition. Except for her disheveled hair, Macia looked and sounded normal. Her eyes were bright and her speech articulate, yet Truth remained apprehensive. She would approach Macia cautiously and see where their discussion might lead. "You seem to be feeling quite well today. Do you know what's brought about this sudden improvement in your health?"

Macia cast a furtive look toward the door and motioned Truth closer. "I ceased taking the medication Mr. Laird brings to me each night. I pretend to take the pill but remove it from my mouth once he leaves the room. And I don't drink any of the water or tea he gives me. He hasn't yet discovered my trickery."

"But what of the nightmares you mentioned? When did they occur?"

"The night I took my final medication. I've not taken it since. I suppose it was three nights ago. I was awake when Daisy brought your baggage and set up the cot, but I pretended to be asleep. I even watched you begin to unpack your clothing."

Now assured that Macia was mindful of their situation, Truth explained the need for their escape. She outlined her tentative plan but also detailed the fact that her move from the carriage house had further complicated her ability to make any definite plans with Silas. "Unlike Janet and Inez, Silas and Daisy can both be trusted. I've promised Silas he can come with us to Kansas. You won't mind if he comes along, will you?"

"Of course not. I trust your—"

Before Macia could complete her sentence, the door burst open. Mr. Laird's jaw was twitching. "I *thought* I heard voices as I was passing." His face contorted into an angry scowl as he looked at Truth. "I told you Macia needs her sleep if she's going to return to good health, and already you've kept her awake with your nonsensical chatter. I don't know what I'm going to do with you, Truth." His voice carried an ominous tone, and she instinctively backed away.

"Do come and see me, Marvin. Please don't be angry with Truth. I'm feeling weak, and I was asking her to go and locate you. She was fearful and seemingly thought she wasn't permitted to leave the room. But I told her she must have misunderstood your directions. Surely she's here to fetch help if needed, isn't she?" She batted her lashes and held onto his hand.

Marvin patted her trembling hand. "Well, yes, of course." He turned toward Truth. "If Macia has any medical need, you are to come and fetch me. Do not hesitate to leave the room for whatever she might need. Do you understand?"

"Yes, Mr. Laird. So long as we both understand and remember what I'm permitted to do."

Mr. Laird studied Macia's face. "I'll be back with your medicine shortly." As he walked to the door, he stopped alongside Truth. "I'm possessed of a sharp mind, Miss Harban. I'll not forget *anything* I've told you."

Truth remained fixed until the door closed. She looked at Macia and held a finger to her pursed lips. "Let me help you back into bed, Miss Macia." She crossed the room and leaned down near Macia's ear.

"He's outside the door—likely watching through the keyhole." She straightened the bedcovers and then helped Macia from her chair. "Now then, let's get you into bed. Mr. Laird will soon be returning with your medicine." They grinned at each other as they finally heard Mr. Laird's footsteps retreating down the stairs.

Once Mr. Laird had given Macia her medicine and then departed again, Macia removed the pill from under her tongue. "I'm accumulating quite a collection." She grinned and placed it in her silver hairpin box with the others. "Now, let's pen that message to Silas."

Worried Janet or Inez might return to their room or be listening outside the door, they kept their voices low as they worded the letter to Silas. They studied the train schedule and completed the missive only moments before Daisy arrived with Macia's supper tray.

Truth relieved Daisy of the tray and then motioned her farther into the room. "Would you give this letter to Silas?" she whispered.

Daisy took the envelope and turned it over in her hand. She nodded and tucked it into her pocket. "Mr. Laird says afta Miss Macia's finished wid her supper, you should bring the tray downstairs an' eat in the kitchen. He says you's to help me clean the kitchen."

"Of course. I'll be down to help you shortly."

Daisy smiled and patted her apron pocket before leaving the room.

Truth waited patiently while Macia ate her supper. She would be glad for a change of scenery, even if it meant washing pots and pans or scrubbing the kitchen floor. She had already grown weary of sitting in Macia's bedroom. When Macia finally wiped her mouth and placed the napkin on her plate, Truth jumped to her feet.

"I'll be back when I've finished up in the kitchen. It may be late before I return." She balanced the tray on her hip and reached for the doorknob.

"I'll wait up for you," she said quietly. "I have a book to read, and I'll be anxious to know if Daisy has been able to accomplish her task."

Truth nodded and hurried off to the kitchen. When she returned several hours later, Macia was asleep. Her book had fallen to the floor, and she was sprawled across the bed. Truth attempted to gently rouse Macia, but when that failed, she gingerly shook her shoulders—all to no avail. Truth's heart thumped wildly, and her mouth felt as though she'd eaten a wad of cotton. She feared Macia was once again languishing in a medicated slumber.

CHAPTER

— 25 —

Hill City, Kansas

J arena sensed that Moses wanted to talk on their return journey to Hill City Sunday after church, but the last thing she wanted was a lengthy discussion. She hoped he would soon tire of her abrupt one-word answers and quit asking questions. Surely it was obvious she didn't want to talk.

"Looks like a good spot to water the animal," Moses said as they drew near to a small tributary of the river. "Close enough to noonday that we might as well have our lunch."

Jarena begrudgingly agreed, although she didn't want to stop. Moses would likely find the silence uncomfortable and ply her with questions. However, this was his horse and buggy, so she took his hand and stepped down after they came to a halt near the water's edge.

Moses handed her the basket, and she spread a tablecloth and laid out the food while he tended to the horse.

He soon strode up from the water's edge and joined her under the clump of trees. "Truly is a fine day, don't you think?"

She offered him a piece of chicken. "It'll do."

"It'll do?" He dropped to a sitting position. "Why, this is a glorious day, Jarena. The birds are singing and there's a fine breeze—even the sun isn't too hot, and that's quite an accomplishment in the month of August."

She could feel her face tighten with irritation. Couldn't he understand she didn't want to talk, that she wanted to spend this time contemplating her future?

Moses bit into a chicken leg and waited. When she didn't comment further, he wiped his mouth. "I know you're angry, Jarena."

"Pappy told you about Lilly?"

"Yes. And whether you want to believe it or not, your father is hurting, too."

"I'm not concerned about him. Isn't it enough that I must deal with Lilly being my mother? Now I must also face the fact that Thomas may be dead—it's more than I should have to bear."

Moses finished the piece of chicken and licked his fingers. "Why?"

She glared at him. "What do you mean, *why?*"

"Just that—why do you believe you're entitled to go through life without pain or suffering?"

"That's not what I believe. But I've already had my share of suffering and bad experiences. Many more than either Truth or Grace has had."

"Ah. So you're comparing yourself to others, and that's how you've come to such a conclusion."

"I truly don't care to discuss this with you. There's absolutely no way you can imagine the pain I've experienced over the past few days."

"No need to talk—you can just sit there and listen." He leaned back against the broad trunk of a cottonwood, and while the horse continued to drink its fill, Moses told her of his past. But this was not the minimal account that he'd given to Aunt Lilly when she had arrived in Nicodemus. Instead, he detailed the complicated story of his childhood.

Although Jarena had set out to ignore him, she was soon captivated by his words. He explained how his mother, a freed slave, had been captured by slave runners and then sold back into slavery and how the man whom he considered his father had left him behind and had gone off in search of his mother—with neither of them ever being heard from again. Then he told her of another slave couple who came from a southern plantation and raised him—the ones whom he continued to regard as his parents.

Moses took a molasses cookie from the basket and broke off a piece. "And don't forget that my blood father was the same white man who had sired my mother. In truth, he was both my father and my grandfather." He leaned back and ate the cookie, staring off toward the water. "Now here's the most important part, Jarena: I wouldn't change one thing in my life. There's been pain and sorrow, but I know that God was always in control."

Jarena gathered up the remnants of food and packed them into the basket. "That's easy enough said, now that it's all behind you."

Moses picked up the cloth they'd been sitting on and laughed. "You're right—it's behind me. But that doesn't change the fact that I lived through it, Jarena. And it was trust in God that carried me through. My life has been far more wondrous than I could ever have imagined as a young boy. All because I trusted God. However, it seems that you're not happy unless *you're* in control."

Where had she heard that before? Her father? Miss Hattie? But this was different. This wasn't about controlling anything or anyone. This was about being deceived. It seemed no one was interested in viewing things from *her* perspective.

"So you're telling me that God is in control of your life and it matters little to you that Truth is off having a good time in New York rather than coming home to plan her wedding?"

He placed the basket inside the buggy. "That's not at all what I said. It matters a great deal that Truth is in New York; it matters a great deal that I never saw my parents again—but I'm not in control of either situation. My anger or worry changes nothing—nor does yours."

"Don't you see? I feel as though I have no one. I don't truly belong anywhere."

"I disagree, but you must finally come to that realization on your own, Jarena."

When they finally arrived in Hill City, Moses helped her down from the carriage. "Thank you for taking me to see . . ." She hesitated and bit her lower lip.

"Your family? They are still your family, Jarena. Nothing will change that except you. Unless you continue to push them away, your father and sisters will feel no differently toward you than they ever have. In truth, I can't understand why you would do such a thing to people who have done nothing but love you." Moses strode back around the wagon and departed without another word.

Jarena ran up the Boyles' porch steps and into the kitchen, thankful that she found no one about. She started emptying the basket onto the counter, annoyed by Moses and his platitudes. "Nothing will change my family except me! Ha! As though I had anything to do with this entire matter." She yanked the tablecloth from the basket and tossed it onto the pile of dirty linens she'd be washing come morning—laundry that Truth should be washing and pressing. Instead, Truth would likely be sauntering up and down the streets of New York, admiring pretty dresses in the shop windows. How like Truth—always avoiding work. She stacked the basket atop several others in the pantry and headed toward the back stairway. Perhaps she could avoid seeing anyone for a while longer.

Laughter rippled from Lilly's bedroom as Jarena reached the top of the stairs. The mirthful sounds of happiness annoyed her. Why should others be amused while she bore such misery? Especially Lilly, the cause of all her pain.

Dr. Boyle stepped into the hallway. "Jarena! Do come in and see how well your aunt is progressing. She has experienced a miraculous recovery over the past twenty-four hours." He waved her toward the bedroom door. "I didn't realize you had returned."

She hesitated. "Yes. A short time ago. I'll stop in the room a bit later. I'm quite weary from the journey home."

Dr. Boyle drew closer. "Oh, do come in just for a minute. I want you to see how well our patient is faring."

Lilly was sitting up in bed, her eyes sparkling and her lips bearing a faint hint of color. She wore a lacy bed jacket and, from all appearances, was as fit as a fiddle. The sight only served to further irritate Jarena. It seemed as if God's blessings were being showered upon everyone but her—even decadent Aunt Lilly.

"You look tired, Jarena."

The woman's words were like fingernails on a chalkboard, yet Jarena instinctively smoothed her wrinkled skirt. "Well, *I* haven't been lying abed."

Lilly folded her hands in a prayerful pose. "And a bit out of sorts, also."

Dr. Boyle pointed to the chair near Lilly's bedside. "Do sit down, Jarena. I'm certain your aunt would enjoy hearing of your visit to Nicodemus. In fact, why don't I leave you two alone to visit, and I'll look in on my wife." Before either of them could answer, he hastened from the room.

Jarena waited only until she heard Dr. Boyle greet his wife before rising from the chair. "I believe I'll retire to my room, also. As you said, I am a bit out of sorts."

"Oh, do sit down, Jarena. Nothing is ever resolved by running away."

Jarena's derisive laugh echoed off the far wall. "You've been running from the truth all your life, *Mother*. Besides, we have nothing to resolve."

Lilly took Jarena by the hand. "Jennie was your mother. I was merely the vessel that gave birth to you. Seems you can talk about forgiveness, but you don't really believe in the concept. Oh, you speak about God's forgiveness, but what about yours? Aren't you supposed to exhibit that same Christlike characteristic? Isn't that what being a Christian is all about? Not just speaking the truth of God's Word but living it?"

Jarena clenched her teeth. "I see. You've lived an immoral life, but now you're an authority on how I should live mine?"

"I told you I grew up listening to all the same Bible verses and preaching as your mother. I know how I'm supposed to live; I just don't do it—and neither do you."

Lilly was wide-awake and waiting when Jarena entered her room with a breakfast tray the next morning.

"I trust you slept well and are in a better state of mind this morning, Jarena."

She ignored the remark and settled the tray on the bedside table. "Is there anything else you need?"

"Yes. Did you think about what I said last night? Or are you planning to keep on wallowing in self-pity?"

Jarena turned on her heel. "You are the most sanctimonious woman I have ever met!"

"Me? I've never professed to be anything except what I am. It's you who sits in judgment of others, not me. I count myself fortunate I didn't believe all your rhetoric about forgiveness. Otherwise, I'd surely feel as if I'd been made the fool."

Jarena's jaw went slack. "So you didn't truly ask God's forgiveness? You said those words only for my benefit?"

Lilly shook out the linen napkin and placed it on her lap. "I didn't mean anything I said, and neither did you, Jarena. Now leave me to my breakfast."

Ezekiel spent much of the next several days praying. When he arose in the morning, he prayed. When he worked in the fields, he prayed. When he ate his meals, he prayed. And when he went to bed at night, he prayed. Although he had long considered himself a praying man, Ezekiel hadn't prayed this much since back when his Jennie had been dying. Course, this felt much the same way—like he was fixing to lose someone he loved. Maybe not to the grave, but he was going to lose Jarena if he didn't do something.

When he and Grace completed the evening meal on Friday, he placed his fork across his plate. "We'll be goin' to Hill City come mornin', so we'll need to get up a little early to make sure we got our chores done afore we leave."

Grace's features brightened, and she squealed with delight. "Truly? Oh, Pappy, that will be such fun! We can see Jarena and Moses."

Ezekiel doubted whether the visit would be enjoyable, but he wouldn't put a damper on Grace's excitement. The girl had little enough pleasure in her life these days. Except for going to preaching services on Sundays, she didn't get to see many folks. Oh, Miss Hattie and Nellie stopped by once in a while, but they'd stopped coming very often. Most of the time Grace was working in the fields, and they'd find no one at the house to offer so much as a cup of coffee or a few minutes of conversation.

Grace was up well before dawn the next day, and Ezekiel surmised she'd likely not slept at all. As he hitched the horses, he prayed Jarena would have an open heart and mind. And, if nothing else, he prayed she would be kind to Grace.

Ezekiel discovered there would be little time for silent meditation on the journey, for Grace's enthusiasm bubbled over, and she talked the entire time. With the exception of their journey to Kansas, Ezekiel had never seen the girl so animated.

Grace sat up straight. "Can we stop and see if Moses is in his office, Pappy? He'll be mighty surprised to see us, won't he?"

Ezekiel agreed, and he brought the horses to a halt in front of the newspaper office. Before he could walk around the wagon, Grace jumped down and raced for the limestone structure. A small bell jingled overhead as she pushed open the door. Moses's astonishment was evident when he looked up from his desk and gaped at the two of them.

Grace clapped her hands together and hurried forward. "We surprised you, didn't we? I'd guess we're the last folks you expected to see walk in your front door." She glanced about the room as she talked. "Is that your printing press? How does it work? I'd sure like to see it operate. You going to be printing a paper today?"

Moses seemed dazed by the barrage of questions. Ezekiel shook his head. "She been yakkin' like this ever since we left the farm. Guess she's jest excited to get away from home fer a while."

Grace pointed at the printing press. "Look at this machine, Pappy. Is this where you put the paper, Moses?"

He nodded. "I promise to give you a demonstration before you leave town, but first I want to know what has caused this unexpected visit."

Grace continued walking around the printing press while Ezekiel took Moses by the arm and explained his concerns regarding Jarena. "Did she talk ta you when you was comin' back from Nicodemus last week?"

"Yes, a little. Right now she seems to believe no one understands her situation and no one has ever been more deeply wounded. I stopped by the Boyles' on Wednesday and asked her about an article she had promised to write for the newspaper. However, she appeared annoyed by my request."

Ezekiel rubbed his chin. "Did she write da piece after you talked to her?"

"Not that I know of—she hasn't stopped by the office. I went ahead and wrote it myself. I can't wait around when I have my own deadlines to meet."

"I understand." Ezekiel genially slapped Moses on the shoulder. "Maybe I kin talk some sense into her. I jest gotta find some way to make her understand. Ain't heard nothin' more 'bout Thomas, have ya?"

Moses shook his head. "No. And I don't expect to, either. Unfortunately, Jarena is holding out false hope that Thomas will return, but I fear she's setting herself up for more disappointment."

Grace remained at the newspaper office to help Moses print some broadsides advertising the upcoming county fair while Ezekiel walked over to see Jarena. The Boyle house was a pleasant structure—nothing like the mansions of the South, of course, but a fine-looking home—especially when compared to the dugouts and soddies that dotted the Kansas landscape.

Hat in hand, Ezekiel walked up the porch steps and knocked on the door. His reflection gleamed back at him from the oval beveled glass in the carved oak door.

"Lilly!" His jaw dropped when his sister-in-law opened the front door. "From all accounts, I thought you was on yer deathbed."

"Come on in, Ezekiel. I was on my deathbed, but I've had an amazing recovery."

Though his shoes bore no visible dirt, Ezekiel wiped his feet several times before stepping into the house. He peered about the foyer, feeling uncomfortable in such fine surroundings. "I come to see Jarena. She hereabouts?"

"She's gone down to the mercantile for Mrs. Boyle. She'll likely return in a half hour or so. Would you like to come in the kitchen until she returns? I was going to make myself a cup of coffee—care to join me?"

He followed Lilly down the hall. "If you don' think the missus will care. I don' want to get nobody in trouble."

"I'm certain both Dr. Boyle and his wife would be happy for you to have a cup of coffee. Sit down." Lilly placed the coffeepot atop the stove before sitting down opposite him. "I guess you and I have a few matters to discuss, also."

"You broke yer promise."

"For what it's worth, I hope you believe that I would have never broken my word to you—I'd have never told her if that snoopy Mrs. Nelson hadn't found the birth paper. I should have thrown it in the fire long ago. But somehow I just couldn't."

Ezekiel folded his hands together and rested them on the table.

"Guess it's best she knows. Livin' a lie ain't no good thing. But she's havin' to deal with too much grief all to once. I's mighty worried what's gonna happen if Thomas don' come home."

Lilly rested her chin in her palm. "All of this falls on my shoulders, except for Thomas. I shouldn't have come to Kansas. If I would have stayed in New Orleans, or even gone somewhere else, Jarena would have never known the truth. But I was so busy tryin' to escape my own troubles that I didn't give a second thought to anyone else."

Ezekiel eyed his sister-in-law suspiciously. He'd never heard Lilly sound so honest and down-to-earth. He wanted to believe she had changed, yet he didn't trust her. He never had. "What's goin' on wid you, Lilly? That bump on the head knock some sense into you?"

Using her apron to protect her hand, she lifted the coffeepot from the stove and poured two cups. After she'd taken a sip of her coffee, she said, "To tell you the truth, it wasn't the bump on the head—it was Jarena."

"Jarena?"

Lilly explained what had occurred at the Nelson house. She spoke with obvious embarrassment as she told Ezekiel how Jarena had found her removing money from the Nelsons' safe and how Jarena had later protected her by returning the incriminating evidence before it would be missed.

"When she thought I was going to die, she forced me to look at myself and the possibility of eternity in hell."

Ezekiel rocked back in his chair. "So *that's* why you's been actin' so kindly. I always did say there ain't nothin' like the fear of meetin' yer Maker to bring folks to their knees."

"That's true. But I think it might be something else I said that's really bothering Jarena. . . ."

———

Jarena shifted the basket of groceries on her arm and impulsively decided to take the rear entrance to the house. Passing by an open kitchen window, Jarena heard Lilly's spirited voice. Who was her aunt talking to? Jarena stood outside the window and eavesdropped for a moment. Her father! He was in the kitchen talking to Aunt Lilly. She placed the heavy basket on the ground, flattened herself against the cool, smooth limestone under the window, and listened intently.

Her breath caught in her throat as she heard Lilly tell of the stinging remarks the two of them had exchanged regarding forgiveness and deliverance. "I thought I could force Jarena to examine her own behavior and beliefs when I said those heated words. Instead of helping, I fear I've served only to make matters worse."

She heard the scraping of chair legs against the wood floor and wondered if her father was reaching out to comfort Lilly. "What's been said can't be snatched back. Jarena's a right smart gal. I been prayin' real hard that God's gonna show her that we was all tryin' to do right by her. And I'm prayin' God's gonna keep His hand of protection on Thomas, too."

Jarena strained closer to the window, not wanting to miss a word of their conversation. A twinge of guilt flitted through her consciousness, but she quickly pushed it aside.

"I thought Moses was the right man for Jarena. In fact, I even tried to do a little matchmaking between them."

"Even though Truth was promised ta him!" Her father's voice boomed out the window.

"Lower your voice, Ezekiel. You'll wake Mrs. Boyle with that hollering. No need to worry. I never could get either of them to look at each other like that. Guess I was thinking of Jarena as my own child and wanted someone for her that would be a better match. I shouldn't have done that."

"Hmph. There's lots of things you shouldn'ta did, Lilly. That's prob'ly the least of 'em."

Lilly's self-conscious laughter wafted through the air. "You're right on that account. Thomas is likely a fine young man. However, I don't want Jarena to suffer through losing someone she loves. She's too young for that kind of pain. I hope she can one day forgive me for the harsh words I said to her."

Jarena slid down the stone wall and dropped to the ground. With her face buried in her skirts, she continued to listen while her father and Lilly discussed her.

"Forgive me, Lord," she whispered. "Please forgive me." Tears dampened her skirt as she buried her face deep into the muslin folds.

Jarena continued to sob until she realized the voices had grown silent in the kitchen. Wiping her eyes, she gathered up the basket and entered the kitchen, startled to find her father and Lilly sitting at the table with their hands joined in prayer.

CHAPTER

— 26 —

New York City

After taking care to quietly close the door behind her, Truth tiptoed down the hall and to the back stairway. With each creaking step, she forced herself to wait and listen, worried that Inez or Janet might appear at the top of the stairs ready to report her to Mr. Laird. She had carefully listened at the adjoining wall, waiting for the two girls to fall asleep. At the sound of muffled snores, she'd finally felt somewhat safe leaving Macia's room. Yet she knew it could all be a ploy, since both girls had proven themselves devious. Ultimately, her need to speak with Silas outweighed her fear. Her plans had gone completely awry in only a short time, and Silas must be warned.

Under shadow of darkness, she exited the house and hurried across the verdant lawn that stretched between the main house and the carriage house, thankful for the moon illuminating her path. Truth prayed no one was watching, for the moonlight that lit her path would also expose her to any eyes that might be peering out from the main school building. She ran from tree to tree, pressing herself against each trunk and waiting for any sign of detection before proceeding onward. She raced toward the final tree, a mammoth oak with sprawling branches, and gasped when an arm suddenly encircled her waist and a large hand covered her mouth.

"Don' scream. It's me. Silas."

The hold softened, and she looked over her shoulder, needing to assure herself that it truly was Silas standing behind her. She relaxed and exhaled, thankful she wasn't looking into Mr. Laird's face. "How long have you been waiting?"

"Not long. I didn't figure ya'd be able to get out afore dark." He checked the house and yard for evidence of observers. "Wouldn'ta been surprised if you hadn't showed up at all. Figured he might have a bell or somethin' rigged up to your door."

Truth's eyes widened. "I never thought of that. Thankfully, Mr. Laird didn't, either. Otherwise, I would have wakened the entire house when I opened the door."

"Well, you's safe, and we'll be outta here come Friday." He patted his pocket. "I did jest like you said. I went and got ever'thing set with the tickets at the train station today."

She sighed. "Friday? I was hoping you hadn't purchased the tickets."

"Why? You changed yer mind 'bout goin' home?"

Truth detected a hint of irritation in his voice. "No. Of course not. But Macia has taken ill again. She's not going to be able to sneak out of the house with me if she's unconscious. Just when I think we have things figured out, something else happens. How are we going to get her out?"

Silas fell back against the tree and breathed deeply. "I think we's gonna be fine if I can talk Daisy into keepin' them other girls outta the way. I gotta drive the Rutledges and Lairds to the theater Friday night. Once I gets 'em there, I'll come back home 'stead of waitin' fer 'em like I normally would."

Truth's heart raced. "And we can use the carriage for our trip to the train station?"

"Right. With all three of 'em out of the house, I can carry Macia downstairs to the buggy and get her on the train. You think you kin get her bags packed without anyone takin' notice?"

"I'll try. Macia's begun sleeping most of the time again."

"I thought she quit takin' them pills Mr. Laird was givin' her."

Truth nodded. "I watched her take them out of her mouth and put them in a small silver box in her bedside table. Perhaps he's figured out what she was doing and found some other way to medicate her. Do you think that's possible?"

Silas shrugged. "You's the smart one, but I figure if Mr. Laird sets his mind to somethin', he's gonna make sure it happens. Ain't no doubt he wants to control her. She's lucky she ain't turned up dead like some of the others."

Truth grasped his sleeve. "What? You never told me about anyone *dying*. You said the other girls got sick."

"Um-hmm. They sure did. And most of 'em finally died."

"And then what?" She shook his arm as though an answer would drop from his shirtsleeve.

He appeared confused by her question. "They shipped the bodies back to wherever they come from—so's their folks could bury 'em properlike."

"But didn't the constables ever come and question anyone? Young girls don't unexpectedly die with no one asking why."

"Don' know, but I never saw nobody ask no questions."

"Didn't any of the girls' parents ever come and talk to the Rutledges or Mr. Laird after their daughters died?"

Silas kicked at a small mound of dirt beside the tree. "I don' know nothin' 'bout none of that. 'Sides, we ain't got time to be worrying 'bout what happened back then. We needs to worry 'bout right here and now. And I think you best get on back to the room afore someone finds out you's missin'."

Truth knew he was correct. A variety of questions came to mind, but she mustn't jeopardize their escape with needless inquiries—at least not now. She could question him further once they were safely on the train and headed to Kansas.

Truth managed to return to the house without detection. She slipped upstairs and slowly turned the doorknob while recalling Silas's comment about a bell. The door opened without so much as a squeak, and Truth sighed with relief as the latch slipped back into place.

"Where have you been?" The words cut through the heavy night air like a slashing sword. She whirled around and saw Mr. Laird outlined by the shaft of moonlight draping the room. He sat in the chair beside Macia's bed with his hands tented beneath his chin. Truth didn't know whether to run back out the door or speak with bravado. There was no way of knowing how long he'd been in the room. Fortunately, neither of the windows in this bedroom faced the carriage house. He couldn't have seen her with Silas. Encouraged by that fact, she decided to speak boldly.

"I wasn't feeling well. I went outside for a breath of air. I know I wasn't supposed to leave the room, but I decided you wouldn't disapprove. And I didn't want to disturb you over such a simple matter."

"You're attempting to play games with me, Truth. We both know you weren't supposed to leave this room, ill or otherwise. If you were in need of fresh air, you could have opened a window. Now why don't you tell me exactly where you were and what you were doing?"

Her mind raced for answers as she attempted to sidestep his interrogation. But nothing, absolutely nothing came to mind. When she remained silent, he stood and approached her. Pinching her chin between his forefinger and thumb, he stared into her eyes. "No need. I already know what you're up to, and it's not going to work."

Her heart pounded an erratic beat that made her feel as though she might faint. "You do?" Her words were no more than a hoarse whisper.

"Of course. I know everything that goes on around here." His eyes gleamed with smug satisfaction. "You forget that I have eyes and ears everywhere, and I can already tell you that you will not succeed."

"I don't know what you're talking about, Mr. Laird."

His scowl created deep creases in his forehead. "Daisy isn't nearly so brave as you. She crumples at the slightest suggestion of losing her employment. Need I say more? You had best heed my words, Truth.

Do not leave this room without my permission. Are we perfectly clear?"

She nodded, and he strode from the room with an air of authority. "But only for the moment," she whispered as he closed the door.

A prayer was on her lips when she fell asleep that night, and she was praying when Daisy arrived with Macia's breakfast tray the next morning. She rubbed her eyes as she greeted Daisy and took the tray.

"You sho' lookin' bad this morning. Didn't you sleep none last night?"

Truth shook her head. "Not much. Have the other girls gone downstairs to breakfast?"

"They's down there, and I's gotta be on my way pretty quick, too."

Truth motioned her closer. "Mr. Laird came to Macia's room last night. He said you told him about our plan."

Daisy leaned close to Truth's ear. "I told him you wanted me to go an' fetch the constable so's he'd help you get away from here. He was twistin' my arm and told me he was gonna discharge me if I didn't tell him what you was up to. I didn't tell him nothin' 'bout your real plans."

"Thank you, Daisy. Do you think he believed you?"

"Oh, yeah, he believed me. I told him you give me a letter to take to the police station but I burned that piece of paper in the stove. I told him I sho' weren't gonna bite the hand that feeds me."

Truth pulled Daisy into a quick embrace before she left the room. She prayed nothing would happen to cause Daisy any difficulty. Though she folded and packed some of Macia's belongings, Truth dared not empty the wardrobe or drawers. What if Mr. Laird or Mrs. Rutledge happened to look in the wardrobe and found it void of any clothing?

The next two days passed in a monotonous pattern punctuated by occasional surprise visits from Mr. Laird and one from the Rutledges on Friday evening before they departed for the theater. Mrs. Rutledge was dressed in a midnight-blue silk gown, with her hair piled high and adorned with bejeweled hairpins. Although her heavily rouged cheeks caused her pale skin to look eerily ghostlike, the woman seemed pleased by her own appearance. She stood before the mirror in Macia's bedroom, smiling at herself as she adjusted her brooch and smoothed her hair.

Mr. Rutledge tugged at his tie. "We promised Marvin we would look in on you before departing," he told Truth. "He's waiting for us downstairs. Come along, my dear."

Turning away from the mirror, Mrs. Rutledge followed her husband toward the door. "I believe supper is going to be quite late this evening. Seems Daisy had the stove too hot and burned both the potatoes and the roast. I'm certain she'll bring a tray once the other girls have eaten."

Truth secretly reveled in the news of burned food. Daisy *had* found a way to keep the others downstairs so the trio wouldn't be seen departing. Waiting only until she heard the horses and carriage at the front of the house, Truth began yanking Macia's clothes from the wardrobe and shoving them into her trunk and bags.

She did her best to rouse Macia, and though her attempts met with limited success, she managed to get her dressed. Rather than endeavor to fashion Macia's hair, Truth located a tall-crowned straw bonnet adorned with wide silk ribbons and flowers and tied it under Macia's chin. The hat was large enough to hide a multitude of hairstyling gaffes.

After what seemed far longer than the hour's wait Silas had projected, Truth heard the sound of footfalls racing up the rear stairway. Truth opened the door a crack and peeked out. She sighed with relief as Silas rushed down the hallway and into the room. He gave Truth an appreciative nod when he spotted the trunk and valises packed and ready to be loaded into the carriage.

Completely unaware of the turmoil surrounding her, Macia was propped into a sitting position in the overstuffed chair beside her bed. Her bonnet was slightly askew, and she snored softly while Silas removed all of the baggage.

When he returned up the stairs for the final time, he gathered Macia into his arms. "You lead the way, Truth, but be sho' you close the door after me."

She did as he instructed, careful to make certain none of the girls had wandered into the kitchen before waving him onward. The entire process had taken nearly a half hour—longer than either of them had anticipated. However, stealth had been required throughout the process, which was something they hadn't taken into account. And though Truth had grave concern over the welfare of Amanda, Lucy, and Rennie, she knew taking any of the girls into her confidence would have been foolhardy. She longed to tell Daisy good-bye and thank her one last time. Instead, she tucked a farewell note, along with several dollars of Dr. Boyle's money, into an envelope and placed it behind a stack of dirty dishes in the kitchen, which was a place no one else would look.

Truth stepped into the carriage and pulled Macia across the seat, hoping to hold her in an upright position until they arrived at the train station. She motioned for Silas to hurry, and she held onto Macia's arm as Silas urged the horses into a run. They made good time until they neared the train depot, where the streets were congested with both people and conveyances.

"What are we going to do, Silas?"

"Ain't nothin' we can do 'cept hope I can get this carriage through. Only other thing would be to leave all the luggage an' carry Miss Macia to the train."

"No. We'd draw attention—two coloreds carrying a white woman down the street. Even if we made it to the train, someone would likely remember or report us to the police."

Somehow Silas managed to keep the horses calm. They arrived at the station with barely enough time to load the baggage and them-selves. However, as they attempted to board the train, the conductor questioned them regarding Macia. "If you don't know what's ailing your mistress, perhaps she should take the train tomorrow. I can exchange the tickets for you."

"Oh no, sir. If I don't get her on this train, she'll never forgive me. She's got to get to Kansas for her wedding."

The conductor stroked his chin. "Getting married, huh? She's probably suffering from a bout of nerves. I would, too, if I thought I was going to have to go live in the hinterlands. You might be doing her a favor to keep her here in the city." He chuckled at his own remark while Silas swayed from the burden of Macia's weight. "Go on and board the train. You're holding up the line."

Truth wanted to tell him that he was the one holding up the line, not them, but she refrained and hurried ahead of Silas to find seats for the three of them. There were few passengers when they entered the

car, and Truth helped Macia stretch across the seat in a reclining position and then covered her with a blanket. Silas and Truth sat side-by-
side on the seat opposite Macia.

Truth poked Silas in the side. "What about the horses and carriage?"

"I paid a friend to take 'em back to the school. He's already on his
way. I told him to tie the horses outside the carriage house and leave
right away. Don' want Mr. Laird to see 'im, but I don' wanna be
accused of being a horse thief, either."

"A wise idea, Silas. It appears you thought of everything."

Truth settled in her seat and watched as the remaining passengers
edged down the aisle. A well-dressed white man stared at them for a
moment and then nodded at Truth as he continued through the car.
His eyes were the color of a soft blue sky, but his look sent an icy chill
racing down her spine.

CHAPTER

– 27 –

They'd been on the train only a short time when the older blue-eyed man approached them. He sat on the seat across the aisle from them, unconcerned that his long legs blocked the aisle. Without the formality of introduction, he focused his attention upon Truth and inquired about Macia's condition. Though Truth thought his prying questions rude and disconcerting, the man's fine suit and southern drawl were a signal she'd best remain submissive. Besides, Silas had begun to tap his foot at breakneck speed, a sure sign that he was on edge.

The man appeared satisfied when Truth explained they were accompanying Macia home due to her unexplained illness. However, his interest was rekindled when he discovered they were returning to Kansas. "Truly? That's where I'm going. I realize I haven't introduced myself. Cummings—Bentley Cummings, from New Orleans."

There was a moment of uncomfortable silence while Mr. Cummings expectantly waited.

Truth lightly touched Macia's blanket-covered arm. "This is Miss Macia Boyle. My name is Truth, and this is Silas." There was no need to give their last names—a Southern gentleman wouldn't expect last names from colored folk.

Silas leaned forward and rested his muscular arms across his thighs. As he arched his thick eyebrows, his forehead creased with tiny worry lines. "You's a long way from home, Massa Cummings."

Mr. Cummings nodded. "Business in New York with several stops along the way. And I'll be making a brief visit in Kansas before I return to New Orleans. I'll be traveling to a town called Nicodemus."

Truth perked to attention. "That's where we live!" She could barely contain her excitement. Word of their little Kansas community had spread to white folks as far away as New Orleans! "Leastways, that's where my pappy has his farm. My sisters live there, too."

"This is quite a coincidence. I knew a woman in New Orleans who left to join family in Nicodemus. I doubt you would know her. . . ."

Truth could hardly believe her ears. "Would her name be Lilly Verdue?"

Mr. Cummings sat up straight. "Indeed. Do you know her?"

"She's my aunt. It was us she came to live with in Nicodemus." Truth could barely contain her enthusiasm. Such a chance meeting seemed impossible.

Mr. Cummings lifted a cigar from an engraved case and snipped off the end. He puffed gingerly until the tip glowed bright red and a narrow rim of ash circled the burning end of the cigar. "Do tell me how

Lilly is these days. It has been some time since I've seen her. I truly cannot imagine Lilly living out on the prairie. She's always been a woman who enjoyed the finer things in life—the kinds of things you only find in a large city."

Truth admitted Aunt Lilly had been unhappy with the small town but had begun to adjust. The man appeared to hang on Truth's every word, and as soon as she completed one answer, he fired another question.

More than once during their conversation Truth wondered if this might be one of the men whom Aunt Lilly had favored with her company—or perhaps he had paid her aunt to cast a spell on some unsuspecting victim. The thought was unsettling.

Although Mr. Cummings might find her question disrespectful, Truth's desire to know outweighed her fears. "How would you happen to be acquainted with my aunt, Mr. Cummings?"

"We had several mutual acquaintances and frequented a number of the same establishments. She's not the proper lady you might think."

His wink was enough to prevent Truth from posing any further questions. She wouldn't defend Aunt Lilly's previous life, but she didn't think Mr. Cummings's behavior was much better. She sighed with relief when he finally excused himself and retired to his private coach.

Ezekiel assisted Lilly down from the wagon. "Maybe Jarena shoulda come along."

"There's nothing wrong with me and no reason to take her away from her duties over at the Boyles'. I'm going to be making a long trip without any help—might as well start out doing things on my own, too. You know I'm in the habit of taking care of myself."

"Miss Lilly!" Georgie's eyes brightened when he opened the door and saw Lilly standing on the porch. "You came back."

"Only to pack the rest of my belongings, Georgie. I'm afraid I must be on my way. Is your mother at home?"

Before he could turn around, Mrs. Nelson walked down the hallway. "What a pleasant surprise, Lilly. You look wonderful. Come in, both of you. I do hope you've returned for good."

"I'm afraid not. I've decided Kansas isn't the place for me, after all. I believe I'll move farther north—perhaps even Canada. I've come to get my things."

"I do wish you'd reconsider. I've missed your help, Lilly." Perspiration dotted Mrs. Nelson's upper lip, and she fanned herself with one hand. "We could surely use some rain, couldn't we?"

"That's a fact. Cornstalks is startin' to curl from this heat." Ezekiel followed Lilly up the steps and into her room, with Georgie close on their heels.

Georgie stood in the doorway and said softly, "I promise to be good if you stay, Miss Lilly."

"Aw, Georgie. My leaving has nothing to do with you or your behavior. In fact, you've become a fairly well behaved young man."

He smiled at the praise and edged a bit farther into the room. "I'd be happy to help you."

"Why don't I call you when I've finished, and you can help Mr. Harban carry my baggage downstairs?"

The boy's eyes brightened.

Lilly hastily gathered her belongings. Although Ezekiel attempted to lend a hand, his skills at folding and packing proved clumsy, and Lilly soon shooed him away from the trunk. When she had completed her packing, she called for Georgie's assistance.

Moments later the boy clomped down the hallway at a run and came to a screeching halt in the doorway. Lilly motioned him forward. "I have something for you, Georgie—a remembrance of me." She held out a white handkerchief pulled into a bundle. She could see from the boy's eyes that he recognized it.

"Is it . . . ?"

"Yes. The rabbit's foot and the glass ball. They hold no power, Georgie. It was your own fear that caused you to obey me—no special power in either item."

He pointed to the amulet hanging on the black velvet cord around her neck. "What about that? How come you wear it if it doesn't have special power?"

"I've worn it for many years. So many, in fact, that I've had to exchange this cord numerous times. You may have it, also, if you like."

"Truly?" He looked up at her expectantly.

Lilly untied the cord and handed it to him. "However, if your mother disapproves, you must throw all these items in the trash without any argument. And I don't want you frightening others with them. Do you understand?"

"Yes, ma'am." He held the items in his fists and admired them. "What are you going to do when you need special help, Miss Lilly?"

She tousled his hair. "I suppose I'll pray, Georgie. What do you think about that?"

"That's what Mama says to do, too."

When the baggage had been loaded and Lilly had said her final good-byes to the Nelsons, Ezekiel drove the wagon back to the Boyles' and helped Lilly down. "What time is that Peterson feller s'posed to come fer ya?"

"Not for at least another hour. Let's go inside and have a glass of water. I'm completely parched." Lilly led the way into the kitchen and poured two tall glasses of water.

Ezekiel took the glass she offered. "Seems like you won over da entire Nelson fambly."

"Only because they don't truly know me."

"Don't be so hard on yerself, Lilly. You's makin' great strides. Jest keep it up."

"I hope I wasn't too hard on *you*. Unfortunately, I think Jarena exhibits some of your unforgiving nature. Jennie was always quick to forgive, but you always did hold a grudge."

He nodded. "Cain't argue that."

"Wouldn't do you any good to try—you'd only lose the argument." Lilly grinned while looking out the window. Jarena was watering the flowers in Mrs. Boyle's garden. "To tell you the truth, I'm still not certain Jarena has completely forgiven me."

"Be patient, Lilly. This was a big shock fer her." He sat at the table, and Lilly sat across from him. "She knows what's the right thing to do, and she'll come 'round."

Jarena gave Lilly a frown when she came into the house. "I thought you told me that problems couldn't be solved by running away. Isn't that what you said?" she asked sharply.

Lilly stood and took a step toward Jarena. "If I remain here, I'll place others in danger. I know Bentley will come looking for me. It's only a matter of time."

"But if you didn't do anything . . ."

"I wasn't involved in those terrible events, but he's not a man who will listen to reason. Jarena, I want to write to you after I get settled in my new place. Will you answer my letters if I write?"

Before Jarena could reply, a knock sounded at the front door. "Anyone home? I got to get moving right away."

"Sounds like Erik Peterson's hollerin' fer ya." Ezekiel pushed away from the table and stood up. "We's coming. Jest hold up a minute."

He proceeded down the hall to answer the door, while Lilly and Jarena followed. Lilly took hold of Jarena's hand as they walked down the front steps. "I told Dr. Boyle good-bye this morning, but I didn't want to disturb Mrs. Boyle. Please give her my thanks and tell her I said good-bye."

Jarena looked away, blinking rapidly. "I'll tell her."

Erik had already placed Lilly's belongings in his wagon and was holding the reins, obviously anxious to be on his way. Lilly hugged Ezekiel. "Thank you for your gift," she whispered.

He leaned back and looked into her eyes. "What gift, Lilly?"

"Your forgiveness." Before he could say a word, she turned and held out her arms to Jarena. The girl stepped forward to accept her embrace. "I know you're still suffering, Jarena, but I want you to remember I love you—I have always loved you. Otherwise, I wouldn't have made the choice to give you up. One day I hope you can forgive me." She brushed a fleeting kiss across her daughter's cheek before holding out her hand to Erik. He hoisted her up onto the box seat of the wagon and flicked the reins. The horses clopped into motion, and dust churned from beneath the wagon as it started down the street.

Suddenly Jarena ran toward the wagon, waving and shouting. "I'll answer your letters. Please write to me. Do you hear me, Aunt Lilly? Promise you'll write to me."

Lilly twisted around and waved in return. "I promise, Jarena. I promise."

CHAPTER

— 28 —

Jarena checked Mrs. Boyle's grocery list one last time and then signed the ledger book. With the purchases safely tucked into her basket, she bid Mrs. Johnson farewell and headed down the street. She hadn't gone far when she noticed a wagon rumbling into town. Three people sat atop the wagon, which appeared to be loaded with luggage and trunks and headed toward the Boyle residence. The girl sitting on the wagon seat looked like Macia Boyle. And was that Truth in the back of the wagon? Jarena shaded her eyes and looked more closely. Was that Erik Peterson driving the wagon? There were two other men in the wagon, as well, but she didn't recognize them.

"Truth!" Jarena's emotions were a strange mixture of excitement and apprehension. Truth was finally home. Jarena could return to her own life back in Nicodemus and Truth could resume her position with the Boyles in Hill City. But did Jarena really want to go back to spending her days cooking and cleaning for her father? Oh, she had forgiven him for the years of lies. But looking into his eyes every day and knowing he was not her real pappy . . . Could she do that? Did she want to?

Truth raised up on her knees and waved enthusiastically. "Stop the wagon. That's my sister!"

The driver pulled back on the reins, and Jarena ran to the wagon, arriving breathless and perspiring. "Truth! I can hardly believe my eyes. I have so many questions."

"Get in the wagon. We're going to the Boyles'."

A young man took the shopping basket and then helped Jarena into the wagon. "This is Silas Morgan," Truth introduced. "I met him in New York. He worked at the academy Macia was attending."

Jarena smiled and nodded at Silas. "Pleased to meet you, Silas. What brings you to Kansas?"

"I's gonna make me a home here." Pride surfaced in his eyes as he made the announcement.

"Good for you." It was the best answer she could come up with. Her sister had arrived unexpectedly and was riding in a wagon with two men she'd never seen before. Jarena had ever so many questions.

Erik brought the team of matched horses to a halt in front of the Boyle residence. "I suppose we should all go inside for proper introductions," Macia told the motley group of passengers, "and perhaps enjoy a cool drink. Is my father at home, Jarena?"

"Yes. He was going to sit with your mother until I returned."

Macia appeared encouraged by the response and led them onward.

Jarena came alongside Truth as they walked up the porch steps. "Who is that finely dressed white man?" she whispered.

"Wait until we get inside. You won't believe the story I have to tell you. But first, do you know if Moses is at the newspaper office?"

"I'm not certain. Why don't I ask Erik if he'd be willing to go and fetch him? I know Dr. Boyle is going to have endless questions to ask you and Macia."

While Erik hurried off to the newspaper office, Macia raced upstairs to greet her parents, momentarily leaving the others in the parlor. The mysterious man brushed the dust from his sleeve and approached Jarena. "We haven't been properly introduced, although I'm guessing you must be one of Truth's sisters."

"And you are?"

"Bentley Cummings—of New Orleans."

Jarena felt the blood drain from her face, and a loud buzzing started in her ears. *Bentley Cummings.* Aunt Lilly was correct: he had followed her. The room began to swirl. She was going to faint. "Excuse me. I'm feeling weak. Likely the heat." She dropped onto one of the overstuffed chairs and dabbed her forehead with her handkerchief.

Truth hurried off to the kitchen and returned with a cup of cool water. After taking several sips, Jarena mumbled her thanks. While the others looked on, she apologetically attributed her faintness to the unexpected return of Macia and her sister. Mr. Cummings and Silas sat down on the settee while Truth fussed over Jarena.

When she was finally in full command of her senses, Jarena grasped her sister's hand. "Sit down and tell me how you and Bentley Cummings happen to be traveling together."

Before Truth could open her mouth, Mr. Cummings explained their happenstance meeting on the train. He then proceeded to convey his overwhelming surprise upon discovering Truth was Lilly's niece. "When I realized Lilly was living in this area and I would be in the vicinity on business, I couldn't pass up the opportunity to see her."

Jarena shook her head. "How very unfortunate that you've come all this way to visit with Aunt Lilly and she no longer lives in Hill City."

Mr. Cummings's blue eyes were ice cold as he glowered at Jarena. "What do you mean?" The knuckles of his clenched fists turned white. "Is she making her home in Nicodemus instead?"

Though her hands were shaking and her underarms had grown sweaty, Jarena forced herself to speak slowly and calmly. "No. She decided to strike out and move to a larger city. She spoke of going to California. She wasn't happy here in Kansas. At least you were already traveling west on business. Otherwise, your trip would have been to no avail."

Mr. Cummings adjusted his vest. "I believe Truth mentioned Lilly worked for the local banker—as a housekeeper and nursemaid."

"Yes. But she's no longer in the Nelsons' employ."

Mr. Cummings stood, looking not at all pleased. "I understand. However, I am in need of a banker. I believe I'll go and meet this Mr. Nelson. I'm certain he will be able to assist me with my *banking* needs." Bentley Cummings stormed from the room, leaving a hint of foreboding hanging in the air like the scent of Aunt Lilly's perfume.

CHAPTER

— 29 —

Truth!" The sound of Moses's voice drifted through the open window of the Boyles' parlor. Truth jumped to her feet and hurried from the room while Jarena watched her. Jarena longed to be happy for the sweet reunion Truth would now experience with Moses. Instead, her heart filled with a stubborn fire of jealousy that refused to be extinguished. Life truly was unfair.

She forced a smile when the twosome walked into the parlor arm in arm. Their affectionate looks were like salt poured onto Jarena's wounded heart. Nothing had changed for Truth. She'd come home to a loving fiancé and untarnished family memories. But what did Jarena have? She was left with little hope that Thomas would ever return to marry her and with the unalterable knowledge that Aunt Lilly was really her mother. Aunt Lilly! Without warning, Jarena's thoughts returned to Bentley Cummings. Could he possibly be her father? She wanted to run after him and see if she could find any resemblance to her own features.

Desperately, she tried to recall exactly when Aunt Lilly had met Bentley Cummings. Was it before or after Henri Verdue? If Jarena was Bentley's child, did he know it?

Truth clapped her hands like an angry schoolmarm, and Jarena startled to attention. "Are you feeling faint again?" Truth asked.

"No. I was lost in my own thoughts. I remembered something that I must take care of. Please excuse me. I'll return shortly."

Before Truth could offer an objection, Jarena brushed by and dashed out the door. Stepping briskly, she hurried toward the bank, all the while worried that Mr. Cummings might already be gone. She walked inside the building, clutching her chest and gasping for air, relieved when she saw Bentley Cummings seated opposite Mr. Nelson. A large mahogany desk separated the two men, who were speaking in hushed tones regarding an investment of some type. Something to do with the railroad.

Both men seemed completely engrossed, and neither looked up when she approached. "I apologize for interrupting your conversation, but . . ." The men leaned back and stared up at her. They appeared to be struck dumb.

Now that she had Mr. Cummings's attention, Jarena had no idea what she wanted to say. Finally she asked to speak to him after he'd completed his business at the bank, and he agreed to meet her outside.

Minutes later, Mr. Cummings walked alongside her down Hill City's dusty main street. Fear had settled on Jarena, and she wondered if she'd made a horrible error. She walked onward, wondering if this man could be her father. Thankful to find the general store void of any customers, Jarena directed Mr. Cummings to the small table and chairs near the back.

"Is there something on my face?" Mr. Cummings asked as he sat down.

"What? Oh, no. Please forgive me. I didn't realize I was staring." She looked away and removed a loose string from her sleeve. "I was interested in learning when you and my aunt first met."

"Why?"

She met his piercing stare. "Since you traveled out of your way to visit her, I assumed the two of you must have had a lengthy friendship."

He stroked his jaw. "And why are you so interested in our *friendship*?"

Jarena's mind whirled in an attempt to formulate a satisfactory reply—one that would convince him. "I suppose I am intrigued by a man who would travel so far out of his way for a mere visit. I wonder if there isn't something else that motivates you, Mr. Cummings."

"And I wonder the same about you, Miss Harban. Did Lilly speak of me?"

"Only once—and rather disparagingly, I might add."

He chuckled. "That much, I believe. However, I think she spoke of me more than once, Miss Harban. Why don't you merely tell me what you want to know—and why you want the information."

Jarena inhaled deeply. "I wish to know how long you and my aunt were together. I want the information in order to establish whether you could be my father."

Mr. Cummings's jaw went slack, and his mouth opened in a look of utter and complete surprise. "Lilly is barren. She couldn't have children—she explained that to me years ago."

"How *many* years ago?"

"Fifteen or sixteen—I'm not positive. We met a few years after her husband, Henri, died. Certainly you don't believe Lilly is your mother." He stared deep into her eyes. "You do!" He laughed aloud. "Impossible! That woman never gave birth to a child."

"At least none that you knew of. She *is* my mother, Mr. Cummings. I have proof of that fact. However, she didn't name my father."

He shook his head. "Lilly never spoke to me of a child." He stood and backed away from her. "I'm not your father. You'll not get a single penny of my money."

Jarena jumped to her feet and faced him. "I don't want your money, Mr. Cummings. And don't worry; I now know in my heart that I am not your daughter. Good day."

———

Truth settled beside Moses, and when Jarena finally returned a short time later, Dr. Boyle motioned her toward a spot on the end of the divan. They were an odd gathering, a mixture of men and women, black and white, old and young. Truth wondered what folks back in Kentucky would think of the unusual assembly in Dr. Boyle's parlor. She steeled herself in an attempt to prepare for the many questions all of them would have. Perhaps if her recitation was detailed enough, the inquiries would be few.

An air of anticipation filled the room, yet it was quiet enough to hear the gentle rustling of leaves outside. Dr. Boyle nodded at his daughter, and Macia began the story. She explained that both her jour-ney to New York and early days at the school had been uneventful until she had fallen ill. Since there was little she recalled after taking to her bed, she asked Truth to continue.

As Truth told the group of the events that took place after her arri-val in New York, there was little doubt they were amazed at all that had occurred, especially her boldness in planning their escape while nearly succumbing to illness herself. They even applauded when she told of Daisy's assistance and Silas's bravery in completing the success-ful escape.

When Macia and Truth had completed their account, Dr. Boyle shook his head. "I believe everything you girls have said, but none of this makes any sense. Why would Mr. Laird or the Rutledges want to harm their students?" He rubbed his open palm along his jaw. "Obvi-ously something is amiss. Why would Mr. Laird have written several times advising me that Macia was feeling better?"

Silas whispered to Truth, and she encouraged him to speak. "Lotsa them girls got the sickness durin' the time I's been working there. I don't understand 'bout the Rutledges' business, but I heard 'em talk 'bout papers on the girls. Miss Macia and Truth figure it's somethin' to do with life insurance. I don' know what that is, but they talked 'bout life papers for them girls. You know 'bout insurance, Dr. Boyle?"

Dr. Boyle looked surprised. "Yes, I understand what insurance is, Silas. Are you certain that's what you heard?"

"Oh, yessuh. I heard 'em talk 'bout them life papers ever' time a fresh group of girls come to the school. When the new ones come, that's when they be in the office talkin' 'bout havin' them girls sign some kind of life papers."

Dr. Boyle glanced at Truth and Macia. "They must have been taking out life insurance policies on their students. Is that possible?"

Macia bobbed her head up and down. "I recall they had me sign papers when I first arrived at the school. I specifically remember because I argued with Mr. Laird."

"But your mother and I had signed all your paperwork," Dr. Boyle said. "I personally forwarded the forms to them."

"That's what I told him, but Mr. Laird insisted I sign a few other documents. I didn't read them thoroughly because Mrs. Rutledge appeared to be upset over the entire ordeal." Macia turned deathly pale. "Do you think they were trying to kill me?"

Dr. Boyle stood and paced in front of the fireplace. He finally came to a halt in front of Moses. "What do you think, Moses?"

"I think this is a matter that needs to be fully investigated. What if I contact one of the newspapers in New York City and advise the editor of our concerns? Perhaps he would be willing to assign a reporter to go to the school on the ruse of writing an article and help uncover the facts."

"Excellent idea!"

Excited voices joined the conversation as they formed a plan to force an investigation at Rutledge Academy. Only Silas appeared apprehensive. "Moses, I's askin' that you please don't be usin' my name when you write that letter to them folks in New York. I don' want 'em knowing I'm out here in Kansas. They's likely to send the law after me."

Moving to Silas's side, Truth gave him a reassuring smile. "Don't you worry, Silas. Moses won't do anything to jeopardize your safety. You have my word."

The affirmation was all Silas needed. He enthusiastically suggested the men make inquiry into the disappearance of Sally Treadwell, a young lady who had become ill and later vanished from the school. He lowered his head and stared at the floor. "Me and Daisy noticed that after any of them girls died at the school, there was always lots of money bein' spent."

An involuntary shudder coursed through Truth's body.

Moses shifted in his seat. "You know of girls that actually died?"

"Oh, yessuh. Probably six or seven since I been workin' fer them people. Strange how them girls was always getting sick. I figured somethin' was wrong, but I couldn' go to no police."

Moses stood. "Perhaps the police won't help, but someone must."

— 30 —

There were few options available for Jarena. Unlike Lilly, she couldn't run off to some unknown place and hide from her past, though she thought the idea a perfect solution. She had carefully folded and packed her clothing in the trunk and had only a few personal items remaining in the room. Pulling open the top drawer of the chest, she removed the leather folder containing her birth record. Aunt Lilly had given her the folder before she departed town—along with her permission to keep or burn the document, whichever Jarena preferred. She was staring at the paper when Truth walked into the bedroom. Jarena quickly closed the folder and placed it in the trunk.

Truth plopped down on the bed. "What's that you were looking at when I came in?"

Jarena bowed her head. She didn't want to discuss her past with Truth right now. Perhaps she never would. Why should she continue to endure the pain of discussing the matter? Let someone else tell her.

"Merely some papers—nothing of interest to you."

"Moses told me about you and Aunt Lilly."

Jarena shrugged. "Everybody has been talking behind my back." Truth's pained expression didn't faze Jarena. She cared little if her words stung. "You need not look distraught. Your life will go on as planned, Truth. I'm the only one who must daily suffer the repercussions of the lie."

"We weren't talking behind your back, Jarena. I was concerned over your odd behavior toward me, and Moses explained about Aunt Lilly—and Thomas. I am truly sorry for all the misery you've suffered. I do wish there was something I could do or say that would help. I love you, and nothing changes that."

Jarena jumped up. "But it *has* changed." She grabbed the folder from her trunk and flung it across the bed. "That piece of paper changed everything. You and Grace aren't my sisters. Your father isn't my father; your mother wasn't my mother. Lies! All of it! Nothing but lies!"

Truth moved toward her. "I can't change any of what happened in the past, but you will always be my sister. A piece of paper doesn't change what I feel in my heart. Say whatever you want, but you won't make me stop loving you. I won't let you push me away."

Jarena buried her face in her hands. "Each time I think I've come to grips with my past, a new situation occurs and the pain once again rises to the surface. I know none of this is your fault, Truth. I've been wrestling with forgiveness since the day I found out. In my mind I know they did what was best, but my heart is filled with such pain and anger."

"What is it Mama used to tell us? Time heals all wounds? Maybe that's what this is going to take—time and prayer."

"So you've grown wise during your short absence?" Jarena wiped her tear-stained cheeks. "Of course, you were always bright—you merely attempted to hide it, along with your ability to sew and clean." Jarena smiled and patted her sister's hand.

"I don't know if I'm wiser now, but I do know that I never want anything to come between us. You're the one I've always looked up to, Jarena. What would I do without you?"

Her firm resolve melted as she looked into Truth's pleading eyes. Rejecting her sisters would only create more pain for all of them. And how could she turn away from the two girls she had practically raised? Nothing could change their bond. Not unless she allowed it. "I'm sorry, Truth. I do love you, and I promise I won't let my feelings for you or Grace change. But you must bear with me if I forget myself and speak sharply sometimes."

There was little doubt the words delighted Truth. She hugged Jarena tightly enough to nearly squeeze the breath out of her. "Thank you, Jarena." When Truth finally released Jarena, her face was alight with pleasure. "As for your sharp tongue, Grace and I became accustomed to that years ago when you were constantly correcting our grammar."

Jarena laughed and nodded. "I suppose that's true enough."

"We best both get to bed. Moses hopes to start for Nicodemus early in the morning."

"And Silas? Where is he?"

"Dr. Boyle offered him Harvey's room, but I think the idea of staying here made him uncomfortable. When Moses offered to put him up at his house, he quickly accepted."

"What's Silas planning to do, Truth?"

"He wants to own a piece of land. Silas reminds me of Pappy when he talks about owning land. I don't think he has much money, so I doubt he can afford to purchase any acreage right away. He's good with horses, and he did lots of odd jobs at the school. Surely someone could use his help."

"I know there are lots of folks who could use his assistance, but whether they could afford to pay him would be entirely another story."

"If all else fails, I'm sure Moses could put him to work setting type at the newspaper office."

"Can he read?"

Truth frowned. "A little. But something will work out. After all, he wanted to come west."

Jarena walked to the open bedroom window and stared into the starlit sky. "But you still bear a certain amount of responsibility to help him, Truth. He wouldn't have come here if it hadn't been for you. Have you noticed the way he looks at you? I believe he cares deeply for you." With her arms folded across her waist, Jarena turned to face her sister.

"No. We're merely friends. In fact, we barely know each other. Silas knew I had marriage plans before he decided to help us. I told him about Moses."

Jarena regarded her sister with misgivings. "You may have spoken the words, Truth, but did you speak them from your heart so there would be no misunderstanding? Were you certain he understood before you convinced him to travel west and give up his previous life? For it's now quite obvious he can't return to New York and resume his position at the school."

Truth looked irritated, and she motioned widely with her hands as she spoke. "He's a man full grown, Jarena. He'll make his way the same as everyone else who's come to live out here. If he wants to leave Kansas, Moses and I will do what we can to help him. If he wants to stay, we'll help him with that, too."

The four travelers had bid their farewells and were settled into the carriage by dawn. Moses drove the coach with Truth by his side, while Silas and Jarena sat behind them. As they set out, Silas began to question Jarena. How far to Nicodemus? Did she think he could find work? Could he purchase land? At first Jarena attempted to answer, but he continued questioning her until she grew weary.

Jarena wanted to shake her sister and force her to answer some of his countless inquiries. "Didn't you ask Truth any of these questions before departing New York, Silas?"

He fumbled with his shirt sleeve and shook his head. "No, ma'am. I s'pose I shoulda, but I wanted to get out of that place. I's wantin' to own me a piece of land more'n anything, and Truth tol' me there was land for the takin' out here in the West."

"There's land to be purchased in Nicodemus. Is that where you plan to settle?"

"Don't know fer sure. I ain't seen it yet. Reckon I could get a job there? Moses says I might be able to hire out workin' for the livery or mebbe helpin' at one of the farms for room and board. But that ain't gonna help me get enough money to buy no land, is it?"

He was a likeable young man, but he sure had a lot of questions. Jarena wanted to offer encouragement. "If all else fails, I know my father could use an extra pair of strong hands. He and my younger sister are attempting to farm both his acreage and the land that lies directly adjacent. Truth may have mentioned that my future husband is off fighting with the cavalry?"

Silas straightened his shoulders as though mention of the military required he come to attention. "No, I don't believe she talked 'bout that. She did say she had two sisters, you and Grace. She said Grace is her twin." His proud countenance reminded Jarena of a young schoolboy who had properly recited his lessons. "You think your pappy might want me to help farm your beau's land while he's off fightin'?"

Jarena simply nodded. There was little doubt her father would be pleased to have the help, especially with the corn nearly ripe for harvest. But sending Silas into Thomas's fields to cut and shuck the corn seemed a betrayal of her loyalty. Oh how she wished Thomas were here to work his own land!

Jarena was thankful to see her father's house come into view. Apparently Grace had heard the wagon approach, for she came scurrying outdoors before the horses had even come to a stop. The moment she saw Truth, Grace began to jump up and down as if her feet were giant springs. When the two girls finally embraced, they bounced and laughed in unison.

"They look some alike, don't they?" Silas said to Jarena as he watched the two girls.

"Yes, but their personalities are completely different. Grace loves to work outdoors alongside Pappy. She's happiest when she's watching things grow, and she's much more thoughtful and quiet—though you wouldn't suspect that from watching her antics right now."

"They's sure happy to see each other." Silas gestured toward the luggage. "Iffen you tell me where to put these things, I can start unloadin'."

Jarena stopped to hug Grace and introduce Silas before leading him inside. "You can put my trunk over there. I can get the rest of my belongings while you bring your baggage inside." Although Jarena wasn't certain what her father would think of having another mouth to feed, she knew he wouldn't turn the young man away—especially if he should prove to be a good field hand.

Jarena stepped to the doorway and called to her sister. "Where's Pappy, Grace?"

"Out in the fields checking the corn. He'll be here soon."

Jarena donned an apron that was hanging near the sink before peering into a kettle bubbling on the stove. Rabbit stew. She could add some more turnips and carrots and make a big batch of corn bread to help stretch the meal. Pappy would expect his food on the table at noon, company or not.

When Ezekiel arrived a short time later, Jarena was ladling the stew into a large crock. "Good to see you, daughter." He kissed Jarena's cheek. "Food sure do smell good, too."

"He's been longing for your cooking ever since you left, Jarena," Grace said. "Seems like I can't cook anything to suit him."

Ezekiel poured water into the washbowl and winked at Grace. "You's doing some better, Grace. Practice makes perfect—you jest don' wanna practice. That apple pie you made a week ago was right tasty."

When Jarena and Truth introduced Silas, Ezekiel welcomed him heartily. "Silas, set down and make yerself to home."

The noonday meal was filled with a lengthy account of the many problems Truth had faced while in New York, along with the details of her subsequent journey home. She saved the final bit of news until last. "You'll never guess who it was that helped us on the train, Pappy."

Ezekiel poured himself another cup of coffee. "Don' reckon as I could. Was it someone I know from back in Kentucky?"

"It was a friend of Aunt Lilly's. Mr. Cummings."

All signs of cheerfulness vanished from Ezekiel's face. "Where's he now?"

"When I spoke with him, he said he had been invited to stay with the Nelsons," Jarena replied.

Ezekiel surrounded his coffee cup with both hands and stared into the dark brew. "He say anything 'bout comin' over here to Nicodemus?"

Jarena shook her head. "I'm not certain he believed me when I told him Aunt Lilly had departed."

"He'll prob'ly come over here to check." Ezekiel pushed his chair away from the table. "Daylight's wastin'. I best head back out to the field. Silas, you wanna come along? Might give you an idea if you want to take up farmin'."

Silas glanced at Moses, who appeared perfectly content to remain at the table. "You go on, Silas. I'm going to town to gather information for the newspaper. I've seen Ezekiel's fields, and I know I don't want to take up farming."

Ezekiel chuckled as he pulled his hat off a peg near the door. "You might want to take a side trip to Stockton while you's this far. Folks is rumoring 'bout one of the railroads layin' track in this direction. Now wouldn't that be somethin' if we was to get us trains comin' right through Nicodemus?"

Once Ezekiel and Silas had departed, Moses appeared anxious to be on his way. However, his offer to have Truth accompany him into town was met by Grace's immediate disapproval. With a good-natured laugh and an admonition that Truth discuss preparations for their wedding, he left the young women to themselves.

Grace gathered a stack of dishes from the table. "Have the two of you set a new wedding date?"

"I don't know if Moses will agree, but I'm thinking the first week in November will allow us enough time to properly prepare."

Jarena sometimes wondered if Truth really wanted to marry Moses, for it seemed as if she kept postponing their wedding. Though the problems in New York hadn't been of Truth's doing, she didn't need to wait another eight weeks to wed. She longed to tell Truth that if Thomas walked in the door, she'd be prepared to marry him that very moment. Of course, Truth hadn't ever been faced with the possibility of losing Moses.

Grace frowned as she grabbed a dish towel and began to dry one of the plates. "I don't think Moses'll want to wait that long. All he talked about while you were gone was that you weren't going to return in time for the wedding. I believe he thinks he's already waited much too long."

"And I may not be here in November, either," Jarena put in.

The twins swiveled around to face Jarena. "Where will you be?" Grace's voice cracked as she asked the question.

"I'm thinking of going to Topeka. Moses mentioned I could go and live there and act as a reporter for his newspapers—send him information and write articles. Doesn't that sound like an excellent idea?"

Grace dried a tin plate and placed it on the top of the stack. "Not if it means you're going to leave us." The girl was near tears.

"No need to cry, Grace," Jarena comforted. "I haven't made a final decision."

When they all came together around the supper table later that evening, an air of foreboding filled the room. Jarena couldn't put her finger on the exact cause. Silas was exhibiting a childlike enthusiasm after spending an afternoon in the fields with her father, but there was something more. She sensed a crackling tension that threatened to explode at any moment, yet the others seated at the table appeared perfectly calm.

As Jarena cut and served slices of apple pie, she realized she'd over-reacted throughout the meal. *Silly girl!* She could have relaxed and enjoyed the time with her family rather than anticipating some worrisome event.

"Sounds like a rider approaching." Ezekiel pushed back from the table and walked toward the door.

Jarena held her breath and waited, listening as the sound of pounding hooves drew nearer and then came to a stop outside the house.

"Ezekiel Harban?" A male voice hollered the question.

"I am. Who's it that's wantin' to know?"

Jarena gasped in surprise as Bentley Cummings pushed her father aside and entered the room. "Come with me, Jarena," he said, pointing his riding crop at her. "I must speak with you." His command nearly shook the walls of the soddy. Why did he want *her*? She clutched the back of a chair as her father started toward Bentley.

"It's all right, Pappy. I'll call out if I need you." Jarena released her grasp on the chair and patted her father's arm. "He won't do anything to harm me."

Bentley was standing by his horse when she stepped outside, staying close to the doorway. "What is it you want from me, Mr. Cummings?"

He removed a large envelope from a pouch slung across his saddle. "If you're truly Lilly's daughter, she'll likely contact you before anyone else. I'm leaving for New Orleans in the morning. Should Lilly return to Kansas or advise you of her whereabouts, see that she receives this. And tell her that I personally delivered it to you."

"That's all you want me to say?"

"Everything else Lilly needs to know is inside that envelope." Without another word, he mounted the bay mare and rode off toward Hill City as though the devil were on his heels.

— 31 —

Nicodemus, Kansas

November!"

"My gown—" Truth began.

Moses cut her short. "Your gown has already been completed. Mrs. Kramer said you could come by for a final fitting anytime. I say we get married a week from Sunday."

Ezekiel jovially slapped his hand on the table. "Sounds like a good day ta me. I'll have the preacher announce it in church come Sunday mornin'."

Truth shook her head, her eyes wide. "I don't think we can have enough food by then, and the other—"

Ezekiel waved dismissively. "Me and Jarena can go talk to Miss

Hattie tomorra. She and the womenfolk will have ever'thing ready in no time."

"But . . ." Truth made eye contract with Jarena as she scrambled for a reply. "Well, I'm not certain Jarena wants to help prepare for my wedding, Pappy. She has other matters occupying her mind right now."

Jarena wasn't sure whether Truth was truly concerned or was merely using her as an excuse to delay the wedding. All she could do was answer honestly. "If you want to have the wedding a week from Sunday, I'll be pleased to help Miss Hattie and the other women. It's up to you, Truth."

Before Truth could respond, Ezekiel slapped Moses on the shoulder. "It's settled then. We's gonna have a weddin' after church a week from Sunday."

Moses's eyes glowed with delight. He leaned sideways and gave Truth a light kiss on the cheek. But Jarena was sure she still saw concern in Truth's expression. Surely she still loved Moses. How could she not? He was kind and patient; he would give her a good life. Perhaps the trauma of all she'd been through in New York had taken more of a toll on her than any of them realized. And there was little doubt Silas was unhappy with the whole conversation. He excused himself with a low mumble.

While the others continued planning the wedding, Jarena slipped outside and approached Silas. "Beautiful night, isn't it?"

"Yes, ma'am. Stars sure is bright out here on the prairie. Never noticed 'em so much back in New York City."

"Are you regretting your decision to come west?"

He shook his head. "No, ma'am. I wants to own land, and there's nothin' gonna change that. One day I'll have me enough money to get started. I's a hard worker."

"I don't doubt that one bit. But you seem . . . You knew about Truth and Moses—that they were going to marry? Before you made your decision to come to Kansas, I mean?"

He shoved his hands into his front pockets. "Truth tol' me. Maybe I jest was hopin' . . . I can see that Moses is a good man for her, though."

The moon dappled his face with light, and Jarena caught a glimpse of his sad countenance. "We're all thankful for what you did to help Truth and Macia, and I know you're going to be happy here in Nicodemus. Why don't you come back inside?"

"I's gonna stay out here a little longer an' enjoy the night."

Jarena doubted there was any more she could do to help Silas overcome his gloom, so she left him to contemplate his future. Only he could decide what path to follow, just as she must decide for herself. Though she refused to give up hope for Thomas, she needed a plan. After all, she didn't want to remain under her father's roof indefinitely. Could her future possibly be in Topeka?

Ten days! Why had she agreed to move forward with so little time to prepare? And why had she agreed to return to her job at the Boyle house in the meantime? When Mrs. Boyle wasn't loudly lamenting the fact that she would soon lose her household help, Truth was busy scolding herself for having approved the rapidly approaching wedding date. In addition, she had waited two days before paying Mrs. Kramer a visit and was now regretting that decision, also. From the loose fit of her gown, it was obvious Truth had dwindled by at least one dress size while in New York. Though all of her clothing had become a bit ill-fitting, Truth hadn't given any thought to a problem with her wedding dress. However, Mrs. Kramer was taking the weight loss as a personal affront. The seamstress acted as though Truth had purposefully set out to make her life more difficult.

Truth slowly turned in a circle while Mrs. Kramer pinned the satin fabric and mumbled disapproving words. When she could listen no longer, Truth firmly planted her feet and frowned. "I, too, would much rather be using my time otherwise, Mrs. Kramer. If you don't want to complete the alterations, I'll take the dress to Nicodemus. I'm certain Jarena can complete the task for me."

Mrs. Kramer nearly choked on the pins she held tightly between her lips. "You'll do no such thing." Several pins dropped from her mouth as she sputtered the remark. "I created this gown, and I'll not have anyone else taking credit for my talent."

Truth arched her eyebrows and shrugged. There was no pleasing the woman. Having a special wedding gown fashioned by Mrs. Kramer had been Moses's idea. Truth had planned to wear a simple dress, but he had insisted she have something special. She didn't know how a dress would make such a difference, for she would be every bit as married in a simple calico as in this flowing satin creation that was causing both Mrs. Kramer and herself far too much time and heartache.

She could only hope that Jarena wasn't experiencing comparable difficulties while making arrangements for the reception that would follow the ceremony. Thankfully, Moses was in charge of plans regarding their wedding trip. Truth couldn't bring herself to tell him she'd prefer to remain at home; after all, she'd been gone nearly all summer. Fortunately, he'd agreed they would be gone no longer than ten days.

"I believe that will take care of all the measurements for today. You can come back on Monday for your final fitting. And no more weight changes—no gains *or* losses!" Mrs. Kramer shook her finger as though she were scolding a naughty child.

"Ten o'clock?"

"Nine! And don't be late—you were ten minutes late today."

"Yes, ma'am. Nine o'clock with no weight variations." The bell above the door clanked a harsh protest as she jerked on the door handle and departed the shop, anxious to be on her way.

Time was melting away like ice on a summer afternoon, and Truth could do nothing to slow the progression. After a brief stop at the general store, she walked briskly to the Boyle home. Macia was likely pacing the floor, for she had invited Jeb Malone and his little sister, Lucy, for supper. Though Macia had insisted she would cook the meal, Truth had little doubt how the tasks would be divided when dinner preparations actually began. Macia had difficulty finding the coffee grinder or a cone of sugar, and her few ventures into the kitchen had always turned into some form of disaster. Truth wondered how Macia could possibly expect to cook and serve an entire evening meal. Even more confusing, why did she want to?

As Truth readjusted the basket of groceries, she recalled a visit with Macia the night before. The girl had vacillated over her feelings for Jeb, and Truth wondered if tonight's meal was intended to impress him, or would this be his proverbial "last supper" with the Boyle family. If it was the latter, Truth knew he would likely be devastated—not to mention the impact such a pronouncement might have upon young Lucy. There was little doubt Jeb's sister adored Macia and had been scheming to have her brother wed Macia since the day they'd met. And even though Jeb appeared more than ready to make his sister's dream come true, Macia had remained either unwilling or unable to make a clear-cut commitment. Possibly the New York experience had impacted Macia more than Truth thought. Selfishly, Truth hoped all would go smoothly at supper, for she wanted nothing more than a peaceful evening.

As she rounded the corner, Truth spotted Macia on the front porch. Wearing an apron and holding a frying skillet in one hand, the girl looked like an armed warrior prepared for battle. Only a dead chicken swinging from Macia's other hand would have made the scene more amusing. When Macia lifted the skillet into the air and announced she was ready to begin, Truth was forced to hold her laughter in check.

With a nod, Truth mounted the steps and walked to the kitchen with Macia close on her heels. Setting the basket atop the chopping table, Truth instructed Macia to combine a bit of cornmeal with flour and then set to scurrying about the kitchen, shelving items in the pantry. What she really wanted was a cup of tea and a few minutes to relax. Instead, she stood watch while Macia added a pinch of salt and pepper and then dipped the pieces of raw chicken into an egg and milk wash before dredging them in the flour mixture. Preparing the meal herself would have been much easier—and faster.

"Put a dollop of lard in the skillet so it can begin melting while you finish flouring the rest of the pieces. You'll need to peel potatoes." Macia looked at her flour-covered hands as though she wasn't quite certain how to accomplish both tasks. Without giving Macia opportunity to object, Truth took over the task of frying the chicken.

However, when Macia cut her forefinger in two different places only minutes later, Truth wondered if there was any task in the kitchen for which Macia was suited. Pointing the novice cook toward the stove, Truth instructed Macia to stand watch over the chicken while she finished peeling the potatoes.

Macia was staring out the window when the unpleasant odor of burning food curled from the stove and filled the kitchen. "Macia!" Truth shouted. "Turn the chicken. It's burning!"

Though she burned her unprotected hand while grabbing the skillet handle, Truth managed to salvage most of the chicken. Lamenting her failure as a culinary artiste, Macia flopped down on one of the kitchen chairs, legs akimbo, while Truth scuttled around her and continued preparing the meal. A short time later, Macia swiped a drooping curl from her forehead and announced she was going upstairs to change her dress. Truth stared after her in astonishment. So much for help in the kitchen!

— 32 —

Hill City, Kansas

Truth glanced at the clock, thankful Macia was at least willing to answer the door. Dr. Boyle would be home any moment, and Mrs. Boyle would soon be making her way into the parlor. Lucy's laughter floated into the kitchen, and Truth wondered if the young girl's joy would turn to tears before evening's end. She uttered a quick prayer as she continued to mash the potatoes.

When Dr. Boyle arrived home, Truth began the final meal preparations. She thickened the chicken gravy and filled the serving platters and bowls. By the time the family had gathered in the dining room, Truth was carrying food to the table. Though she thought Macia might at least help serve the meal, it was obvious she had reverted to the role of hostess. At present, she was successfully coaxing a smile from her mother. Fortunately, Mrs. Boyle had rested all day, and Truth surmised the older woman would remain in good spirits.

After the group joined hands, Dr. Boyle offered a prayer of thanks for their meal, and plates were soon being filled with the fried chicken and mashed potatoes. Jeb and Dr. Boyle launched into a discussion of the railroad, each anxious to offer opinions regarding the possible routes that might one day be laid through northern Kansas. It was obvious both Mrs. Boyle and Macia were bored with the conversation, but neither interrupted. Truth was about to remove the plates and serve dessert when the railroad conversation finally lulled.

Without hesitation, Mrs. Boyle took command. "Macia has an announcement to make, don't you, my dear?"

Macia startled, eyes wide and fingernails digging into the table-cloth. She looked like a housecat caught in a raging thunderstorm. "I have something to say that may come as somewhat of a surprise to all of you—except Mother."

Macia's fear was palpable as they silently waited for her to continue. Truth studied Mrs. Boyle, wondering if she had something to do with Macia's upcoming announcement. The older woman appeared compla-cent, which was likely not a good sign that the news was going to bode well for Jeb and Lucy. Mrs. Boyle had never wanted Macia to marry the blacksmith.

Macia took a sip of water and cleared her throat. "I've made a deci-sion regarding my immediate future."

Jeb's eyes widened, and Lucy scooted to the edge of her chair.

"Mother was corresponding with her friend, Mrs. Donlevy, before I departed for New York."

"Actually it was after you took ill in New York, but that fact is of little consequence," Mrs. Boyle interjected. When Macia didn't continue, Mrs. Boyle announced, "What Macia wants to tell all of you is that she has decided to accompany Mrs. Donlevy to Europe. She will act as a traveling companion on the voyage and tour Europe with Mildred. Isn't that exciting news?"

Lucy gasped; Jeb's fork clanged as it dropped from his hand and chipped the edge of the china dinner plate; Dr. Boyle stared in astonishment; Mrs. Boyle smiled, and Macia looked as though she might faint. Though Truth longed to run from the room, she forced a smile and calmly offered dessert.

No one acknowledged her offer. In fact, no one said a word until Lucy tossed her napkin onto the table and ran from the room. Without taking time to excuse himself, Jeb hurried after his sister. Truth dropped into one of the recently vacated chairs and waited.

Dr. Boyle's hand shook as he pointed his index finger at his wife. "Whose idea was it that this announcement be made at supper rather than in private? You, Margaret? Macia? Did you know about this, Truth?"

Truth immediately shook her head. "Oh no, Dr. Boyle. I didn't know anything about any of this." She stood up, wanting to distance herself from the entire situation, but Dr. Boyle waved her back down.

"I want this matter sorted out right now. Someone owes me an immediate explanation of how these plans were formulated without my knowledge. *Margaret?*"

Mrs. Boyle fidgeted in her chair before finally speaking. "I feared Macia would return from New York with no aspirations for her future.

I want more for my daughter than a life in this dreary town. She deserves more, Samuel."

Macia remained silent—like a lifeless rag doll placed in a chair at the dinner table—expected to be seen but not heard.

Mrs. Boyle straightened her shoulders and continued. "Once she's traveled abroad, she will be better prepared to make a decision regarding her future. If Jeb truly cares for her, he'll wait another six months. At the end of that time, if Macia wants to return and marry, I won't interfere or object."

Pulling a handkerchief from her pocket, Mrs. Boyle wiped the corner of her eye. "If she marries Jeb now, we both know she'll never have an opportunity to travel abroad. I want her to experience more before she agrees to remain in this town."

"I suppose you make a valid point. Nevertheless, I still don't concur with the way this has been handled," Dr. Boyle said, a hint of anger returning to his voice.

Mrs. Boyle once again dabbed her eyes with the lace-edged hankie. "I'll concede that making the announcement at supper was a distasteful idea, but I feared Macia would lose her courage if she attempted to speak with Jeb alone. After all, young men can be quite persuasive." She sniffed, and Dr. Boyle reached across the table to pat his wife's hand.

"Now, now, stop your weeping, my dear. I suppose if Macia truly wants to travel for six months, that's not too much to ask. However, that means we'll need to seek help for you here at the house. You must remember, Truth will be leaving us very soon."

The tears in Mrs. Boyle's eyes were soon replaced with a gleaming twinkle as she explained how she'd been feeling much better of late and was certain she'd do fine until they could find someone to help with the house. Truth wondered if Dr. Boyle thought it amazing that his wife rallied when things went her way. The abrupt onsets and cures of the woman's undiagnosed maladies were always truly convenient. Possibly Dr. Boyle had decided long ago to take his wife's opportune ailments in stride. In any event, the entire evening had been completely unsettling.

"At the moment, however, I'm feeling a bit tired," Mrs. Boyle submitted. "I wish to go up to my room now."

Truth had to work very hard not to roll her eyes.

————

It was nearly ten o'clock when a tap sounded on Truth's bedroom door and Macia whispered her name. Truth briefly considered pulling the sheet over her head, but she knew Macia needed a listening ear. After talking with her father, she had finally gained enough courage to go and speak with Jeb and Lucy—likely not a pleasant experience for any of them.

Macia sat down on the chair beside Truth's bed. With her head bowed until it nearly touched her knees, she rocked back and forth. "I don't know if Jeb is ever going to forgive me for giving in to my mother's wishes—or for hurting Lucy."

The sheet rippled as Truth turned on her side. "You can't blame him for being angry, Macia. He told you long ago he didn't want Lucy hurt again. He may never be willing to overlook what's happened, but you can't change it now." She pulled her arm out from under the sheet.

"You best be prepared, for he may wed someone else before you return from Europe."

Macia's lower lip was trembling when she lifted her head. "You think he would do that?"

Truth nodded as she plumped her pillow with two swift punches. "I couldn't blame him if he did. Why on earth did you ever agree to such a thing? So far as I can see, your mama's the only one happy over your decision."

Macia endeavored to explain, though she faltered without her mother's prompting. Still, it was evident she was truly attempting to do the right thing. And Truth knew what that was like.

A tear dropped onto the bed sheet, and Truth took Macia's hand in her own. "You can't change what's been done, but we can pray that God will set things on the proper path for you, Macia—and that Lucy and Jeb will find it in their hearts to forgive you."

As they bowed their heads, Macia's tears continued to flow. Truth doubted Macia would follow her heart.

CHAPTER

— 33 —

Jarena had survived her sister's wedding unscathed . . . mostly. She had experienced both joy and pain, along with a generous portion of guilt. For the most part, however, Jarena was genuinely happy for Moses and Truth. She only hoped that one day she would experience the pleasure of being a bride herself.

Truth was strikingly beautiful in the satin gown that had been fitted to Mrs. Kramer's exacting requirements. Jarena had never seen Moses, who looked quite handsome in his morning coat, appear happier than when he saw his bride enter the church grasping her father's arm. Nevertheless, the finely bedecked couple seemed somewhat out of place in the small church with its limestone walls and log benches that were notorious for implanting splinters in many of the congregants' backsides. Fortunately, the weather cooperated and the reception went on until well after bedtime. Even Miss Hattie admitted the music and food were to her liking.

Before Truth and Moses departed on their wedding trip, Jarena had agreed to make a brief return to the Boyle residence. Though Jarena was certain the temporary employment was intended to lure her back into a full-time position for the Boyles, she didn't intend to acquiesce. When she had learned of the Boyles' oldest son's impending visit in order to accompany Macia back east, that had been enough to entice her into a brief return. Carlisle Boyle was Jarena's final link to Thomas—the only person she knew who had served with him in the army. She had decided she would gladly cook and clean in the Boyles' home in exchange for any information about Thomas she could extract from Carlisle.

In retrospect, Carlisle's visit had been a blessing. During his time at home, he told Jarena of Thomas's dedication to the military and his selfless attitude both at the fort and in the skirmishes in which they'd been engaged. She soon realized there had been more battles than Thomas had ever written her about, likely because he hadn't wanted to worry her. And although Carlisle was no longer privy to news concerning the men at Fort Concho, he agreed there was hope that Thomas might one day return. She was thankful for his encouragement—and she told him so. Even though her family thought she should move forward with her life, Jarena was not about to give up hope.

With Macia and Carlisle headed east to meet Mrs. Donlevy in Baltimore, Jarena was anxious to return home. With a final promise from Mrs. Boyle that she need stay for only one more week, Jarena set off for the general store to stock the shelves of Mrs. Boyle's pantry before her final departure. As she neared the Malones' house, young Lucy came outside and hollered a greeting. Since Jarena's return to the Boyle household, Lucy hadn't come calling, although the girl had previously been a frequent and welcome visitor.

Life had changed for young Lucy since Macia's decision to travel abroad, and Jarena couldn't help but take pity on the girl. No doubt, her days were lonely with only an older brother at home. She returned Lucy's greeting and swung her empty basket. "I'm going to the store. Would you care to walk along with me?"

The girl bobbed her head with enthusiasm. "Will you wait until I ask Jeb?"

Jarena agreed, and minutes later Lucy came running pell-mell toward her. "Jeb says I can go with you."

"Good! I've been meaning to stop by and tell you that I have several books Macia asked that I give to you. Perhaps you could walk me home and we'll get them when I'm done shopping."

Lucy clutched Jarena's hand tightly. "I don't know if I should accept a gift from Macia." The girl's eyes shimmered with pain as she spoke Macia's name.

"If you don't want to keep them, you could at least spend some time with me over the next few days and we could read them together. Would you like that?"

"Yes . . . but are you leaving, too?"

Jarena nodded. It might have been better not to have mentioned the books or spending time together. She had hoped to provide a bit of diversion for Lucy, not cause her more disappointment. "However, I'll be in Hill City one more week, and while I'm here, I'd like to get started reading those books. What do you say we set a time to get together each evening? And perhaps you could come to Nicodemus and visit me some time soon."

Skipping around to face Jarena, Lucy danced backward as they continued down the street. "Oh, I would like that! I never get to go anywhere."

She shouldn't have made such an offer, Jarena told herself. If she moved to Topeka, the girl would be disappointed when she didn't get to travel to Nicodemus. She walked through the open door. "Good morning, Mrs. Johnson," she greeted.

Ada Johnson glanced over her shoulder as she continued to stock the shelves with the shipment of goods her husband had brought from Ellis the day before. "Good morning. Let me know if you need any help. Oh, and there's a letter for you, Jarena." Mrs. Johnson nodded toward the stack of mail that hadn't yet been sorted into the small wooden cubes along the wall.

A letter! Jarena's stomach muscles tightened into a knot of apprehension. Could it possibly be from Thomas? "May I?" she asked, pointing at the heap of letters.

The woman nodded, and Jarena began shuffling through one pile of envelopes while Lucy busied herself with another stack. Jarena kept her attention focused upon the handwriting on each envelope, longing to see Thomas's familiar script.

"Wait! Here it is." Lucy pulled an envelope from the pile and thrust it at Jarena.

The missive didn't bear the handwriting for which she'd been searching. In fact, it wasn't from Indian Territory at all—it was from Leadville, one of the boomtowns out in Colorado she'd heard folks mention from time to time—and the script was obviously feminine.

"Who's it from?" Lucy's eyes sparkled with excitement as she leaned across the counter to gain a better look at the envelope. "I never get mail from anyone."

"I'm not certain, Lucy." Jarena tucked the envelope into her skirt pocket and picked up her shopping basket. "Why don't you find me a spool of thread. Dark blue. If you don't see any, Mrs. Johnson will help you locate it. I'm going to gather the other items on the list."

Even though the envelope didn't bear the name of the sender, Jarena assumed the letter was from Lilly. Who else would be writing to her from such a place? Yet Lilly had told them she was going to head north to Canada—which was exactly why Jarena had told Bentley Cummings her aunt had probably headed to California.

———

Neither Lucy nor Jarena mentioned the letter after their return from the store. It wasn't until Jarena was preparing for bed that she withdrew the envelope from her pocket and opened it carefully. She sat down in a rocking chair near the foot of her bed and unfolded the pages, first glancing at the signature on the final page to assure herself the letter was from Lilly.

When she had finished reading her aunt's letter a short time later, Jarena leaned back in the chair and closed her eyes. How could she possibly be this woman's daughter? She felt no connection to her—nor did she want to. Though the pages were filled with interesting tidbits about Lilly's life in Leadville, there was no explanation as to why she had chosen to settle in Colorado rather than traveling north to Canada as planned. Jarena surmised the decision had been based upon the possible exploitation of a fellow traveler Lilly had met on the train, especially since her letter included references to her recent purchase of a millinery shop and an investment in a silver mine.

Jarena was mindful Lilly hadn't departed Hill City with enough money for such costly investments. All of Mr. Nelson's valuables had been returned; she'd seen to it herself. She leaned back in her chair and imagined Lilly sidling up to a wealthy gentleman on the train, pilfering his riches with the ease and pleasure of a cat lapping up a bowl of milk. She shuddered at the thought. She truly didn't want to think ill of Lilly, yet how else could the woman accomplish so much in this short period of time? Perhaps she would write and ask what had happened to her aunt's talk of thankfulness to God for sparing her life and restoring broken relationships. Ha! The woman was a fraud—always had been and always would be.

On the final page of the letter was an inquiry regarding Bentley Cummings. Obviously Lilly remained fearful of the man. The letter asked that her mail be directed to general delivery in Leadville and was followed by a heartfelt request that her whereabouts remain a secret from anyone who might know or have contact with Bentley Cummings. Wouldn't Lilly be distressed to learn that Macia and Truth had traveled with him on their return journey to Kansas? Or that Jarena had told him Lilly was her mother—that bit of information had nearly caused him to come undone. She would consider penning a letter to Lilly once she returned to Nicodemus. In addition, there was the dispatch from Mr. Cummings. If nothing else, she should forward Bentley's letter to Lilly. No telling what information that missive might contain.

Jarena sat in the pew alongside Dr. Boyle. When young Lucy discovered Mrs. Boyle was suffering from a headache and wouldn't be attending the morning services, she moved to take the seat beside Jarena. Mrs. Boyle had insisted she would be fine for an hour or so by herself. And although Jarena agreed, missing the Sunday morning services at the Boyles' church wouldn't have distressed her in the least. She surveyed the crowd and wondered what the members of this serious congregation might think if they heard a sermon preached in Nicodemus. They'd surely clutch at their chests when someone shouted a heartfelt amen or hallelujah. The idea nearly made her giggle aloud.

When the service ended, Jarena hurried to Truth's side. "Were you still planning for me to come over to visit this afternoon?"

"Of course!" Truth looped her left arm around Jarena's right arm. "I'm preparing chicken and dumplings and even made a layer cake for dessert."

"And it didn't even topple over this time." Moses kissed his wife's cheek and winked.

Lucy had followed along behind Jarena and giggled at his remark.

"Don't laugh, Lucy," Truth said. "One day your husband will make fun of *your* layer cake, too."

"I'm going to be like Jarena. I'm not going to get married."

Jarena's breath caught in her throat. She wanted to grab the child's face between her hands and explain that this solitary life wasn't of her own choosing, that she wanted nothing more than to walk down a church aisle and wed Thomas Grayson. She wanted to be exactly like Truth and the other women in the congregation—married to the man she loved, baking uneven layer cakes, and looking forward to a future filled with laughter, happiness, and children.

Moses captured one of Lucy's braids between his fingers and gave a gentle tug. "Jarena is going to marry one of these days, too. She's merely waiting for the proper time. Isn't that right, Jarena?"

"That's right, Moses." Jarena was thankful he hadn't said she was awaiting the right man, for such words would have cut her to the quick.

———————

Once they'd finished the noonday meal, Moses excused himself and retreated to his library. He'd spoken of a book he'd been wanting to begin. Though Jarena doubted he was anxious to read, she appreciated his kindness in allowing her time alone with her sister. They'd begun to clear the dishes when Jarena said, "I received a letter from Lilly yesterday."

Truth looked up. "Truly? Where is she? Canada? Did she mention Mr. Cummings?"

"Indeed. She asked whether he'd actually come to Kansas. However, she's not in Canada. It seems she went only as far as Colorado—Leadville. She did ask that we not divulge her whereabouts to outsiders."

Truth picked up the bowl of green beans and returned it to the kitchen. "I won't say a word, but I wonder what made her change her mind about Canada."

Jarena followed along behind her sister, carrying a stack of dirty dishes. "I have no idea, but she's invested in both a millinery shop and a silver mine. And she's asked me to join her."

Truth's eyes widened with surprise. "What? In Leadville? That's ludicrous. Surely she doesn't think you would do such a thing. You wouldn't, would you?" Truth dropped the damp dishrag into the sudsy water and turned to look at Jarena. "Would you?"

CHAPTER

— 34 —

Nicodemus, Kansas • October 1880

The journey to Nicodemus should have been uneventful. However, they were only a few miles outside Hill City when Truth began to voice a succession of arguments against Aunt Lilly's proposal that Jarena move to Colorado. Although Jeb had offered to drive Jarena home, Moses and Truth had insisted they would see to the task themselves. Jarena now realized why! Truth was consumed with presenting all the possible pitfalls of a move to Colorado. To make matters worse, each time Jarena attempted to divert the conversation, Truth signaled for Moses to take up the cause. Quite frankly, Jarena was now confident Jeb's company would have been preferable to that of her sister and brother-in-law.

When they finally arrived in Nicodemus, Moses assisted the two women from the buggy. Jarena sighed with relief, pleased to be set free from their sermonizing. "Please don't mention any of this in front of Pappy. No need to upset him with any of this foolish talk."

Truth brightened and grasped Jarena's hand before she had a chance to enter the house. "Then you agree with us? You're not going to consider going to Colorado?"

Jarena peeked out from beneath the brim of her lace-trimmed bonnet. "*You've* made the decisions regarding *your* life, Truth. I suggest you let others do the same."

"Now, Jarena. Don't go and get your back up. You know we're only attempting to look out for what's best."

Jarena exhaled in exasperation. She gave momentary thought to stomping her feet just like the twins used to do when they were little girls wanting their way. Perhaps such childlike behavior would finally capture Truth's attention. "And I'm telling you I don't want you or anyone else making my decisions. Do you understand?"

Grace emerged from the cornfield and came running toward them with the skirt of her dress whipping about her legs like a ship's sail gone awry. "Truth! Jarena! I'm so happy to see you." She squealed and made a headlong dive for Truth that nearly sent both young women toppling to the ground. Jarena laughed at the sight, thankful the frenzied leap had been directed at Truth rather than herself.

Grace leaned back and looked at her sister and then at Moses. "You're going to stay and visit for a day or two, aren't you?"

"Only until tomorrow. We must leave early—the newspaper. But it won't be long until we move to Nicodemus, and then you'll quickly tire of having us around."

Grace's smile turned into an effective pout. "But you won't move here until Harvey Boyle finishes school and comes back to Hill City. That's not so soon."

"Now, now, Grace. You know Truth will want to oversee construction of the new house once the roof is on—and that's not far off."

Truth looped arms with her twin sister. "Yes—and I'll need lots of help making decisions about the house. Unlike some people, I appreciate the opinion of others."

"Only when they agree with you," Jarena whispered as she brushed by her sisters. "Pappy and Silas out in the fields, Grace?"

"We've started cutting in the far field, but now that Pappy's got Silas working with him, he doesn't care much whether I'm out there helping. He'd rather have me spend time improving my cooking." Grace giggled. "I know he's gonna be glad you're back home for good, Jarena. He got used to having you for those couple weeks before you went back to help at the Boyles'. Now that we've begun the harvest, he's gonna want some of your corn pudding."

Truth nodded. "We all know how much Pappy wants Jarena here at home."

Jarena gritted her teeth. Truth's attempts were annoying and obvious. Besides, she was having enough trouble trying to decide about her future as it was.

Apparently Moses had now tired of their haggling. "I'm going over to see how the roof is progressing on our house. Tell your father and Silas I look forward to visiting with them this evening."

Truth hurried forward to kiss him farewell. "Don't forget to ask if there's been any word regarding the new printing press."

Grace followed Jarena into the house. "You're in a sour mood today."

"I'm sorry. I promise to try and do better. Tell me, how have you and Silas been getting on? From what you said earlier, it sounds as though he's showing promise as a farmer." Jarena wondered if having Silas begin to take over in the fields was difficult for Grace.

"He'll learn—he's kind of slow at first, but once he catches on, he does good. He likes being out there working, that's a fact. Pappy has to force him back to the house come suppertime. He's already trying to figure out how long it's going to take before he can afford to buy his own piece of land. I think maybe he's hoping you'll sell him Thomas's land."

Jarena bristled as she removed her bonnet. "You can tell him Thomas's land isn't for sale. We're going to farm that land ourselves when he returns."

"Silas didn't mean anything bad, Jarena. He was just—"

"Thinking that Thomas is dead. Like all the rest of you. But I know he isn't, and you'll not convince me otherwise." Her anger continued to rise along with the heat of her words. "Not until I have more proof than a letter saying he didn't return to the fort with his company. He might have survived. You don't know that he's dead!" She shouted and waved toward heaven like a fire-and-brimstone preacher at a tent revival. "Only God knows, and I trust that He's going to bring Thomas back to me."

She fell into a chair, spent, while her sisters looked at her as though she'd gone mad. Perhaps she had. Why was she clinging to hope? Why did she suddenly believe she should trust the Lord for Thomas's return?

Trust—the barrier she had struggled against all her life—the adversary she had never conquered. Trust!

So many thoughts raced through her mind that she was surprised when words from the Psalms came to the forefront: *"The Lord is my rock, and my fortress, and my deliverer; my God, my strength, in whom I will trust."*

For now, for today, she would depend on the Lord for Thomas's safe return.

———

Jarena's sisters quickly retreated outdoors. Truth said she needed to stretch her legs after their lengthy buggy ride, but Jarena suspected both girls wanted to escape in case she veered off into another unexpected tirade. Not that she blamed them. She'd likely frightened them out of their wits as she had ranted and flailed her arms.

Perhaps there'd be no further mention of her peculiar behavior if she began the supper preparations before Truth and Grace returned. She retrieved a clean apron from her trunk and got started. Her father had pushed the trunk to the foot of her bed, right where it had been before she departed for her first journey to work for the Boyles. She unfastened the hasp and lifted the heavy lid. There, on top of her belongings, was the mysterious envelope from Bentley Cummings. She picked up the missive and turned it over as his words played back in her mind. *"Should Lilly return to Kansas or advise you of her whereabouts, see that she receives this. And tell her I personally delivered it to you."*

Jarena pulled Lilly's letter from her reticule and placed both documents side-by-side on the wooden kitchen table. One bore Lilly's precise feminine script; the other displayed Bentley's irregular, mannish handwriting. Lilly's envelope was rather small and thin, while the one from Bentley was much thicker. Startled by the sound of her sisters' laughter, Jarena grabbed the letters and forced them into her skirt pocket. Ignoring the faint sound of a rip, she pushed until the envelopes were safely tucked out of sight.

Grace poked her head in the door only long enough to say they were going to the river and would return shortly. Jarena nodded and waited only a moment before reexamining the envelopes. In her haste, she had torn the flap on the larger envelope—the one addressed to Lilly and carefully sealed by Bentley Cummings. She would need to remove the contents and place them in another envelope so Lilly wouldn't think she'd intentionally opened her mail. Of course, she could merely explain what had actually happened, but Lilly would never believe such a story.

Jarena pulled the contents from the torn envelope. Her jaw went slack as she unfolded the outer page. In the center of the paper was a picture of Lilly with her name clearly printed beneath the likeness. A reward of five hundred dollars was being offered for her return to New Orleans. The poster stated she was wanted for the murder of Sephra Rigilou and the kidnapping of her son, William. The paper shook between Jarena's fingers. A five-hundred-dollar reward! Had Mr. Cummings continued traveling after leaving Nicodemus, handing out these posters along the way? If so, Lilly wouldn't be safe anywhere!

Jarena slumped into a chair and unfolded the letter that had been tucked inside the poster. Jarena scanned the page and then dropped it on top of the poster. The letter was clear. Even though there was no proof, Mr. Cummings had convinced the authorities in New Orleans that Lilly was responsible for Sephra's death. However, if Lilly would return his son unharmed, he could assure her safety from the law and would willingly give her the reward money.

Jarena attempted to weigh the information she'd just learned. Bentley wouldn't absolve Lilly if he truly believed she had killed Sephra and kidnapped his son. And if Lilly had been involved, did he actually think she would believe him and produce his son? Was this purely an attempt to gain information from Lilly—determining her guilt or innocence? Two things were certain: Bentley wanted revenge and, guilty or not, Lilly was his target. Lilly would understand this was nothing more than a ruse . . . wouldn't she? After all, she was a worldly woman.

Surely a woman of Lilly's age and experience also would realize Leadville wasn't a safe hiding place. Too many itinerant men who had possibly seen that wanted poster. Men who wouldn't care if they claimed their fortune from a mountain stream or from the bounty on a woman's life. Truth could put her worries to rest. Jarena would not be heading off to Leadville.

She gathered the papers together and placed them in her trunk. She would write to Lilly in the morning—after the others were gone from the house—when she could think clearly.

Her sisters returned a short time later. Truth came in while Grace stood outside the door holding a line with two large fish. "Look what was on the lines I set this morning. I'll clean them if you're willing to fry them for supper."

Jarena laughed at her sister. "I think I'm getting the better part of that bargain. Truth, why don't you get me some potatoes from the root cellar and I'll fry some to go along with that fish."

Grace peeked back in the doorway, the fish still dangling from her line. "Best plan on some corn, too. Pappy's sure to bring enough ears for supper."

———

As Jarena began to clear the dishes from the table, she heard her father ask, "How'd you find things in town, Moses? I took a look-see after church on Sunday and it appeared like the men was makin' good progress on the newspaper office."

"I agree. If the printing press arrived tomorrow, it could be set up. They've done a fine job. Unfortunately, the house isn't coming along so well. I don't think they've done much on the roof since the last time I was over here."

Ezekiel wiped his mouth with his checkered napkin and placed it on the table. "I reckon that'd be true. The men's been helping with a barn raisin' over near Millbrook. Fire took the old barn. Jest finished gettin' it up yesterday."

He didn't need to say more. When a family was in need, all those who could help turned out to lend a hand. The new construction of a fancy house didn't take precedence over a man needing a barn to store his crops for the winter. It was the way of things on the prairie.

"Just so long as they have it completed before the snow begins to fly. Harvey Boyle wrote to tell me that he'll finish his schooling and return to Hill City by the end of November. Once he's home, Truth and I will be moving to Nicodemus. Truth wants to spend Christmas in her new home."

Jarena tried to suppress her jealousy as she watched Truth beam at her husband. Everything seemed to be falling into place exactly according to their desires. Why was her own life so different?

But then came the still, small voice in her head: *Trust—continue to trust.*

The next morning Truth and Moses left to return to Hill City. Jarena waited until Grace and the men departed for the fields before penning her note to Lilly. Finally satisfied with the contents, she carefully tucked the letter into an envelope along with the letter and poster from Bentley and headed off for town. Once she'd delivered the letter to the post office, her duty to Lilly would be done. She only hoped the woman would be careful, for Jarena feared Bentley Cummings was not a man easily discouraged.

The horse clopped along the familiar road into town, and though Jarena held the reins, the animal didn't need her assistance to find its way. As the wagon rolled into Nicodemus, Jarena scrutinized the little community with fresh eyes. The town was coming into its own and beginning to take on its own unique personality. Somehow Jarena had developed a fondness for this place that she had, at one time, never wanted to inhabit. It was good to be home.

She stopped in front of Mr. Wilson's two-story general store, a limestone building he had lovingly constructed. The structure also housed the local post office, a fact that greatly pleased the proprietor. After posting her letter to Lilly, Jarena retrieved a list from her pocket. A tow-headed young man stepped forward. "I can help you fill your order, if you like."

Jarena smiled but held onto the paper. "Thank you, but I'm checking your prices and quality. I want to see what Mr. Green has available in his store and compare his prices before I make my final selections."

The boy sighed. "We'll fill your order for a nickel less than Mr. Green. You go and write down his prices on your list and come back. I'll figure 'em up, and we'll give you a better price. I promise."

Jarena nodded and exited the store, happy to learn the competition between the two general stores was keeping prices low. She slowly made her way through Mr. Green's store, her shoes clicking quietly on the wood floor as she moved from shelf to shelf, marking down prices on the sheet of paper.

"He's at it again, isn't he?"

Jarena startled and turned around. Mr. Green's round face drooped, with the fleshy folds nearly covering the collar of his white shirt. He was pointing at Jarena's piece of paper. "Wilson! He's told you he'll sell to you for less than my prices, hasn't he?"

She wanted to flee from the store, but Mr. Green's rotund body was blocking her only line of escape. "You go back over there and tell him I will *not* be undersold. If he lowers your bill by . . . by—well, whatever he offered . . ."

"A nickel."

Mr. Green glowered as he rubbed a beefy hand across his bald head. "Then I'll lower the total price another seven cents. You tell him I can go on as long as he can. He'll not steal another customer from me with his conniving ways." He marched down the aisle and waved Jarena forward. She was the soldier, and Mr. Green was the officer sending her into battle. "And for your information, I carry a higher quality of goods than Mr. Wilson does. And you can tell him I said so. And a better selection, too!" Mr. Green stood in the doorway of his store, continuing to holler after Jarena as she hastened across the street.

If the two men did this for long, they'd end up filling her order for free. She smiled at the thought as she entered Mr. Wilson's mercantile. Unfortunately, Mr. Wilson nullified his son's earlier agreement, conceded defeat, and sent Jarena back across the street to Mr. Green. Jarena managed to complete her shopping at Mr. Green's mercantile with a nice discount—once she convinced him he should honor his word. The savings paid for both an extra cone of sugar and the postage on Aunt Lilly's letter. It had been a most satisfying morning!

Mr. Green placed her purchases in the back of the wagon while Jarena excused herself. The sound of banging hammers mixed with the jovial shouts of workmen beckoned her. She wanted to see the newspaper office before heading home.

Moses was correct: The limestone building was nearly complete. She wiped a thin layer of dust from one corner of the recently installed windows and peeked inside. The workmen were mounting the new cabinets that would hold all of the wooden type. The highly polished multidrawer cabinets had been handcrafted by John Willbanks, one of the Exodusters the town had sponsored after Grace's impassioned speech on Emancipation Day. She smiled as she inspected the office—no cottonwood in this building. Instead, special-ordered soft pine grooved and tongued floors had been fitted tight by the carpenters.

She returned to the wagon, pleased and impressed by what she'd seen. Her articles for the newspaper would actually be printed in that very office—if she decided to write them.

Strangely, she no longer harbored a desire to leave this place and move to Topeka. Living with her father might prove difficult, but living in Topeka, she decided, wasn't the answer she was looking for, either. There was no reason she couldn't remain on the farm and write for the newspaper.

— 35 —

Nicodemus, Kansas • December 1880

A new carpet of snow covered the prairie in a thick white wrapper that brightened the countryside appreciably. Jarena's father had welcomed the fleecy coverlet that would protect the winter wheat he had planted for the first time this fall. It was an experiment of sorts. When the farmers in Nicodemus Township had discovered other farmers were having good success with Turkey Red, a hard winter wheat introduced by the Russian Mennonites who had settled in the state, many decided to try the crop. In September, Ezekiel, with Silas's help, had sown several acres, and he now rejoiced each time the skies released a snowy cloak of protection for his fields.

Jarena was busy preparing a savory rabbit stew when Silas and her father returned from the barn. Snowflakes followed them into the house and skittered across the floor, melting as they approached Jarena's feet. "Close the door!" she called. "We're quickly losing what little heat this stove is putting out."

Ezekiel stomped his feet on the rag rug and winked at Silas. "She won't mind leavin' that door open when she sees Truth and Moses is right behind us."

Jarena smiled broadly. "Truly?" Her smile soon faded to concern. "What brings them out in this weather?"

"Why shouldn' they come visit? The snow's stopped."

"For the moment, but look at the sky. Those are snow clouds."

Ezekiel shook his head. "You worry too much. This ain't no blizzard, gal, so don't go frettin' when there ain't no cause."

She knew her father's admonition was sound, but whenever the snow began, she remembered the blizzard years ago when Thomas had headed off for Hill City to fetch the doctor and nearly frozen to death. Better if folks stayed home in bad weather. There was no need borrowing trouble.

Before she could reply to her father's comment, Truth and Moses entered the house, both of them stomping and shaking off the snow. "Sorry for the mess," Truth called to her sister. "Where's Grace?"

"She's on her way in from the barn," Jarena answered. "What brings you two out on a day like this?"

"A day like this? Why, it's wonderful outdoors—especially snuggled under blankets in the sleigh." Truth held up a pair of ice skates and waved them as Grace came into the house. "I brought my ice skates along in case you want to go skating later."

Jarena frowned and shook her head. "I doubt the river is frozen enough for skating. Best you both stay indoors."

Moses pulled a chair close to the stove. "That sounds like an excellent suggestion to me." He rubbed his hands together. "We have a bit of news to share with you."

Truth hurried to his side while Jarena held her breath. Were they going to announce that Truth was expecting a baby? If so, Jarena knew that envy would besiege her like a hungry wolf stalking its next meal.

Moses retrieved an envelope from his jacket pocket and held it up. "I received a letter from the newspaper in New York. They assigned a reporter to investigate Rutledge Academy. I shared this news with Dr. Boyle only yesterday; and now we want to tell the rest of you—especially you, Silas."

Jarena slowly exhaled and sat down. Guilt quickly laid claim to her thoughts. How could she begrudge her own sister the joy of a child? How selfish! Yet the truth was there to face her. She was relieved and, yes, even a little pleased that the news was about Macia's school.

"Isn't that astonishing, Jarena?" Truth was staring at her wide-eyed.

"What? I'm sorry, I didn't hear . . ."

Truth tapped her fingers on the table. "And you accuse *me* of daydreaming!" She giggled and gave Jarena a fleeting embrace. "The newspaper reporter from New York, Mr. Campbell, discovered the owners of the school had been purchasing life insurance policies on some of the girls without their knowledge. They had purchased one for Macia Boyle."

"What? Why would they do such a thing?"

Truth sighed. "Because if the girls die, they collect the money on their lives."

Silas shook his head. "And there was several girls that died while I was at dat school. Reckon Macia woulda been next iffen Truth hadn't been watchin' out for her."

"Not just me, Silas. If you hadn't helped, I never could have gotten her safely back to Kansas. We would have remained there, and likely we both would have died."

"This letter explains everything," Moses told the group. "After being questioned by the police, Mr. and Mrs. Rutledge and Mr. Laird admitted to involvement in poisoning five girls and collecting insurance money. Mr. Laird apparently conceived the plan, but the Rutledges went along, willing to share in the spoils and permit his evildoings."

Ezekiel thumped his coffee cup on the kitchen table. "And to think I's the one who let you go to that place. I wouldn't never forgive myself if something woulda happened to ya, Truth."

She gave him a warm smile. "Nothing happened, Pappy. I'm home safe and sound. And that's not the very best news." She reached into the big front pocket of her coat. "Silas, this is from Dr. Boyle. A reward for your courage and assistance in returning us safely from New York. Dr. Boyle asked that we deliver it to you."

Silas untied the string, opened the brown paper, and gasped. "It's money! More'n enough to buy a piece of land."

Grace rested her open palm across her heart and beamed. "It's what you prayed for, Silas! God answered your prayer."

From the look on his face, Jarena wasn't certain her father was quite so happy at the thought of Silas purchasing his own parcel of land. After all, the young man's willingness to work was a valued asset in her father's fields. Now that he had the money, she wondered if Silas would ask to purchase Thomas's land. Likely not—Grace would surely tell him the purchase of Thomas's land was a forbidden topic.

Jarena's thoughts were interrupted by Truth's invitation for the family to join them at their new house for Christmas dinner. "Moses and I are hoping you'll agree." Instead of looking to their father for affirmation, Truth was focusing on Jarena. "Well? What do you think?"

Ezekiel leaned forward. "I's thinkin' it's a fine idea. We's gonna be in town for church meetin' on Christmas—preacher says he's got a fine sermon already prepared." Ezekiel chuckled. "Prob'ly the same one he preached last year. We can jest all come to your place afterward. Ain' that right, Jarena?"

"Of course. That will be great fun." Jarena knew her agreement was expected. "You let me know in advance what you'd like me to prepare."

"I was hoping Pappy would offer us one of the hams."

Grace poked Truth in the arm. "And I'm guessing you want Jarena to bake it for you—along with an apple pie, too!"

"We'll likely need at least two pies. Moses and Pappy are both fond of mincemeat." Truth grinned as she looked from her husband to her father and back again.

The twins were enjoying the verbal exchange, and Jarena played along with them and added her agreement to whatever they suggested, though suddenly she felt very old—as though she'd already lived her life and the final curtain was falling. It ought not be that way, but thus far, she'd not experienced any of the life for which she longed.

But she knew something that would bring a smile to her face, and she jumped up from her chair. "I believe I'll go and check on those baby chicks. It's cold, and I want to make sure they are warm enough out in the coop." She grabbed her cloak and hurried outside, ignoring Grace's protests that she'd already given them sufficient care.

The clouds hung heavy in the sky. Intermittent snowflakes dropped from the heavens and danced on her face before melting and trickling down her cheeks like tears. Grasping the hem of her cloak, Jarena swiped the fabric across her face and dried her cheeks. She hesitated as she reached the barn. For a moment, she thought she heard sleigh bells jingling in the distance. She shook her head. In addition to indulging in self-pity, she was beginning to hear things.

The heavy wooden door creaked and groaned in protest as Jarena pulled on the handle. Again, she heard sleigh bells. She turned and squinted toward the horizon. There *was* a sleigh in the distance. She wasn't imagining things after all! But who would be out for a sleigh ride in this weather? She laughed at the thought. Moses and Truth thought nothing of traveling in the snow; in fact, they planned to return to their home in town later this evening. Apparently she was the only one who gave the weather more than a passing thought.

"Helloooo!"

She didn't know who was shouting from the sleigh, but she waved in return. Whoever it was, they'd likely stop for a cup of hot coffee if one was offered. She pushed the barn door closed and walked toward the road while straining to see. Will Southard? What was he doing all the way up here from Ellis?

She cupped her hands around her mouth and shouted, "Will Southard. Is that you?"

The horses clopped to a halt and snorted puffs of frosty air from their large nostrils. The animals shook their heads, tossing their frost-laden manes in the cold air and causing the harness bells to jangle a melodious greeting.

"What brings you from Ellis on this cold day, Will? Weather's going to turn bad on you before you can get home."

He nodded. "I know. I'm hoping you'll offer a cup of coffee and put me up for the night if need be." He waved at the blanket-covered mound behind him. "As a way of thanking me for bringing you a special Christmas present," he added.

Jarena wondered if Moses had ordered a special gift for Truth and had it delivered to the farm in order to surprise her. "Christmas present? You must be mistaken. I'm not expecting anything from Ellis. I don't think any of us placed any special orders."

The blankets shifted, and Jarena watched as the wool coverlet dropped away to reveal the Christmas gift. "Thomas!" Her high-pitched cry of delight streaked across the still, snow-covered prairie. "When did you . . . ? How did this . . . ?" She couldn't complete a full sentence, nor could she seem to move!

"Aren't you going to come closer?" Will asked with a laugh.

The question jarred her into motion. She sprinted to the side of the sleigh and then stopped short. "Thomas! What happened to you?"

"Indians," he said as he arranged himself in a seated position and straightened the patch over his left eye. "But I'm alive, and I'm not complainin'." He grasped her hand. "I'm not the man who left here, Jarena, but don't pity me. I can already see you're pained by what you're seein', but I don't want nobody feeling sorry for me—least of all you. Understand? I lost an eye, but my leg's healin'. It's gonna be fine in another few weeks."

A lump formed in her throat and rendered her speechless. She tipped her head in agreement, unable to speak. Will circled the sleigh, and with a surprising nonchalance, assisted Thomas out of the sleigh and into the house while her family hurried to welcome the men and then fetch coffee and food, all of them acting as though nothing were unusual.

Thomas thanked them for the coffee before he requested a few moments alone with Jarena. She swallowed hard as she neared his side, hoping to rid herself of the lump in her throat that wouldn't seem to diminish.

"Please, sit down." There was an ache in his voice she'd never heard before. He took her hand and looked deep into her eyes. "I wanna tell you what happened. Why you ain't heard from me. When I'm done, I want a promise from you."

She bowed her head, knowing if she spoke it would be through tears. And she knew Thomas didn't need tears. He needed her to be strong. Biting her lower lip when it began to tremble, she listened while he told her of a battle with Victorio and his men. How a bullet ricocheted off a rock and hit him beside the left eye. The only thing he remembered was the flash of light before he fell to the ground.

"I don' remember any of what happened after that. I don't know how long I was there, but the men who found me said I'd wandered across the Rio Grande and into their village. When I got there, I didn' even know who I was. I'd lost my memory. 'Course, from my appearance, they knowed I was one of the buffalo soldiers. The womenfolk nursed me back to health—even made this patch for my eye." The black fabric had been embroidered with brightly stitched flowers and tied around his head.

"As I started to heal, my memory slowly returned. When I finally got back to Fort Concho, I found out the army had listed me as dead. There was a note in my records showin' Moses was notified. I coulda written you as soon as I got back to the fort, but they said they'd be sendin' me home for good—what with my eye and all. I figured I might jest as well wait and surprise ever'body." He waved his arm with bravado. "So here I am, determined to farm my land right here in Nicodemus, jest like I planned."

"And I'll be at your side, Thomas," Jarena whispered. "I've been waiting so long. . . ."

He rubbed his thumb across the back of her hand and shook his head. "No. We cain't get married, Jarena. Leastways not right now. Maybe never. That's the promise I was talkin' about. I'm not the same man what left here, not the man you was plannin' to marry. So I want you to promise me that if another fella comes along, you won't hold off because of me. To tell you the truth, I wouldn'ta been surprised to find out you was already married to some lucky fella."

A swell of indignation rose in Jarena's chest. "How could you think such a thing? Did my letters not speak what was in my heart? Didn't I promise to be here waiting for you?"

"No need to get angry. You's a pretty gal, Jarena, and I figure there's plenty of single fellas lookin' for a wife in these parts. When I couldn't get word to you, I thought ya'd take me for dead and move on with your life."

"Well, you should have known better than that! I'm not a fickle woman, Thomas!"

He chuckled and brushed her cheek with his hand. "I can see that.

But here's the thing. With this bad leg and only one eye—this isn't somethin' either one of us was intendin'. I don' think we should be plannin' for the future right now."

After all this waiting, after trusting God for his return, was Thomas now going to reject her? "Nobody ever plans on facing difficulties, Thomas." Apparently she was going to have to argue him into marrying her.

"That's true, but I know myself. I'll likely be pretty ornery to get along with when I start trying to keep up with my farmin' chores and such. Sometimes I get mighty bad headaches, and it wouldn' be fair to you."

Her pulse quickened, and she could feel her temples throbbing, racing to keep time with each rapid heartbeat as she gathered both of his hands in hers. "I'm pushing my pride aside, Thomas, and I'm going to say what's on my heart. I love you and I want to marry you. I must know if you feel the same."

He hesitated and then lifted her hand to brush it with a soft kiss. "You know I love you, Jarena. I've loved you since the first day we met. But I couldn't stand it if you grew to hate me. I wanna do the right thing by you."

"Then marry me. That's the right thing—the only thing."

He drew her into his arms and softly kissed her lips. "If you're sure that's what we should do."

She returned his kiss. There was no doubt: this was the man for whom she was intended. This was the person she wanted to spend the rest of her life with. Injured or not, she loved him with all her heart.

With God at the helm of their marriage, they would face these new hardships with a steadfast love and trust in Him. Working together, their life on the prairie and their love for each other would shine as brightly as a Kansas morning sky.

ACKNOWLEDGMENTS

Special thanks to:

The stalwart pioneers who willingly sacrificed to settle the
  Kansas prairie
The staff of the National Park Service, Nicodemus
  Historic Site
The staff of the Kansas State Historical Society
Mary Greb-Hall
Mary Kay Woodford
Angela Bates-Tompkins
Deletria Nash

Books by Judith Miller

FROM BETHANY HOUSE PUBLISHERS

BELLS OF LOWELL*

Daughter of the Loom

A Fragile Design

These Tangled Threads

LIGHTS OF LOWELL*

A Tapestry of Hope

A Love Woven True

The Pattern of Her Heart

FREEDOM'S PATH

First Dawn

Morning Sky

*with Tracie Peterson

Bestselling Author
TRACIE PETERSON
EMBARKS *on a* NEW SERIES

Leah Barringer's life in the rugged Alaskan Territory
changes unexpectedly when the man her heart can't forget
returns after ten long years. But unbeknownst to her,
Jayce is a wanted man. Can the past be made right...
and can she surrender her heart again?

Summer of the Midnight Sun by Tracie Peterson
ALASKAN QUEST #1

◆ BETHANYHOUSE